A WEB OF DECEIT

Gary D. McGugan

A Web of Deceit
Copyright © 2021 by Gary D. McGugan

Cover and book design by Castelane.

This book is a work of fiction. Names, characters, businesses, organizations, places, events, and incidents are the product of the author's imagination or are used fictitiously. Any resemblance to actual persons, living or dead, events or locales are entirely coincidental.

ISBN 978-1-9995656-7-1 (Paperback)
ISBN 978-1-9995656-8-8 (eBook)

1. FICTION, THRILLERS

For Ali,

Warm Wishes!

Gary McGugan 04-09-22

Also by Gary D. McGugan

Fiction
Three Weeks Less a Day
The Multima Scheme
Unrelenting Peril
Pernicious Pursuit

Non-Fiction
NEEDS Selling Solutions
(Co-authored with Jeff F. Allen)

What People are Saying About Books By Gary D. McGugan

"The chapters in this fast-paced plot jump from character to character, all interlinked by the hand of fate – some scheming, some grieving, and some learning valuable lessons about how stuff really works in the world beyond the headlines."
~ *Barbara Bamberger Scott, Feathered Quill*

"If his audience thought crossing the finish line in Three Weeks Less a Day was epic, they better fasten their seatbelts and get ready for another thrilling ride to be had in The Multima Scheme. Bravo Mr. McGugan. I am a fan and am thrilled with the momentum of this series!" ~ *Diane Lunsford, Feathered Quill*

"Gary McGugan skillfully crafts an intricate tale of suspense, thrills, and non-stop drama, and I was thoroughly captivated by Three Weeks Less a Day." ~ Sheri Hoyte, Reader Views

"The challenge that McGugan faces in creating this second novel is to stay true to the more significant plot-line of the series. There is also the added problem to create a sequel that would be complete enough that readers could just read the follow up without being lost. It becomes a balancing act, which McGugan has admirably pulled off."
~ *Norm Goldman, Bookpleasures.com*

"Thoroughly enjoyed Unrelenting Peril, the third installment in the story of the Multima Corporation. It is definitely the best of the three books! I was so absorbed in the story it was difficult to put the book down. The author's writing style, which was excellent already, keeps getting better which each book. I can't wait to read the next one!!"
~ *GoodReads Reviewer, Mary*

"Action-packed and filled with enough thrills to give readers chills, Pernicious Pursuit is a no-holds-barred suspense story that will keep you hooked." ~ *Rabia Tanveer for Readers' Favorite*

For everyone touched by
losses, misery and isolation
in the COVID-19 pandemic.

Multima Corporation

Suzanne Simpson
Chief Executive Officer

James Fitzgerald
Director (Board)

Wilma Willingsworth
President Financial Services

Angela Bonner
Forensic Detective

Gordon Goodfellow
President Supermarkets

Dan Ramirez
Chief of Security

Heather Strong
Chief Financial Officer

Betsy Forsia
Financial Director

Kim Jones
Section Head

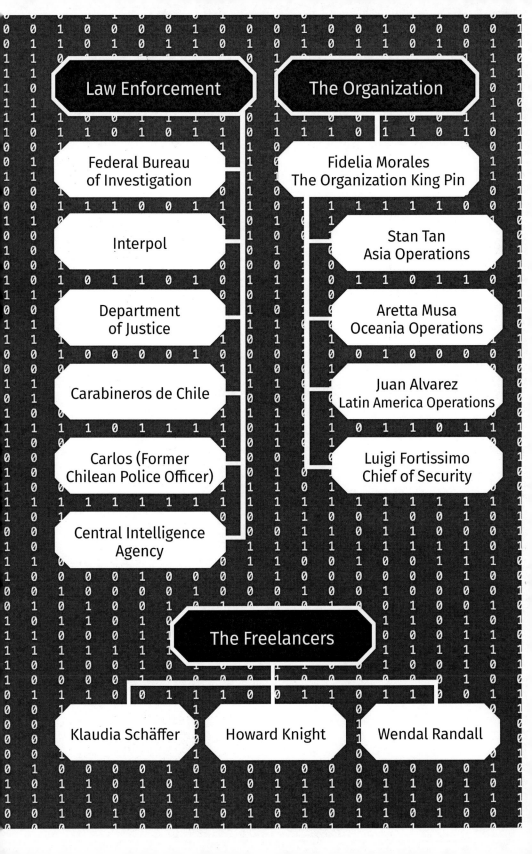

Law Enforcement

- Federal Bureau of Investigation
- Interpol
- Department of Justice
- Carabineros de Chile
- Carlos (Former Chilean Police Officer)
- Central Intelligence Agency

The Organization

- Fidelia Morales
  The Organization King Pin
  - Stan Tan
    Asia Operations
  - Aretta Musa
    Oceania Operations
  - Juan Alvarez
    Latin America Operations
  - Luigi Fortissimo
    Chief of Security

The Freelancers

- Klaudia Schäffer
- Howard Knight
- Wendal Randall

"Oh, what a tangled web we weave,
when first we practice to deceive!"
(Sir Walter Scott, 1808)

ONE

Ft. Myers, Florida, Tuesday January 28, 2020

Suzanne Simpson glanced up from her scrutiny of the previous day's sales results at Multima Supermarkets when she heard a light knock before the click of an opening door.

"There are two FBI agents in the lobby asking to meet with you urgently," her executive assistant Eileen announced with a tone of surprise. It was extremely rare for anyone to ask for a meeting with a chief executive officer without the courtesy of an appointment.

"Did they explain their purpose?" Suzanne was equally caught off guard. She had no idea what they might want to discuss.

"No. They flashed their identification at our receptionist, said the matter was urgent and they needed to see you, personally."

With a silent nod of consent, Suzanne signaled her assistant to bring them up. She tucked the reports into a top drawer of her expansive mahogany desk and tidied up other piles of paper and reports on a distant corner as she considered the possibilities. Was there some sort of threat against the company? A threat to her own safety? Possibilities seemed limitless so she'd hear them out for a few minutes.

Eileen showed up a few minutes later, and ushered the agents into Suzanne's spacious, tastefully decorated office suite on the fourth floor of the building. Both wore dark blue suits and somber expressions.

"Good afternoon, gentlemen." Suzanne stepped out from behind her desk, flashed her most charming smile and extended her right hand in welcome.

"Good afternoon," the older one replied sternly. At the same time, he reached into the pocket of his suit jacket rather than shaking her proffered hand. "My name is Agent Burke with the Fort Myers office of the Federal Bureau of Investigation, and this is Agent Douglass. Are you Suzanne Miriam Simpson?"

Agent Burke held his identification shield close to her face while he waited for an answer.

"Yes, that's me. How can I help you?"

"We're acting on a warrant for your immediate arrest issued at 2:53 this afternoon by the Department of Justice on five separate charges under section 1956 of The Money Laundering Control Act of 1986. We need to take you to the US Attorney General's office. Please turn around."

"I have no intention of turning around or going anywhere," Suzanne replied as calmly as possible while her knees trembled. "I'm calling our legal counsel immediately."

She reached for the phone on her desk, but Agent Douglass grabbed her wrist and held it firmly before she could push a button. Agent Burke stepped behind her and grasped her free hand, then pulled back her arms and secured both with a loud snap. *Handcuffs!*

"What's going on here? This is outrageous." Clearly tipped off by Eileen, Alberto Ferer's voice boomed with authority as he burst through an open door and strode into Suzanne's office.

"They've put me in handcuffs," Suzanne said before the agents could answer.

"I'm her legal counsel. And I demand to know what you're doing here and why you've detained her." Alberto stood just inside the door, his arms straight, fists clenched, jaw tight with indignation.

Once more, the FBI agents flashed their identification badges without any apparent emotion. One pulled a piece of paper from his pocket and waved it at the attorney as he reiterated their intention to lay charges related to money laundering against Suzanne and two other officers of the company.

Agent Burke took the lead, and his tone was conciliatory if not accommodating. "If you're Ms. Simpson's legal counsel, you can meet us down the street in the US Attorney General's office in a half hour. We have other agents currently apprehending your Chief Financial Officer, Heather Strong, down the hall. If you're representing her too, you can join us after we finish with Ms. Simpson."

Agent Douglass carried on in a more assertive tone as he reached out with a business card. "Right now, our Chicago office is also at Multima Financial Services, arresting its President, Wilma Willingsworth. She'll be charged with the same offenses. If you want to set up legal counsel to meet with her, call this number."

"Why are you laying charges without even interviewing Suzanne?" Alberto wanted to know. "She's one of America's most respected business executives. She doesn't deserve this kind of treatment regardless of your suspicions."

"Just following orders," Agent Burke replied. His tone became testy as he added, "The warrant demands immediate apprehension and constraint. The higher-ups consider all three women to be flight risks. Now step aside, please."

"I'll be right over," Alberto told Suzanne with a resigned shake of his head and an empathetic grimace. The FBI agents marched her out of the suite directly in front of Alberto, underscoring who was in charge.

A few steps later, they led Suzanne past her executive assistant, who stood beside her workstation, dabbing her eyes with a tissue. Maintaining her CEO persona, Suzanne stopped for a second. "Don't worry, Eileen. Everything will be alright. We'll get this all sorted out."

Neither agent said a word as they steered her along the narrow corridor, astonished employees gawking from individual offices. Taller than most women, Suzanne matched the agents' brisk strides as they led her into the elevator, then down to their car parked immediately outside the entrance to the building.

The drive took only minutes before they arrived at 2110 West First Street. She recognized the unassuming white stucco building with an orange tile roof. It was a short walk from her favorite tourist spots, the Edison and Ford homes. She'd visited the popular attractions on the shore of the Caloosahatchee River a couple times since moving to Fort Myers a year earlier.

The car slowed to enter a driveway, eased into a parking enclave, and stopped at a side entrance to the building. A crowd waited there. Journalists and television crews with mobile transmission vans clustered loosely in parking spaces usually reserved for people with mobility issues.

The impatient mass swarmed toward the FBI car before it came to a complete stop and its doors opened. The relative anonymity she enjoyed in the charming, laid-back Florida city was about to evaporate into an unwelcome notoriety.

Humiliation—gross humiliation—overshadowed everything as Suzanne tried valiantly to collect her thoughts and maintain her dignity. Cameras flashed continuously, reporters shouted out questions, and someone jabbed a microphone into her face as she walked between the bulky arms of the FBI agents. Both kept vice-like grips on her upper arms.

Suzanne fought back tears of anger and despair and was grateful for the good luck she wore sensible shoes that day. With heels any higher or less sturdy, she couldn't have kept her balance and composure as persistent media people jostled each other for position. And the pantsuit was a good choice too. No need to worry about a troublesome skirt or gust of wind. At the same time, the agents marched her forward at a quicker pace. They intended to embarrass her, not to allow bodily harm by the gathered crowd.

Someone from either the US Attorney General's Office or FBI must have tipped the media off about her arrest for so many to gather so quickly in the sleepy downtown core of Fort Myers. Despite a frenzied attempt to find other possible reasons, Suzanne could think of only one. Humiliation. They'd invited the media to a staged scrum to humiliate her.

Her head down, Suzanne squeezed through the glass doors, both agents pressed against her, until Agent Burke turned away to slam the large door behind them. Agent Douglass continued to lead her off to the left of the lobby where a handful of curious workers glanced up from computer screens to scrutinize their latest felon. Suzanne wasn't the first woman escorted through their workspace, nor was she the most famous.

Agent Douglass smiled ruefully as he pointed to a chair at a small round table in an equally tiny room.

"It's not as luxurious as your suite over at Multima, but it's the best the US system of justice can offer you for the next few hours." His tone almost conveyed empathy. "Someone will bring you a pitcher of water in a few minutes. Burke and I'll be back when your attorney arrives."

Agent Douglass reached behind Suzanne's back and released her handcuffs before he left. She heard the snap of an electronic lock activate an instant after the door completely closed. Then, almost total silence enveloped a space that confined her communication, movement and spirit.

Whatever can the Department of Justice be thinking?

A respected, publicly traded company on the New York stock exchange, Multima Corporation's financial affairs were scrutinized by dozens of independent analysts every day. Hundreds of people continuously monitored every aspect of the company's widespread activities from every possible angle. Those experts, of course, included the two women arrested with her.

Wilma Willingsworth—her former CFO and now president of Multima's Financial Services division—was considered one of the fifty most respected financial executives in the nation. Heather Strong, who'd replaced Wilma as CFO, had been a direct report for several years when Suzanne ran the Supermarkets business. Heather's dedication and her penchant for meticulous compliance with every accounting rule and government regulation were legendary.

Suzanne saw both women as impeccably honest and ethical stewards of every detail of the financial operations at Multima. How could the Justice Department get this so wrong?

A polite knock interrupted her thoughts before a young woman entered while Alberto Ferer held open a solid door. She carried a tray with a large pitcher of ice water and a half-dozen plastic glasses, set all of them on the table, then turned to leave without greeting or looking at Suzanne.

Alberto handed a plastic key card to the departing woman, then glanced at the ceiling before taking a seat beside Suzanne at the table.

"Assume everything we say is recorded," he said in a stage whisper. "Just in case."

"What's going on, Alberto?"

"The FBI agents will be here in a few minutes to read your Miranda rights as a formality. They don't intend to ask you any questions today. Curiously, they have a warrant but the background file justifying your arrest hasn't arrived yet." Alberto's tone stayed just above a whisper. He shrugged his shoulders and shook his head. Raised eyebrows and unusually deep creases in his forehead implied exasperation.

"Do they intend to hold me here?"

"Yes. But we'll fight that. On the way over, I called Jeb Kastigate. You probably see his law firm advertising on TV all the time. Jeb's coming personally, and he's the best in the business. His office is just around the corner, and he'll be here any minute now. Don't answer any questions until he joins us."

"You know we don't engage in money laundering, Alberto. Who or what could be behind this?" She began to think more logically as her heart rate slowed.

"No idea. My assistant is trying to reach Dan Ramirez in corporate security. Apparently, he's in Washington today, meeting with some of his old cronies from the FBI. She'll ask him to find out what he can," he whispered.

"Did you arrange attorneys for Wilma and Heather?"

"I called the best criminal defense firm in Chicago for Wilma, and Kastigate is bringing one of his people to assist Heather. We'll sort out the appropriate legal roster after we get everyone released, even if it means posting bail. That's the priority."

Shortly after, the two FBI agents returned with an agitated Jeb

Kastigate in tow, loudly demanding to know why the media zoo was milling about outside. The agents ignored his protests and ceremoniously activated video cameras and recording devices with several switches mounted on the wall next to the door. Burke read Suzanne her Miranda rights and then told her they'd be recording their conversations.

"First of all, we'll prepare for the booking," Agent Douglass said, glancing toward her to make eye contact for a second or two. "We'll start with a photo and fingerprinting in a few minutes. We're waiting for a file supporting the formal charges to arrive from the Justice Department in Washington. We expect it before the end of the day."

Despite her barely concealed fear, she tilted her head upward, just enough to convey a measure of defiance.

"You staged this mockery of justice and subjected this woman to a media perp walk without even reading the evidence against her?" Jeb Kastigate raised his voice another notch and added an indignant thrust of his ample chin, his eyes glaring at the FBI agents.

Neither agent responded to his accusation. Both looked directly at Suzanne as Burke continued.

"We've alerted a federal judge about our intention to formally lay charges and requested a first appearance today. She'll decide if you're going to spend some time with us in custody or if she'll grant bail with you posting a bond. It's a little unusual, but if your attorneys behave, she's agreed to work late and hold a hearing by video this evening."

"Never mind the smart talk about behavior," Jeb retorted the moment the FBI agent paused to take a breath. "That gang outside has already raised suspicions about manipulation of the media for nefarious purposes. If you folks have any ideas about jacking this lady around with red tape and process delays, prepare for some nasty publicity about the treatment of one of America's most upstanding business executives. I promise it won't be pretty."

Agent Burke glared back at the attorney for a moment but made no immediate reply.

"You're planning to try the charges in a federal court," Jeb Kastigate continued. "Did your judge indicate her inclination related to posting bail?"

Agent Douglass answered. "Her assistant said she'd want to carefully read the charges before deciding, but the judge generally leans toward bail rather than detention in these types of corporate cases. The assistant thought the bond amount might be high, though, with confiscation of passports and other conditions likely."

"Ms. Simpson, you'll need to go through their booking process and pose for a photo that they'll probably share immediately with the media outside." Kastigate's voice had suddenly become calm and reassuring.

"I suggest you try to maintain the most neutral facial expression you can. Stay patient. I'll commence the bonding process so we're ready when the judge decides. Give some thought to what security you can pledge to support a security bond. As you heard, it may be a large amount. My guess is several million."

Hold it together. Don't give them the satisfaction of tears.

TWO

Aimé Césaire International Airport, Martinique,
Tuesday January 28, 2020

As though dropping him off for a short business trip, Fidelia Morales gave Howard Knight a quick peck on the cheek before he stepped out of the SUV. With a casual wave, she sped off, leaving him on the sidewalk outside the airport departures area.

She knew Giancarlo Mareno would never have let Knight off with anything less than gruesome torture and death. But her boss's preoccupation with exacting revenge from her former lover wasn't her battle. Once Howard had wounded him with a first shot from a hidden weapon, Fidelia had quickly finished off Mareno with three quick spurts from her powerful Smith & Wesson 460XVR. It was messy, but over quickly.

Fidelia would take his place at the head of The Organization.

She still felt something for Howard, even if he'd disappointed her more than once. She had even offered Howard a chance to join her again in The Organization, but he declined. Just didn't have the appetite, he claimed. Within seconds, she'd decided to let him continue to run for now. With what she was scheming, there was always a chance he might just be useful again one day.

Her drive was a short one. She only needed to circle the airport perimeter and navigate up the dark, hidden gravel path that led to a remote building beside a concealed opening in a fence. From there, they'd access the private jet parked in the darkness in a rarely used corner off the main tarmac.

Luigi was waiting when Fidelia pulled up.

"Put this in a plastic bag. I want to keep the fingerprints," she instructed her chief of security.

"Both are gone?" Luigi Fortissimo scowled as she gingerly passed him the weapon for safekeeping.

"Neither will be a bother in the future," Fidelia responded coyly.

There was no need for her co-conspirator to know all the details. "Is the jet refueled?"

Luigi responded with a simple nod, then swung on his heel toward the aircraft.

"Is everything ready in Italy?" Fidelia asked as she followed him. He appeared to nod.

Exhausted from lack of sleep and the drama surrounding Mareno's death, Fidelia dozed for almost the entire flight and arrived in Lugano, Switzerland refreshed and ready for their next mission. From there, it was a forty-five-minute drive south to a house on a steep bluff of Lake Como.

After he learned of Mareno's death, the Italian crime boss had agreed to meet her almost at once in a familiar location.

Fidelia knew the man well, and she loathed everything about him. She waited outside while Luigi and his team checked all around the property to be sure the guy had come without reinforcements. Before she stepped through the doorway of the remote house overlooking the lake, she loosened the top three buttons of her silk blouse and parted the material slightly.

Sure enough, before hellos were done, the jerk's eyes drifted to the uncovered space around her breasts and fixed there. He was well acquainted with her barely covered cleavage. Giancarlo Mareno had loaned Fidelia to him to use and abuse several times over the past two decades. The lewd grin of the guy's bodyguard suggested the pair had surmised her invitation promised more than conversation. They probably thought she would offer anything for protection.

Fidelia suggested they open a bottle of wine and dispatched Luigi to an adjoining kitchen to retrieve some glasses. Meanwhile, she forced herself to joke and make mindless small talk with the men. When Luigi returned, he carried the bottle. Another bodyguard carried a tray of glasses and a corkscrew. They set everything on the table before Fidelia rose to serve the wine as expected. As she stood up, her men attacked.

Luigi seized the Italian crime-boss from behind with a powerful grip on each shoulder. He applied enough pressure on the sensitive nerve points for the man to fall face forward, his head banging the table with a violent thump. Her other bodyguard grabbed the guy's protector at the same instant and incapacitated him before either could cry out.

With the noise and commotion as their signal, three more of Luigi's men burst through the front door carrying zip ties they wrapped tightly around the upper bodies of both. Within a minute, both men had been neutralized. Luigi motioned for his companion to release his paralyzing grip on the bodyguard's neck, at the same time allowing the Italian to raise his head.

"We already told you Giancarlo Mareno is dead," Luigi said without emotion. "The media will probably announce it soon. We want you to understand how it's going to work now. Going forward, you'll send your monthly commissions to Fidelia. She'll also need your oath of loyalty."

"Let's be reasonable, Fidelia," their captive said, barely concealing both condescension and contempt. "Let's talk about this before you make a big mistake."

"There's nothing to discuss," Luigi replied. "Either you agree to send Fidelia ten percent of your take every month—just like you did with Mareno—and swear your loyalty to her, or you die. Which will it be?"

"Luigi, for Christ's sake! No woman can run The Organization. That's just ridiculous." Intelligence was clearly not the guy's greatest asset.

Fidelia watched impassively as Luigi pulled a knife from a concealed pouch. In one skillful motion, he reached forward and drew a deep laceration across the entire front of the Italian crime boss's throat. Blood spurted in every direction, staining the table and everything in its path. She glanced over at the man's horrified bodyguard. His shock was profound and his fear evident.

"How about you?" she asked the speechless and terrified man. He nodded repeatedly, his eyes now pleading for mercy.

"From this moment on, you report to Luigi here. What he tells you to do, you'll do without hesitation and without question. Do we understand each other?"

The terrified Italian bodyguard continued to nod agreement, his eyes begging her to spare him. This guy knew Luigi well. He'd probably even watched Luigi do his enforcer work on occasion. Everyone knew Fidelia's chief of security had served Giancarlo Mareno with blind loyalty for years—until he had agreed it was time for the boss of all bosses to go.

No other personal meetings were necessary. The terrified Italian bodyguard executed his orders and instructions precisely while three of Luigi's men oversaw his work. On each phone call, he performed exactly as demanded. He graphically relayed to each person on the list—with a suitable amount of passion and grief—how his boss had been eliminated while he watched.

From the jet a few hours later, Fidelia made calls to the other five most influential crime bosses in Europe. Spain. Portugal. France. Germany. Greece. Her polite demands for monthly protection payments and loyalty produced predictable, immediate and positive responses. Each leader swore his allegiance to her and hastily confirmed where he should send his monthly payments.

The Americas fell into line once they arrived in New York. It was Luigi who talked individually with the leaders of the drug, prostitution, gambling, loansharking, and theft activities. He calmly outlined Mareno's misfortune and explained the way they could avoid a similar fate. As expected, none objected. In less than a day, Fidelia and her security chief were back in the jet.

To complete her consolidation of power, they needed Stan Tan's support. He would bring Asia in line. For years, Singapore had cracked down on organized crime more effectively than any other major economy. Its autocratic government had eliminated most of the fringe elements and squeezed even The Organization into a secretive, tightly controlled bubble.

But Tan had managed the transition masterfully. He gradually shifted more and more criminal operations away from the higher-risk prostitution and drug businesses to focus on cyber activities. Consequently, the Chinese, Japanese, Korean, Indian, and Indonesian elements of The Organization not only respected Stan Tan, they also admired him. He was the essential missing link in her plan to modernize and restructure The Organization.

At the beginning of their next flight, Fidelia spent about an hour reviewing all the details Luigi's people had coordinated with Tan's people for accommodation, travel from the airport, and security around their hotel. When she was satisfied her companion had done his job well, she slept. Tan was the smartest of them all and she'd need every ounce of energy she could muster to win him over.

THREE

Aimé Césaire International Airport, Martinique,
Tuesday January 28, 2020

Dumbfounded, Howard Knight mentally processed the incongruity of it all.

He didn't have a watch or phone, but a hint of dawn to the east suggested it might be about six o'clock in the morning. Exterior lighting brightened the outside area adequately, but the airport interior lights were dimmed completely, and no one hung about any of the check-in counters yet.

He listened for sounds of activity but heard only a faint buzz of insects and occasional chirps from birds. There were no moving cars, no planes in the sky. He shuddered as he took in an eerie darkness, the unsettling quiet, and an uncharacteristic lack of activity. The place seemed more like a morgue than an international airport.

Howard spotted some outdoor benches farther along the building at what he supposed was the arrivals area and ambled off in that direction, assessing his current situation. Despite viciously beating him unconscious a few hours earlier, the bastards hadn't discovered the money in plastic bags strapped inside his underwear. Fifty thousand American dollars, plus a couple thousand euros. Money shouldn't be a problem for a while, but that amount wouldn't last forever.

His clothes were a problem. His bizarre attire would surely attract unwanted attention when people started to arrive at the airport. Howard wore a massively oversized golf shirt—four or five sizes too large—and Bermuda shorts far too broad for his slim stature. He had grabbed the sportswear from a closet in Giancarlo Mareno's house. He had no choice. His own garb had been splattered with blood and gore when Fidelia shot and killed the crime boss in cold blood.

The morbidly obese thug probably weighed four hundred pounds. His clothes made lanky Howard look like a bum or buffoon, with the shorts bunched up tightly around his waist by a belt while the bottoms dangled like inverted denim funnels about a foot above his ankles.

Before he and Fidelia had fled the scene of the murder at Mareno's mansion in Sainte Anne on the other coast of Martinique, Howard had taken a moment to study his appearance in a bathroom mirror.

His face was a mess. Darkened, blood-shot brown eyes puffed partially closed, swollen from the beating. His nose was broken and hung dejectedly to one side with dried clots blocking each nasal passage. His lips were enlarged and his jaw was almost immobile. A front tooth was chipped. Blood matted his shaggy, disheveled hair. And the back of his head throbbed incessantly.

Other than clothing and a money belt, Howard had nothing. He'd lost the backpack with his phone and meager possessions when Mareno's bodyguards first tackled him to the ground and beat him unconscious on the tarmac of an airport in Austria hours earlier.

Fidelia took the handgun he'd used to incapacitate Mareno before she finished him off. At least there was no weapon left behind with his fingerprints on it.

But the cursed warrants for Howard's arrest were still active, and police around the globe could identify and detain him from Interpol's Red Notices. Fortunately, a forged European identity card nestled discreetly among the American dollars in his money belt. Still, authorities in Martinique and elsewhere would surely want to see a passport instead.

He couldn't stay on the island. He didn't speak French and didn't look like a tourist. But he also couldn't expect to board a commercial airline from the island either. People here might be a little laid back, but they weren't stupid. That thought caused another shudder and reminded Howard it was too dangerous even to sit for a while on an empty airport bench.

Instead, he got up and headed toward one end of the airport, searching for the private jet section. Palm trees along the parking lot and roadway swayed in the morning breeze as he walked, creating a serenity totally at odds with the usual sounds of an airport. At the end of the arrivals area, Howard found only the typical car rental offices with no other apparent facilities or direct access to the tarmac.

He gazed dejectedly through a chain-link fence and detected motion on the far runway, out beyond the terminal buildings. Howard cupped his eyes and peered into the darkness at a long strip of asphalt where he heard a growing roar in the distance. Seconds later, a small, unmarked white jet streaked along the runway, then soared rapidly upward.

It was the same all-white plane he'd seen on the ground in Austria— the one Mareno had stepped down from seconds before thugs from The

Organization appeared out of nowhere. Before Howard could react, he'd lost consciousness. Hours later he realized they'd bundled him inside the private jet and were transporting him to this Caribbean island.

He had no doubt the plane climbing into the early morning carried Fidelia. His former lover. The murderer of Giancarlo Mareno. And now the new head of The Organization to boot.

With a shake of his head, he reversed his path and wandered back toward the spot where Fidelia had dropped him off. On his way, he noticed a cleaner inside, pushing a cart with several mops. He waved for the man to come to the next locked door.

"Can you help me?" Howard shouted through the glass door in English.

"What you want?" a heavily accented voice replied.

"The private jet terminal." Howard paused, then shouted out a French word he remembered. "*Privé*, jets *privé*."

The cleaner nodded, pointed in the opposite direction, and waved his hand to suggest a left turn at the first street. He also shouted, "Two kilometers," then helpfully held up two fingers to confirm the distance.

Howard set off following those vague instructions and eventually found a street where he supposed he should turn left. Sure enough, after about a kilometer more, he noticed a compact general aviation terminal right at the end of the street, with a small restaurant called Chez Maimaine directly across.

It was little more than a cafe. Howard approached its front door and peeked into a darkened interior. His shoulders drooped as he noticed the business hours. Twelve to three daily. With no other immediate alternative, he crossed the street. The doors to the private aircraft terminal were unlocked, its interior lights glowing.

"Is there anyone here?" Howard called out before he poked around the small open area serving as a lounge for pilots. No one answered, nor could he detect any sounds other than the subdued hum of a small refrigerator.

"Just act as though you belong," his father had often counseled when he was a youngster. "When people see you acting like you belong there, they assume that you're probably okay." That strategy had worked remarkably well throughout his life.

Howard headed toward the Nespresso machine, made himself a cup of coffee, found a three-day-old English-language newspaper, and got comfortable in a chair with a view of the tarmac. A few hours dragged past before anyone else arrived. According to a wall-clock, it was almost eight-thirty when a small gray plane pulled into a parking slot just in front of the terminal.

A pilot disembarked after a few minutes and hurried toward the terminal. Howard watched him intently for a moment, then raised his spread newspaper to cover his face. The pilot offered a cheerful "*bonjour*" as he entered the room, closing the door behind him. Howard muttered a bored "hello" in return. The pilot wandered off to a toilet without further comment. A few minutes later, he came out, left the building, scurried to an adjacent parking lot, got into a car, and drove away.

That pilot was the last person Howard saw for another two hours. After eleven o'clock, private jets landed more frequently. He repeated his routine of raising the newspaper above his face for each arrival, attracting little attention and minuscule bits of conversation. Unfortunately, none of the pilots displayed the characteristics Howard sought for his mission. A cleaner arrived just before noon, but the stooped and elderly man also left him alone after a cursory glance and nod before going about his work.

At that point, Howard hadn't eaten in almost two days. His only nourishment on the flight from Europe was a bottle of water. Since arriving in Martinique, he'd drunk only coffee, with a couple glasses of water from the dispenser on the opposite side of the room. Apparently lounges no longer offered even chips or nuts for their itinerant guests.

Finally, a few minutes after one o'clock, a pilot who suited his purpose stepped down from an unmarked jet. Lithe, oozing confidence, the tall young man walked with a swagger that comes with power and money. Designer sunglasses and jeans, expensive shoes, and a three-hundred-dollar golf shirt completed the package. He looked part Latin American, but his skin tone was dark enough to have an African influence.

Howard looked over the top of his newspaper to inspect the aircraft more closely. It was a Bombardier Global 5000, the most sought-after level of luxury in the private jet market. The plane was popular with large corporations but also appealed to less savory types of buyers. People like successful drug distributors, for example.

"Hello there." Howard lowered his newspaper and smiled as broadly as the searing pain around his mouth and jaw would allow.

The pilot turned in Howard's direction, but held his gaze for several seconds before he answered. "Hello. Do we know each other?"

"I don't think so. But I could use some information about your jet. I'm thinking about buying one. Are you headed over to Chez Maimaine?"

The pilot nodded so Howard added, "Can I buy you lunch and ask a few questions?"

With only a moment's hesitation, the fellow nodded before they strolled together to the small restaurant across the street. They talked only about the weather while they walked. They settled into wooden chairs on opposite sides of a small square table, covered by a red-and-white checkered tablecloth, in the corner farthest from the door.

After both ordered, Howard posed a few questions about the plane. He wondered about the interior comfort and finishing touches, then wanted to know about handling in turbulence and costs of operation. Until the food arrived, he kept their discussion focused on the aircraft and showed enough knowledge to signal his familiarity with private jets.

After their Caribbean creole dishes arrived, Howard first took a few moments to gulp down several mouthfuls of the food he had craved for hours. After swallowing with a swig of water, he broached his real purpose for their lunch.

"Who might a guy with some cash—but temporarily without documentation—talk to about a flight to another island?"

"What happened to the documentation?" the pilot asked.

"A business deal gone bad," Howard replied. "As you can see by my rearranged face, I'm lucky they let me go with just the loss of my passport. But you can also imagine why I'd like to leave this idyllic island as soon as possible."

"Where you want to go?"

"Eventually, I want to return to Canada. But if I can get to Barbados, I have connections there who can help me get a new passport first. Any chance you're heading that way?"

"Not directly. But I will stop there for a few minutes later in the day. I need twenty thousand US dollars in cash to get you to the tarmac. Nothing to do with immigration control or anything else. And I need it upfront," the pilot said nonchalantly.

They ate the rest of their meals in silence. Before leaving the restaurant, Howard made a quick stop into the tiny *toilette* beside the kitchen. When he came out, he paid their lunch bill in cash with Euros, then sauntered with the pilot to the parked aircraft. Inside the jet, the pilot held out his hand before he closed the door. Howard counted out US hundred-dollar bills pulled from the left pocket of his oversized shorts while the pilot watched and counted with him.

"Sit wherever you like," the pilot said without a smile, gesturing around the sumptuous beige leather interior.

Howard chose a large leather seat that swiveled, on the left side of the plane, just behind the cockpit, and buckled himself in for the ride.

Within moments, they'd taxied to the takeoff position. Soon after, the engine screamed along the tarmac before the small jet climbed steeply to cruising altitude.

It seemed like just minutes later they began a descent.

After a long look out his window, Howard noticed the distinctive twin peaks of Les Pitons and concluded they were headed to St. Lucia. The island was among his favorites and he leaned closer to the windows to better admire the lush, green vegetation. Many claimed the island was the greenest of the Caribbean, and his view from the sky won a vote of agreement.

He unbuckled his seat belt and moved forward to the cockpit. The pilot saw him coming in a rear-view mirror, motioned for him to take the seat beside him, and handed him a headset.

"We'll touch down in just a few minutes at George Charles Airport, the smaller one. Here's a cap. Pull it down over your face as much as you can. After I open the door, follow me down the steps and into the terminal. There's no immigration check or anything like that. They know I'm only there for a few minutes. Go into the bathroom, stay there for about five minutes, and then meet me back in the lounge. After, we'll leave for Barbados."

Howard watched their landing through the cockpit windows, exhilarated by the approach, touchdown, and screeching brakes as the plane slowed. Intrigued by all the tarmac activity, he looked from side to side as the jet wended its way toward a terminal for private aviation. It was the same every time they let him into the cockpit. He felt like an elated ten-year-old as he took it all in.

On the ground, he followed instructions as precisely as possible. Still, the pilot motioned for him to hurry as soon as they met again in the tiny lounge area. On their way to the plane, Howard wasn't surprised to see a cleaner descend the jet's steps. The fellow carried a large, green trash bag that appeared full and heavy. He was even less surprised when the cleaner gave a friendly wave to the pilot before he scurried off in a golf cart toward the maintenance buildings. Of course, the aircraft interior had been spotless when they'd left it only minutes before.

Without waiting for an invitation, Howard followed the pilot into the cockpit and buckled up for departure. Within minutes, they were airborne. The pilot switched off the radio with air traffic control and spoke to Howard on another channel.

"We'll cruise for about a half hour, then I'll reduce altitude and land in Bridgetown. Do you know the airport?"

"I visited there on commercial flights but don't remember much about it," Howard replied.

"As we approach the island, go back and sit on the left side of the jet. I'll bring us in from the South so you can follow the coastline from Bridgetown—the big city there—right out to the airport. You'll have a few minutes to study the landscape and get your bearings."

"Any suggestions for immigration control?"

"Come in with me like you did the last time and go into the toilet. The boys all know me and they know I'm only making a quick stop. They won't call any immigration guys over. Go to the third stall, the one on the end. Stand up on the toilet and you should be able to reach the false ceiling."

"And what? Just pull myself in with a chin-up?" Howard hadn't worked out in a gym in over two months, and the task sounded far easier than it was likely to be.

"You look fit enough. Pull yourself up into the crawl space above the false ceiling and stay up there until after dark. Everyone leaves then, but the doors stay unlocked. Don't forget. On your way in, grab a bottle of water from the refreshment table. It'll be a little hot up there."

"How do I get out of the airport?"

"After the guys all leave for the day, just walk out the front door. Outside, turn left and walk toward a car park beside the building. Walk all the way around the parking lot. You'll come out to the main road and you're on your way."

"No cameras or security to deal with?" Howard inquired.

"Of course." The pilot tossed back his head and laughed. "They have both. You'll have to figure that part out yourself. Remember, my twenty grand doesn't include immigration services."

FOUR

Ft. Myers, Florida, Tuesday January 28, 2020

They made a seemingly simple process as time-consuming and complicated as Suzanne could imagine.

The FBI wasted more than an hour taking her photo and fingerprints in two separate rooms, with two different teams. They had the decency to let her brush her hair and apply a touch of lipstick before they clicked the camera. Thankfully, she wouldn't look as bad as some arrest photos released to the media.

But her hands trembled involuntarily as a technician forcefully pressed her thumb, then two fingers, into the grimy pad where they captured her identity prints. The process humbled Suzanne. *How powerless people without the means to hire a top-notch attorney must feel.*

Despite Jeb Kastigate's vociferous demands, the Attorney General's office refused to press the bureaucrats in Washington to relay details of the specific charges more urgently. After finally receiving them, they frittered away precious hours before sending them on to the federal judge.

The judge was away on an evening dinner break when the documents arrived in her office. She required more than an hour to study the ten-page text before she consented to an initial hearing that evening. To no one's surprise at the FBI, the technician responsible for setting up the videoconference had gone home to Lehigh Acres and had to make the forty-five-minute trip back again to set up secure audio and video equipment.

It took only five minutes for the judge to rule that Suzanne Simpson could be released with a bail bond of ten million dollars. She must also surrender her passport and let FBI agents install an electronic tracking device on her ankle. Both were to ensure the CEO would not leave the city of Fort Myers for any reason before her next hearing on the fourteenth of February.

Heather Strong stepped before the video camera after Suzanne's dismissal. Her release on bail followed predictably.

To say she was exhausted was an understatement, but Suzanne found the courage to wear her new ankle bracelet as a badge of honor rather than a loss of freedom. Immediate rest was impossible as she left the Attorney General's Fort Myers office a few minutes before midnight. Instead, she plotted while Alberto Ferer drove her back to the offices of Multima Corporation in his cramped Nissan sports car.

Suzanne had already set several frantic wheels in motion for damage control at the US headquarters of her massive Fortune 50 company. Back from Washington, Dan Ramirez would meet them in the boardroom, providing any information he was able to glean from his contacts there.

Heather Strong and her attorney were also on the way. Eileen had already returned to the office to organize a videoconference with Wilma Willingsworth and her attorney in Chicago. Alberto also wanted to compare notes with them about the Justice Department charges and prepare a communique for release before the TV business networks started their day.

Her executive assistant had also phoned members of the board of directors across various time zones. She woke several from deep slumber to alert them to Suzanne's arrest and ask them to join an emergency video board meeting at five in the morning, Eastern time, to approve that draft media release.

Of course, Multima's director of corporate and investor relations hadn't yet begun work on a document for the media. Eileen had interrupted him sleeping soundly only minutes earlier, and Edward Hadley raced toward the company headquarters while Suzanne and Alberto made their five-minute trip.

"How are you holding up?" Dan Ramirez said with genuine concern as he stood up when she walked into the meeting room.

With her day-old makeup, and after wearing a now-wrinkled pantsuit for almost twenty-four hours, she imagined her appearance looked anything but corporate. The company's chief security officer probably wanted to assess her state of mind before giving his report, and his intense gaze might even suggest he was reassessing her character. It could be justified under the circumstances.

"Tired. So don't speak too quickly or use too many big words." Suzanne didn't bother with her trademark smile. "What did you learn?"

"Unbelievably, it appears the order to arrest you came from exceptionally high levels. My source tells me the Attorney General admitted as much when the FBI pushed back on making a quick arrest. Apparently, he told the Assistant Director to start clearing out his desk if he didn't carry out the order by four o'clock."

"Wow!" Alberto exclaimed. "You spent a lot of time in the hierarchy over there. When's the last time an Assistant Director of the FBI heard an order like that?"

"Only once before. A case of suspected terrorism," Ramirez replied. "According to my source, the Assistant Director himself didn't see the exact charges against Suzanne—or any evidence—before he relayed an order to the folks in Fort Myers."

"Do we know yet what they're basing the charges of money laundering on?" Heather Strong asked as she stepped into the meeting room, her face pale and voice uncharacteristically timid.

"Not really. The Justice Department is using language like 'a pattern of irregular transactions' and 'significant transfers of large amounts of US dollars overseas.' Even the FBI people think the entire exercise is based on wobbly logic. The evidence they've seen is scant on details." Dan paused and looked first at Heather, then focused back on Suzanne. She signaled that she was ready to begin the videoconference.

"Wilma, have there been any unusual transactions from Financial Services that might attract this kind of attention?" Suzanne looked directly at the camera, tilting her head inquisitively and making sure her tone sounded curious rather than accusing.

"Only the five hundred million we transferred to Luxembourg to buy the small credit union in France. You remember, the one we'll use to manage the private label credit card program for Farefour stores in France and Belgium? You'll also recall we had that transaction vetted by Dan's team and even ran it past the European Central Bank to be sure they were comfortable."

"That's what I thought." Suzanne turned away from the camera and addressed her CFO, Heather Strong. "Any unusual payments from Supermarkets? Or out of your shop at headquarters?"

Heather still carefully monitored Supermarkets. Her replacement was gradually working into her new role as financial director, and everyone around the table knew Heather was usually aware of even small transactions with suppliers.

"None from here," Heather began. "Supermarkets started buying some coffee directly from a growers' cooperative in Colombia and some fresh fruit and vegetables directly from Peru and Chile to eliminate middlemen. None of those transactions are in the millions of dollars.

They probably average about ten thousand dollars, and Supermarkets has been reporting them to the Fed religiously."

The room grew quiet as everyone considered any action or transaction that might have created doubt in the minds of regulators. The silence lasted a minute or more until the participants began to squirm in their chairs and clear their throats. Suzanne leaned forward and stared into the camera as she changed her tack.

"Wilma, I expect you'll want to contact some of your sources at the Fed to learn what you can. Do you see any legal issue with her doing that, Alberto?"

"Unless they're folks you know well, I doubt they'll return your call. I might advise against contacting even good friends there right now. Conversations may be recorded and used as evidence against you later." After a short pause, he added words of caution. "I'd rather see Wilma focus on an internal investigation of every foreign transaction over the past couple years."

"You want to see if there's a pattern of transactions under the $10K threshold?" Wilma clarified. Her tone of voice sounded an octave higher than usual, and she held her hands in a tight grip, probably unsettled by the uncharacteristic drama.

"Yeah. And we should probably do the same at Supermarkets."

Another uncomfortable pause followed. Everyone knew Wilma and Heather would launch investigations without any further need to discuss them. But there was still an aura of bewilderment around the table. No one understood why the Justice Department would take such dramatic action, so thoroughly humiliate Suzanne, and cast such an unfavorable light on their proud corporation. Dan Ramirez broke the silence this time.

"I know you folks want to get working on the communique you need to release to the media. I have neither the word-smithing skills nor legal expertise to contribute much," he said with a smile to lighten the mood. "But there are a couple pieces of gossip I learned in Washington you all might find of some interest."

"Sure, Dan. I know you haven't slept yet. Give us your gossip and then feel free to slip out whenever you like." Suzanne matched his Cheshire cat grin.

"There's no confirmation yet, but the CIA thinks Giancarlo Mareno of The Organization may have been killed." Ramirez paused and panned the room slowly after he heard a collective gasp. "That sophisticated software they use to pick up and record conversations—the ones using keywords—apparently overheard a conversation from the Caribbean island of Martinique. From that recording, they gleaned he was murdered at his home there. They've dispatched resources from Fort-de-France to confirm it."

"I never wish for anyone's death," Suzanne said circumspectly. Bile formed in the depths of her throat, but Suzanne was determined not to display the visceral hatred she felt for the scum who'd plotted incessantly to steal her company. Two years of threats, fear, and even a colleague's death formed her thoughts of Giancarlo Mareno and his gang of thugs. Instead, she maintained her CEO composure.

"But if that information proves correct, our lives might become a little more predictable. Would you agree, Dan?"

"Who's taken over from Mareno? I guess there's a chance The Organization might abandon its attempts to take over Multima Corporation. But there's no guarantee whoever replaces him won't be as dogged and ruthless. However, I think my other piece of gossip might make your lives even more unsettled," Dan Ramirez said.

"The folks at the CIA are terrified about this coronavirus from Asia we've heard about. Apparently, the World Health Organization has European Union countries reporting on every incident of the disease. My CIA sources tell me the WHO is quietly whispering about the possibility of a pandemic. They've waved big reg flags at the White House every day for weeks now but aren't getting the President's attention at all."

"Oh my God," Suzanne gasped. *A pandemic?* "Eileen, round up the executive team at Supermarkets and get them on the line next. We'll need to jump on another videoconference right after we get the media release approved by the board."

FIVE

Inch Marlow, Barbados, Tuesday January 28, 2020

Howard Knight followed the advice of the pilot who brought him to Barbados in the private jet. He hid in the ceiling above the airport restroom and waited until he was sure it was dark outside. Then he slipped out the section of false ceiling above the toilet and lowered himself gingerly, his feet balancing on either side of the bowl.

After replacing the ceiling section above, he waited another few minutes and listened for sounds. With high levels of airport perimeter security, lounges at private jet terminals around the world often remained open almost twenty-four hours a day to accommodate wealthy and demanding patrons. Still, it wouldn't be safe to leave the bathroom until he could be sure the staff had left and no guests wandered in for a break.

He carefully opened the door just enough to detect any motion or noise. When he found none, Howard poked his head from the bathroom door and peeked all around the room. It appeared empty. Staying close to the wall, Howard edged his body along the short corridor until he had a full view of the room. A digital clock on the wall facing him announced the time was 20:12, or 8:12, in the evening.

Howard continued to edge toward a large window at the front and checked outside for any signs of activity or movement. All appeared clear.

Turning his attention inside again, he looked for emergency supplies and a first aid kit. Like every other Caribbean island, Barbados was vulnerable to hurricanes. Every public building had flashlights, candles, and basic medical needs stored in a prominent and easy-to-access location.

Within minutes, Howard found what he was looking for in a recessed closet just behind the coffee maker. He checked the flashlight. It still worked and he jammed it inside his pants pocket when he saw the expected glow. Just in case, he also grabbed a handful of bandages and tape, shoving them deep into another pocket of his oversized shorts.

To complete the pilfering, Howard picked up bottles of water in each hand and headed toward the door. Opening it slowly, he squeezed outside, staying as close to the building as possible. If cameras were surveilling the area, he'd make it as difficult as possible to discern his image among the shadows.

Two completely darkened private aircraft sat on the tarmac nearby, probably parked there for at least the night. Farther away from the building, the large section of the airport for commercial flights also appeared quiet. About a half-mile away, a British Airways jet was parked on the tarmac close to the terminal. Well beyond it, one Lufthansa plane unloaded passengers and cargo.

Creeping tightly against the building, Howard headed from the tarmac toward the parking lot in the back. There, he surveyed the terrain and saw two abandoned jalopies sitting in a back corner. To his right, a driveway appeared to connect with a street. Peering intently into the darkness, he searched for surveillance cameras but found no vantage point to position a camera. Last, he checked the sky. Slow-moving, low clouds concealed the moon, and only a few stars twinkled through occasional breaks in the cover.

Howard set out in the darkness, wary of potholes in the parking surface and driveway, not daring to turn on the flashlight. When he reached the paved street, he looked left. About a hundred yards along, a separate parking area stretched out to a road with occasional cars passing to or from the airport. Minutes later, he arrived at that intersection, huffing and puffing like an old man. The beating had taken a greater toll than he realized.

Flying in, he'd decided his route should be away from the airport, toward Bridgetown. So he set off in almost total darkness, walking on the right side of the road facing oncoming traffic. After a few minutes, he turned on the flashlight to navigate the frequent uneven surfaces close to the roadway. There were few dimly lit streetlights, so it was important to alert drivers to a pedestrian on the narrow roadside. Two taxis rushing to the airport had already brushed past so tightly he felt the heat of their exhaust as he trudged along.

From the private jet, Howard had also spotted several small hotels and resorts along the coastline southwest of the airport. He committed to memory a landmark to guide his hike that night. It was the Sol service station about two miles from the airport. With a left turn there, a winding road led around the perimeter of the airport and down a steep hill. At the bottom, a partially lighted street ran toward the village of Oistins.

Howard grinned broadly as he recalled the village from earlier visits to Barbados. Its raucous Friday evening fish fries were renowned across the small island. On earlier, more relaxed visits to the island, he recalled walking for hours on the pristine white sand beaches, entranced by large, rolling waves gliding effortlessly into nooks along the coastline. Near Oistins, he should be able to find a place to take refuge until he found a way off the island.

Feeling exhausted, hungry and lightheaded, Howard pushed on until he arrived at the Sol service station and made the turn. He'd already downed both bottles of water he'd snatched from the airport lounge and was tempted to buy more as he passed a couple tiny grocery stores still open for business.

But it was too risky. Someone might report a stranger. Instead, he headed carefully down the hill with its two steep sections. Soon, Mike's Convenience store came into view just as he reached the expected crossroad. Uncertain of the best street to access the coastline, he willed himself to keep moving for another half-mile before he veered left again at Ealing Park South.

The street was a perfect choice. Howard followed it about a mile— all the way to the end. There, he came upon another narrow roadway running along the coastline, the moon reflecting off the water beyond the houses lining the street. Howard spotted a potential refuge. An inconspicuous sign on the left side of the road announced, "Bound Stone on the Sea." The small, unremarkable inn appeared ideal from the street.

Still dressed in the baggy, oversized clothing he stole from Mareno's home—and displaying the ravages of a vicious beating—Howard straightened his shoulders, held his head high and forced himself to put one foot before the other for another few yards. It took longer than he expected.

"Look like I belong," he whispered to himself before he summoned enough energy and plodded toward the water where some lights sparkled invitingly from a restaurant nestled next to the sea.

"Good evening, sir. How can I help you?" A casually dressed young Bajan stepped out from behind a curtain inside. He looked like he could be a server.

"I'm looking for your front desk. I'd like to see if you have a room available for tonight."

The young man examined his visitor quizzically for a long moment with a dark scowl and little attempt at friendliness. They were about the same height, but the server avoided making eye contact and seemed more focused on Howard's appearance. He glanced at the drooping nose, scrapes, and bruises, but showed more interest in the odd-fitting wardrobe.

"The front desk is closed, but I'll check to see if someone else can help you." He disappeared again behind the curtain.

Howard leaned unsteadily against a wall beside the entrance to the restaurant and looked around. It had two distinct sections—an enclosed seating area with a half dozen tables and an outdoor patio that seemed mere feet away from the Caribbean Sea. Waves lapped against the rocky shoreline with a soothing resonance, and moonlight glistened on the water's surface. A potentially romantic atmosphere. But the place seemed strangely quiet for that time of evening.

Only two couples sat in the entire restaurant space, separately and on opposite sides of the outdoor terrace. Both spoke in muted voices. Fortunately, neither couple glanced in his direction.

Howard took three deep breaths to slow his racing heart and turned to the adjacent building housing the guest suites or rooms the establishment offered. Lights shone from only two rooms. January was one of the prime months for tourists in Barbados. Why would such a lovely, quaint inn have so few guests?

"Good evening, sir." A woman's voice with a pleasant lilt interrupted his thoughts. "We rarely have guests check in at this time of the night."

An attractive, middle-aged woman of color smiled as she made the comment, but an inquisitive tilt of her head and raised eyebrow signaled she expected an explanation.

"Good evening to you." Through the fog of fatigue, Howard gauged which explanation might be most effective. During his walk from the airport, he had formulated three possible replies. He went with "I don't usually look for a room this late in the day. And I won't bore you with all the details. Let's say I've experienced unplanned misfortune with a jealous husband and need a place to stay for a few nights."

The woman started to smile but caught herself before her lips completed the exercise. Instead, she grimaced. Her dark eyes still sparkled with amusement as she scanned him again, apparently trying to fill in gaps in his story with clues from his outfit.

"Well, I can certainly understand that a jealous husband might do that kind of damage to your face, but what happened to your clothes?"

"Borrowed," Howard said with a shrug of guilt. "The offended husband took my clothes. And my passport."

"Misfortune is right. So, I imagine he took all your money and credit cards too?"

"Luckily, no. I can pay cash for a room."

The woman's jaw dropped, her eyes wide with intrigue, as she shook her head slowly in surprise and perhaps disbelief. She said nothing for more than a minute. Howard studied her face, then filled the silence with a reality check.

"You're probably wondering why I'm here looking for a room rather than returning to the place I rented for my stay in Barbados, am I right?"

"We're on an island so small you can travel anywhere you want by taxi or bus in less than an hour, so yes. I'm more than curious to know why you don't just ask me to call a taxi. It would cost far less than a room."

"I don't actually have a place. I was on a cruise stop and signed up for a day trip to Harrison's Cave. The tour guide was a lovely woman. One thing led to another and we ended up at her place after the tour. I expected only a short time there. But our encounter was so delightful I stayed longer to—shall we say—multiply the experience."

The innkeeper strolled toward the front of the property and motioned for Howard to follow. Clearly still curious about his story, and apparently more relaxed about the absurdity of it all, she encouraged him to keep talking.

"So, this woman proved so appealing you lost track of time and forgot to go back to the ship?"

"Exactly. I had no idea there was a husband involved. I thought I'd stay the night and figure out whether to catch up to the ship in another port or just fly back to Canada in the morning." Howard lied with conviction in his tone despite his dry throat.

As they approached the front entrance, the woman pulled out a key, unlocked and opened a door, and motioned for Howard to follow her inside.

"How many nights are you planning to stay?" She switched suddenly to business, shuffling some papers behind a wooden counter.

"I don't know for sure, but I would guess it might take a week or more to get a new passport sent here from Canada. Do you have a room available for a week?"

"I have several rooms available for more than a week," she replied, shaking her head with apparent sadness. "That virus people are talking about is already causing serious problems for us in Barbados. I had seven cancellations today alone. This will not be a good year for us. We have only two-bedroom or three-bedroom suites here. Which would you prefer?"

"Has the virus arrived here in Barbados?" His brain immediately lurched into action as he recalled stories he'd heard in Europe.

"Not yet." Her tentative smile betrayed her confidence, but Howard needed somewhere to stay while he regrouped and recovered.

Once he confirmed a suite with two rooms was more than adequate, she told him the rate would be one hundred US dollars a night for accommodation only. One hundred and fifty if he wanted a suite and three meals a day. He agreed to the higher price, stepped outside to take cash from his concealed money belt, then counted out eleven hundred dollars. With a rueful grin, Howard told her to keep the difference for her excellent service and expected discretion.

As expected, the woman didn't make further inquiries about identification nor request he fill in paperwork. She slipped the cash into a pocket as she passed him a large metal key for suite 208, at the end of the hallway on the second floor, overlooking the sea.

With the most charming smile he could manage given the continuing pain in his face, Howard said good night and shuffled up the stairs toward his room. With one hurdle passed, his thoughts immediately shifted to the next urgent matter—where to get a fake Canadian passport in Barbados?

SIX

With a defiant scrawl, and under the watchful eye of her assistant, Eileen, Suzanne signed off on a communique just approved by the board of directors. The world would now know about her arrest.

During that meeting in the wee hours of morning, individual board members were generally supportive. However, a couple conveyed visible concern about the seriousness of the money laundering charges and the impact they might have on Multima's business interests. No one implied she should step aside, but the questions, frowns and tense upper bodies suggested more unease than Suzanne had anticipated.

As chief legal counsel, Alberto Ferer had handled most of their questions and guided the board about the language Multima should use to communicate her legal dilemma. Suzanne had listened intently except for her brief—but strong—opening denial that neither she nor her colleagues knew anything about any money laundering.

"James Fitzgerald is still holding on line three," Eileen reminded her softly.

"Right! Thanks, I almost forgot about him." Suzanne grimaced at her forgetfulness as she shoved a felt pen into a desk drawer before reaching for the phone on her desk. "Ask the folks on the videoconference with Supermarkets to hold tight while I talk with James. I don't expect to be long."

Her former peer—and now a director—had asked to speak with her offline during the earlier videoconference board meeting, and he wasted no time when she picked up the phone.

"Have you checked the European stock markets this morning?" He was probably well aware she'd been too busy with the arrest and its aftermath to check the news on anything but her personal crisis.

"No. Do we see some activity?" Suzanne reached toward a desktop monitor at her side and clicked it on.

"I texted a stockbroker friend in London while I was waiting for you to finish up with the media release. He tells me it's bad. Something is going on with Farefour shares this morning." Farefour was Multima Corporation's recently acquired French subsidiary.

"It seems odd because we own more than fifty-one percent of the shares," James continued, "and effectively control the company. Still, buying and selling activity on the EuroNext exchange in Paris is feverish. In the first hour of trading, there's been more volume than we usually see in an entire day. And prices are down dramatically."

"That doesn't bode well for Multima shares when the market opens in New York, does it?" Suzanne asked.

"Not at all. My friend in Europe wonders if someone has launched the attack on Farefour to trigger a panic on Multima shares as soon as the markets open here."

"Is there anything we can do but ride it out?"

"Not much, I'm afraid. Panic is tough to contain. But there's one dramatic course of action you might want to consider, if your attorneys agree."

"You're not going to suggest an interview with CBNN, are you?" Suzanne's posture stiffened. A media interview ranked at the bottom of any list of things she wanted to do that day.

"Yeah. I know your attorneys will probably have conniptions even thinking about the idea, but a strong TV denial might be the only way to moderate a plunge in share prices. I realize it's counterintuitive, but I wonder if someone is taking a run at us—expecting you'll find it hard to quickly defend against those money laundering charges hanging over your head."

"You heard Alberto Ferer relay Jeb Kastigate's caution. Directors should avoid any public comment about the case. He's concerned anything we say might jeopardize our defense. He reiterated his worry to me very forcefully." Suzanne's voice reflected a surrender to her attorney's advice.

"I did. And I won't try to convince you to do something you're not comfortable with." James reassured her in his most soothing tone of voice. "But here's what I suggest you consider. The selling in Paris seems to be triggered by computer trading. There's no chance the algorithms are going to wrest control of Farefour from Multima. Even if one single buyer scooped up all the shares available, you'd still have the controlling vote. However, if they apply the same strategy when the markets open in New York—and enough other shareholders bail out as the share price declines—things could get really complicated."

"But wouldn't any attacker need to declare its position as soon as it holds ten percent of the company?"

"Yes. If they're playing by the rules. But my friend in Paris thinks numbered companies are buying most of the shares in Farefour. If that same pattern develops in New York, a dozen different entities could buy enough shares to hold solid positions. If those unidentified numbered companies are owned by only two or three entities—who then coordinate their ownership clout—they could win control of enough Multima shares to force their way onto our board without ever announcing their positions." James put emphasis on the last phrase.

Suzanne understood at once the urgency he conveyed. Every business executive dreaded a hostile corporate raider trying to win a seat at the table to influence company decisions. Fitzgerald was the most rational person she knew and unquestionably experienced in the world of finance. He wouldn't add to her wall of worry if he hadn't carefully thought through all the implications. That he wanted her to consider ignoring the advice of her attorney signaled the level of his concern.

"Okay, James. Here's what I ask. Why don't you have a conversation with Alberto? Let him know I suggested it. Walk him through the scenario you described. If he buys your concern, perhaps both of you can run the idea past Jeb Kastigate. I won't lie. The idea of doing a TV interview this morning terrifies me. However, if you, Alberto, and Kastigate all agree on parameters, I'll discuss it and might consider doing it."

With a glance at her wristwatch, Suzanne confirmed twenty-four hours had elapsed since she slept last, and her body protested with slower reactions and profound fatigue. However, rest and a refreshing shower would have to wait until the end of an early conference call with the Supermarkets team.

"I made an executive decision," Eileen explained as she reminded Suzanne the participants waited on a line. "There were some protests when I requested a video connection. Not dressed yet, no time to apply makeup, haven't shaved. You can imagine. So, your call will be audio-only this morning."

The executive assistant laughed as she justified the change in plans. Suzanne forced an expected return chuckle and waved away any concern. Over the more than ten years they had worked together, Suzanne had learned to trust the woman's instincts implicitly. She had never met a person who could judge a mood or measure the sensitivity of issues as quickly and accurately as Eileen. If she decided audio was better that morning, audio it would be. She pressed the speaker icon on her phone.

"Before we start, Suzanne, I want to let you know we have a guest on the line for the first few minutes." Gordon Goodfellow, president of Multima's Supermarkets division liked to make announcements formally. "Dr. Joanne O'Rourke works with the Fulton County Board of Health. You probably remember meeting her at company social events; she's Jeremy Front's partner."

Suzanne remembered the woman and immediately welcomed her to the conversation. She took mental note of how skillfully Goodfellow handled her introduction in case Suzanne hadn't recalled the few occasions they'd met previously.

"Dr. O'Rourke, thank you for joining us. I imagine you weren't expecting to get dragged into a Multima conference call when you went to bed last night. Still, we'll all be grateful if you can tell us what you know about this virus we hear about in the news."

"Of course, Suzanne. Thanks for recognizing I haven't had much time to prepare, but this coronavirus is serious. I appreciate the opportunity to give you a heads up about what we know." Joanne O'Rourke used a tone that conveyed gravity without panic. "It's probably going to change the way we live for a while."

Pausing only to take a breath from time to time, Dr. O'Rourke held her telephone audience spellbound as she described the characteristics of the newly discovered virus. She emphasized how rapidly it was spreading and the number of countries already reporting breakouts. She took pains to describe why the new virus was far more contagious and harmful than the flu.

Then she warned them of its potential to kill more people than the influenza pandemic a century earlier, when millions lost their lives in the US and around the world. She ended her summary with a description of draconian steps the Chinese government had taken in Wuhan, the modern metropolis where the coronavirus started.

"We understand they've entirely sealed off this city of about twelve million people and shut everything down. Factories, offices, schools. Everything except grocery stores. And they're encountering shortages of essential food products. Trucks and trains have difficulty delivering goods into the city," the doctor explained. "It's too early to say we'll have to do the same thing here. But you should probably discuss what processes you'll need to incorporate to keep your employees and customers safe if we can't get this under control right away."

With that advice, Joanne O'Rourke excused herself from the call to rush into her office for another meeting. The Center for Disease Control had scheduled a conference call to brief boards of health across the country.

For almost a minute after the doctor left, their call remained silent. It seemed everyone needed some time to absorb and process the barrage of information and gravity of the situation. Suzanne chose to step over to a marble credenza between her desk and a window overlooking the beautiful Caloosahatchee River to make a coffee. She took a sip from her cup, glanced wistfully at the river, then was first to speak.

"Sobering, isn't it?" she asked rhetorically, still trying to decide where to begin. "Gordon, what preparation has your team done so far?"

"Not enough. But Joanne planted thoughts in Jeremy's ear a few weeks ago, so we've actually started the process."

With that understated introduction, Goodfellow asked the doctor's husband, his director of store operations, to give an overview. Jeremy Front performed brilliantly. He outlined some of the actions they'd need to take with employees, including providing them with Plexiglass barriers.

His team had done research, found companies who could manufacture and install the protective barriers, and worked up an estimated budget in the millions of dollars to equip all their stores. They were ready to go if the pandemic moved into any of the areas where Multima operated. But he recommended holding off implementing the plan until absolutely necessary. Customers might not like the barriers if they didn't understand and appreciate their importance.

"With the food industry's gradual shift toward part-time employees, there'll likely be challenges getting employees to come into work if they consider the store or warehouse environment unsafe," Multima Supermarkets' director of human resources said when it was her turn to report.

They'd need to reconsider the length of shifts, stress management, and employee education to help them avoid catching the virus. With a grave expression, she cautioned that Multima might also need to pay workers considerably more during the crisis—a form of danger pay.

Although Suzanne was nearing exhaustion, for almost an hour she paced slowly around her expansive desk, sipped strong coffee, willed herself to focus, and remained actively engaged with pointed questions and comments in turn. At the end of the briefing, she thanked the team for its early diligence and suggested they schedule the same group to meet by videoconference every week to review the situation and react as necessary. Then she ended the meeting with an exhortation they'd all heard before.

"Let's boost our orders and inventory the way we do before hurricane season. You know how people rush to our stores to stock up on supplies if they sense a crisis unfolding. Let's get lots of sanitizers and wipes on order, and we'll probably go through tons of bottled water...and toilet tissue too," she exclaimed with a broad grin. "Like we always do when folks decide to hoard."

As the conference call ended, she looked up to see Eileen ushering a pale Alberto Ferer and a red-faced Jeb Kastigate into her office suite. Both men appeared uncomfortable as they fidgeted and wrung their hands while she assessed their emotional landscape. Waving toward the sofa and comfortable chairs in the area left of her desk, Suzanne invited them to sit. At the same time, she ordered yet another black coffee from Eileen.

"Jeb insists you not do a CBNN interview, and I'm inclined to agree with him," Alberto said. "James Fitzgerald explained the business reasons, and he recommends you do an interview. However, Jeb thinks the risks are just too high."

Suzanne made her way to an antique wood-frame chair with a subdued floral design in needlepoint, and sat facing them.

Kastigate wasted no time with pleasantries. He leaned forward on the sofa, puffing out his chest, waving his hands in a wide arc to each side.

"Yeah, I understand the business goals too, but you have no control over the line of questioning once the interviewer gets started. James and Alberto have both assured me you're polished and skillful working with the media. But we must expect the Justice Department will analyze every sentence of the interview and have behavioral psychologists assess every facial expression you use. One unguarded split second could give them ammunition we can never offset later with facts."

"But we're innocent," Suzanne protested. "Why should I fear questions or body language if we're not guilty of any of the charges they've laid?"

"You know the adage. It's not what you know, it's what you don't know that bites you every time," Jeb countered. It was an expression drilled into future executives at every business school in America.

For about a quarter-hour, they respectfully parried back and forth, considering how they might try to control a TV interview. Or if they could control who asked the questions. Or if they could find a CBNN producer who agreed to supply questions in advance and stick to those questions. With logic and reason, the criminal attorney shot down every avenue Suzanne explored, while Alberto Ferer watched from the sidelines. Finally, Kastigate forced an end to their discussion and drew a line in the sand.

"I feel so strongly about this issue that I would be forced to resign as your attorney if you decide to have an interview with CBNN or any other media outlet. Until we can get a handle on the government's case, we have to avoid any negative fallout." The lawyer stood as he made his proclamation, signaling an end to his submission.

Unmoved, Suzanne stood and offered her hand in farewell. "I respect your position, Jeb, and will consider your comments carefully before I make a final decision."

She courteously saw both men to the door of her suite and summoned Eileen from her workstation. Once inside, she gave her executive assistant one instruction.

"Do you remember Beverly Vonderhausen, the criminal attorney in Atlanta?" Suzanne waited for Eileen to nod before she continued. "I need a second opinion. Please get her on the line."

SEVEN

Inch Marlow, Barbados, Wednesday January 29, 2020

A sharp knock on the door jolted Howard Knight from a deep sleep. Momentarily disoriented, he jumped from the bed, then remembered he was in a suite at the Bound Stone Apartments on the Sea in Barbados.

Quickly, he slipped on the oversized shorts he'd left lying on the floor and peeked out the front window from a corner of the inner curtain. It was the manager who had checked him in the night before. She carried a large tray with a tall carafe and a covered plate beside an overturned cup. Howard released the security pin on the door and opened it wide so she could enter. Brilliant, strong sunlight flooded into the room, followed by warm air carried by a breeze off the water.

"I'm sorry to wake you, but the kitchen is closing until lunch, and I promised you three meals a day for the rate you paid," the Bajan woman said with a broad smile and carefree manner.

Howard studied her. Dark eyes dimmed the radiance of her smile, and a furrowed brow implied some level of discomfort with either Howard or the situation. After a quick assessment, she moved toward the room's only table to set down the tray.

"I'm sorry, but I missed your name when we met last night." She turned from the table, offered her hand, and tilted her head expectantly.

"I was tired yesterday. My name is Smith, John Smith," Howard lied with ease, and without hesitation, as he extended his own hand. "It's I who should apologize. I appreciate your discretion and hospitality. May I ask your name?"

"Narissa," she replied, a lilt in her voice. "I hope you don't mind me disturbing you, but you looked hungry, even last night. I slapped myself when I tried to sleep but realized I hadn't offered you anything before we closed."

"Don't worry," Howard said with a casual wave. Despite the lingering pain around his nose and jaw, he made a special effort to smile as warmly as possible. One never knew where a conversation with a helpful woman might lead.

"For lunch, I can bring you something again if you wish. I expect you don't want too many people to see your face in that state." Narissa's eyes showed concern, not alarm. After only the briefest of pauses, she continued. "I have a doctor friend in Oistins. Would you like me to ask her to visit today and try to repair your nose and tend to some of those cuts and scratches inflicted by the jealous husband?"

She suppressed a smirk as she asked the question, then looked up at him, feigning innocence. It appeared she didn't buy his story entirely after she'd had time to think about it. But she also gave no sign of remorse. He'd still need to be careful, though.

"Yes, that would be helpful. Is your doctor friend as discreet as you in these matters?"

"She'll be no problem. If you can pay her fee for a home visit, she'll keep the matter to herself. I think she charges about a hundred American dollars."

"Yes, please ask her to come whenever it's convenient." Then Howard remembered things moved at an entirely different pace in the Caribbean. He added, with just a little more emphasis than necessary, "Whenever it's convenient today."

"Sure. It will probably be this evening after she closes the office." Narissa started toward the door but stopped before she reached it and turned a questioning gaze on him. "Oh, do you need the telephone number for the Canadian High Commission? That's what they call their consulate office here. I looked it up for you on Google."

"I think I'd rather visit the High Commission in person. Do you know where it is?"

Narissa reached into a pocket, retrieved a phone and punched some keys. Carefully, she read the address to Howard, then explained the best way to get there. She watched Howard's nods and expressions to be sure he absorbed all the details. "Oh, and they're closed on Saturday and Sunday, so you might want to go there tomorrow to be sure you get your new passport within a week."

Howard followed her advice. The next morning, he headed out with his ball cap pulled down over his face, a reset and bandaged nose, and fifty Barbadian dollars in small bills, all neatly arranged by Narissa. She'd even gone with him out to the street and pointed him in the right direction. For a moment, he wasn't sure if she might give him a farewell peck on the cheek.

A white van with "11" painted on it arrived moments after Howard staked out his space at the designated corner. It stopped long enough for him to get in and close the door, but screeched off in a burst of energy before Howard could take an empty seat in the third row at the rear.

The acceleration caused him to lose his balance, thump his head on the roof of the van, then tumble awkwardly into the vacant spot. The driver continued his manic pace with abrupt stops and fitful starts every half-mile or so. It was left to an attractive young woman traveling with him to collect three dollars from each passenger whenever she considered it safe enough.

Of course, Howard had no intention of visiting the Canadian High Commission. The folks there would have no interest in providing documentation for a battered American with a highly improbable story. Instead, he intended to find and nurture a local connection to help.

Once the van deposited him at the marketplace, he looked for the sea and followed its shoreline toward a cruise ship docked less than a mile along the road. The kind of people Howard wanted to meet usually hung out near the cruise ships where they found willing customers to buy their wares.

He needed only a few minutes to find a merchant selling shorts and T-shirts who also pointed him toward a restroom where he could change. Within moments, he was a walking advertisement for Barbados but thankfully wearing clothes that fit him.

Howard came upon an outdoor cafe and claimed a seat at the front with a good view of passing traffic. Before he finished drinking his cup of coffee, a candidate materialized.

The young man was dressed casually in shorts, a T-shirt, and sandals. He was of average height and a small goatee decorated his chin. He was unremarkable in every respect but his swagger. He sauntered with no apparent destination and looked about with an air of indifference. His heritage was difficult to discern. Skin coloring suggested some Indian or Latin influence, while his long, curly hair looked oddly out of place with his other mostly Anglo-Saxon facial features. However, he appeared to be a man of the world.

When the candidate glanced over, Howard smiled and waved for the young man to approach the outdoor table. The fellow looked around, made sure he was indeed Howard's intended target, then slowly meandered over.

"Are you familiar with Bridgetown? Howard asked.

An exaggerated nod with a partial smile was the only reply.

"Can I buy you a coffee and ask you a few questions about the city?" Howard asked. This time, the fellow stepped back, theatrically slid out a chair, and sat down without any further comment. But his smile broadened to become more friendly and welcoming.

For a few minutes, Howard asked a few banal questions about the sights of Bridgetown, things to visit and places to eat. The young man answered each question patiently but didn't volunteer more details than needed. When he thought the timing appropriate, Howard asked, "Do you know where a guy can safely buy a couple ounces of weed? Is it legal here?"

"No, it's not legal. But it's widely available for about twenty US dollars an ounce. If you use it out of sight, no one will bother you."

After a couple clarifying questions, the fellow offered to take Howard to a place where he could buy some marijuana, and they set off down the street after paying the bill. No more than two hundred yards along the avenue, the young man pointed toward an alley and said they should turn there. Once they were around the corner, he stopped, looked in all directions, and pulled a plastic bag from a deep pocket in his jeans.

"Forty US if you want two ounces." He handed the tiny plastic bag to Howard, expertly shielding it from passersby in any direction. As soon as he pocketed the two twenty-dollar bills, he turned away from Howard and said with a grin, "I'm here every day if you want some more. No need to buy me coffee."

Howard didn't use marijuana. He hadn't taken a single toke since that night in Ochos Rios, Jamaica—about thirty years earlier—when he performed somersaults from a balcony into a backyard pool while mellow, nude and stoned. Whose house, he never knew. But he was smart enough to realize that continuing to smoke weed might become dangerous to his well-being. This purchase would stay at the inn when he checked out, a tip for helpful Narissa.

On his way back to find a number 11 van at the marketplace, Howard looked for a shop that sold mobile phones and found one two blocks away. He bought a throwaway model with unlimited data for a month. It was all he needed for his research.

From experience, he knew that folks who sold drugs in the street also knew other useful people operating outside normal boundaries of the law. Twice more, Howard made the dangerous journey in the back of the number 11 van into Bridgetown to meet the amiable young supplier.

Before he set out on the fourth day, Howard told Narissa the Canadian High Commission needed a new photograph to email to

Ottawa. She rummaged through a cluttered drawer behind her counter and found him a plastic razor and some scissors. With a chunk of soap and an hour of effort, he removed all evidence of a beard. Before he left, the woman also offered to apply some concealer to hide the residue of scratches and bruises.

After making his daily purchase of cannabis Howard asked the young fellow about getting a good, forged Canadian passport. Without a moment's hesitation, the Bajan man immediately guided him to a modern printing shop near the perimeter road of the city.

As they entered and walked past a service counter toward the rear of the shop, Howard's young supplier casually slapped the outstretched hand of a clerk in a universal gesture of brotherhood. Behind the swinging door, the resourceful rascal introduced a man he said could help Howard.

Three days later, Howard picked up the finished product. With what appeared to be a precise duplication of an official passport, his new document identified him as Mario Bartoli, a citizen of Canada. He smiled as he inspected his new photoshopped passport image. It made him look younger than his fifty-six years and showed no evidence of the wear and tear his body felt from the savage beatings a few days earlier.

Armed with his new ID for travel, Howard headed back to the Bound Stone Apartments on the Sea for one last night. It had taken several days of persistence and research, but he had crafted a workable plan to leave the island and begin an arduous process to normalize his life. His sole goal at this point was to become invisible.

He wouldn't contact the FBI to re-enter the witness protection program as Fidelia had suggested. Instead, he'd head off in a direction neither The Organization nor any legal authorities searching for him would expect. All he wanted was to be left alone.

Mid-morning the next day, he put on new clothes he'd discreetly bought during each trip to Bridgetown. With new jeans, a sweatshirt, and hiking boots, he'd travel less conspicuously. A new backpack held a supply of toiletries, underwear, and socks to freshen up every day. And most important of all, two new phones with five hundred dollars of airtime loaded on each, nestled deep inside the storage pouches of the knapsack. Neither should cause concern or alarm for security checks and immigration clearances. Both were clean.

Packed, Howard watched from his outdoor balcony and waited for Narissa to wend her way toward the restaurant by the seashore as she usually did about that hour. He wished he could say goodbye properly and thank her for her help. But should the authorities catch him at the airport, it would be easier for her if she knew nothing of his planned departure.

Once he spotted her from the back, he dashed to a stairwell, making for the exit, and strode quickly toward the intersection where number 11 vans stopped. Within minutes, one screeched to a stop. Seconds later, Howard was seated in the rear, heading away from Bridgetown at the van's usual frenetic pace.

Relieved to survive another ride unscathed when they lurched to a stop, Howard made his way inside Grantley Adams International Airport. There, he paid cash for a one-way ticket for one of Copa Airlines' several remaining seats on a flight to Panama City. His flight would leave at 2:35 that afternoon and arrive early evening. From there, he'd buy another ticket for a direct, non-stop flight to Toronto.

Then he'd try out the new passport with Canadian immigration authorities.

EIGHT

Singapore, Friday February 7, 2020

From a spacious suite on the twentieth floor of the swank Five Seasons Hotel in the heart of Singapore, Fidelia Morales glanced at a TV screen dominating one wall in the living area. Dramatic photos from that day's *Singapore Straits Times* newspaper caught her eye as they scrolled across the screen every few seconds. The one announcing the death of Giancarlo Mareno was old news. But another shocking picture showed starkly bare shelves of a supermarket in Hong Kong. Panic buying reflected the growing gravity of a virus spreading from China.

A moment or two later, another photo displayed thousands of couples in a Unification Church in Gapyeong, South Korea. Over 20,000 people were gathered there for multiple weddings. The striking contrast nudged her to break the silence and comment.

"Can you imagine that, Luigi? All that news about some highly contagious coronavirus in China. And they still squeeze a huge number of people inside a church for a mass wedding. Wanna bet there's a breakout in Korea soon?"

Luigi Fortissimo didn't see any relationship. "That picture's in South Korea. What makes you think there's any connection?"

His tone wasn't dismissive, but Fidelia interpreted his query through a lens she'd honed since her teens. Guys usually just didn't get it as quickly. If she led them through her thought process, they usually caught up.

"What are the main industries in Wuhan?" She answered her own question without bothering to wait.

"Electronics, Automotive, and Aviation. Wanna guess the main industries in South Korea? Electronics, Automobiles, and Textiles. Now, let's Google how many flights a week travel between the two. Five per day. Shall we say about two hundred people per flight? That makes about seven thousand people a week. We put twenty thousand people together in one event near Seoul? I think the odds are good one of those people

51

hugging and kissing recently visited Wuhan. Let's watch the news over the next few days."

She threw back her head and laughed as his expression changed from skepticism to wonder, then conviction.

"You're right." He shook his head in amazement. "I wonder what the travel numbers are between Singapore and Wuhan. Maybe we should get out of here too."

Fidelia didn't reply. They'd leave the nation-state when their business was done, and it might take a while. One of two important meetings on her agenda that day was with Stan Tan, head of The Organization's affiliate in Singapore and the missing piece in her plan to consolidate power. Before that meeting, she and Luigi planned a pivotal briefing with Wendal Randall.

Fidelia glanced at her watch, realized he'd knock on the door of her suite within minutes, and drew a deep breath as her thoughts switched to the eccentric technology whiz.

Wendal was a good-looking guy about five years younger than Fidelia. He wore a buzz cut—with slightly more hair than simply shaving his head—and had a tall, lean frame. His face was more cute than handsome, with a narrow chin, thin lips, and a pouting jaw. His eyes were brilliantly blue, but dark, sagging bags underneath always offset them. He looked permanently tired.

It wasn't his looks that attracted Fidelia; it was his brains. Before he'd made several foolish mistakes that led to his banishment as head of the technology division at Multima Corporation, Wendal had been considered the Steve Jobs of his era. Now he worked with her in a unique role yet to be fully defined.

True, Fidelia slept with him from time to time. Primarily, she needed to keep him motivated. But he also satisfied her normal sexual urges adequately when they surfaced. Luckily for her, he had two qualities—great intelligence and an oversized penis. Also useful was his tendency to think with his dick rather than his brain.

Fidelia had quickly learned she could easily control the emotionally immature genius by giving and withholding sexual favors. In the few months he lived at her compound in Uzbekistan, Wendal had earned his keep many times over. His best achievement? Inventing a new spying technology that allowed her to dispose of Giancarlo Mareno and seize control of his massive crime empire.

As a bonus, he created sophisticated algorithms that generated an unexpected bonanza. Last week, her technology genius had managed to covertly manipulate the price of some company's shares on the Paris stock exchange and earned three hundred million dollars in a single morning.

After a perfunctory knock on the door, a bodyguard outside in the hallway used his key to enter the suite and show in the expected visitor.

"Hello, Wendal." She greeted him with a formal handshake. "Let me introduce Luigi Fortissimo. You know he's chief of security, right?"

She scrutinized both men's behavior as they shook hands and exchanged meaningless greetings. She had meticulously trained both men to compartmentalize her relationships with them. Neither should give any signal of intimacy with her.

Satisfied both had controlled their body language as expected, she got right to the point.

"Bring us up to date on your meetings with Stan Tan this week."

"He's a cagey one," Wendal said with his usual boyish grin. "I can see why he's eluded government enforcement so effectively for the last two decades. He's brilliant."

"I know you're impressed with his knowledge of technology. What was he willing to share with you?" she pressed.

"So far, nothing specific. He's polite. He spends time with me and doesn't rush our conversations, but he's as tight-lipped as anyone I've ever met."

"Were you able to plant the app?"

"Yeah. It's been inside his phone since our first meeting, and I've accumulated a fair bit of new knowledge." Wendal nodded his head enthusiastically. "Like we suspected, he's really the brains behind the North Korean hacking success. I've had almost daily intercepts of conversations between him and the Great Leader. Seems they've been buddies since the Korean attended university in Switzerland."

"How about India?"

"Same. Your guess about his relationship with the Mumbai telephone support centers was spot on. He's using resources there to hack American companies who offshore their computer systems activities, exploiting gaps in security he was able to penetrate," Wendal continued.

"How does he feel about us setting up operations here?" Fidelia asked.

"His reaction was curious. He seemed a little surprised when I broached the subject, but he seemed quite open to the idea of us using Singapore as a temporary base. No objections. No expressed concerns."

"Maybe he thinks it will be easier to penetrate our systems if we're closer to him," Luigi offered as his first contribution to the discussion. "Weren't you under the impression his minions tried to attack our firewalls just a couple weeks ago?"

"Yeah. There's no doubt the servers trying to hack our equipment in Central Asia were connected to Tan. Still, I doubt our proximity would influence his thinking much unless he thought it might be easier to compromise one of our people. He might be able to focus on finding a weak link in our organization if we're all living here."

"If we limit our team here to you and the two technicians you brought from Central Asia, are you confident we're safe with those women?" Fidelia asked. She took care to not reveal her suspicion. Might Wendal himself become a weak link?

"I think so. But we're all human, right? He may be able to learn something we don't know and use it to penetrate our security. Would you consider bringing him in as a partner?" Wendal wondered.

Fidelia smiled. They got it. Luigi had made precisely the same recommendation that morning. Both were starting to think more like her. For the next two hours, Fidelia led the men through a process of identifying all the risks they could collectively imagine. They talked about technical connections, IP addresses, the Dark Web, and tracking devices.

She goaded them into ever more minute details about electronics and technology—subjects she'd known little about a few short years before. When the security guard in the hallway called to announce the Singaporean crime boss's arrival, Fidelia smiled at both men with satisfaction. They were ready to do business.

All three stood up to welcome their guest. Fidelia stepped forward to offer her hand. In return Stan Tan, sporting a colorfully decorated mask over his mouth and nose, bowed his head slightly as he pressed his palms together in Namaste, the Hindu form of greeting.

"With the spreading coronavirus, it's better we keep our distance and not make contact." His sparkling eyes projected brightly above a mask-covered smile. "I hope you take no offense."

"Of course," Fidelia replied. She intensified her grin to warmly convey both welcome and understanding. "Did they take your temperature at the front door downstairs?"

"Yes. As of this morning, all hotels were ordered to monitor every guest entering their buildings. It's just a precaution. However, after our horrible experience with SARS a few years ago, our government authorities learned they must act quickly and decisively at the first sign of a disease," Stan Tan explained. "In America, SARS wasn't such a big deal, but with us so close to China, the virus was devastating. Our economy only recovered fully in the last few months before this new mess."

After they took their seats, Fidelia offered coffee or tea. Tan refused again with a shrug of apology and a reminder he shouldn't touch more than necessary in the suite in case he was unknowingly carrying the dreaded contagion.

In normal times, a meeting between two powerful crime bosses would have taken place over a feast of local delicacies, delivered to the suite by white-gloved waiters serving exquisite food from covered silver-plated trays. Stan Tan had already told Fidelia he'd meet with her for a brief discussion but would decline any food or refreshments because of the virus. Instead, they chatted about the disease for a few minutes. Tan had an amazing amount of knowledge about the coronavirus and took the disease seriously.

American-based television networks, where they got most of their news, had so far carried very little detail about the virus. They adhered to their President's view that it was a Chinese event Americans had no reason to fear. But Stan Tan's perspective was completely the opposite. He repeatedly pointed out to his visitors how seriously Singapore's government treated the issue, and the dramatic impact the coronavirus would probably have on The Organization.

"My people abandoned the drug and prostitution businesses here long ago because of government harassment. But our friends in Japan, China, and Indonesia tell me their businesses have already dropped significantly because of the pandemic."

Tan made a dramatic thumbs down gesture to emphasize the severity. "In China, where they have shut down everything, revenues were off by more than ninety percent these past two weeks. If this virus continues spreading to other countries—and they close everything for any extended length of time—their economies will suffer like no other time since the global depression of the 1930s."

His dire warnings and troubled body language were precisely what Fidelia hoped to hear and see. She had already slid forward in her comfortable armchair and straightened her posture, ready to pounce verbally at the first appropriate opening.

"We agree. One of the main reasons we had to take out Giancarlo Mareno was his inability to see that our business climate was changing entirely." Fidelia's intentional reference to Mareno's murder was designed to underscore her willingness to use violence to achieve her goals if necessary. When Stan Tan blinked nervously and furrowed his brow, she continued.

"We think the future of The Organization depends on superiority in cyber technology. Like you, we see an opportunity to siphon-off billions from inadequate security. Banks, governments, and corporations should be our new earnings base. Working together, we think the income opportunity is almost unlimited if we're patient and don't become too greedy."

Stan Tan looked from Fidelia to each of the men, warily and deliberately.

Looking for a signal of trouble or surprise?

Apparently satisfied, he asked a non-committal question. "What do you propose?"

Fidelia let Wendal Randall take the lead, just as they'd agreed when they plotted their strategy. He had the technical knowledge to frame their idea most rationally without divulging more detail than required. He was also a guy. Without showing her chagrin, Fidelia set aside the unquestioned importance of male supremacy everywhere in Asia.

It took only a few minutes for Wendal to plant the seeds of their proposal. He spent another short amount of time expanding the idea with a couple examples of ways their new partnership could benefit everyone. Fidelia was satisfied with how skillfully her ally used the pronoun "we" throughout his presentation. She liked that. It wasn't his usual style, but it was essential to make it easy for the Asian crime boss to say yes. He needed to see a partnership of equals rather than a new arrangement that implied submission to a woman's demands.

She watched nods of understanding become more frequent and definite. Tan's upper body relaxed, and he shifted his hands from the armchair to his lap as he listened. His eyes grew increasingly animated and less wary. When it came time for him to ask questions, the soft-spoken Asian had only a few. Fortunately, they were all framed as clarifications rather than objections.

Luigi listened and watched impassively. But she caught a tightening of her security chief's jaw when Wendal confirmed only he and two technicians would stay with Fidelia in Singapore in their new arrangement. The implication that a full security detail wouldn't be necessary probably irked the lifelong enforcer and bodyguard.

It probably also reinforced the reality that their sexual liaisons would become less frequent. Fidelia made a mental note to assuage any lingering concerns when they had a farewell romp that night.

In less than an hour, a deal was done. Stan Tan pledged his loyalty and promised to bring onside The Organization leads in Japan, China, South Korea, Indonesia, and India. They confirmed his share of the take—five percent of total revenue generated from illegal cyber activities.

Without prompting, Tan invited Wendal Randall and his two technicians to live in his ultra-secret compound in Chatsworth Park. There, behind walls of technology, they could block infiltration attempts by Singapore's government or other potential hackers. She saw the benefit and silently weighed the risks. In the end, she agreed.

Fidelia offered to buy a condominium Tan owned in Sentosa Cove for five million dollars, two million more than its assessed value. She'd live there when she was in Singapore. In return, Tan's people would arrange all necessary immigration and government approvals through his impeccable network. He also offered to provide local security.

As the door to her suite closed behind their new partner, Fidelia wanted to spring from her chair and high-five Wendal and Luigi in delight. But that wasn't The Organization's way of celebrating victory. Instead, she popped the cork on a chilled bottle of expensive champagne and offered each a glass. Discreetly, each raised their glass and gave a nod with only faint outlines of smiles.

Regardless, she was now the unquestioned head of the most successful criminal element in the world. Now, she'd ensure it would shift in a much different direction.

NINE

Ft. Myers, Florida, Friday February 7, 2020

Beverly Vonderhausen's approach to Suzanne's potential CBNN interview dilemma was decidedly different from the forceful insistence of Jeb Kastigate.

"I get it," she said the instant Suzanne outlined her quandary. "Your business advisors are pressing you to do more than make a formal statement. You're torn between an obligation to Multima Corporation and its shareholders, with concern for your own personal interests. How can you balance that conflict with the criminal charges against you?"

"Exactly," Suzanne replied. "I know we're not guilty of any illegal activity. But if it destroys shareholder value in the company, it'll be a hollow victory when I'm exonerated."

"Right. We may be able to find a way, but as your advisors there in Florida already told you, it comes with significant risk," Beverly cautioned. "I suggest we wait until the stock markets open and see precisely what kind of damage we're dealing with. If there's a disaster like a 'stop trade' order, I can prepare three options for us to consider within an hour."

A week later, Suzanne was grateful for that simple but profound advice. James Fitzgerald also recognized the wisdom of waiting when she relayed her new attorney's advice to him. Alberto Ferer remained opposed to an interview but was relieved the delay bought more time.

Ultimately, there was no need for an interview. Shockingly, Multima Corporation shares didn't tank at all that Thursday morning.

About a half hour before the New York Stock Exchange opened, share prices for Multima's subsidiary in Paris bottomed, then inexplicably increased in value gradually. Surprisingly, Farefour's share price continued to climb after the markets opened in the US. Prices for the company's shares finally closed at their highest level of the year.

In New York, Multima Corporation share prices also dipped slightly at the day's opening, but soon reversed course and rose again. By midday, trading volume was light, and movements in price were minor and relatively steady. Multima's shares finished the day with prices at a new fifty-two-week high.

The outcome pleasantly astonished James Fitzgerald. He spent much of the next several days using his enviable network of contacts in the financial world to ferret out the underlying cause. Why had Farefour prices plummeted so dramatically for most of the day in Paris, only to recover minutes before the American stock exchanges opened?

"We traced the phenomenon to several computer servers in the Cayman Islands," he reported to Suzanne during a mid-week telephone call. "Someone triggered highly sophisticated computer trading algorithms generating hyper buying and selling activity and pushing prices downward. Those same servers reversed the pattern at two o'clock in the afternoon—Paris time—and sold all their positions in Farefour before the markets in Europe closed. Someone made a considerable amount of money with one day of trading."

"You think it was just a sophisticated, opportunistic trader?"

"Maybe. But the pattern of buying and selling was a concern. We should probably get Dan Ramirez to draw on some of his FBI contacts to see if we can identify who was behind it. Clearly, it was someone with very deep pockets. They created a free-fall in share value with only minimal sales and bought increasingly larger quantities as the prices plummeted. That's exactly the opposite behavior we expect from computer-driven trading." James's subdued tone reflected his bewilderment.

"It's as though somebody was prepared to lose a substantial sum of money. Or perhaps they orchestrated the plunge—knowing they'd strategically reverse it—then sold off as share values recovered. Is that right?"

"That's my fear," James repeated.

Dan Ramirez contacted the FBI and learned they'd detected evidence of price manipulation. But when police in the Cayman Islands tried to investigate the building associated with the internet address, they found a vacant office in a business tower with no evidence left behind. The room had been professionally sanitized. Then the situation shifted from unsettling to downright bizarre.

Every day that week, Suzanne and Beverley Vonderhausen huddled by videoconference to plot a defense against the Justice Department charges of money laundering. After each session, Suzanne took away a list of reports and research her attorney recommended, checking to ensure nothing untoward had occurred.

Forensic accountants from Multima's auditing firm also pored over mounds of data generated by hundreds of reports from the company's subsidiaries. They didn't find a trace of anything either suspicious or illegal.

Beverley continued to press the Justice Department for more information. One day, she demanded an immediate deposition of the government's witnesses to understand better the evidence that led to money laundering charges. After a couple follow-up calls, Beverley reported that deposition meetings should be scheduled soon. On her third call, the attorney with the Justice Department became strangely uncommunicative and noncommittal.

Suzanne worried more. Sleep became elusive as her brain refused to shut down at night. Why was Multima targeted by the Justice Department? Dozens of competitors purchased far more products from overseas than her buyers. None of them had heard a peep from the FBI or anyone else. OCD, the accounting firm that audited their books every year, had lauded Multima's controls and processes. And did the White House somehow fit into the morass that haunted her? It continued night after night.

Today, her attorney was astounded. The Justice Department's spokesperson had informed her they would drop the charges. Suzanne's jaw sagged as she leaned back from the video camera to mask her shock.

"I almost fell out of my chair," Beverly said. "In twenty-three years of practicing law, I have never had charges dropped by a government agency before the first depositions. It's almost inconceivable."

"When you say the charges are dropped, does that mean they've abandoned their case against us altogether?"

"Exactly. I have a document right in front of me confirming it. Perhaps someone in a position of authority at the Justice Department reviewed the evidence and concluded there just wasn't enough to merit their case."

"Perhaps," Suzanne mused. She took a sip of coffee to buy some time and process the welcome but bewildering development. It seemed too easy to be true. She chose her next words carefully.

"My chief of security got the impression from one of his contacts at the FBI that those charges emanated from someone in or near the White House—and over the objections of higher-ups in the FBI. Wouldn't the Justice Department normally pursue the matter fully to satisfy whoever gave that order?"

"You'd think so. If your information is correct, I guess someone in the White House must have changed their mind and decided the charges were no longer worth pursuing."

"Could there be another motive?" Suzanne took care to make her tone sound curious rather than fearful. But the entire affair didn't compute logically for her.

"The only alternative that comes to mind is a possibility that someone else is pulling the strings, and the person who pressured the FBI might also be just following orders."

Suzanne shivered at the thought. She finished the call and rose from her desk to join the headquarters team for their daily videoconference with Supermarkets. The meeting room down the hall from her office suite was a two-minute walk. On her way, she glanced at a television mounted on a side wall. A bright banner crept along the bottom of the screen, flashing its message in brilliant red and white.

GIANCARLO MARENO—KINGPIN OF CRIMINAL ELEMENT
THE ORGANIZATION—FOUND DEAD IN MARTINIQUE

Suzanne stood transfixed, waiting for more details. As they appeared on the screen, she read the follow-up details.

Sixty-eight-year-old mastermind of The Organization found dead in mansion on Caribbean island of Martinique last Friday. Multiple gunshot wounds. French police released details today after autopsy and identification. No heir apparent. NYC police fear increased gang violence.

Suzanne took a deep, calming breath as she processed the news. The rumor Dan had heard in Washington was right. The ogre who had doggedly tried to wrest control of Multima Corporation from her for the past four years—the man she feared most—was dead. It would be reasonable to feel relief, perhaps even some elation. Instead, her knees trembled and her hands visibly shook. Was there a connection between Giancarlo Mareno and the White House? Was it possible the influence of The Organization penetrated even there?

TEN

Bridgetown, Barbados, Friday February 7, 2020

Howard Knight set out on his travel marathon from the departures lobby of Bridgetown's international airport. His passport forger had helpfully added a stamp from the Barbados immigration authorities, certifying his supposed arrival two weeks earlier. Consequently, the Bajan inspector barely glanced up before adding his own stamp and waving Howard through the line-up.

His Copa Airlines flight to Panama was in business class, enjoyable, and not at all crowded. Howard had correctly guessed most executives would travel toward Barbados on a Friday morning, not so many in the opposite direction. Service was attentive but not overbearing. He used free in flight Wi-Fi to research stores at the Panama international airport, then hotels in Toronto.

The moment the doors to the plane swung open in Panama, Howard dashed from the aircraft toward the Hugo Boss menswear shop. There, he bought the most expensive pair of jeans in the store, an overpriced casual red shirt, a beige lightweight sweater, and a black rain jacket that offered little warmth. However, he expected his garb would appear somewhat more reasonable for a returning Canadian than golf attire alone.

His strategy worked. Howard looked as though he belonged there when he presented his fake passport and customs declaration to a Canadian immigration official in the wee hours of the morning at Pearson International Airport in Toronto. When answering the couple questions about his recent travel and goods purchased abroad, Howard stifled any semblance of an American accent and used as few words as possible. The young female officer smiled, welcomed him back to Canada, and waved him toward an exit.

Sheraton Hotels had a luxury four-star hotel within the airport, but Howard wanted a less-known brand off site. His main need was an IP address in Toronto for a few days. Plus, it was better to be well away from the airport and less visible. He wanted to reduce suspicion in case curious minds were tracking him or some astute law enforcer matched his face to the Interpol Red Notice for his arrest.

A quick Google search reminded Howard of a possible candidate—the Tiantang Hotel in the heart of Toronto. He had stayed there on previous business trips to Canada and thought it was a great hotel with spacious rooms and lots of facilities. And they had rooms available for the next three days. He couldn't reserve without a credit card but had no doubt rooms would remain available on a blustery Saturday morning in February.

Howard shivered as he stepped from the airport arrivals area into the frigid outdoor weather. The weather app showed thirteen degrees Fahrenheit, and he yanked up the collar of his lightweight jacket to cover his lower face and venture out. It would get better.

Half the downtown core of Toronto was connected by a heated network of well-lit tunnels and underground shopping malls that made winter wear unnecessary. People called it The Path, and spending time down there would soften the cold shock to his body after the balmy weather in Barbados.

Minutes after checking into the five-star hotel, Howard connected to its free Wi-Fi service. There, he navigated to a site for the government of Vietnam, where he made an online application for a thirty-day tourist visa.

After all his soul searching in Barbados, he had eventually decided to travel eastward, using a rationale he hoped neither The Organization nor Interpol would expect. His only mission at this stage in his life was to live free of The Organization's malicious mischief. To confuse them all, he intended to head directly toward an area the spreading coronavirus had already infected.

Such an apparently bizarre decision seemed necessary. While Fidelia Morales had assured him she no longer sought retribution for the money Howard had embezzled from The Organization, he knew others pined for an opportunity to punish him. The Organization's plants within Interpol would undoubtedly still encourage police forces around the globe to watch for and apprehend him.

His first choice had been the Cayman Islands. That's where the money was. But traveling to or from Cayman to almost anywhere involved a stop in the US. Howard knew The Organization had successfully infiltrated the FBI and Homeland Security. Even connecting flights through the US could be perilous.

That was one of the reasons he chose to get a fake Canadian passport and travel through Toronto to wherever he might ultimately decide to go. Plus, most countries around the globe welcomed polite and friendly Canadians more willingly than Americans.

So Howard hung out in Toronto. He first paid cash for another new disposable phone with a three-month prepaid text and voice plan good anywhere in the world. It was surprisingly hard to find, but with a few questions to shopkeepers and Google maps, he eventually discovered a tiny store in Chinatown that accommodated him. A day later, he bought yet another burner from another outlet down the street with yet another plan. Then, he visited the Toronto branch of TVB Bank, the one he used in Cayman.

There he went through the bank's voice recognition process and requested a pre-paid credit card. The customer service representative didn't blink when Howard asked her to load fifty-thousand US dollars and take it from his main account. Between the cash in his money belt and the amount available on the credit card, Howard had enough money to live comfortably in Asia for several months.

Unusual doubts about the wisdom of his plan crept into Howard's thoughts. It was rare for him to second-guess decisions, but so much had gone wrong the past few months his confidence took a hit. That second night in Toronto, he didn't sleep. Instead, he tossed and turned, re-evaluating risks. He weighed alternatives again, tried to identify possible complications, and considered his options. Before dawn, he slammed his right fist into his left hand and exclaimed, "Let's just do it."

He did more research about his future destinations, then explored shops and restaurants in The Path until he received confirmation of the visa Tuesday afternoon.

With that news, he immediately went back to bed. The coming few days would be long, arduous ones, so Howard willed himself to sleep shortly after noon and slept until the phone alarm awoke him at seven. After a shower and a final five-course dinner in the hotel dining room, Howard left for the airport and his midnight departure for Taipei.

Wary that Interpol would probably still be on the lookout for him, his greatest concern was facial recognition software. Canadian police paid more attention to world-wide warrants than many countries, so he wouldn't be safe until he landed safely in Asia. Thankfully, his forged passport had already passed the test once, and he expected exit formalities in Toronto for a Canadian-documented traveler would be cursory.

The spreading coronavirus provided an added opportunity. Howard wore a mask that covered his lower face completely whenever possible. He had noticed several passengers wearing masks in the arrivals lounge three days earlier and bought two colorful ones. They might not trick facial recognition software, but it was worth a try.

There were no glitches boarding the flight, and he slept several hours in relative comfort. When he awoke as the plane descended, it was already Thursday morning, Taipei time. Howard deplaned and spent a few hours inside the airport waiting for his flight to Vietnam. By late afternoon he had reached Ho Chi Minh City, often still referred to as Saigon.

Clear of Vietnamese immigration control, he set in motion a plan to effectively disappear in Asia. It carried risks, but Howard had researched the landscape and strategized. He avoided the usual areas where western tourists tended to stay and where police might focus their attention in case facial recognition software prompted them to search for him in Saigon.

Instead of a well-known hotel near the airport or deluxe accommodations in the center of the city, he chose to head for the bustling quarter where Asians of little means usually congregated. From the Internet, he found what appeared to be basic, but functional, accommodation in District 1 of Ho Chi Minh City. When he showed the address to an available taxi driver outside the airport, the man took a long look at Howard's face. He appeared to be curious, even surprised, at the destination.

Less than thirty minutes later, the driver pulled up against the curb of a busy street and a sidewalk with hundreds of people scampering in all directions. Howard barely had enough space to open the car door and slide out without being jostled by the bustling activity. There was no hotel in sight.

Down that alleyway, the driver motioned. The passageway he pointed toward was too narrow to be considered a street. Little wider than Howard's height, dozens of pedestrians, bicycles, and scooters darted in all directions, so he squeezed his way along the alley taking in the sights as he advanced tentatively.

Several tiny bars and restaurants with outdoor tables encroached on the limited space in the passageway. He noticed a laundry. Women from a dozen massage parlors aggressively encouraged passersby to stop for a while. Some had breasts peeking out from scanty tops, others wore skirts so short Howard noticed their private parts weren't entirely covered. All smiled invitingly.

The third tiny hotel on the left was the one he was looking for—Sonnie's Guest House. With frontage no more than fifteen feet wide, it was easy to miss. But the bright yellow sign caught his attention. He climbed four steps to the entrance, swung open a door, and noticed a large placard in English asking guests to remove their shoes. Howard complied, then took three steps from the door to the check-in counter. A barefoot teenaged girl stood shyly, then bowed in welcome as she greeted him by name but with her voice raised to form a question as she pronounced it. Probably her only foreigner booked that night.

As the young woman accepted his one hundred US-dollar payment for three nights, she apologized. No breakfast was included, but she pointed out there were many nearby restaurants open at any time. Her English was clear and easy to understand. Howard glanced to his left as she completed her paperwork and selected a key for his room. An aged Vietnamese woman sat in a squat fabric chair slightly behind the lobby area, dozing in what appeared to be living quarters.

Accustomed to foreigners lugging massive pieces of baggage, the young woman expressed surprise Howard carried only a small backpack. He offered no reply as they climbed the three floors to his assigned room, where she asked if it was alright and passed him the key.

"Before you leave, one request. Would you be able to find me an English-speaking tour guide with a private car? I'd like to visit the Mekong Delta tomorrow."

"I can try for you," the girl replied. "Unfortunately, many of the tour guides haven't returned from New Year's celebrations. They go back to their original homes in the countryside for two or three weeks. This year, many haven't come back because our tourist business dropped so much with the virus."

"How much does it usually cost for a Mekong Tour?" Howard asked.

"Usually it's about fifty US dollars. But that's for a group of six to eight people. I've never arranged a private tour."

"An American friend was stationed down in that area during the war," Howard lied, careful to create adequate cover for his fake Canadian passport. "I'd really like to visit there tomorrow. Tell your tour organizer I'll pay eight hundred dollars for a private tour. But it has to be tomorrow."

About a half hour later, the young woman knocked on the door of his room again. A van would pick him up the next morning at seven. She would take him to meet the driver.

Howard slept for a few hours, then left the hotel to find dinner. He'd eaten only airline or airport food since his last feast in Toronto, and his stomach growled in protest. Darkness had set in while he napped, but the alley was brightly lighted and still packed with people.

Cautiously, he wended his way along the narrow passageway in the opposite direction until he reached its end. There, he turned left and walked past three intersections to a busy nearby street. Finally, he discovered a Thai restaurant, enjoyed a good meal, then returned to his basic accommodation at Sonnie's.

The young receptionist looked as though she had just left her bed when Howard met her the next morning. Dressed but disheveled, her long hair jutted out in several directions as she slipped on shoes at the doorway and headed back along the alley in the direction from which Howard had arrived originally.

There was little activity along the alley, but a few places served breakfast or tea to local customers as the pair wended their way to the busy cross-street. As promised, a driver and van waited at the alley entrance, parked snuggly against an already cluttered sidewalk. The young woman protested gently when Howard slipped a gratuity of thanks into her hand but smiled humbly when he insisted.

He climbed into the first row behind the middle-aged driver, who grinned warmly as he welcomed Howard into the vehicle. The fellow slipped on a face mask, used passable English, and gestured that Howard, too, should cover up. Traffic was relatively light, and the driver seemed relaxed and confident. As they drove out of the awakening metropolis, he asked if there was a special place in the Mekong Delta Howard would like to visit.

"Yes. I want to go to Ha Tien in Kien Giang Province. An American friend visited there during the war and asked me to walk around and take pictures for him. Do you know the way?"

"Of course," the driver replied. "Are there other places you'd like to visit like Can Tho or Bac Lieu? We can go there as well if you wish."

"No, let's go to Ha Tien. I'd like to spend the entire day there."

Three hours later, they arrived at their destination. The driver pulled into a small parking area attached to a tourist office and asked if Howard wanted to walk around on his own or would like him to come along and translate as needed.

"I've actually changed my mind. I'd like to stay overnight." Howard pressed a wad of Vietnamese Dong into the astonished driver's hands. "I'll pay you now for the trip. Give me a card with your phone number. I want you to pick me up here and take me back to Saigon. I'll give you another two hundred dollars if you meet me here at four o'clock tomorrow afternoon. Oh, and give me a card with your phone number, just in case I change my mind about the time."

The perplexed driver studied Howard for maybe twenty seconds before he responded.

"Are you sure? Two hundred dollars just to wait here overnight?" His eyes searched for validation, and a tilt of his head questioned the motive behind such extravagance.

"Yes, I'm sure." Howard gave the driver's shoulder a dismissive tap of assurance and a broad grin. "Two hundred dollars should cover a hotel room, food, a few beers, and maybe a massage or two?"

Within a half hour, Howard sat alone at a sidewalk cafe where he could study passersby. He watched faces as he sipped his coffee. About an hour later, he spotted his target and offered to buy him a cup of strong Vietnamese coffee in return for some information.

As expected, the cocky young man with an expensive-looking knock-off watch spoke some English and accepted his offer. After a half hour of banal conversation, Howard thought he had the right guy for the job. He broached the subject of the famously porous border between Vietnam and Cambodia.

"If I wanted to make a one-way trip over to Krong Kaeb in Cambodia at night, do you know someone we could trust to do that?"

Without warning, the young man jumped to his feet and ranted in Vietnamese as he backed away from the coffee shop table. Howard understood nothing, of course. But realized some passersby were looking at him with something more than curiosity. Undeterred, he calmly left more than enough Dong on the table, and purposefully headed toward the other side of town.

Can't be right all the time.

Farther along the street, Howard slowed his racing heart and found another coffee shop to try again. It was only a matter of minutes before a lithe, more-than-middle-aged man with a limp and bent posture slowed, then approached him slowly.

"I know lots of people who'd do it and stay silent," the man said quietly. His black eyes gleamed with interest before he added. "If you pay enough money." Clearly this guy had seen what happened at the last coffee shop.

Howard motioned that he should sit down and have a coffee with him.

"Would I pay that money to you or a boat driver?"

"Me. If you give me three hundred US dollars, I can find someone to take you after dark. The trip takes about two hours."

"And we could land somewhere secluded? Without attracting the attention of immigration authorities?" Howard pressed to be sure the man understood his intentions.

"That would be another two hundred dollars." The fellow displayed no emotion.

"Is there any chance you know someone who could discreetly give my passport an exit stamp that looks official?"

"That would be another hundred dollars. If you want a Cambodian visa and entry stamp, that will also be two hundred dollars." The man showed increased enthusiasm. His eyes widened and his smile broadened.

"So let me get this straight. I give you five hundred for a boat ride to a secluded spot. Another three hundred for Vietnam and Cambodia exit and entry stamps. A total of eight hundred dollars. You can do everything we discussed by this evening. Is that right?"

"Yes. If you add another two hundred dollars, I'll forget we ever had this conversation."

"Okay, a thousand dollars to get me there with all the documents properly stamped and everything kept completely secret. I'm okay with that. Now, is there any chance you have a Cambodian friend who might have a good used scooter for sale? And be willing to deliver it with a full tank of gas to a remote location in the middle of the night?"

Their deal was sealed with a handshake.

Posing as a tour guide taking in the sights around the town, the wily entrepreneur also escorted his foreign guest to two different printing shops at opposite ends of the town. When they finished the passport and visa forgeries, they wandered out of town to one of the nearby tributary waterways of the Mekong Delta. There, Howard's new Vietnamese friend negotiated boat trip arrangements for later that night with a woman built like a wrestler.

On their way back to town, they slipped into a quiet wooded area on the outskirts. By phone, the versatile fixer arranged for Howard to buy a three-year-old Yamaha scooter in "excellent" condition. He would pay the seller five hundred dollars when they met up at the point the boat driver delivered him to the shores of Cambodia around midnight. The scooter seller didn't speak English but assured them he would call Howard's phone if they had any problem meeting up.

Before the end of the day, the helpful Vietnamese man limped back to the coffee shop with Howard.

Despite the inherent risks in his plan, Howard was confident he could find his way back to the muscular woman and her boat after dark and had no further use for his temporary companion. Before he said goodbye and shook the gnarled hands of the helpful guy with both of his, Howard reached into his backpack. He pulled out a business card and an envelope that already contained another two hundred US dollars.

"Call this man at four o'clock tomorrow afternoon. Ask him to meet you, then pass him this envelope." Howard took a long look directly into the fellow's grateful eyes. They clasped hands in farewell, and Howard took care to grip the man's hand again for just a moment longer than necessary. In return, the man nodded, lowered his head, and set off in the opposite direction.

Finding the heavy-set woman in her village again that night proved uneventful. She squatted against a tree, smoking a cigarette just feet from her boat. She stood up the moment she spotted him walking toward her and wordlessly cast them from shore as soon as Howard took a place at the opposite end of the boat to ballast their weights. The wooden vessel first seemed less stable than he had expected, but the woman navigated expertly through the calm, tree-lined tributaries and out into the bay.

Moonlight glistened on the surface and the water's waves gently rocked the boat in a constant rhythmic motion as the woman increased the speed of their puttering vessel toward the shoreline of Cambodia. Howard looked in all directions but didn't see any other boats traveling about. Many were anchored closer to the shore and appeared to be fishing boats. He couldn't tell with certainty but expected many of the local fishers slept overnight on their small vessels.

Less than two hours after they set out, the woman shut off the outboard engine and glided the boat close to shore. Howard turned from his seated position and saw a flashlight waving slowly among the trees and shrubs behind the shoreline. Moments later, with a solid thump, the boat slid onto the tops of weeds along the shore and stopped with a sudden jolt. His boat driver dismissed him with a wave of her hand and the outline of a smile.

Wordlessly, Howard thanked her with a wave and a grin of appreciation. She nodded and gestured for him to get on his way. A hand reached out from the shoreline to grab Howard's. With a surprisingly firm grip, the small man with a flashlight tugged him from the boat and into the murky water along the shore.

On land and swatting mosquitos every few steps, Howard followed the young man through a heavily forested area for about a half hour before they came upon a gravel pathway. At its end, a scooter was stashed behind several dense shrubs. Breaking the silence, the man started the two-wheeler and held out his hand for money. Without speaking, Howard reached into his pocket for American dollars and counted out the agreed five hundred.

As soon as he finished, the man said something in local Khmer or Chinese—Howard had no idea which—and pointed with an exaggerated gesture down the pathway to his right. Howard checked the throttle, made sure the clutch and brakes worked, then headed off in the direction the man pointed. A major paved road appeared within a few minutes and he pulled off to its side.

Just months earlier, Howard had used a scooter to escape violent pursuers and Interpol roadblocks in Portugal and Spain. At that time, he rode for only a few hours at night, every night, for more than a week. Driving in the darkness, with only the beam of his headlamp, didn't alarm him. Instead, it brought a certain comfort. His pale skin color and foreign appearance weren't so visible. He wouldn't attract as much attention as he might during daylight hours. So he took his time to get his bearings and plot his route.

Using his new phone and GPS app, Howard keyed in the name "Siem Reap" and waited for directions to his destination. Within an instant, the app outlined his route on a digital map and instructed him to continue along road NR3 through the town of Krong Kaeb to route AH123. Total travel time estimated: eight hours. With a little luck, Howard should arrive at his destination in time for breakfast.

Of course, there were no markers visible on the roadside. So, Howard simply took a leap of faith and followed the blue highlighted path on his app for about an hour. When he stopped again to check his progress on the GPS, it appeared all was good. He took a few gulps of water from a bottle in his backpack and ate a protein bar to keep his energy level up. Before setting off again, he flexed and stretched his wrist muscles for a few minutes to eliminate developing tightness. He dreaded the discomfort he knew would come.

Howard kept his attention focused squarely on the road as giant potholes became his enemy. Large, unexpected sections of broken pavement jarred his tires and made controlling the scooter at times precarious. However, from his research on the plane, he recognized the Phnom Voar mountain range when it appeared on his right. Reassured, he motored steadily until his phone informed him the road was now named NR41 and he doggedly continued his northerly trek.

Over the ensuing few hours, roads gradually improved, a clear signal he was approaching the capital, Phnom Penh. It was about two o'clock in the morning when Howard entered the suburbs of the sprawling metropolis of more than two million. He was struck by the prevailing darkness. There were traffic signals and basic lighting at major intersections, of course. Still, it appeared many streets lacked adequate illumination and most office towers were completely dark.

Surprisingly, an occasional speeding truck passed him in the streets. Howard, in turn, passed an occasional *tuk-tuk*. The curious contraptions—designed with a small motorcycle engine powering crudely designed tricycles and seating for up to six small passengers—puttered noisily through an otherwise quiet city. Drivers seemed courteous and left lots of space as they passed. No one showed any curiosity or concern about a foreign man on a scooter at that time of the morning, including the gas attendant who filled his tank at the only open station he'd seen for miles.

From Phnom Penh, Howard continued in a northwesterly direction along AH11, which eventually became NR6. Every hour or so, he stopped, checked his GPS, took a few swigs of water, and ate another protein bar. High energy was a crucial part of his plan to remain alert and on track in a country he had never visited and knew little about.

A glorious sunrise raised his spirits while he made his last stop to refresh. Brilliant red and orange hues promised a hot and humid day to come, and the thin clouds on the horizon reflected bold colors in formations that implied mystery and hinted at some spiritual influence. The next stop would be Siem Reap.

A few minutes after eight o'clock that Saturday morning, Howard wheeled off a paved road leading into town and then onto a roughly finished gravel surface when his GPS instructed him to turn right at an alleyway. About a hundred yards along, he spotted a sign for Aunt Martha's Villa on the right side.

To his pleasant surprise, the guest house looked unexpectedly cozy. He parked his scooter alongside others in a corner on the same graveled surface as the street and walked along a short stone walkway toward the entrance. On his right, people ate breakfast in a partially enclosed area with a half-dozen tables. Tall shrubs and trees shaded the courtyard nicely, and a small patch of grass was trimmed short.

When Howard stepped into the lobby area, he was pleased to see it was about five times the size of the hotel he stayed at in Saigon. Like his earlier frugal accommodation in the seedy part of the Vietnamese city, a sign instructed him to remove his shoes. Careful to not offend his hosts, Howard slipped off his shoes and shuffled across the lobby in sweaty socks.

Check-in was brief, efficient, and pleasant. A cheerful young woman spoke English well and smiled often. When she asked for a credit card, Howard told her he'd pay cash in advance for a week. After punching a quick sequence of numbers into a calculator, the woman requested one hundred and ninety-six US dollars—and pointed out that breakfasts were included.

As Howard followed the attractive, bare-footed young woman up a stairway to his assigned room at the end of a hallway on the second floor, he relaxed. A broad smile formed. His choice of hotels seemed a good one. After all, Trip Advisor pointed out the location was a mere five-minute walk from Siem Reap's entertainment district, and beer was fifty American cents there, every day after noon.

Could there be a better place to hide out for a few weeks?

ELEVEN

Atlanta, Georgia, Thursday February 13, 2020

Time never stood still for the chief executive officer of a major global corporation.

Fortunately, retrieval of Suzanne's passport and bond in those first hectic days after the Justice Department's shocking about-face had been Beverly Vonderhausen's priority. Despite the government's official surrender, both women couldn't quite believe the authorities had dropped all charges of money laundering against her.

Suzanne wanted to show appreciation for her attorney's efforts smoothing the waters so quickly, and offered to buy dinner in Atlanta before a flight to Europe. Beverly met her at the Fulton County Airport and was waiting near the entrance when Suzanne stepped down from a Bombardier Global 5000 corporate jet Multima had bought in 2019. She'd discreetly waited until her father, John George Mortimer, had died. He'd always argued the company already had enough jets in its operating divisions without another one at headquarters.

A pang of grief surfaced as Suzanne thought about the founder of Multima—even though eight months had passed since cancer finally claimed him. She wiped an unexpected tear away and took a deep breath before tugging open the doors to the terminal and warmly embracing Beverly.

They'd known each other since Stanford but never became close friends. In fact, Suzanne's most distinct memory was their amicable rivalry to briefly attract the attention of a back-up quarterback on the college's football team. That memory gave her smile a little more sparkle and underscored a healthy respect for her attorney. Beverly had clawed her way to the top of the legal profession, and that always deserved admiration.

"Let me give you these first." She handed an envelope to Suzanne with a flourish. "Your passport and a receipt for the electronic transfer of the bond back to your account."

"I don't have the words to thank you enough for everything you did for me. Thank you so much." Suzanne gave Beverly another quick hug.

"Will you drive to Smyrna? I reserved a table for us at Scalini's. I used to eat there all the time when I lived in Atlanta." Suzanne punctuated her comment with an enthusiastic lick of her lips.

Beverly agreed. After they arrived at the Italian restaurant, they devoured meals both described as "scrumptious," and caught up on each other's lives for about two hours. It was only after Suzanne presented her credit card to pay the bill that Beverly shared one lingering concern.

"They've officially dropped the charges, but bits and pieces that dribble out in conversations I've had with people in Washington just don't pass the smell test," Beverly said. She crinkled her nose for emphasis.

"Why? What's going on?"

"It's no secret our current Attorney General is closer to the White House than any in recent memory. Some fear he's too close. Maybe under the control of the President—as though he's indebted to him. I've spoken with five different sources who are usually very reliable. Each told me they suspect your money laundering charges originated with someone very influential in the White House."

"I trust your assessment, Beverly. But that seems almost unbelievable. I'm not political at all. I don't even know anyone close to the White House!"

"I understand your bewilderment. It's the same for my sources," Beverly said. "Have someone you trust take a close look at all your company records. I sense the issue may raise its ugly head again, and I suggest you make doubly sure none of your subordinates is acting as a lone wolf in a subversive way. Maybe you could ask a trusted colleague or former executive to pore through the company's cross-border transactions?"

"Maybe. I have someone I might approach. But isn't it hard for the Justice Department to bring charges again once they're withdrawn?" Suzanne asked.

"Not at all. And the way this government operates, it wouldn't be surprising. Look how many U-turns they've made in the past three years." Beverly's arched eyebrows conveyed her obvious distrust.

With that ominous warning, the women headed back to the private aviation terminal to meet Suzanne's refueled plane, ready for departure. Her next destination was a two-hour flight to Teterboro Airport in New Jersey.

Immersed in reports she needed to finish, Suzanne looked out the window only when the plane pulled up to the private jet terminal. She spotted her colleagues all huddled just inside the main entrance at the front of the building.

As soon as the jet doorway opened and the stairs lowered, Wilma Willingsworth led the parade out the doorway and toward the jet, wheeling her luggage for a pilot to stow. Behind her, James Fitzgerald toted his carry-on bag effortlessly. In contrast, his female companion drew her heavy winter coat tightly around her, then pulled up its hood before she traipsed behind the others, coaxing an overweight bag with uncooperative wheels.

Suzanne had never met the woman James had asked to bring along on the flight. At first, she silently wondered if James might be using the opportunity to pursue something amorous. But she willingly agreed when James explained why. Angela Bonner was her name, and James wanted her to accompany him when he visited EuroNext Paris—the French stock exchange.

He'd dug deeper into the mysterious trades that caused chaotic price swings in Farefour shares days earlier and hadn't found a satisfactory explanation. He remained troubled by the selling activity that first pummeled their share prices, then caused them to recover so dramatically in the hours before the New York stock exchanges opened.

Angela was a financial forensics investigator from Chicago, with impeccable credentials. She had flown to New Jersey earlier with Wilma and James on a smaller corporate jet used for travel related to the Multima Financial Services division. One other great asset Angela brought was a command of French. According to James, the woman not only spoke French fluently, but as a student she had also interned for two summers at EuroNext Paris.

As they all settled in after introductions, Suzanne proposed they review their game plan before everyone got a few hours of sleep. Once the jet rumbled down the runway for lift-off, they fell into deep discussions, with their luxurious seats turned inward to form a conversational circle around a low table fixed to the floor.

"Let's quickly review our logistics to make sure we're all on the same page," Suzanne began. "I appreciate you all cutting into your weekend time to get this trip in, but Michelle Sauvignon insisted we get as much accomplished as quickly as possible. According to her, the World Health Organization will declare the coronavirus a pandemic, and she suspects travel to Europe may be restricted soon."

"Michelle is Suzanne's chief operating officer for Farefour Stores globally," James piped in for Angela's benefit. "She's based in Paris and they've been friends since college."

"I have my meetings with the European Central Bank scheduled for ten in the morning," Wilma said. "Farefour's CFO will meet us at Orly when we land in Paris. She'll go with me to the meeting in Frankfurt with the ECB. First, I'll deal with their enforcement branch about the money laundering concerns. In the afternoon, we'll talk about the approvals we still need for bank licenses in the Eastern European countries. We'll have dinner with the President of the ECB and bring the jet back to Paris by about midnight."

"Right. Eileen already told the pilots to stay flexible. If you need more time, call them and let them know. Our priority should be to allay any concerns the ECB might still harbor. If you need more time on Saturday, don't rush back to Paris." She swiveled her seat to the other side. "James, you and Angela have meetings planned for all three days. Is that correct?"

James nodded to his companion. Reading from notes on her phone, Angela Bonner rhymed off the times, names, and titles of seven different people they were scheduled to meet at the stock exchange the next day. Then she repeated the process for Saturday, naming the three different investigators she'd been collaborating with in Paris. For Sunday, their only scheduled meeting was a private lunch with the president of the stock exchange to discuss their findings.

Angela definitely had the credentials and her network seemed impressive. But Suzanne wondered if James was aware of the glint of adoration in his eyes when he watched her speak.

"Impressive," Suzanne exclaimed, all business in her manner. "You might want to include Michelle Sauvignon for your Sunday lunch discussion. She tells me the president of EuroNext has been giving her some grief about the delay in moving our corporate headquarters from Fort Myers to Montreal. We promised to do that when we acquired Farefour. We've set up an office, but it's really just handling the Canadian businesses so far, and I've got that on my agenda with her today."

From their logistics planning, Suzanne moved the discussion to more ominous matters. Dan Ramirez had sensed some unexplained connection between the erratic trading of the Farefour shares a few days earlier, The Organization, and the White House. Was such a bewildering relationship possible?

Suzanne was determined to find out. They spent the next few hours of their overnight flight plotting how they could use each of their European meetings and resources to ferret out information without creating more suspicions about the complex global business activities of Multima Corporation.

As a result, sleep was short and elusive for all of them.

TWELVE

Even with Stan Tan's influence, Singapore's laws required Fidelia to leave Singapore for at least forty-eight hours and re-enter the country with a new visa application and supporting documents. For the past two years, she'd traveled on a passport issued by Uzbekistan. That arrangement resulted from her close relationship with its Deputy Minister of Finance and, technically, she should return there to complete her paperwork for Singapore.

But Fidelia grew increasingly stressed about how contagious the emerging virus was proving to be. Should she contract the virus, medical treatment in an impoverished Central Asian country might prove inadequate. There was no reason to take that chance.

A quick call to her friend in Uzbekistan confirmed he could file the documents for her at the Singaporean consulate in Tashkent. He'd get her the required visa. When it was ready, he'd forward it electronically to Fidelia. To satisfy Singapore's exit-and-return requirement, she could travel wherever she chose.

After a quick huddle with Luigi, they concluded he would go back to New York and work from there for a while. His part of their deal was to maintain loyalty among the American factions of The Organization. The first few months under her command and control would be critical. She needed him to keep a close watch to ensure all expected commissions arrived on time.

In short order, they decided Luigi would leave behind one bodyguard from his team and he'd fly home on their borrowed private jet. Fidelia would choose another place to hang out while her contacts in Uzbekistan sorted out her documentation details, and she'd fly there on a commercial airline.

Her farewell night with Luigi was not a great one. His performance in bed often related directly to his daily call with his wife in New York. Long before, Fidelia realized her security chief had complex and deep-seated problems—especially in his relationships with women. He could be dominant, submissive, and occasionally a partner to make his Italian forefathers proud. For their last night, he showed none of those characteristics and simply couldn't get it up. And she no longer felt it her responsibility to do all the work. So they eventually slept in separate rooms.

"Don't worry about last night at all." Fidelia leaned toward him—using a sultry tone she knew amused him—as they sipped coffees with a room service breakfast. "I know it was an exceptional thing. It happens to all guys once in a while. I know how you feel about me. Next time it'll be great. I can't wait."

"Don't bullshit me. I know you wanted it last night. I'll get Viagra next time."

Male egos need so much coddling. It took considerable skill to avoid an eye-roll and keep her facial expression serious.

"As you wish. I've already reserved the last weekend in March on my calendar for us. You won't disappoint me."

After considering several possible destinations for her quick exit and re-entry from Singapore, she settled on Australia. It was summer there, but the intense wildfires seemed finally under control. Should COVID-19 catch up with her, medical care in the economically advanced country was excellent. Most importantly, she'd have an opportunity to solidify her influence over Oliver Williams, The Organization's boss for Oceania. She hadn't seen him for a while.

She decided to take Wendal Randall along. The best way to win over the heart and mind of the crime-boss for Australia and New Zealand would be to wow him with technology that could enrich them both. Wendal could easily find an opportunity to prove the value she brought in return for Williams's unquestioned loyalty.

There was a bonus. Fidelia found herself increasingly attracted to the bright young stud. A couple good romps with Wendal would keep him highly motivated too. That was important. And, after Luigi's inability to perform, there was no harm satisfying her own sexual desires either.

Booking tickets to Sydney for a flight was a breeze. Most Australian tourists had already canceled holiday plans to Singapore. It was just too close to China. Passenger counts on scheduled flights had been light for a few weeks.

Their massive Singapore Airlines Airbus A380 took off on schedule, and the crew proved again why they enjoyed a reputation for the best service in the sky. Everyone on their eight-hour overnight flight wore a mask that covered both mouth and nose. Some passengers even declined the flight attendants' offers of food and drink.

Fidelia sensibly chose to have a good meal, then converted her swank leather chair into a bed and private sleeping area by pushing a few buttons. With soothing music from her headphones, she slept for more than five hours. It would be enough to get her through the first day in Australia.

Arrivals control on the ground in Sydney took longer than expected. Medical authorities had started screening passengers, and everyone needed to line-up to have their body temperature recorded. Then, security people shuffled them off to another area where nurses asked questions. Where had she been in the two weeks before? Any symptoms of the virus? Any indications of a cold or sore throat?

Immigration authorities took an unbelievably long time scrutinizing documents, studying the reports attached by the health inspectors, and asking more questions. Where was she going in Australia? How long would she stay? Where could she be reached? It seemed to go on endlessly. But an hour after she left the plane, she was able to join up with Wendal and their bodyguard again and claim her single piece of luggage.

A tall, slender blonde woman made silent eye contact with Fidelia after they stepped through the sliding doors of the arrivals level at Sydney Airport. She gave a slight nod of recognition. The woman motioned to the end of a barrier where she followed them and took their luggage.

Outside the terminal, the woman guided her guests to a large SUV. Protected from the view of passersby, she pulled a wand from the front seat and carefully passed it over the fronts and backs of Fidelia, her bodyguard, and Wendal without conversation. Satisfied they carried no weapons, she motioned for them to take a seat inside, and loaded their bags. Within twenty minutes, the vehicle pulled up to the rear door of a nondescript family restaurant near the airport.

Fidelia recognized the building. She had last visited Oliver Williams to discuss his call-girl operations. More than five years had passed since that trip, but Fidelia noticed little change to the building's boring yellow brick exterior, oversized parking lot and low-profile neon sign.

Back then, her job was to coordinate The Organization's prostitution activities for Giancarlo Mareno. The jovial and gregarious crime boss from Sydney had been one of their best performers. His discrete operations in Australia and New Zealand generated some of the best prostitution revenues in the world. And he was a reliable customer for Asian women and girls.

Oliver Williams stood up from behind his desk to greet her when they entered his surprisingly spacious office in the back of the restaurant. He towered more than a foot over Fidelia. Two even larger men stood on either side of him, a few steps behind. None of the three smiled or showed any emotion. Fidelia's first impression as she extended her hand in greeting was a shocking change in Williams's appearance. He'd lost at least fifty pounds since she saw him last.

His face was different too. Pale cheeks sagged. Blue eyes now seemed gray, and his forehead and temples were creased with permanent lines of worry, or pain. When the crime boss finally forced a small smile of welcome, his thin lips parted only enough to display a glimpse of badly yellowed teeth. His handshake lacked its usual enthusiasm and felt limp in hers. *What's with this current run of limp men?*

"How are you?" Fidelia asked. Still grinning, she forced the tone of her question to conceal concern about his health. But she noticed instantly the stark contrast between his current haggard appearance and the image she had retained. Her next thought was Giancarlo Mareno's constant refrain about interacting continuously with subordinates in person and often. Things change.

"Had a few health problems recently," Williams grunted. "Nothin' to worry too much about, though. They tell me it's all under control now."

They continued to size each other up for a few seconds. Fidelia sensed enough concern to deal with the issue directly. "What happened?"

"Cancer. I'm getting chemo treatments now. Prognosis is good." The usually talkative Australian was clearly holding something back and coughed twice before he could say more. Within seconds, another revolting cough erupted from deep in his chest, gagging him.

Fidelia pointedly looked at the ashtray on his desk. Mid-morning and it was already half filled more than a dozen cigarette butts. A stench in the air stung her healthy lungs. There could be little doubt about the type of cancer he had.

"Tan said you wanted to talk about the future when he called. What's up?" Williams asked before another sputtering cough, one tinged with a hiss of accumulated phlegm, had his chest heaving erratically.

"He filled you in about the process going forward, right?" Fidelia looked him directly in the eye.

"Yeah. Congratulations. But there won't be much money to send you for a while. Business is the shits." Williams managed to get it out without coughing, but also without any enthusiasm. She waited for him to explain why.

"Visits to the women are down eighty percent this month. Drugs down fifty percent. Loans about the same, but delinquency's up fifty percent. Protection's almost zero. The owners almost dare us to burn their places down so they can at least collect insurance money. Even thefts are off. Only the food and liquor companies are shipping any significant quantities for us to hijack. Most warehouses are locked up tight with nobody working inside."

"Yeah, and it's just the beginning of a pandemic," Fidelia said. "We see it everywhere. Some of the experts say we're in this mess for a couple years."

"Another month like this and I'll have to cut loose some of the women. Can't afford to keep 'em if there's no customers. Now, the North Koreans and Chinese are pissed and making threats. I told them no more girls for now, and both said they'll just find other ways to get Australian dollars. We caught a pair of chinks cutting into our heroin business over in Perth last week. They had bad accidents with a power drill before they confessed and told us who they were working for. If you don't keep those bastards from poaching on my territory, there won't be no money at all to send you."

Williams's vehemence was so intense he managed to sputter all that out before another round of hacking and coughing. He covered his mouth, but Fidelia cringed at the number of germs that must still be escaping around his closed fist every time he coughed. And probably lingered in the stagnant air of the poorly ventilated office. She was tempted to yank out the face mask in her bag.

Civil conversation continued for a few more minutes before Fidelia tired of the repetition and bitterness. Williams pledged his loyalty, but it was clear his support was both limited and tentative. She decided to point their conversation in a different direction.

"Where's Aretta today?" Aretta Musa was a Nigerian-born woman Fidelia had recruited to serve as one of Oliver Williams's girls. A gorgeous prodigy, the woman now oversaw all The Organization's prostitution business in Oceania. Fidelia liked her.

"She's in Melbourne today. Trying to find a way to improve business," Williams said.

"Let's get her back here. I want her to join our talks tomorrow. For today, I'm jet lagged. Wendal and I'll go to the hotel and get some sleep. Let's start tomorrow at nine." She stood to end their meeting.

Apparently surprised the meeting ended so quickly, Wendal lifted himself from his chair a moment or two later. Williams made no effort to stand.

"When we check-in, take a separate room," Fidelia instructed Wendal after the blonde driver dropped them off at the grand entrance to the Five Seasons hotel. "We're both going to be busy this afternoon."

"Why? What's up?"

"I need you to find out what's wrong with Williams. Can you hack into some local hospitals and labs and see if there are any records?"

"Sure. Shall I try to track down his doctor too?" Wendal asked with his usual enthusiasm for a chase.

"Great idea. Call me as soon as you find out." Fidelia punctuated her directive with a promising smile, just to be sure.

Inside the hotel, Fidelia wasted no time. She made one call to Aretta Musa, leaving a message for her to meet at their usual rendezvous spot at nine that evening. Then, she scanned all the data stashed in her computer spreadsheet about Aretta. Next, she compared that data with other leaders of The Organization's business operations in Australia and New Zealand. With painstaking care Fidelia compared each of the individual records she had maintained over her three-decade career.

All that work, all those long hours, the spying, the working behind Giancarlo's back, always worrying that he might find out and kill her—it had all been for moments like this. She was prepared.

Fidelia had first discovered Aretta Musa working in an office in Nigeria. The law graduate sat in on a meeting between the partners of her legal firm and Giancarlo Mareno. He'd wanted to learn about loopholes in Nigerian law that could be exploited to capture and kidnap young girls without detection.

Aretta was a tall, exceptionally beautiful black twenty-five-year-old at the time. Her name translated to 'a charming and enchanting woman' in English, and her posture and manner fit the description perfectly. When Fidelia offered her a job recruiting young women for export—with a salary of one hundred thousand dollars—it took less than ten seconds for Aretta to accept.

She later confided she had been earning less than five thousand dollars annually at the time, despite graduating with the highest grades in her university program. Aretta also shared that she'd won her job with the prestigious law firm only because she'd reluctantly agreed to service all the senior partners on demand. Sometimes three or four of them in a single day.

Fidelia launched the woman's career with The Organization on an extraordinary trajectory. After Aretta had successfully recruited more than five hundred girls from remote areas of Nigeria in her first year,

Fidelia recommended Aretta run the Australian prostitution business for Williams. In that role, she showed remarkable management skills and grew the business by fifty percent in the following two years.

So Fidelia didn't hesitate. Once Wendal's afternoon hacking medical computers definitively confirmed the Australian crime boss was dying of stage-four lung cancer, she made her decision. If she didn't act now, within months there'd be a territorial war for control of Oceania. She couldn't afford that.

"What's the most important lesson you've learned from my mentoring these past years?" Fidelia asked as her clandestine meet-up with Aretta drew toward a conclusion.

"Any further progression in The Organization is entirely up to me," Aretta said with an even tone. "I should have a plan and be prepared to execute it on a moment's notice."

"Exactly right. And now is the time to act. I'll support you. Do it tonight. Then meet me at Oliver Williams's office tomorrow morning at eight." Orders delivered, Fidelia stood up and left the cafe.

———•———

Aretta lured Oliver Williams to his secluded country estate near Sydney. It was where she usually met him for unhurried liaisons. Until then, it was always Oliver who summoned her to perform, but he apparently found nothing untoward about his subordinate's late-night plea to meet for a few minutes.

From behind a curtain in the living room, Aretta confirmed he had come alone as usual. For a second, she toyed with the idea of doing it without the sex, but decided there was too much risk if her timing wasn't perfect.

She dimmed the lights just the way he liked it and checked in a mirror the fanciful short dress he'd bought for her, with cleavage forming a provocative V all the way down below her navel. And she waited seductively on the sofa where their sexual adventures usually began.

She did everything he asked without gagging, even though he coughed often as she performed her duties. Then, she snuggled against him to ask about the upcoming meeting with Fidelia. He told her not to worry. The new female crime boss just wanted to show some muscle. She should just tell Fidelia how bad business was. He had her back. The reassurances seemed hollow and condescending, but Aretta waited patiently until his coughing attacks became more pronounced.

When Williams decided to scamper back to his wife, Aretta walked him to the front door as usual. He liked her to parade nude, give him one last kiss and feel, and wave farewell from the open door.

As his tongue probed deeply into her mouth, she gently put her fingers right behind his ear, then applied increasing pressure on his Mandibular nerve at precisely the sensitive spot. As she passionately pressed her tongue farther into his mouth, she suddenly pressed down on the nerve with a lethal grip.

His knees buckled almost at once, and he tried to fight her off, but growing paralysis made the attempt futile. She pulled her tongue from his mouth just before he sank toward the floor, keeping her left hand tightly clamped on his sensitive nerve. Her strong grip kept him partially upright.

Aretta stole a glance at his face. His eyes bulged. His sallow face was red. With her right hand, she reached into a large urn on a shelf at shoulder height and pulled out her hidden semi-automatic handgun. She released the pressure on his shoulder. Before he could react, she aimed the gun, pulled its trigger, and held it tightly for two seconds.

Oliver Williams expired almost immediately from the half-dozen shots to his chest and face. The silencer on the gun assured no curious neighbors or unwelcome visitors. But Aretta herself screamed out in horror at the sight of the splattered gore.

Instinctively, she dragged the body farther inside and slammed the door. Then she ran for the bathroom and threw up repeatedly. She had never killed before.

When her gut-wrenching repulsion finally subsided, Aretta washed and dressed quickly, then meticulously wiped down the spots she had touched in his home that night. She left the bloody mess of Williams's body just inside the door and locked it on her way out.

The police would probably make only a halfhearted effort to find the crime boss's killer, at any rate. They'd likely announce that his death appeared targeted and there was no danger to the public. Aretta rushed home and showered for more than an hour. Without any sleep, but with a change of clothes, she headed to the restaurant Williams had used as an office and met Fidelia precisely at eight.

———•———

Overnight, Fidelia had called Luigi, made him aware of the issues, and instructed him to put together a team for the next morning. He chose four enforcers from the lending business and told them to report to Fidelia's bodyguard. That unit carried an enviable reputation for brutality among both the citizenry and other sectors of The Organization. They met the bodyguard at the restaurant's unlocked back door and quietly disposed of the sole sentry without a fuss before the women arrived.

"Now, you must complete the consolidation of authority," Fidelia said when she heard Aretta's story and offered suggestions on how that should happen. The two huddled behind the closed door of Oliver Williams's former office until nine o'clock when four others filed in somberly.

First, they surrendered their weapons to the enforcers outside the door, then each took a seat in one of the chairs facing Aretta. She sat with her posture erect, face unsmiling, looking a bit like a schoolteacher.

Fidelia observed the proceedings from one end of the desk with an unobstructed view of the whole room. She didn't invite Wendal to this part of the meeting. It was just her and Aretta with the bodyguard and the guys. Each of the arriving men displayed varying degrees of discomfort. A cough or two. Squirming. Clearing throats. Glances at each other.

"Where's Oliver?" the head of the Australian illicit drug business finally wanted to know.

"Oliver Williams is no longer with us," Aretta replied, looking at each of the men individually for a second or two. Her eyes settled on the questioner last. No one spoke.

"Things will change going forward." Aretta paused again. Apparently satisfied with no immediate reaction from the men, she resumed in an even and unwavering tone.

"I'll continue to oversee the prostitution business for the time being, but the weekly percentages you paid to Oliver for protection of your businesses come to me now. Starting today, I expect you to show me the same loyalty you gave Williams."

All four men looked stunned and glanced from Aretta to Fidelia, then at the two big brutes standing behind each woman and glowering down at the gathering. Only one spoke up. It was the man who had served Oliver Williams the longest. The guy who ran the protection business.

"This is bullshit," he said with disdain. "I report to Oliver Williams and demand to know where he is and what makes you whores think any of us owe you anything."

A nod from Aretta to the thug standing behind Fidelia was barely perceptible. But the man lunged instantly, grabbed the leader of the drug business by his throat from behind, and hauled him to his feet before anyone could react. The enforcer standing behind Aretta drew a powerful semi-automatic handgun from his jacket pocket and pointed it menacingly at the remaining three. Although they had started to stand, all slowly slunk back into their chairs without protest.

Within seconds, the enforcer choking the drug-business guy dragged his astonished prey from the room. Before the door closed, everyone seated heard three pops from the corridor—pops no louder than bursting balloons—before a muffled cry and a loud thump as a body hit the floor.

"Any further discussion on the subject of leadership?" Aretta asked calmly.

The meeting with the remaining crime-bosses was uneventful. Fidelia outlined how The Organization planned to support their businesses going forward. Aretta covered the nitty-gritty of remittances, communication, and reporting protocols. All would change from the days of Oliver Williams. She made it clear no exceptions would be tolerated. The men appeared to reluctantly accept the new order, and each swore an oath of loyalty to the African woman.

Wendal arrived later that afternoon and became the star for the rest of that momentous day. With his powerful laptop computer attached to a wide-screen TV mounted on a wall in Aretta's new office, he demonstrated the mind-blowing technology he expected the Australian branch of The Organization to learn to use.

It took him three hours of clicking, punching keys, and manipulating data at blinding speed. His hands blazed across the keyboard in a blur as he watched for tiny signals on the massive screen. Finally, he announced they were in. The files displayed on the monitor were inside MacMaster Bank, the largest investment bank in Australia.

He spent most of the afternoon demonstrating how to skim five basis points from every trade the bank executed.

"It's only five cents on every hundred dollars traded," he explained patiently. "But this afternoon, algorithms diverted more than a million dollars from MacMaster Bank to our account in the Cayman Islands. They won't even notice it until they try to balance their books at month-end. By then, I'll have created a new algorithm to skim the funds in a different way. They'll have to figure it out all over again. Or they may just raise their customer fees a bit to offset unexplained losses."

"You need to find a technology whiz like Wendal. Maybe a gamer from one of our gambling websites. Or a university research nerd. You get the idea," Fidelia said to Aretta. "When you find one, Wendal will send one of his technology experts to train your person. We'll share the income fifty-fifty."

On their last day in Sydney, Fidelia rewarded Wendal with several hours in bed. When she invited him to her room the night of his triumph over MacMaster Bank, his adrenalin rush and enlarged penis combined to produce a quick but satisfactory orgasm. She let him stay the night. Adding to her pleasure, he awoke the next morning with an erection that led to multiple delightful climaxes until they ordered room service at noon.

Fidelia turned on the TV while they waited for food. The first story carried by ABC News crept across the bottom of the screen with a grand announcement in a red banner.

ECB to Withhold Approval of Polish Licenses for Multima?

"Look at this, Wendal," Fidelia called out with a smug grin. "Your former employer is in trouble again."

"Poland? Is that related to the money laundering charges? Didn't they drop them after Mareno died?"

"They did. But this one may not be The Organization. I think it's somebody else. I'll get Luigi to find out who's involved, but you might want to get those algorithms ready to go again. You might be able to scoop another few million. Let's watch it closely for the next few days."

After a leisurely lunch and shower, they dressed and left for the airport. Their four o'clock flight left on time, and Singapore Airlines again impressed them with outstanding service in the first-class cabin. Everyone used face coverings when not eating or drinking, but the staff made the voyage a pleasure regardless.

On arrival in Singapore eight hours later, Fidelia chose to split from Wendal and the bodyguard. She needed to present visa documents sent from the government offices in Uzbekistan. There was no point complicating the process with a male companion.

"We'll separate here," Fidelia said to Wendal as they walked from the aircraft into the terminal. "Let me know if you find anything on that Multima Financial rumor. And do a good job with our project in Australia. Once you pull out our first hundred million, I'll have you over to the Five Seasons for a night or two."

With a sassy wink and toss of her long hair, she swung on one heel and veered off to the immigration line for travelers entering Singapore with visas. The next stage of her remake of The Organization was about to get underway.

THIRTEEN

Paris, France, Friday February 14, 2020

Suzanne's roommate from college, now her chief operating officer for Farefour Stores globally, met the Multima entourage at Orly, the international airport located on the outskirts of Paris. As usual, Michelle Sauvignon bubbled with enthusiasm and good cheer. That morning, she seemed even more exuberant than usual. Suzanne realized why as soon as they settled into the rear seats of the Peugeot limousine waiting for them at the doorway of the terminal.

"You're engaged! When did this happen?"

Beaming, Michelle theatrically twirled her hand in the air to show off a ring—particularly the spectacular diamond in its center. The chic executive was in her early fifties, taking a first stab at marriage. In contrast, Suzanne had married much earlier, and then divorced a few years afterward. Michelle had climbed the corporate ladder instead, with increasingly important postings around the world. She could barely contain her delight with the latest development.

"Last weekend. I saved the news until we met up," Michelle gushed. "You'll be so jealous when you meet him. He's everything I've ever looked for in a guy!"

"Tell me all about him," Suzanne pleaded, matching her friend's enthusiasm and expression of joy.

"His name is Guillaume. Guillaume Boudreau. He's a couple years younger than us. You might have heard of him. He's CEO of *Les Entreprises Diverses*, one of France's largest corporations. They make all kinds of rubber and plastic products." Michelle paused until Suzanne made the connection and nodded, then rushed on without any prompting. "We met more than a year ago and have seen each other every few weeks for the past several months. In December, he asked me to move in with him. The weeks since then have been the happiest of my life!"

"Sounds wonderful!" Suzanne tried to match the same intensity of delight but missed the mark slightly in tone. She compensated quickly with body language, grinning broadly, and reaching across to give her friend a genuine hug of congratulations.

"I want you to meet him tonight. If it's okay with you, I invited him to join us for dinner," Michelle said. "And I asked him to bring along another guy Guillaume and I both know well. You'll like him, too."

Suzanne didn't let an internal grimace make it to her face. However, the significance of the day's date, Valentine's Day 2020, wasn't lost on her. She wasn't a hermit and didn't dislike men, but she always found friends' efforts to fix her up with someone an unnecessary distraction.

Years before, she'd concluded that chief executive officers—male or female—were really married to their corporations. The commitment of time, energy, and focus required to lead a successful company left little space for a spouse. An occasional dalliance perhaps, but anything longer-term spelled trouble. She didn't dampen Michelle's excitement, but doubted the evening would lead anywhere special.

Their moods and focus shifted upon arrival at the Farefour headquarters in the La Défense area of Paris—a ten-minute walk from the iconic Grande Arche. In that section of Paris, prestigious French businesses flaunted their success with magnificent towers and grand architecture that rivaled cities like New York or Tokyo. A Canadian subsidiary of Multima Corporation might now own Farefour Stores, but citizens there still prized the company as one of France's most respected retail chains. Both women were acutely aware of their responsibilities leading a business icon, particularly now.

For the rest of that first day, it was all business. As in Hong Kong a few weeks earlier, panic buying and hoarding had begun in Europe, and there was chaos in the supply chains feeding Farefour Stores. Michelle's management team briefed them on the latest rapidly changing developments with polished PowerPoint presentations and mountains of data.

People were buying many staples. Few Europeans had large refrigerators or separate freezers in their homes, so stocking up was focused on packaged and tinned goods. Pastas, rice, sauces in jars, flour, and similar items flew off the shelves as quickly as employees could stock them. Sanitary wipes, sprays, and cleansers had already disappeared from store inventories and the warehouses that supplied them. Line-ups at checkouts were long, and employees were overworked.

Presenters took pride in the phenomenal sales volumes they reported, but cautioned the stores' performance might plummet if suppliers didn't respond more quickly. Their shelves would simply become bare. The morning's conclusion: they needed to conduct a blitz buying spree with the chain's primary manufacturers and processors, and it had to happen that afternoon.

Long lunch breaks in Paris were almost a business ritual, but that day everyone settled for baguettes ordered from a local shop. They gobbled down their sandwiches as they debated solutions and developed strategies in meeting rooms. Product group by product group, teams huddled over speakerphones and pressed the companies who delivered their goods to make more available, more quickly.

Suzanne and Michelle spent the entire afternoon moving from office to office, lending their support and exhorting their colleagues to demand more and call in favors. When they regrouped to recap of the day's activities, Suzanne listened intently and mentally tabulated the progress Farefour's buyers had made. It was impressive.

Suppliers had agreed to ship mind-boggling quantities of the popular products over the coming weekend when they'd typically be closed. They also promised to buy massive amounts of ingredients and materials to make more in the coming days. And most promised to ramp up production quantities to previously unheard-of levels.

Their pandemic-sensitive celebration of success was different. Instead of the usual high-fives, Suzanne and Michelle stood at the head of the massive conference room table wearing masks as they positioned their hands in namaste. Then, together, they bowed deeply, recognizing and thanking their staff for a remarkable achievement in only a few hours.

Minutes later, Suzanne's jubilation faded abruptly with a call from Germany.

"The ECB is definitely withholding approval on the banking license for Poland," Wilma Willingsworth said. Her tone was grim and her message bleak. "Worse, they're also putting our other European licenses under review. We can't increase our book of business until they finish their investigation."

"We can't write any more loans until they investigate us?" Suzanne said with a gulp of dismay. "What happened?"

"They haven't stopped us from doing business completely. For example, we can't issue any new credit cards, but we can renew mortgages—provided our loan balances don't rise beyond current levels. It's a pain, but we won't have to close up shop completely." Wilma paused for a moment to let that information sink in before she carried on.

"Everything looked like it was a go for Poland. Just before we were set to wrap up our discussions, an aide came into the meeting and whispered something into the ear of the Director-General. She excused herself and came back about fifteen minutes later. Her face was the palest I've ever seen, and she wasted no time explaining her absence. They had just received new evidence from the USA regarding our involvement in repeated cross-border money laundering over a prolonged period."

"What...what is going on?" Suzanne stammered in shock.

"She wouldn't share any specifics with us but said she hoped we, and our auditors, would cooperate fully with her investigators. A bit more positive news, though. I persuaded her not to issue the review order today. She'll give us the weekend to work informally with her investigators to get to the bottom of the accusations."

"Are you planning to stay there in Frankfurt or fly back to the USA to do your digging?"

"I think it's probably better for me to stay here and try to ferret out what I can from the European Bank investigators. Heather Strong is better placed now to dig into our records. I'll get my people in Chicago to work with her. Still, if there's something amiss, it's much more likely to be in Supermarkets than Financial Services. In my division, we just don't have many international transactions. I combed through the books when I moved there last year."

Within minutes, Suzanne directed Heather Strong to use whatever resources the CFO needed—from anywhere in the company—to root out the source of these claims.

"Let's ask Harrison over at OCD to use his accountants to probe the records at Supermarkets and Financial Services." Suzanne referred to the Managing Partner at their auditing firm.

"And let's be sure to have them review every transaction from our new office in Montreal, too," Suzanne added.

"I understand the urgency." Heather Strong had joined their call from headquarters in Fort Myers. "But it's Presidents' Day weekend. I'm not sure I can reach Harrison. And many of his top people may have already left for weekend trips."

"Eileen has his cell number if you need it. This is a non-negotiable, Heather..."

Her unfinished phrase sealed the discussion. Suzanne's team knew she was almost always willing to listen to objections and usually welcomed opposing views. On those extremely rare occasions she shut down debate, everyone knew further opposition was pointless. The destruction of hundreds of weekend plans was about to begin. It was unfortunate but necessary.

James Fitzgerald and Angela Bonner waited for Suzanne back in the lobby of the San Régis, one of the finest hotels in the world. Both stood chatting near a beautiful wall that was ornately decorated with gilded gold trim. As she swept into the lobby, their expressions telegraphed concern, and Suzanne invited them up to her suite. Michelle Sauvignon's assistant had already handled the check-in, and a butler left a plastic key card on a walnut dining room table as he warmly welcomed her to her suite.

As soon as the pleasantries and coffee service were out of the way, James Fitzgerald began.

"We had a productive day, but not a good one. There's something very wrong going on in the Caymans, but we can't figure it out. Tell Suzanne what you learned, Angela."

"Our formal meetings were all very polite, but blasé. Everyone at EuroNext acknowledged the trading pattern with Farefour shares was badly distorted on January 29. They all agreed the numbered companies pushing down the prices of the shares must have been working together. They also concurred that the unknown entities must have been in cahoots as the share prices soared in the afternoon. However, everyone claimed it was impossible to track the source of the odd computer trading pattern." The forensic investigator shook her head in disgust and disbelief.

"Angela tried everything to get them talking about what they knew, but every time she explored a different angle, they shut her down," James Fitzgerald chimed in.

Suzanne sensed it was better to listen first, then ask questions later. She took a sip of her coffee. Once she set the cup back on the saucer, Angela continued her narrative with a mischievous grin.

"They didn't realize I speak French. After about two hours of roadblocks, we gave up. As we were getting up to shake hands and say our goodbyes, I overheard one of the younger women ask if they shouldn't let us know about the South American angle. The guy shut her down with a warning shake of his head, and I just pretended not to hear anything."

"We got a potent reminder of why it's always important to exchange business cards with everyone at a meeting," James Fitzgerald exclaimed with barely concealed glee.

"Before we left the meeting, Angela handed her card to everyone there, including the young lady. That woman called Angela on her cell phone before we even got to the Metro entrance. Asked if she could meet us somewhere private. Within ten minutes, we met with her in a coffee shop."

"It was clear she was uneasy about meeting us," Angela continued. "But I'd given her a knowing look in the eye when I handed her my card. She realized it was wrong for the EuroNext exchange officials to withhold a vital piece of information that might be very important for our safety."

Angela let James Fitzgerald deliver the bombshell.

"It seems Interpol—that association of international police forces headquartered in Lyon, France—is also investigating the same numbered companies. They think those outfits in the Caymans are connected to a notorious drug lord operating out of Colombia. She wanted us to know we must be very careful if we continue our investigation."

"Wow," Suzanne murmured. "This just gets weirder by the hour."

They agreed to digest the disturbing news for a bit. Suzanne took that break to fill them in about the licensing issues Wilma encountered with the European Bank and the new threats to Multima Financial Services' lending activities. They bounced ideas back and forth for a few minutes before Suzanne decisively set them in motion.

"Let's cancel those meetings you've scheduled with the independent investigators tomorrow. With organized crime possibly involved, I think we'd better bring in Dan Ramirez from security. As for your lunch with the president of the EuroNext exchange, let Michelle and I handle that. I need both of you back in the States."

Suzanne paused for another sip of coffee. They needed time to process her about-face before she set them off on a new mission.

"I'll get the pilots to come back from Frankfurt. They should be here within an hour or two. I want both of you to use the corporate jet and fly back to Atlanta. If we have a problem, Wilma thinks it's probably within Supermarkets. I trust her intuition. And I'd like you guys to ride herd on the OCD forensic investigators and help Heather Strong sort out this money laundering mess."

Before the pair left again for Orly, Suzanne called her chief of security, Dan Ramirez. They brought him up to date with what they knew about the mysterious buying and selling in Farefour stock and the apparent South American connection. Then Suzanne brought up the issue of cross-border money flows.

"Can you get some of your people up to Atlanta today? We have a huge problem brewing with the European Central Bank over here. They told Wilma someone in the US tipped them off about new allegations of

Multima laundering money. We've got two days to find out what's going on or the shit hits the fan."

"I'll have to cancel some weekend leaves, but I can get a pair of forensic experts in Atlanta tonight, and I'll get there tomorrow," Dan Ramirez volunteered. "I think we should be worried about this side of the Atlantic too. If the Feds have already shared something with the folks in Europe, we should expect some flack here again right after the long weekend."

"Agreed. That's why I'd like you to spend some time with your former colleagues. Can we get some of your old cronies at the FBI to dig a little? Let us know who's causing the problem? And what evidence they have? For the audit resources, right now it must be like searching for a needle in a haystack." Suzanne had tempered her desperation with a softer tone.

Their conference call ended with Dan Ramirez undertaking to do what he could with the FBI and promising to keep in touch with James Fitzgerald and Heather Strong as they spearheaded the weekend's desperate search.

As Suzanne closed the door behind them, she glanced at her watch. Only minutes remained to prepare for the dinner Michelle Sauvignon had arranged with some blind date. After a quick shower, Michelle let her hair drip dry as she applied make-up quickly and did a cursory inspection. She sighed at the discovery of specks of gray shooting up among the roots of her brunette shoulder-length hair. A visit to the stylist was imperative as soon as she returned to Fort Myers, and maybe time for a color-change too.

Michelle had warned Suzanne they'd eat on an outdoor patio at one of the best restaurants in Paris, and temperatures outside were in the mid-fifties. It would get colder after dark. Suzanne squeezed into a pair of Michael Kors jeans, buttoned up a warm long-sleeve top, and tugged a large turtle-neck wool sweater over her head before she dried and brushed her hair into place.

Since she'd become CEO of Multima almost three years earlier, two bodyguards traveled with Suzanne everywhere. Jasmine Smith-Field, a muscular woman of color who'd served with the US military in Iraq during the wars, had been her most constant companion. Suzanne trusted her judgment implicitly.

Jasmine had already checked out their route to the restaurant while Suzanne met with her visitors in the suite. Her protector gave her the okay to walk to the restaurant rather than use a limousine. Suzanne liked fresh air and physical activity after a strenuous day, so the pair joined Willy Landon—her even larger and more muscular bodyguard— who typically watched her suite from the outside.

A fifteen-minute walk later, Suzanne met Michelle Sauvignon, her fiancé Guillaume and Stefan Warner, the blind date. First impressions were surprisingly positive. Stefan was good looking, appeared very fit, and was considerably taller than Suzanne. She had to look up to take in the details. Long, wavy black hair, stylish eyeglasses, sparkling blue eyes, and a tight smile caught her eye as he stretched out his hand.

"I'm delighted to meet you, Suzanne." His English had a noticeable German accent, and he shook her hand with one pump in the stiffly formal way they liked to greet each other in Germany. Unsurprisingly, he applied the correct amount of pressure to her hand, and parted his lips only enough to form the outline of a smile.

"*Enchanté*." Suzanne beamed with practiced charm.

Michelle Sauvignon jumped in to let Stefan know Suzanne spoke French. "She's *Québecoise*, you know. Except for her accent and occasional odd Canadian expression, she speaks just like us," Michelle teased.

For reasons Suzanne never understood, Parisians always liked to point out the small differences between French spoken in Quebec and Paris—even among friends. Suzanne didn't react, and Stefan appeared more comfortable as they switched to French.

"We already told Stefan about your role at Multima," Michelle said to Suzanne. "You might be interested to know he's a doctor—a doctor of business."

"As in a business consultant?" Suzanne asked. A more charming smile flashed this time.

"No. I have a doctorate in international business. I lecture at the École Polytechnique."

His tone was casual and unassuming. Instantly, Suzanne was impressed with his credentials. A German scholar teaching at one of the best universities in France. The guy must be well beyond ordinary. She signaled her interest in learning more with a tilt of her head and most engaging smile.

Maybe it was the wine, or the stimulating conversation with an intellectual, or a combination of both. Regardless, Suzanne and Stefan came to dominate the conversation around the table that evening. At one point, Michelle's surreptitious wink and knowing smile conveyed her delight at how well the pair were connecting.

Stefan seemed enthralled with the complexities of Multima's businesses around the globe, and Suzanne found his probing questions challenging and thoughtful. He clearly understood the corporate world. When she switched their conversation to arts and culture, Stefan was even more impressive. She listened intently as he politely argued with Guillaume and Michelle about the most illuminating museums in Paris. He knew them all intimately and described each with passion. But he also displayed an engaging sense of humor.

In fact, they all laughed often—not forced, polite chuckles—but genuine hearty guffaws and giggles. Before Suzanne realized it, the number of guests on the patio had gradually dwindled. Their table and the small one in the corner for her bodyguards were the only ones occupied. She checked her watch and expressed shock at the late hour.

"It's been great joining you all for dinner." Suzanne picked up her bag to leave. "I've been going for almost forty hours with only a short nap on the jet. And Jasmine has our morning run scheduled for six."

"Who's Jasmine?" Stefan wondered. Suzanne pointed to her bodyguards in the corner, also rising from their table.

"Jasmine and Willy are my security detail. They follow me everywhere. But you're also welcome to join us for the walk back to the San Régis, if you wish," Suzanne offered, a little more quickly than she intended.

As they turned on the sidewalk and headed toward her hotel, Stefan offered his bent arm in a chivalrous gesture. Suzanne was indeed tired and wore four-inch stiletto heels. She wrapped her hand comfortably in the crook of his elbow and held it there as their conversation and laughter continued all the way back to the San Régis. Jasmine and Willy stayed well back out of earshot, with their usual discretion.

Regardless of their good cheer, Suzanne took care to signal Stefan nothing more would happen that night. At this stage in her life, she was no prude. But she rarely slept with someone until she knew him really well. Surprisingly, there was a tug of temptation to break that rule with this guy. But not that night. She was exhausted. Still, she didn't rule out the possibility for another day.

"It's been a great evening with you, Stefan," She stood on her toes to give him an inviting smile and polite peck on the cheek before she swept into the bright and well-appointed lobby alone.

Maybe later?

FOURTEEN

Fidelia noticed a difference entering the country right after leaving Wendal Randall and her bodyguard in the arrivals area of Singapore's over-the-top international airport. Things were different in the Asian city-state. One Chinese woman, impressed with the unique architecture in an opulent section where people lined up for immigration control, drew the ire of a uniformed officer. He demanded she put away her camera instantly. No photos allowed.

In the line-up Fidelia joined, four or five people ahead of her chatted among themselves casually while they waited their turn. The same uniformed officer curtly instructed them to make a single line, in straight rows, while they waited. He showed no humor when the young people laughed uneasily as they followed his orders.

Earlier, public health officials had tested everyone's body temperature digitally as they left the aircraft. Armed police stood by to assure full compliance. And posters everywhere warned people to stay two meters apart because of the coronavirus.

When an immigration officer finally pressed a button to release a stubby metal barrier, Fidelia stepped forward and adopted her most submissive posture. Shy smile. Eyes downward. Her posture conveyed a docile and unthreatening manner in every way she could imagine. Despite Singapore's professed welcome of all races and cultures, the officer handling her case apparently hadn't got the memo.

First, he wanted to know from where she was coming. Then, he had to know the cities she visited in Australia. After that, in an overbearing tone, the names of people she met there. Why did she want to live in Singapore? Where would she stay? How long? After several minutes of interrogation, he called a specialist who led Fidelia to a small room with two uncomfortable plastic chairs and a tiny desk.

The immigration specialist grilled her for another half hour. Many of the details the woman wanted to know were already answered in documents she held in her hand. It appeared to be a test of truthfulness, but Fidelia had committed the entire document to memory. She confidently responded to each inquiry without hesitation.

Before they released her from immigration control, another public health official posed a dozen questions about her health. Took her temperature again. And warned her not to go outside the Five Seasons Hotel for the next fifteen days. Then she instructed Fidelia to download a tracking app and checked it was correctly installed on her phone.

As a final step, the immigration officer kneeled on the floor and wrapped an electronic bracelet around Fidelia's ankle. With a flourish she locked it, then warned her sternly not to remove the device—for any reason—before visiting an immigration office at the address on the card she handed her. And only after fifteen days, she emphasized.

At an airport exit, Fidelia met the guy who had driven Wendal and her to the airport a few days earlier. He was waiting with her bodyguard. Within minutes, she sat comfortably in the firm leather rear seats of a gray Mercedes Benz, speeding toward the downtown core on virtually deserted roadways at two o'clock in the morning.

A flood of emails had popped up on her phone when she turned it on to download the coronavirus tracking app. As she skimmed through the list, one message caught her eye. With a silent grimace, she forwarded it to Wendal and highlighted the "urgent" icon before sending it. There were problems in the Cayman Islands. But he was an hour ahead of her leaving the airport and might already be in bed.

With pursed lips, she pressed the speed dial and had him on the line after a half-dozen rings. Her conversation was brief. "Sorry to wake you, big guy. I need you to check your email and get back to me before you sleep again."

The Five Seasons hotel butler assigned to her floor recognized Fidelia the moment she stepped off the elevator. As usual, he greeted her politely by name with a warm smile and a deep bow of respect. Together, they inspected the five-room suite to ensure everything met her expectations before he offered to bring anything more she needed. The genial host had just carefully backed out of the doorway when her phone rang. It was Wendal.

"Your information was right. There's been a slip-up with the guys in South America. Someone forgot to scrub an IP address, and the French stock exchange authorities have made a connection between the Cayman Islands accounts and Colombia."

"I was hoping the guy at Interpol was wrong," Fidelia groaned. "How do we fix it?"

"They've already cleaned out the Cayman offices. Now, we'll have to do the same in Colombia, within the next few hours. Then we'll have to reset IP protocols for all the servers to somewhere else," Wendal explained. "We'll likely be down for only a couple days if they move fast enough in Colombia."

The guy who ran The Organization's activities in Latin America was a young wannabe playboy named Juan Álvarez. Fidelia checked the date on her calendar and guessed she'd find him at his summer home. She was right, but was also not surprised when a woman with a sensuous young voice put her on hold while she looked for her boss.

The plaything was probably one of the girls from his prostitution business. Apparently, Juan was sunbathing on a beach across from his home in the San Rafael quarter of Punta del Este in Uruguay. She'd run over there with his phone right away. Fidelia knew the house and realized it would take a few minutes. She used the time on hold to organize her thoughts.

Like other Argentinians, Juan loved to spend time across the Rio de la Plata in Uruguay. In the middle of a South American summer, his countrymen numbered in the hundreds of thousands visiting the small country. Fidelia's call would cut his vacation short, but that's what happened when people screwed up.

She liked the guy. He'd spent about a year with her in Uzbekistan before Wendal arrived. She'd plucked him from the Argentinian prostitution business he ran under Giancarlo Mareno. Juan Álvarez ran his business well, and she saw good potential for him when the time was right. And he made love expertly.

Fidelia had no qualms about using him the way men everywhere use women. She too had sexual needs, and he satisfied them very well. Of course, when she saw potential in a promising young guy, she took extra care not only to satisfy his desires but also trained him to want more.

So, when Mareno needed a change of control in the Latin American operations, she persuaded him that Juan Álvarez was the right man for the job. As a result, his loyalty to her was unquestioned. There had been no need to visit him in person to extract his oath of allegiance after she got rid of Mareno and seized control of The Organization.

Still, Juan was expendable. If he didn't get his IP protocol problem fixed within the next twenty-four hours, it would be over. A new leader couldn't show weakness when mistakes were made. Watching Mareno for thirty years, she'd learned that lesson well.

And it was the only reason she waited patiently on the phone while

Juan's young thing ran along the beach to get him on the line. This matter was just too important. While Fidelia waited, she took stock of her progress to get where she was. And remembered why it mattered.

———•———

She'd grown up in a poor, undesirable quarter near the core of San Juan, Puerto Rico. But she'd been lucky. Her brain worked well—apparently very well compared to others. Fidelia went to schools run by the Catholic Church and showed up every day. She liked most of her teachers and was considered the top student in her classes.

From secondary school, Fidelia won a scholarship to Columbia University in New York for her undergraduate and law school studies. There, she ranked among the top five when she received her JD, before accepting an entry-level job as a junior attorney with a high-powered New York firm. Things started out all right, but Fidelia soon realized her bosses assigned her nothing but mind-numbing documentation reviews. The male lawyers got all the good cases and resulting high incomes. Her career went nowhere.

She even slept with two persistent senior partners, hoping to move forward in the firm. It was all to no avail. More frustrating was her inability to progress financially. New York was an expensive place to live, and she fell more into debt every month. A friend eventually taught her how to make "date money" on the side and connected her with a madam who supplied well-paying men to augment her paltry salary as a junior attorney.

Fidelia knew the Church considered it a sin, but imagined that God must be somewhat understanding on that one. Actually, it was His loyal servants who first coached Fidelia to use her hands and mouth to deftly create sexual ecstasy. Through her middle and high school years, two supposedly celibate priests and a wayward nun had each paid her generously to keep secret their regular clandestine sexual liaisons. It turned out they did her a big favor.

Within weeks of "dating" for money, Fidelia found herself consistently earning thousands of dollars a week. Far more than her lawyer's salary. As a result, life became much better. So, she became a full-time call girl and was eventually discovered by Giancarlo Mareno. She remembered their first conversation as clearly as if it were yesterday.

"I'll pay you a million dollars a year to start," the crime boss said. "And five percent of all the income we generate." The million-dollar salary caught her attention.

"Working with you, how?"

"I want you to find other women just like you—charming, exquisitely beautiful women who truly like to satisfy their customers. We control thousands of women around the world and need a constant supply of new ones. Select the best of those women, train them, and oversee them. I'll take care of you."

Fidelia did the math quickly. She accepted his offer within seconds. It was a "no-brainer," as her attorney colleagues used to say, and her subsequent rise within The Organization had been nothing short of meteoric. Salary and bonuses stretched into the millions of dollars each year. Most found their way to numbered offshore bank accounts.

Before she eliminated Mareno and claimed his billions, her dozens of secret offshore accounts already held hundreds of millions. All outside of the purview of greedy governments. Now, having won the grand prize, she had no intention of losing it.

—•—

"You have a problem to fix," she began as soon as Juan Álvarez said hello. "It's mid-afternoon there. Get in your nifty jet and get to Colombia. The problem needs to be handled before midnight today."

Juan began to protest the short notice but thought better of it and stopped after about three words. Fidelia then gave him the low-down on the Interpol tip. She told him to choose a new location, somewhere in Chile this time. Then, she instructed him to talk to Wendal about more secure IP protocols for the new servers. He said he got it all.

It was approaching three in the morning in Singapore when she finished her call with Juan Álvarez, but Fidelia had one more task. With a cheap throwaway phone, she called another number in France, this time in Aix-en-Provence.

"Call Deschamps at Interpol," Fidelia began. "Tell him you're sending over your youngest girl in Lyon. Find out which place he'd like to use. Then take the travel agency helicopter to get yourself up there too. Make him a very happy man all weekend long."

FIFTEEN

James Fitzgerald briefly wrestled with his priorities after settling into the plush seats of the Bombardier Global 5000 Suzanne Simpson had loaned him to return quickly to the US. Since his divorce two years earlier, he had lacked female companionship. The woman accompanying him on the trip more than piqued his interest. One reason he'd invited her was to leverage the time in Paris to perhaps kindle a romance. She appealed to him on every level.

But he quickly decided getting to know Angela Bonner better was less urgent than a few hours of sleep. For forty years, corporate priorities had always come first, and it was a tough habit to break.

The day ahead would be a crucial one for Multima Corporation. While he was now only a member of its board of directors, the European Union's threat to impose sanctions on the banking licenses of Multima Financial Services was particularly annoying. After all, it was he who had created and built the division into a global powerhouse.

Dan Ramirez, Multima's chief of security, met them at the general aviation entrance of Fulton County Airport as arranged. After they were all seated in the company's Cadillac SUV, James noticed his long-time friend and colleague looked exhausted. He must have driven almost the same number of hours from Fort Myers as James and Angela spent flying from Paris.

"Did you get any sleep last night?" James asked as Ramirez squinted into the bright morning light.

"No. I just arrived a few minutes ago and had breakfast down the road while I waited for you." The former high-ranking FBI official used a just-the-facts-ma'am tone. The habit had carried on well beyond his law enforcement service.

"I guess you probably don't have much news to report yet." James wanted to be prepared for any developments before they reached the office.

"Unfortunately, I was on the phone almost the entire time I was driving up here." He nodded toward Angela in the rear seat. "Are we okay to talk openly?"

James gave a nod. Within a few seconds, he was glad he chose sleep over sex on the overnight flight. Dan's disturbing news report went on for several minutes.

"When the FBI makes a call to almost any Latin American police force with a request for action, the response is usually immediate. Last night, a former colleague who runs the South American file sent the National Police of Colombia out to visit the address you got from the young lady at EuroNext in Paris." Dan smiled before he continued.

"It was a warehouse in an industrial section of Medellín. When they got there, they found a truck backed up to the door of the place. A guy came out with an armful of laptop computers. When they confronted him, he threw them on the ground and tried to run off. The police chased him, but he was too fast. They couldn't catch him, so they chose to shoot. The shot was high and hit him in the back of the head. Blew him up."

Riveted by the tale, James listened. Angela loosened her seatbelt and leaned forward between the front seats so she could hear better. After a sip from his cardboard cup of coffee, Dan continued.

"Unfortunately, as the officers were returning to the building, they noticed another guy throwing something into the truck's fuel tank. A second or two later, the whole thing exploded. The guy at the truck tried to leap away but wasn't fast enough. Flames engulfed his entire body before the police could get to him."

"Sounds like organized crime to this layman," James ventured.

"Yeah. That's what the boys at the FBI think too. They're sending two agents to Colombia this morning to investigate further. But there's more," Ramirez said, then paused.

James Fitzgerald was known throughout the company as the guy who tolerated only a single piece of paper on his desk. Uncomfortable focusing on more than one subject at a time, "there's more" was the last thing he wanted to hear that morning and his colleague knew it.

"While I was talking to my guy at the FBI, he told me accusations about Multima's involvement in money laundering have surfaced again." Dan took another sip of his coffee and glanced briefly toward the rear seat to be sure it was okay to continue.

"Seems the Justice Department got a tip overnight from an informant in Germany. The European Central Bank has uncovered some new evidence. The FBI didn't know anything about it. They're flying an agent over there this morning."

"Shit! The ECB promised Wilma they wouldn't release any info to US authorities before Monday. Now we're in trouble on both sides of the Atlantic."

"And maybe more trouble than we thought," Dan continued. "It looks like the audit team from OCD has indeed found some accounting irregularities at Supermarkets."

James hoped the barrage of bad news was finished and muttered thanks as they drove into the parking lot of Multima Supermarkets' headquarters. His overloaded brain struggled to sort through the multitude of implications this info dump foreshadowed.

None of the emerging scenarios looked favorable.

SIXTEEN

Singapore, Sunday February 16, 2020

Wendal Randall moved in for the kill. He felt a primeval excitement surging as he tried to slow his heart rate and keep his hand from shaking. Wendal loved everything about video games and devoted most of his nights to his passion, sleeping as little as possible. His opponent would soon take an unsuspecting step around the corner, and he'd strike a fatal blow. That's how it worked with the horror video game S.T.A.L.K.E.R.

This latest version out of Ukraine was set in the area surrounding the Chernobyl disaster site in an alternative reality. A supposed second explosion occurred at the nuclear power plant sometime after the first and caused strange changes in the area. S.T.A.L.K.E.R., as an acronym on Google, grabbed Wendal's attention instantly. When he realized it stood for Scavengers, Trespassers, Adventurers, Loners, Killers, Explorers, and Robbers, he was sold. And for the past three weeks, Wendal felt like a sleep-deprived zombie.

Once the satisfying rush of the kill subsided, he shut off the laptop computer connected to a massive screen on the wall of his borrowed suite in Singapore. He leaned back in his executive-style chair and parked his feet up on a cluttered desk. Wendal needed a few minutes to reassess his current situation.

Stan Tan seemed a perfect host. Upon Wendal's arrival, Tan showed his guest to the small, separate three-room house tucked away in the massive back yard of the mansion compound. Then Tan told Wendal to do whatever he liked with the place. The only rule was to do it inside the house. Everything was secret that way. The structure was essentially a technology cocoon where nothing could be tracked, overheard, or spied upon.

Outdoors it wasn't so secure, but Wendal spent little time getting in touch with nature, so it made no difference. Technology had always been his passion. Even as a boy, video games, computers and science had always consumed him.

Some people called him a genius, though Wendal thought that description was a little exaggerated. At one time, a fawning American business magazine referred to him as the Steve Jobs of his generation. That was probably an exaggeration too. He'd started only one new computer company so far. By the time he was Wendal's age, Jobs had founded two.

But Wendal believed the best was yet to come. He was still in his mid-forties, very healthy, and more ambitious than ever.

Fidelia Morales might think of him as merely a sex toy, but she wouldn't be the new head of The Organization without him. His app to intercept voice communications without physically planting listening devices on subjects had won Fidelia her job. Wendal first realized the ultimate potential of that discovery during the bizarre days he and a female German companion were captured by the FBI and secretly spirited away to Guantanamo Bay, in Cuba of all places.

Rogue agents had seized them both as they stepped down the stairway of a private jet Howard Knight had organized to get Wendal home in a hurry. The FBI whisked the pair away in the middle of the night to a waiting helicopter that took them to Cuba. There, guards treated them like the handful of Middle Eastern terrorists the US government detained. For months, an unholy alliance between the FBI and CIA confined Wendal and his companion with threats of a trial for trumped-up charges of some national security violation. All because he'd unwittingly brought a hooker back from Germany.

Bizarrely, their capture and confinement related to a global search for that same Howard Knight. Wendal didn't know it at the time, but Knight was the financial genius behind a massive criminal element known as The Organization. However, the financial wizard had apparently crossed the crime boss Giancarlo Mareno and was then a fugitive on the run.

Unbelievably, the FBI was also after Knight. For some reason, agents in Cuba thought Wendal and the German whore had enough technical expertise to hack communication lines and pinpoint Knight's precise location. The agents figured they could capture the fugitive, then milk information from Knight and the woman he was traveling with. They were convinced that could lead to the arrest and imprisonment of key figures in The Organization.

As far-fetched as their scheme seemed, it turned out the woman from Germany was more than a lady of the night. She was also a technical whiz. And she wasn't actually German. She was a former technologist with a Russian government security agency who had bailed out and moved to

Germany after she learned she could make twenty times more money recruiting girls and women to serve as prostitutes for The Organization.

The FBI eventually offered to drop all the trumped-up national security charges against the pair. They also offered to provide new identities in the witness protection program—but only if Wendal and the woman could find Howard Knight before The Organization did.

Klaudia, the Russian-German woman, put Wendal on the path toward their stunning discovery. She remembered some experiments the Russian agency undertook to deal with dissidents and thought they could replicate it. The FBI supplied powerful computer servers and a couple brilliant resources from their technology group at Quantico to help. Within only a few weeks, the pair indeed found a way to penetrate telecom servers in Latin America. They intercepted one conversation Knight's companion had with an Eastern European friend that led to an apartment in Buenos Aires.

Hours later, Argentinian secret police snatched Knight and his companion outside that apartment complex. Within a short time, an FBI jet from Argentina arrived at Guantanamo Bay carrying Knight and a woman named Fidelia Morales. Before the new captives arrived in Cuba, Wendal had already dreamed of developing a revolutionary new technology to make himself a billionaire.

However, his new identity in the witness protection program—together with its smothering rules and suffocating bureaucracy—didn't satisfy Wendal for long. To put it simply, his life sucked. Although they hid him in northern California, it was boring, uneventful, and going nowhere within mere months.

That's what led him to track down the same Fidelia Morales he'd met in Cuba. By then, she was living in Uzbekistan. It was surprisingly easy to find her once he spent some time on the Dark Web, a popular spot for criminals and other lowlifes. Naturally, she didn't use her real name. But Wendal had dug into everything he could find about Fidelia Morales and her life before she "retired" from The Organization.

The woman's history was impressive, and she had been very active on the Dark Web. Wendal first hacked into servers of service providers used by The Organization. From information gleaned there, he built an algorithm to find messages she had sent to contacts in the world of human trafficking.

It was there he came across the guy from South America and started a dialogue. Shockingly, he was able to provide an IP address to track Fidelia. This led to an obscure village called Muynak in Uzbekistan, located up at the top corner of the country near its border with Kazakhstan.

Wendal engaged in several months of coded conversations and secret planning with her before Fidelia consented to a clandestine meeting in Singapore. After their initial get-together, weeks of planning followed before she spirited Wendal and his two Californian technicians into Uzbekistan and her secluded compound.

After settling into the remote location, Wendal became her most valuable resource in all matters related to technology almost at once. There was no doubt she depended a great deal on his know-how. But oddly, she seemed to think she controlled him. For a while longer, he'd let her continue to think so. Eventually, she'd learn.

"Are you ready to play now?" A young female voice in the background giggled.

When Wendal swiveled around to face his video game partners, they were already undressed. Their tongues explored each other's mouths with exaggerated passion as hands gently caressed aroused nipples. They knew their sexual escapades turned him on, and tonight was no different.

He watched until they had worked their way down each other's bodies to their pubic regions, inserted their fingers, and penetrated each other enough to squirm in delight. Then Wendal ambled to their side of the room, squeezed his tongue into the mishmash, and waited for their attention to shift. As usual, it took only a few moments before he could feel them reaching to unbutton his clothes.

Moments later, excited tongues explored every nook and crevice of his body as they undressed him. Their sexual fervor grew with his erection and climaxed only when all three lay exhausted on a giant mattress in the middle of the floor in the room where they worked and played.

Once again, Wendal grinned. How absurd for Fidelia to think she controlled him with the reward of a night in her bed.

SEVENTEEN

Paris, France, Sunday February 16, 2020

Suzanne slipped out of bed with her phone's first ring. One glance at the number confirmed the early morning call would probably take more time than ideal under the circumstances. She didn't dare greet her caller with a whisper, so she chose a tone just above a murmur instead.

"Hi, Eileen. Give me a moment." She glanced at still-sleeping Stefan as she grabbed a robe from the closet, then scooted silently toward the living room, still debating whether she should just have them all call back after she was dressed and comfortable.

A quick glance at the clock on the wall of her spacious suite at the San Régis Hotel confirmed it was six fifteen in the morning in Paris. That made it about fifteen minutes after midnight in the eastern US. Empathy with her team won out. At least she had savored an enchanting dinner with Stefan, followed by a couple hours of exquisite sex and a few hours of sleep. Her callers had been slogging on the job for eighteen or more demanding hours. She told Eileen she was ready.

James Fitzgerald quarterbacked the call, but about a dozen other team members also clustered in the main conference room at Multima Supermarkets headquarters in Atlanta. He realized they'd interrupted her sleep and graciously offered a few moments to let her brew a coffee and fully wake up before they began. Though grateful for the offer, she declined. She wanted to know what they'd found.

"It's going to take a few minutes for me to tell the story." Methodical as always, James slowly outlined what they'd learned in Atlanta.

"The picture doesn't look good. We encountered more than a few twists and turns before we got to where we are. One of the bright young gals on the OCD forensic auditing team noticed something curious with a few invoices for fruits and vegetables purchased by the produce department. I'll let her explain."

"There were several relatively small invoices—all less than the usual ten-thousand-dollar verification threshold—for fresh blueberries." The young auditor sounded like a recent university grad, and her voice began tentatively. She nervously cleared her throat before continuing.

"What struck me as unusual were the dates on the invoices—July 2018. I wondered why Multima would buy blueberries from a supplier in Chile, in July. Blueberries are plentiful here in Georgia in the summer. Why didn't Multima buy locally? Then it struck me. If blueberries were in season in Georgia, in the Northern Hemisphere, they probably wouldn't even be harvesting them in the Southern Hemisphere in July. So, I googled it. Sure enough, the blueberry season in Chile is typically November to March."

The young woman had a flair for the dramatic and paused to let the implications set in.

Anticipating bad news, Suzanne took advantage of the pause.

"Let me interrupt you for a second. I think I need that cup of coffee before we go much farther." Still holding her phone, she dashed over to a Nespresso machine and loaded it. Once she had pressed the start button, she said, "Continue."

"Well, I checked the supplier's name on Google and couldn't find a website for the company. I tried everything I could think of. I checked the names of the produce suppliers in Chile, company registrations, even different spellings of the supplier's name. Nothing came up, so I reported that to my supervisor."

"That was just before we arrived," James chimed in. "So, we got the entire team together and did a blitz on all South American produce invoices since 2016. A clear pattern emerged. We found a few thousand relatively small invoices—always just below the ten-thousand-dollar reporting threshold—from a couple dozen South American suppliers. Those suppliers submitted invoices and were paid every month of the year, regardless of the growing season."

"Fraudulent invoices," Suzanne whispered in disbelief. "Stretching back four years."

The implications sent her reeling. Four years was significant. During two of those four years, she was still the president of Multima Supermarkets. The fraud began on her watch.

"I'm afraid so," James replied. "We can't find anything on the Internet about any of the companies in question. At this stage, it looks like more than fifty million dollars over the four years."

Suzanne took a deep breath. Fifty million was a considerable amount, even though it really represented no more than a rounding error for a company with sales of over fifty *billion* dollars a year.

Her current Chief Financial Officer oversaw Multima Supermarket's financial operations at that time. "What do you think about all this, Heather?"

"It looks like I really slipped up on this one," Heather responded with her usual candor. "I vaguely remember noticing something odd about that vendor and recall requesting a more granular summary from Kim Jones, the section head, a couple times. I don't remember ever getting her report, but the amounts were so small they didn't show up on my radar for more rigorous follow-up."

"Okay. What does Kim Jones say now?" Suzanne demanded to know.

"Unfortunately, Kim is no longer with us. She left the company last week. We've tried her phone and last address. The phone number was disconnected, and her apartment is empty. No one knows where she's gone." It was James Fitzgerald who had the courage to confirm the dreaded news.

Dan Ramirez followed with what they were doing to find the missing former employee.

"We filed a missing person's report with the Atlanta and Georgia state police departments. I've talked with one of my contacts at the FBI to get them working the back channels for anything they can find about her whereabouts. They'll use facial recognition software to see if they can place her at Hartsfield-Jackson or Miami International any time in the past week. My people learned she had a reservation with Delta for a flight to Miami three days ago but never showed up."

"This does not sound good at all." A classic understatement, but Suzanne needed to buy some time to regroup. She felt a little flushed, and her heart was racing much more quickly than usual, but she wasn't prepared to let her CFO off the hook too easily.

"Heather, who was this Kim Jones reporting to?"

"Her immediate supervisor was the accounts payable director. That director reported to Bessie Forsia, who replaced me. She's in the room in Atlanta," Heather offered.

"Hi, Bessie. What can you tell us about these payments?" Suzanne asked.

"It looks as though I dropped the ball on this one too. I remember Heather flagging one of the payments and recall asking Kim's superior for more info. Unfortunately, I didn't see it as a priority, and with everything else going on, it slipped through the cracks."

"Mistakes happen." Suzanne took a long, deep breath. Still, her voice hardened more than expected. "But we're talking four years of mistakes here. Get someone on your team to rework our policies and procedures. We won't tolerate a repeat of this, and I'll have to report this major lapse to the board of directors. James, would you oversee a fix as part of your growing list of director's responsibilities, please?"

"Sure. I'll work with Bessie and Heather to get it done as quickly as possible. But I think we first need to focus on the damage already done." Tactfully, James shifted the conversation again. "There's no doubt the payments caught the attention of regulators. Surely, the money flow gives the appearance of a pattern created to avoid central bank scrutiny in both the US and the receiving country."

"Fair enough," Suzanne said "But we're the victim in this fraud. We had nothing to gain by making these payments. In fact, we lost fifty-million dollars. Whatever gave the banking authorities the impression we're laundering money?"

"Let me handle that one," Angela Bonner interjected. "The European Central Bank apparently created a very sophisticated algorithm to track transactions. It watches for patterns and creates a red flag when any consistent pattern develops. Ninety-nine-point-nine percent of the time, the pattern is boring and reflects money ending up in a legitimate bank account in a regulated country. These payments were all transferred several times between several banks before they ended up in accounts in Valparaíso, Chile."

"Let me guess," Suzanne said. "That bank account is for a numbered company that can't be traced."

"Precisely," Angela replied. "And that's bank accounts—plural. And they're all empty. Whoever is behind this has highly sophisticated programming and technology expertise. But it looks like they didn't think this all the way through. Either they didn't know the ECB could monitor those transactions or they didn't care."

Suzanne retrieved her espresso from the machine and listened to the briefing for almost an hour. First Angela, then James, then several people from the OCD auditing firm took turns filling in missing theoretical pieces of the puzzle. Tapping everyone's creativity around the table, the group tried to hypothesize who might have created the fraud and why it had proved so successful. No consensus developed.

"Here's the dilemma as I see it." James set out to summarize in his usual deliberate style. "The ECB already knows everything we now know. The people there saw the patterns and realize all the money was eventually funneled to a few accounts. But they don't see Multima as a victim. They must think someone at Multima is the ultimate beneficiary of the fraudulent transfers. Otherwise, why didn't we—or OCD during their audits—figure it out? Why did the company allow it to go on for almost four years?"

A total and awkward silence followed as all the participants realized the implications. If the money laundering was for the benefit of someone within Multima, it could be more than illegal money transfers—it might be embezzlement. Either way, she had to act quickly.

In Paris, Suzanne imagined the discomfort everyone around the table must be feeling. But she had little doubt her own inner turmoil was greater. What could she have done differently when she was in charge at Supermarkets? What should Heather Strong have done differently? And why was Heather so noticeably quiet during the theorizing? Was she just shell-shocked with all the events or was there more?

It would have been so much better for this call to be video rather than just audio.

"How do we resolve this by the end of today?" Suzanne asked, knowing she wouldn't like the answer. Angela Bonner jumped in.

"By the end of today is impossible," she answered, her tone matter of fact. "But I believe the problem is solvable. We need to put a team on the ground in Valparaíso, Chile. From there, we can access company registrations, meet banking authorities, and tap less conventional information sources. Chile is an exasperating country for foreigners to do business in. However, I have resources there I've worked with and trust. It might take a couple months. We can find the answer, though."

"I sense a big 'but' in your argument," Suzanne concluded.

"Right. *But* you might not like the answer."

Their course of action was clear, whether Suzanne would be happy with the outcome or not.

Within minutes, they had linked in Wilma in Frankfurt and finalized a strategy. James, Angela Bonner, and the observant young woman from OCD would leave that night for Chile, using Multima's corporate jet. OCD's partner in Atlanta would enlist his counterpart in Chile and arrange for three forensic accountants from their Santiago office to meet in Valparaíso Monday morning.

And Suzanne would fly to Frankfurt to meet up with Wilma. Their mission: buy more time from the ECB. A long sigh of resignation punctuated her sudden pang of disappointment as the call ended and participants scurried off with their immediate individual priorities defined.

The dreaded "corporate curse" raised its ugly head again. Mere hours had passed since she reveled in an intimate, late-evening dinner with the charming Stefan Warner, one that led to the best sexual encounter she could remember. For now, it would have to end there. Once again, a business crisis drowned personal interests with a compelling priority.

It was a curse that had cost her a marriage, eliminated a Japanese lover, and cast a cloud over any possibility her captivating encounter with Stefan could ever be more than a taunting memory. Before she left her suite, she'd already decided to let him know they'd need to slow it down. They could see what happened in a few months. She'd tell him before leaving for Frankfurt in a few hours, but not before a last breakfast.

Suzanne quickly wiped away an entirely unexpected tear.

EIGHTEEN

Siem Reap, Cambodia, Thursday February 20, 2020

A few days into Howard Knight's stay at Aunt Martha's Guest House in Siem Reap, Cambodia, the young woman at the front desk finally showed a hint of interest. How it evolved was somewhat surprising, even for a man of the world like him. Until then, he'd probably asked a dozen unimportant questions about directions or information about local points of interest. But on the fourth day, he casually asked her name before stepping away from the check-in counter.

"Chantou," she replied, with a charming smile and cute tilt of her head. "It means flower in Khmer."

"What a lovely name." Howard notched up his own charisma, warming his smile.

That first unexpected, simple exchange sparked a more extended conversation. Chantou wanted to know what "Mario" meant in English. He'd used the name Mario Bartoli from his fake passport only a handful of times over the past two weeks and was momentarily puzzled. But Howard recovered, grinned broadly and told her his Italian mother chose that name because it implied manliness.

She was intrigued by his supposed Italian heritage, told him she loved translated Italian movies, and thought the language sounded very romantic. They both laughed and shared a few stories about growing up with their respective names before she suddenly switched subjects. Why hadn't she seen him with any Cambodian girls? Unclear what answer she was looking for, he opted to obfuscate.

"Why do you find that unusual?"

"Most of our single, male foreign customers seem attracted to young Cambodian girls. In turn, girls in Siem Reap like most foreign men. So, guests usually come back to our rooms with companions. But I haven't seen you with any girls."

Her smile was coy, eyes sparkling mischievously. Pure curiosity led Howard to ask a few more questions. He learned young Cambodian women actually liked the gifts they received from foreigners much more than the men themselves. Gifts like watches, jewelry, perfumes, and stylish clothes seemed to be preferred.

He had never pined for girls or young women, always preferring more mature partners, such as his latest lover, Janet—who was at least half his age when she was killed. This hotel receptionist appeared still in her teens but oozed charm like a seasoned veteran. He flirted more, just to test the waters.

"How about you? Do you like foreigners when they visit or do you have a Cambodian boyfriend instead?" he teased.

"I'm much older than those younger girls, older than you think." She stood more upright and giggled. "I prefer good food and talking with foreigners. It helps me learn more languages. And I have fun."

Howard couldn't resist the temptation. Almost quicker than a blink of an eye, he learned spicy Indian was her favorite food. She had no plans for that evening, and she would love to meet him at her favorite restaurant at seven thirty. Precise directions followed, complete with a hand-drawn map, her tone hushed and almost conspiratorial. That she didn't want either their plans or destination overheard fanned his intrigue.

He scouted out the Indian restaurant she had named as he ambled aimlessly around town that afternoon. Its owner was pleased to book a reservation for that evening but less enthusiastic when Howard asked if it were possible to partition off a tiny private area for the couple. Private sections caused problems and cost him revenue because diners took longer to eat, he argued.

After a few minutes of verbal sparring, Howard offered to pay a five-dollar surcharge, and they completed arrangements for dinner. Satisfied, the restaurant owner bid farewell with a traditional namaste clasp of his hands and a giant grin that seemed almost a leer.

As Howard sat on an outdoor patio and sampled fifty-cent beers, he let his mind wander. When he so casually followed his father's encouragement to join The Organization after college, he never imagined how hard it would become to leave. Imprisoned with a life sentence couldn't feel much more confining. And only time would tell if Fidelia would honor her promise and Interpol find more pressing fugitives. In the meantime, he'd look for joy where he could.

He had last made love with Janet Weissel in the hours before Howard was snatched from his home in Overveen, in the Netherlands. That was almost three months ago.

A pang of fresh regret haunted him momentarily as images of Janet's battered, dead body—strapped upright in an airline seat beside him—flickered in his memory bank. Earlier, he'd pushed thoughts of her as far away as possible to engineer an escape from both Interpol and The Organization. Released, those memories flooded back with surprising power and clarity.

Although their relationship spanned only a couple years, their long walks together, their exploration of an entirely new life in Europe, and passionate hours in bed had been filled with tender and loving experiences he sorely missed. His eyes grew moist and his voice became hoarse when he asked the server for a bill.

By the time he took a last swig from his fourth glass of beer, Howard decided to buy Chantou a nice gift. Within a few minutes, he found a shop that sold fake Apple watches for about fifteen dollars. He bought one with the most bells and whistles.

His earlier melancholy disappeared entirely during their dinner. The restaurant owner took personal care of their evening. He recommended the lamb vindaloo and other dishes from his kitchen, served them gracefully, and discreetly left the couple alone to talk for long periods without interruption.

Chantou surprised him. She had attended and graduated from the country's best university in Phnom Penh. English was her major. She had read and enjoyed dozens of English novels and talked knowledgeably about authors like John Grisham (her favorite) and James Patterson. While a student, she had also traveled throughout Cambodia and recounted some of her adventures with joyful passion.

Howard found it necessary only to throw in a question from time to time for Chantou to regale him with answers.

"What do you think of the Cambodian royal family?" he wondered as the main course was served. Before he realized it, over two hours had passed, the bottle of Sula white wine was empty, and the owner gently hinted the establishment was about to close.

When they stepped out of the restaurant, Chantou delicately took his hand and tugged him toward a side street that led to a slow-moving river flowing through the center of Siem Reap. As they strolled along the stream in darkness, Chantou asked questions, and Howard told stories.

He lied about a lifelong ambition to be a writer. He created fantasies about the multitude of factors that had conspired to thwart his eagerness to put his thoughts on paper. Should she query him again, he told stories he could remember easily—leaving out minor details that might trip him up later.

As they approached Aunt Martha's Guest House, he grinned with satisfaction as he thought about the character he had created for Mario Bartoli, someone who existed only as a name on his fake Canadian passport.

At the street where they turned toward the inn, Chantou abruptly stopped and looked up invitingly into Howard's eyes. He paused a moment to be sure. When her lips parted ever so slightly, he kissed her and was surprised by her responsiveness and passion. The kiss lingered and she pressed her body closer to him until they both needed to take a breath.

"Would you like me to come up to your room?"

Howard nodded.

"When we get inside, go upstairs. I'll join you in a few minutes and let myself in."

He followed her instructions and waited. When there was no sign of her after about a half hour, Howard turned on the television and watched a BBC news program. After the program ended, he concluded she had changed her mind, undressed, and went to bed.

Sometime later, he awoke with a start as a warm hand massaged his chest gently and long hair tickled his cheek. He detected a faint alluring scent of fine perfume. Chantou touched his lips with her forefinger, then followed up with her tongue. He had no idea for how long, but they made love. First tenderly, then passionately, and finally with a burst of celebration, they held each other tightly and silently savored their climax.

When he woke up later that morning, she was gone.

NINETEEN

Valparaíso, Chile, Saturday February 22, 2020

When James Fitzgerald and his group left Atlanta, sleep eluded them for most of the ten-hour overnight flight. Sumptuous leather seats on Multima's corporate jet were unquestionably comfortable enough to bed down, but the occupants were engrossed in a desperate exercise. Their situation looked bleak.

Multima probably had only a few days left to solve the mystery of apparently fraudulent supplier invoices. Europe's central bank still thought those billings were created to illicitly launder the company's money offshore. If James and his team couldn't find out who was behind the morass—and exonerate Multima management—Multima's European financial business was effectively dead. Billions would be lost and the future of the entire company in peril. On a more personal note, the company's directors might be held liable by litigious shareholders, putting his own wealth at risk.

Suzanne had asked James to run with the ball, but Dan Ramirez had created one almost insurmountable hurdle. The company's security chief demanded they undertake their investigation in Chile without communicating with an agent Multima often used to liaise with suppliers in the South American country. The local agent was probably complicit in whatever went on down there.

Chilean police could better investigate the agent covertly, while James and his team followed the money trail. Suzanne agreed. His team would need to work with a single former police contact Ramirez would arrange before they got there.

James's team of four was a good one, with three exceptionally bright women. Angela Bonner had established her credentials in forensic accounting and had already helped him immeasurably when they were in Paris. For a substantial fee, the OCD accounting firm had supplied two of its skillful resources, Patricia González and Maria Green. The new additions brought essential Spanish language skills.

For hours on the plane, they debated possible sources of information, offices to contact, and potential lawyers in Chile. Then they listed specialized resources back in the States they might use to pry open difficult-to-open doors. When they weren't strategizing, they executed. Dozens of emails were sent. They explored more than a hundred websites and saved links as reference material. Everyone made notes and created spreadsheets to capture growing amounts of data.

Throughout the night, James maintained his soft-spoken tone, his manner deliberately kind and cordial. Patiently, he probed their individual outputs and prodded each to dig deeper and scrutinize details meticulously. Chile was in a time zone an hour ahead of Atlanta, so it was impossible to talk with people on the ground throughout the flight. However, by the time the aircraft began to descend for landing, they felt prepared.

The team landed in Chile at Aerodromo Redelillo, a small regional airport near Valparaíso on the west coast. They chose that beautiful, sprawling city on a hillside because most of the companies who received payments from Multima Supermarkets were supposedly located in its surrounding areas. From there, they could access government offices easily and travel to nearby rural villages, if necessary.

That morning was crisp and bright for a summer day, with temperatures in the mid-sixties. James watched his companions draw deep breaths and quicken their pace as they debarked at the end of a terminal reserved for private jets and scuttled into the building.

A huge man wearing a leather jacket and fedora met them inside. He looked directly at James, tipped his hat, and nodded once. The faint outline of a smile appeared on his aging face, but the bushy dark brow stayed furrowed, his black eyes piercing the group, assessing their worth.

"*Buenos días señor y señoras.* My name is Carlos." His gentle tone didn't match his hulking presence. "Dan Ramirez stole my entire night's sleep with his sad story of your problem."

He still didn't smile. Wary, the women deferred to James, so he stepped forward to offer a firm handshake and express gratitude for the man's willingness to help. Sleepless as well, he had no need to apologize to this new companion. Instead, James asked if Carlos had a vehicle, started the entourage in the direction he pointed, then tested him as they walked.

"I realize it's only eight o'clock on a Sunday morning. Will you need time to rest before we begin?"

"No. Dan emphasized the urgency, and I owe him more than one big favor," Carlos said. "He got me out of a very tough spot with my job a few years before I retired. Dan told me it's urgent, so I'll do whatever you need, whenever you need it."

From the first moment he helped them with their luggage as they checked into the warm, mahogany-paneled lobby of the boutique hotel Casa Higueras, Carlos worked with dogged determination and without complaint.

Sunday morning, he helped the hotel round up a half-dozen electronic whiteboards from around the city and installed them along the walls around the perimeter of the entire living area in James's massive suite on the top floor of the hotel. Spectacular views of the magnificent city built on a mountainside became restricted, but business priorities came first.

James sent the team out shopping, and they found burner phones with voice and data plans to keep in touch during their stay. Then Carlos contacted a friend in Valparaíso, who opened his shop to print business cards with telephone numbers. James wanted everyone to give out business cards at every visit, mindful of their recent experience in Paris where leaving a card behind had led to a breakthrough.

He gave everyone a few hours to sleep after lunch. They'd all been working for more than twenty-four hours, and the worst of their schedule was still to come. At precisely five o'clock that first evening, a hotel receptionist roused the team to meet in James's suite again.

Using the whiteboards, he led brainstorming sessions to develop questions for team members to pose in meetings the following day. Board after board filled up as James made notes of the ideas from everyone—especially from Carlos, who saw the value his policing experience brought to their efforts. His enthusiasm grew by the hour.

While they toiled in Valparaíso, Multima's chief legal counsel worked the telephone from Fort Myers to schedule meetings with three different law firms in the city. By nine that first night, James's team had a plan and schedule in place. He ordered dinner for everyone in his suite, and they got to know each other better over good food and wine.

Monday, James asked Carlos to drive the three women to the lawyers' offices. At the same time, he—along with three new accountants sent from OCD's Santiago office—researched other sources online from his suite.

Carlos waited in his SUV while Patricia and Maria took turns grilling the lawyers. Usually, Patricia worked through the extensive lists of questions they'd developed on the whiteboards. Maria quietly translated the attorneys' answers into English for Angela, who only occasionally asked follow-up questions for clarity.

By the end of the day, they shared their findings. They all agreed they had much better insight into how businesses in Chile were registered, structured, and regulated. Everyone expressed satisfaction with the day's progress before dinner arrived in James's suite at about nine in the evening.

On Tuesday, Carlos chauffeured Patricia, Maria, and two OCD associates from Santiago, to registration offices in Valparaíso and the administrative regions both north and south of the city. All five pored over computers, microfiche readers, and paper files. Their mission: to trace names of shareholders and executive structures of incorporated companies identified only by sequences of anonymous numbers.

Back in James's suite at Hotel Casa Higueras, James and Angela built elaborate charts with information emailed or texted back from the team in the registry offices. By the time Carlos returned in the evening—with the four young women in tow—whiteboards displayed the ownership relationships and control for all the identified companies. Still no pattern developed. None of the numbered companies seemed to have balances in their accounts. They were left to find and pursue former owners or directors.

On Wednesday, James asked Carlos not only to drive the women to more than a dozen banks but also to join those meetings and press reluctant bank managers for information. He wanted the retired police officer to add his expertise to learn the whereabouts and status of dozens of individuals they had discovered related to the numbered companies involved in the fraud. Every meeting finished in frustration as managers maintained the imperative of privacy over any other interest. That day ended about nine with dinner in James's suite, but enthusiasm ebbed low.

Thursday morning, James dispatched Carlos to Santiago with all the women in his big SUV. Angela and the OCD accountants from Florida planned to visit banks there and return the loaned Chilean resources to their regular work. James stayed behind to bring Suzanne and the Multima team up to date on their progress so far. Although he didn't feel very successful, the team back in Fort Myers applauded his progress and pledged more support to ferret out other contacts in Chile.

Dan Ramirez agreed to press the Chilean police to lean on senior management at the uncooperative banks. Wilma Willingsworth seemed most vocal about calling in some favors, and Alberto Ferer pledged to increase legal pressure.

By the dinner hour, Angela reported back that their day in Santiago was marginally more productive. They had uncovered more personal names attached to the numbered companies. Also, a few leads surfaced about banking relationships in Santiago. James relayed the info back to Fort Myers with little optimism but eternal hope.

He didn't hear from the team in Santiago on Friday until they knocked on his suite's door about nine in the evening. Expressions were downcast. Few words were exchanged. Their body language projected dejection. James opted to tack in a different direction.

"I can see it's been another tough day. Let's forgo a recap and relax for a while."

"Tough doesn't begin to describe it," Angela ventured. "Whoever the mastermind behind this scheme is, he or she is brilliant."

"Brilliant and ruthless," Patricia added. "When we talk to people, they aren't just uncooperative, they're terrified. We can see it in their faces."

"That's right," Carlos concurred. "I've seen murder suspects less fearful than these functionaries answering seemingly easy questions."

Tactfully, James ordered in dinner rather than pressing for information. He asked about their drive from Santiago, the scenery, and their impressions of the Chilean capital. With a good meal, fine red wine, and an abrupt change of focus, he tried to shift the glum mood.

Just as the team decided to break up and return to their rooms, a telephone rang. Everyone looked at their phone. It was Patricia's. She called out a friendly greeting and listened. After only a moment, the team watched Patricia pull a pen from her bag and make a note as she said, "Can you repeat that name and address for me?"

When Patricia finished the call, her furrowed brow rose and a faint smile formed.

"That was the bank manager we first met on Tuesday. In one of her files she found an account with the same address as a woman here in Valparaíso. The last name of the woman is the same as one identifying a partial owner of three of the numbered companies. But she couldn't find a phone number."

Within minutes, they decided someone should visit the woman at the address passed on by the caller that evening. Carlos, Patricia, and Angela would check it out.

Even with the GPS, it took Carlos almost an hour to find the apartment building, and Angela Bonner rang the doorbell with a sense of unease. It was nearly eleven o'clock at night. Anyone would be nervous answering a bell at that time. A middle-aged woman opened the door a crack and peeked through the opening.

"What do you want?" she asked in Spanish.

"Are you Señora Antonella Ortez?"

"*Si.*" The woman's reply was just above a whisper, and her expression couldn't conceal the fear her sad brown eyes projected as she peered down both directions in the hallway.

"We ask only a few minutes to get your advice." Carlos matched her soft tone. "I worked for the police in Santiago for twenty-five years, and we're looking for an acquaintance of yours. Can you help us?"

The woman kept the security chain fastened, but opened the door slightly wider.

Patricia took the lead. Pointing toward Angela, she used her reassuring smile and Latin charm to explain the connection.

"Our friend here is looking for a gentleman named Manuel Ortez. She invested with him in a food business identified only by a number, no company name. Recently, he disappeared and she's worried about his safety. Someone told us you may know where to find him. Before we go to the police, Carlos here suggested it might be better for us to talk with you privately. May we come in for a moment?"

After a long moment of hesitation, curiosity apparently trumped fear, and the woman unlatched her door, silently motioning for them to enter.

The woman answered only after they were all inside the living room, although the door still sat slightly ajar. "I haven't talked with Manuel for a few days. I'm not sure I can be of much help to you."

Carlos took the lead. "We understand Manuel is your son. Is that correct?"

"Yes, but he no longer lives here with me. He lives in Santiago. Has something happened to him?"

"We're not sure. When did you talk with him last?"

"About a week ago. He was leaving on a business trip to Colombia for a few days. Said he'd call me when he returned."

"Did he tell you who he was meeting in Colombia?"

"No. He tells me nothing about his job. I'm not a businessperson. I'm a widowed housewife."

For another few minutes, Carlos applied his well-honed investigation skills while his female companions observed. Despite his noble efforts, his questions led nowhere. The woman either knew nothing about her son's activities or skillfully denied knowledge. When it appeared they would gain nothing more from his questions, Angela asked if she might use a restroom. It was urgent, she pleaded in English before Patricia translated.

Permission granted, Angela dashed down the hallway to the end and closed the bathroom door. She waited inside for a reasonable amount of time, then flushed the toilet and washed her hands. Back in the hallway, she deliberately slowed her pace. Then she stepped back to close the door behind her.

As she swung around, she took in small details about the bedroom next to the bathroom. Something caught her eye. Angela took a second look as she headed back toward the group in the living area.

Moments later, the team politely apologized again for their intrusion, thanked the woman for her help, and retraced their steps to the car. Angela spoke first.

"Carlos, did you notice if the woman had any particular accent when she spoke?"

"No, she sounded like a native Chilean from this region of the country."

"How about you, Patricia? Notice anything amiss?"

Patricia shook her head, and Angela took another moment before she asked, "I wonder, then, why does the woman prominently display a Russian flag on her bedside bureau?"

———•———

Saturday morning, a few minutes before their scheduled meeting time, James heard a knock on his suite's door, and Carlos burst into the room when James unlocked it.

"I just saw a story on the morning news, on TV," he said breathlessly. "Sometime after midnight, witnesses saw a man leading a woman who appeared drunk into the tallest apartment building in Valparaíso. About ten minutes after they went inside, a woman fell to her death from a balcony on the top floor."

James tilted his head and glimpsed over his eyeglasses, but said nothing. Sure enough, Carlos had more.

"When police forced their way into the apartment, they learned it was a vacant, unrented Airbnb suite. The woman on the ground carried no ID. They showed a picture of the body on TV, looking for help in identifying her. It was the woman named Ortez we visited last night. We were with her about an hour before her death!"

Carlos's face became pale. When James handed him a bottle of water, his hands trembled, and his wide eyes darted about restlessly.

James didn't know what to ask, so he moved away and switched on the TV as though seeking validation of the unsettling news. Seconds later, they heard blood-curdling screams from the hallway.

Carlos reached into his jacket pocket for a weapon as James flung open the door to his suite and looked down where the screaming women pointed. A small dead pig lay just beyond the doorway, with its throat slashed from one side to the other and blood pooling around its mostly detached head.

Without a word, Carlos took a running jump over the dead swine and sprinted down the hallway toward a stairwell exit, his gun drawn and ready for action.

James comforted the women, helped them into his suite with an outstretched arm, and then called the front desk. While he waited for them to answer, it dawned on him. Only moments earlier, Carlos had entered the room with his news.

Had someone who knew precisely where they were just delivered the frightening message? Or did Carlos stage the scare for some other unsavory purpose?

TWENTY

"I think you all should return immediately," Suzanne declared the moment she heard the disturbing stories. "Clearly, we're dealing with something way out of our league. The money-laundering allegations are serious, but your safety is far more important."

"I won't argue with you about Patricia and Maria," James reasoned. "But we have Carlos here. Angela and I think we can carry on if you'll authorize a few more security resources."

"It's too dangerous. Let me call Eileen. She'll have the company jet on the way to pick you up within an hour. When you're safely back here, we can all discuss with Dan Ramirez how his security team can carry on with the research."

"We appreciate your concern, Suzanne. But let's not be too hasty." James slowed his pace, always a sign he'd already thought it through and wanted to be heard.

"I'm listening." Suzanne maintained a calm demeanor, but this incident caused a headache to come from nowhere—not an unusual occurrence when she felt extreme stress.

"Before you call Eileen, let's loop in Dan. I'll explain the circumstances to him. If he agrees with me, he might send a couple of his people down with the jet to pick up the OCD women. Added to Carlos, that would give us three armed specialists. Angela is also licensed to carry a weapon."

"That license would be for the US, of course," Suzanne pointed out. "I'm wary of the whole idea of you continuing down there. But I'll hear you out. Let's get Dan's opinion before we decide."

She put the call on hold and dialed Dan Ramirez. By the time she reached him and connected them all again, James had put his phone on speaker too. Angela, Carlos, Patricia, and Maria all took part in the call. For the rest of the morning, it turned out.

Suzanne let James take the lead after giving the briefest of background info to the call. Initially, Dan Ramirez's reaction was identical to hers.

They all needed to get out of Chile as quickly as possible. James again begged to slow it down a bit. Then he delivered a potent reminder of the many reasons he had been one of Multima's most skillful and successful executives for over thirty years.

She imagined him mentally shifting gears as he asked permission to provide some background on why they'd met with the dead woman in the first place. When Suzanne and Dan both agreed, James took control of the conversation. He did it slowly, methodically, and cleverly.

Gradually, he drew in each of the people on his team in Valparaíso to explain the aspects of the investigation they had conducted and what they had uncovered. They explained their background research, summarized each of the visits, and shared some of the frustrations they encountered. Whenever Suzanne or Dan needed clarification, James or one of his team addressed their concern with facts and without emotion.

Finally, after James had taken considerable time to describe the environment they worked in, he brought everyone back to the shocking news report of the woman's death. He let Angela voice their collective opinion.

"We think the woman is a relatively innocent victim. She seemed to understand little of her son's activities. We saw no evidence of business acumen. In fact, she seemed to be genuinely concerned about her son's whereabouts. The only thing we found odd about our entire encounter was a small Russian flag we noticed beside her bed."

"Why do you think a Russian flag is significant?" Dan Ramirez asked.

"When Angela first told us about seeing the flag, we didn't attach too much significance to it," Carlos explained. "But when we got back to the hotel, I decided to do a little research. It took a while, but I was able to access a security site I probably shouldn't still have access to."

"Don't give us any more background. Just tell us what you found."

Suzanne found it rare for Dan Ramirez to be so rude. *Oh! Right. It's better not to know the details.*

"Sure. I understand," Carlos said. "It turns out someone named Manuel Ortez once shared the same address as the dead woman, and he has a rather complex background. He has a police record for several small-time crimes like burglary here in Valparaíso. In Santiago, he graduated to more serious stuff like armed robbery. He was also charged with extortion but got off on a technicality. But most interesting of all, from the time he was seven until the age of fifteen, he lived with his Russian father in Moscow."

A hush fell over the conversation. Everyone on the call contemplated the implications of Carlos's pronouncement.

Almost certainly, Manuel Ortez spoke Russian and had contact with at least one person there. The woman who might be his mother had fallen from a high apartment balcony less than an hour after meeting with James's team of investigators. Such falls were terrifyingly similar to frequent news reports of sudden deaths out of Russia. Add in the slaughtered pig dropped in the hallway outside James's suite hours later, and all this on the heels of an intensive investigation into fraudulent invoices to Multima Corporation.

Suzanne spoke first. "Does all this suggest some connection to Russian criminals?"

"Not automatically," Dan cautioned. "Russia's a big country with a lot of people. It's possible Manuel Ortez's father was just a wayward sailor who wanted to raise his son in his home country for a few years. But I think there are a lot of dots out there just waiting to be connected. We can try to interest some capable folks at both the FBI and the Investigations Police of Chile right away."

"That's why I think it's helpful for Angela and me to stay here," James argued. "If we just hole up here inside the hotel, we'll be okay until you can round up some FBI and Chilean police support. Carlos is with us. He's armed. And he thinks he can get some additional resources to help keep the bad guys at bay."

Suzanne was leaning toward changing her mind, but she needed first to underscore their primary objective.

"You got my email about the meeting Monday with the European Central Bank. Michelle and Wilma gave it their best, but they couldn't sway the regulators. They described the bleak picture for our balance sheet should the ECB put any further restrictions on our European banking activities. The bastards didn't even flinch when we showed them the negative impact on the economies of several individual countries as well."

"They can be brutal," James sympathized. "But you did get some extra time."

"Yeah. They gave us thirty days. We're now down to twenty-four. That's what we can't lose sight of. As terrifying as it sounds to have Russian hoodlums sniffing around, the ECB is probably more urgent. Do we see any other way to build a story the regulators can accept? Something to buy more time?"

"They haven't bought your arguments that Multima is an unknowing victim so far," James said. "It seems to me we'll only satisfy them when we point to a specific individual or group with a clearly defined motive and rock-solid facts."

"What do you think, Dan?" Suzanne used a tone balancing both continued apprehension and possible deference to Dan's judgment.

"It's a tough call. I see where James is coming from. It's up to us to solve the case if we need it done quickly. But I share Suzanne's concern for everyone's safety. Here's what I suggest."

As though he'd had hours to think about and fashion a solution, he rattled off a proposed game plan. First, get at least half a dozen police cars around the hotel. A highly visible presence should deter any immediate threat. Next, book the two women from OCD on the first direct, non-stop flight out of Valparaíso to anywhere in the US, then on to Atlanta with American police protection. His people would arrange everything once they knew precisely where the women would land.

He'd also contact the FBI and request at least three agents accompany him on the Multima corporate jet to Chile. Plus, he'd bring along more from the Multima security team. He'd also ask the FBI to contact the Chilean Investigations Police right away and get a name and number for Carlos and James.

Suzanne accepted defeat graciously. "Okay. It sounds as if I'm the only one reluctant to have James and Angela stay there. But if you're sure it's something you want to do—and you don't put yourselves in harm's way unnecessarily—I'll go with the majority."

Seconds later, the plan outlined by Dan Ramirez was underway.

As she finished the call, Suzanne glanced up from her phone just as a red banner crept across the bottom of the TV screen mounted on the wall beside her desk. It caught her attention for its odd confluence of events. While a potential pandemic raged—and with panic buying of seemingly everything in her supermarkets that day—the Dow Jones average of blue-chip American stocks reached an all-time high. *That paradox seems almost unbelievable.*

TWENTY-ONE

As a wall-mounted TV screen flickered to life, Fidelia Morales noticed stock market results for the previous day showed red everywhere. After finishing the week before at all-time highs, it seemed the business world was getting a dose of reality. Some blamed the decline on unsettling news related to the mysterious coronavirus.

The World Health Organization seemed under increasing pressure to declare the rapidly spreading virus a pandemic. A day earlier, the media had reported that over seventy-three thousand people had been infected with the coronavirus. New cases of infections popped up outside China—where it had originated—in the US, Italy, Iran, UAE, and South Korea.

Fidelia scoffed as she heard a TV personality say more than five hundred of Korea's cases were traced to a single evangelical Christian church. She wished Luigi was there so she could nudge his elbow and point out how right her predictions were a couple weeks earlier.

But Luigi was in New York and would be there until the end of March. Wendal was still trying to get the numbers up with hacking thefts in Australia. He had dispatched one of his technology assistants to Sydney to successfully train Aretta Musa's recruit, and the early results were impressive. Their scores were already into the tens of millions. However, it would still be a while before they reached the magic hundred-million-dollar goal.

Her technology genius called while she thought about his latest successes.

"The new app is ready to go. It does everything we expect. But I've got one big concern. Timing is everything. Unless you have someone on the inside to perform on command, we run the risk of getting caught."

"Why?"

"The worm self-destructs, but I haven't found a way to delay it if the other guys aren't buying at the price we want. I don't think it's workable until we influence somebody on the inside, and it needs to be someone near the top."

Wendal's cautionary news caught her off guard, so she told him she'd try to think of a company they could influence. There was no rush.

Instead, Fidelia devoted every spare hour to her own body. The Five Seasons hotel was almost empty. Upscale customers fled Singapore immediately after the first cases of the mysterious virus were discovered. So, hotel management instantly agreed to her request to have the fitness room cleaned and sanitized every afternoon at one. They also agreed she could use the gym exclusively for the following two hours. When she finished there, she practiced yoga and stretched in her suite for another hour.

After only a few days, she felt rejuvenated. Her muscles showed improved definition and tone. Her weight was back to its trim hundred and ten pounds. And she found herself sleeping better at night. Still, she got up early every morning to walk for an hour before breakfast. As she explored the city on foot, she marveled at how the city's pace had changed in those couple weeks since the Prime Minister first asked the people of Singapore to stay home.

Broad streets looked almost like a ghost town. Almost no cars, trucks, buses, or taxis on the roads. On sidewalks, Fidelia encountered only one or two other pedestrians as she chose different routes. One evening she walked to the Little India sector with her bodyguard. She was astonished to see most stores and restaurants closed in an area of the city that usually bustled with commerce and activity. Another evening jaunt over to the casino found it closed—even the outdoor observation level.

But the city was still safe. Hospitals efficiently contained the few virus cases that surfaced. Few deaths were reported. And neither the government of Singapore nor the local crime boss Stan Tan paid any attention to her.

Back in America, Luigi reported that remittances from all segments of The Organization were flowing into her bank accounts as expected. On the surface, life appeared to be good, and that gave Fidelia cause to worry. Wrenching control of the most powerful criminal element on earth should have been more difficult. She knew that.

Every scenario she had imagined during her years of dreaming and scheming suggested she should expect resistance in one quarter or another. But the elimination of the asshole who'd controlled Italy, and of Oliver Williams in Australia, proved uncharacteristically uneventful. No one else had challenged her authority. All segments fell in line as directed. Was it because the misogynistic bastards hadn't yet figured out how to deal with a woman?

Only South America remained unsettled. Back from another evening walk, Fidelia glanced at her phone and quickly calculated the time in Argentina with an eleven-hour difference. It was eight-thirty in the morning—time for Juan Álvarez to be on the job. A different young, sexy voice answered the phone this time, and Fidelia instructed her to get him out of the shower and on the line. This time, it took less than a minute before she heard his voice.

For telephone calls, she no longer used the secret-code screening system Giancarlo Mareno had trusted for several years. Instead, all her phones used apps created by Wendal Randall that distorted every conversation. Anyone she spoke with on the line heard her normal voice. Someone trying to tap into, or record the call, heard only an annoying buzz. For two years, it had proved secure.

"What's happening with the relocation of the server farm?" Fidelia wanted to know first.

She couldn't resist smiling every time she used the term. Calling a bunch of computers hidden in some secret location a "farm" had at first seemed odd. Then she learned the technology did indeed create a harvest—just like a real farm. With the server farm, though, output was far more productive. Harvests were measured in millions of dollars.

"It's up and running again." Juan Álvarez sighed theatrically to convey there had been problems. "We found a place that's perfect in Valparaíso, Chile. We already own the building. It's in a very secure neighborhood. But we had to spend a fortune to get new computers so quickly."

"What happened?"

"I told you about the guys in Colombia already. We lost both, and the computers were damaged in the fire. We managed to steal them back from the police, but we also had problems with the back-ups in the cloud. The data was all there, but the guys did something to scramble access before they bailed out in Colombia. Technicians here needed five days to solve the problem and reload the back-up data on the new servers. Then, the algorithms didn't work properly, so another team had to rework them. Late last night, we finally got everything working."

"The money is moving again?" Fidelia wanted to confirm it. She was really only interested in the bottom line, not the details.

"Yeah. You probably lost about a week's worth of interest on some accounts, but remittances are all flowing again."

"A week's worth of interest is a few million. Don't forget that." Fidelia's tone was frosty. "Did we find out how the European Central Bank found the farm?"

"Sort of. We traced it to an IP address in West Virginia. Believe it or not, the IP address belongs to the American CIA. It's a secure address, but we managed to get in the back door the same way as before. They still haven't discovered the gap. We scanned the database to isolate the message they sent. It wasn't even encrypted. However, we lost track of where it went from there."

"Text me the IP address. I'll see if Wendal can track it."

"You want me to dig a little deeper?"

"Yeah. A lot deeper," Fidelia replied. "When I heard the ECB held up Polish banking licenses for Multima Corporation because of questions about money laundering, I knew they weren't acting on information we planted. The Organization's attempt to disrupt Multima ended with Mareno's death. I have no interest in supermarkets."

Finished with Juan, Fidelia prepared for her next call while she waited for the text with the IP address to arrive. She had already decided the unease she felt with Juan's explanation required an outside opinion. Her next call would not be to Wendal as she had implied. There was someone better. It had been so long since she'd talked to the woman she needed to look up the number in her contacts. It was still early evening in Germany, so she wasn't concerned about the hour. But she did have some misgivings about making the call.

Her former close friend had asked to escape from The Organization forever and Fidelia had granted her that request. But there was no one who could track Internet activity better. Once more, she felt compelled to draw her friend into a drama the woman detested intensely. But, as usual, she answered on the third ring.

"Klaudia. I need to ask a favor."

TWENTY-TWO

Siem Reap, Cambodia, Wednesday February 26, 2020

Chantou came to visit Howard Knight in his room at Aunt Martha's Guest House every night the rest of that week. Sometimes she waited until he was in bed asleep. Other nights she came earlier and talked and giggled quietly as they exchanged stories or shared life experiences. They gradually developed an unspoken bond of affection.

Like every other morning, Howard sat alone in a quiet corner of the covered open area that served as a breakfast room at Aunt Martha's. But today, as he sipped strong coffee, he also kept an eye out for Chantou to appear at the front desk. He wanted to ask her out on a real date.

As usual, she had slipped from his bed sometime after he fell asleep and before he could propose his idea. Leaving that way followed her pattern of making love passionately for more than an hour until he drifted off to sleep and erotic dreams. Then, she would quietly leave his room without disturbing him.

When he woke up this morning with his body fully recharged, he decided not to wait until lovemaking distracted them that evening. Instead, it was time to venture out of the hotel and see some Siem Reap sites. Who better to serve as his personal tour guide than Chantou?

His chair in the corner let him survey everyone in the breakfast room without attracting suspicion. By leaning a bit to the left, he could also see inside the small lobby with a direct line of sight to the front desk where she would eventually appear. While he watched, he pondered his dilemma.

———•———

Chantou's visits provided a welcome temporary relief from his constant dread of capture by local police acting on an outstanding Interpol Red Notice for his arrest. Giancarlo Mareno had orchestrated the entire Interpol fiasco when Howard had escaped from the crime boss's minions in Spain at the end of last year.

Those thugs were in good health when Howard got away from them. They had simply let down their guard for a few moments and he "escaped". But those captors died sometime later—either by suicide or murder. He had no idea which. Regardless, Mareno leveraged those deaths to convince corrupt officials at the summit of power in Interpol to issue a Red Notice for Howard and pull out all the stops to capture him and hold him in custody.

He'd eluded The Organization once, only to again fall into its kingpin's hands when Howard tried to rescue his captured lover. It all ended terribly. Tragically, Janet Weissel perished from vicious blows delivered by Mareno. Later, the crime boss himself died when first Howard, then Fidelia Morales, shot him at his home in Martinique. Of course, killing Mareno was self-defense. They were all there in the first place because he intended to torture and eventually execute Howard.

When they parted on the island, Fidelia had assured Howard The Organization would no longer officially pursue him. She'd call off the huge reward Mareno had offered for his capture, but she couldn't promise others in the criminal element might not seek retribution of their own.

Just thinking about it caused Howard's hands to tremble and his heart rate to surge. Now a mysterious virus spreading across the globe added complications. How could he avoid it? What would happen if he contracted it? What kind of healthcare was available to a foreigner in a tiny, underdeveloped country like Cambodia?

———•———

"Where're you from?" The question came from an older fellow with little remaining white hair, a ruddy complexion that suggested lots of time in the sun, and an accent that sounded Canadian. He had sat down at the table next to Howard's and hadn't yet ordered breakfast. He made no apology for interrupting Howard's morning reverie.

"Toronto." Howard hoped his brief response would discourage a follow-up question but wasn't surprised when the man asked another.

"Toronto. That's kind of curious. I find Canadians usually answer that question with a simple 'Canada.' Americans tend to lead with the name of the city where they live. What part of Toronto do you live in?"

Howard paused before he answered. He'd given no thought to what part of Toronto he should consider home for his fictitious persona. He'd only stayed at downtown hotels the few times he had visited.

"Downtown," he finally said. Then, to deflect the fellow's interest, "How about you? Where are you from?"

That was all it took to get the guy talking about himself. Over the next few minutes—with only a brief break to order from the waiter—the elderly man offered more information than Howard could ever want.

Seven months of the year, the fellow lived in a retirement community in some small town in Southwestern Ontario. Howard had never heard of it. Each year he traveled throughout Asia from December to April. He needed to escape the bitter winters in Ontario, and Asia was a cheap alternative place to live.

So far this season, the guy had spent December in Indonesia and January in Thailand. This month and next, he had planned to stay in Cambodia, then visit Vietnam in April. But this new coronavirus had him worried. He might have to spend more money and go to a more developed country—like Singapore.

After the fellow's eggs and vegetables arrived, and between large mouthfuls, he recounted his visit to an elephant preserve. Assuming Howard would be interested, he described his harrowing trip up winding mountain roads in the back of a pickup truck with a half-dozen other people. He described the colorful wool apron the sanctuary hosts gave everyone to wear, pulled out his phone to show pictures he took, and pointed out odd elephant habits he'd noticed.

When Howard tried to project disinterest by looking at the time on his phone, the fellow switched to his escapades in Siem Reap and recited a review of every restaurant in the entertainment district.

He took particular care to highlight establishments that offered fifty-cent beers. It seemed they all offered much more delicious food and more attentive service than those charging the ridiculous price for beer of a US dollar or more.

Howard told him he didn't drink much beer. Startled by that possibility, the older gent changed gears and asked a question.

"Have you been out to Angkor Wat yet?"

"No, is it worth the trip?" Howard took care to ask his question in a tone that didn't project enthusiasm, just enough interest not to be rude.

"Hard to say. If you're into archaeology and all that old stuff, it's probably pretty interesting. I found it a long day. Very tiring in the sun, with not much shade out there. I suppose it depends how good your guide is."

At that point, Chantou gave him a cheerful smile and wave from her post at the front desk. It was enough for Howard to politely thank his fellow traveler for the information, wish him a good day, and dash away from the breakfast area.

Listening to the old fellow hadn't been a complete waste of time. Indeed, he had provided what Howard needed to find for a date with Chantou: A destination. Now he had it. He'd entice her to become his guide for a day as they toured Angkor Wat.

It turned out to be more complicated than expected. Sammy, Chantou's cousin, apparently was the dedicated inn resource for tours of Angkor Wat. It was he who owned the tuk-tuk needed for transportation. He also had more than five years' experience as a guide, and he needed the business. There were far fewer tourists right now because of the spreading virus.

Howard watched the back and forth between Chantou and her cousin. The usually cheerful, vivacious young woman conversed with her gaze cast down to the floor, her voice soft and her manner submissive. It continued for several minutes. She made little headway and began to appear flustered.

"Excuse me." Howard interrupted with a broad smile and a wave of his hand. "How much do you charge to rent your tuk-tuk for a day?"

Sammy was surprised. Although he understood English quite well, he asked Chantou to translate for him into Khmer. He appeared unsettled when she finished.

"You want to rent my tuk-tuk? Do you know how to drive one?"

"I think so. You can test me to be sure, but I've traveled lots with scooters. Mine's parked over there." Howard pointed to the scooter he'd bought and ridden from Krong Kaeb a week earlier.

"You don't need a tuk-tuk then. I'll ride on the back!" Chantou squealed in delight, slapping her cousin's shoulder playfully as she sensed advantage in their quarrel.

"But we need you here," a woman's voice admonished in English for Howard's benefit. Chantou's mother.

Another conversation ensued, with cousin, mother, and Chantou arguing in Khmer about some new point of difference. After a couple minutes, it was decided.

"We still need you to pay the tuk-tuk fee of twenty-seven US dollars because you will be taking me away from my work," Chantou explained. "My mother says I can go only if you pay our regular fee."

Howard drew thirty dollars from his pocket and set them on the counter without comment. The mother nodded. Sammy snatched the bills with a surly snarl and stomped away. Chantou announced triumphantly that they'd do the trip the next morning. Howard took a long look at the departing cousin and made a mental note to dig deeper into Sammy's relationship to her.

When she let herself into Howard's room that night, her arms were loaded. Chantou carried a backpack stuffed with goods and told him they must get up at four-thirty the next morning. She showed him bottles of water and small boxes that held their breakfast-to-go. At the bottom of the backpack, he noticed a mask, a cap, a change of clothes, and a package of condoms.

She wanted to have sex right away so they could sleep well ahead of an exhausting day. Excited about their plans, she began undressing and teased Howard to hurry up. In bed, Howard slowed the pace, caressing her gently and kissing her tenderly.

She responded with passion and their session became deliberate, extended, and ultimately fulfilling. Both fell asleep soon after, and Howard forgot completely about circling back about Sammy. They awoke the next morning to the intrusive sound of his phone alarm.

It was still pitch dark when they made their way to the scooter parked outside. The harsh, sputtering start of the engine seemed strangely out of place as it shattered the silence of the neighborhood. As Howard had found earlier on his drive from Krong Kaeb, streetlights in Cambodia were sparse. Since he had no idea where the famous temples were located, he reached for his phone to program the GPS. Chantou hopped up on the seat behind him, wrapped her arms around his waist, and whispered she'd show him the way.

At the first main street they crossed, tuk-tuks and other scooters appeared. An occasional SUV also joined the parade out of town, all seemingly headed toward the world-famous archaeological site dating back to the twelfth century. Why such an early departure?

"It's the most spectacular sunrise in the world," Chantou promised.

They pulled into a large parking lot beside a giant complex where dozens of people lined up for tickets to visit the historical treasure from sleepy cashiers enclosed in glass compartments. Others—trying desperately to earn income for the day as guides—accosted them every few steps until Chantou chased them away with curt rejections in Khmer.

On the scooter again, for another fifteen minutes she guided Howard along a paved road with lots of twists and turns. Then, she pointed to a parking area lined with merchants selling everything from coffee to sunglasses. They secured the scooter to a tree with a plastic-coated chain device Chantou pulled with a flourish from a pouch in her backpack, then joined the throngs ambling in darkness toward the famous temple.

For another hour, the crowd milled about, looking for the most opportune place to catch a prized photo of the sun peeking over the main temple at Angkor Wat. Serious photographers installed tripods and checked angles. Couples walked arm-in-arm to make the occasion as romantic and memorable as possible. Children of tourists scooted about looking for mischief while parents promised an upcoming event that would be awesome and create memories for a lifetime.

Howard tugged his hat down low on his forehead and continued wearing the face mask Chantou had thoughtfully brought along for their scooter ride. She wrapped her arm around his waist and cuddled in tightly as they found a bridge with a low wall to lean against while they waited for sunrise. And she talked.

Proud of her education and heritage, she sounded like a guide as she explained the background of Angkor Wat. Chantou clearly loved history. Her enthusiasm grew as she pointed out the site was the largest religious monument in the world, the most important in all of Cambodia, and the product of both Hindu and Buddhist influences. As her passionate narrative came to an end, they both watched the sun rise from the horizon in respectful silence, almost as though it was a religious experience rather than a daily occurrence.

The day was cloudy, so they didn't see the full magnificent patterns and brilliant reds or oranges of touristy photos promoting the temple, but it was satisfying regardless. After a half hour of watching the sun creep higher above the horizon, the crowd started to move on.

Howard and Chantou followed the masses. For the entire morning, their pace was relaxed as they ambled along paths, climbed stairs, peered into ancient halls, and enjoyed each other's company. Chantou's black eyes sparkled, expressing delight and amusement. She was clearly smiling continuously behind her colorful mask.

They used Howard's scooter to travel among the other temples, structures, and monuments at the sprawling tourist destination. For lunch, the couple took away food from a parking lot trailer to picnic in a secluded wooded area Chantou found. Later, she urged Howard to buy a bottle of wine from a Dragon Fruit orchard vendor and guided him to another hidden stream off the road where they drank from the bottle and lounged in the shade.

By late afternoon, with temperatures soaring into the nineties,

Howard jokingly pleaded for relief and they reluctantly returned to Aunt Martha's Guest House. The front desk was unattended when they entered the lobby. Chantou noticed the anomaly instantly, slipped off her shoes, and carried them in her hand as she motioned urgently for Howard to follow her up the stairs.

In his room, she acted quickly. As though their time together was about to end, she unbuttoned her top and slipped it off. Her breasts were bare. Without hesitation, she tugged off her shorts to reveal she was wearing nothing beneath them either. With arms wide apart, she leaped from the ground toward Howard, who caught her around her buttocks. Secured, she wrapped her arms around his neck before she thrust her tongue deep into his mouth. When she finally came up for air, she jumped from Howard's arms and yanked off his golf shirt.

"Let's get you undressed, too, and have a shower together." She teased him with a playful jut of pert breasts and a flick of her tongue around her lips.

Their shower together stretched longer than expected as kisses grew from flirtatious to passionate. Touches began tenderly and tentatively, then became bolder. With a first sign that the shower's supply of hot water was exhausted, Howard gasped in shock, then swooped Chantou into his arms. Five steps later, he gently deposited her on the bed before he grabbed a towel and soaked up most of the water from their dripping bodies.

They held each other tenderly but firmly and made love more passionately than ever before. Howard held himself back as long as he could, but still penetrated deeply with each thrust.

Chantou moaned her satisfaction. Her eyes sparkled and her face lit up until they climaxed in unison exactly as Howard had hoped. They lay together that way for several minutes, holding each other, each gently stroking the other's body. Neither made any profession of love, but he surely sensed something special was happening.

They moved from the bed only after they had decided to go out for dinner before the restaurants closed. This time their individual and chilly showers were quick and functional. They giggled about how much better the earlier session in the shower was.

At dinner, Howard remembered to circle back to the question of the cousin. He tried to make light of it.

"Sammy looked a little annoyed yesterday when we eliminated him from the tuk-tuk to Angkor Wat tour. Is there anything about him I should know?"

"To be honest, Sammy isn't really a cousin. When I left home for university in Phnom Penh, my parents needed someone to help them in place of me. He was a teenager from the neighborhood whose parents died when he was young. He lived in tough conditions, so my parents helped him out. When I returned from university, they let him create the tuk-tuk business and continue to live with us."

"I thought I spotted a spark of jealously or anger when you won the argument yesterday," Howard pressed.

"Maybe. My parents have tried to match us up, but I have no interest in him. It's not just that he is younger than me. I'm also a twenty-three-year-old Cambodian woman. I make my own decisions and will choose my own man." She leaned in suggestively.

Howard didn't pursue the matter any further and changed the subject. But that small revelation delayed his sleep for several hours. Later that night, he thought about Interpol and the Organization from every perspective he could imagine. He thought about Sammy, his mannerisms and his aspirations. And he considered his growing affection for Chantou. Could she be the one to replace the void Janet had left?

Although their day had been idyllic, a complete reassessment of Siem Reap felt necessary. A potentially jealous, jilted suitor could be a dangerous thing. In male-dominated Asia, that danger seemed magnified.

With more than a tinge of regret, he decided he had to act.

TWENTY-THREE

Sydney, Australia, Wednesday February 26, 2020

The newly hired hacker in Australia outdid himself. With training by Wendal's young technology whiz, combined with the guy's diligence, they surpassed Fidelia's goal of a hundred million dollars a month in less than ten days. So, Wendal reported the milestone to her in a late-night call.

"Come on over." Fidelia's laugh morphed from delight to seductive in seconds. "Have your little helpers left you enough energy?"

"I always have enough stamina. Those little helpers are all business." Surprised she either suspected or knew about his sexual escapades with the two technology whizzes, he tried to shut down that line of thinking at once. "In fact, something happened with the hacker in Australia. Aretta Musa asked me to send one of the girls back to train a recruit—a woman this time."

"What happened to the first guy you trained?"

"According to Aretta, he just disappeared. Didn't show up for work."

"That doesn't sound right to me. Did she have an explanation?"

"No, she just asked me to send someone down, and I put Jennie on a flight last night. She's been working there most of the day." Wendal sensed there might be something he was missing. "Should I have checked with you before I sent her?"

"No. But I'm going to call Aretta and have a chat while I wait for you to come over." Fidelia's tone turned seductive again with the last phrase.

When her bodyguard unlocked the door to let Wendal in, Fidelia, wearing sheer lingerie, was perched provocatively on a plush leather sofa, sipping a glass of red wine. She motioned for him to come over and pointed to the wine bottle and glass.

Wendal shook his head no, then ambled at a leisurely pace toward the controls for the suite. He dimmed the lights, then found romantic music he knew Fidelia preferred, and set the volume just loud enough to muffle their sounds from the bodyguard in the hallway.

Their familiarity required little conversation. Both knew why she had invited him, and Wendal wasted time no time stripping off her flimsy gown. She undressed him with teasing gestures and hints of her tongue. With light touches to his lips, chest, then promisingly lower, she aroused his passion. He felt his erection building more quickly than expected.

It felt longer to him, but it was probably only three or four minutes before she welcomed him into her mouth while she stroked his testicles and caressed his groin. Fidelia was truly amazing. Her lovemaking was so expert, she made every time feel like their first. Her touch, passion, even her moans of encouragement seemed to be different each time. The way she explored his orifices, or probed with her darting tongue, heightened his senses and carried him to repeated delight.

Still, he always found one thing odd about their sexual encounters. Fidelia always wanted to be on top, and it was she who determined the pace and depth of his thrust. She was the only woman he ever recalled doing that. But he wasn't complaining.

For a couple hours, Fidelia urged him to perform again and again. When he was entirely spent and she apparently satisfied, a long silence hung over them before she told him how great it was. With a peck on his cheek and a gentle squeeze of his genitals, she slipped out of bed and showered. When she returned, she was wearing lingerie again. She planned to talk.

"I want you to go to Sydney in the morning. Something's not right there, and I want you to check it out. There's a flight about eight; I already checked."

"Okay." He drew out the word to appear perplexed, adding a tilt of his head and a blank expression. She didn't react, so he carried on. "Sure, I can go. But what's up?"

"Not sure. That's why you need to check it out. Aretta admitted she's in over her head with the technology. She also said your girl, Jennie, was alarmed to see something had changed in the algorithms since she trained the previous guy. They were trying to figure it out when I called."

"It can't be too serious. Jennie would have phoned if it was. Why don't we just give her a call now and check it out?"

Fidelia concurred, and they got Jennie on a speakerphone. Wendal felt the blood rush from his brain as the girl gave her report. Not only was the guy she trained missing, so was about twenty-five million dollars. They had scooped it out of three Australian banks the previous day, but the algorithm didn't deposit any of the money in the designated Chilean accounts. It had just disappeared.

Five hours later, Wendal filed onto a Qantas Airlines flight with a few other surly, early morning passengers, then fretted the entire journey. Food and refreshment were the least of his concerns in the plush first-class section. Instead, huddled over his laptop for almost the entire flight, he probed the Dark Web with encrypted Wi-Fi access and mounting angst.

It didn't get better. After Aretta's flunky met him at the airport, and James arrived at the back of the nondescript family restaurant where Aretta worked from her office, she broke the news right away. Her people in drugs had just come across the missing hacker's body.

It was an opioid overdose in a seedy part of Sydney. Aretta had no idea the guy used drugs. None of her people in the illicit business knew him either. He'd never been a customer, they swore. And his body showed no evidence of other drugs or habit. Her people were asking around to see who'd sold the guy the opioids, but they had come up empty so far.

Aretta's new hire to replace the guy wasn't up to the challenge. She simply didn't have the technology smarts needed. So, Wendal and Jennie pounded the keyboards of their laptops for several hours that first day instead. They found no trace of the route their twenty-five million Australian dollars followed after leaving the banks. Every path led to a frustrating dead end. When Wendal finally found it necessary to admit defeat, he called Fidelia. She was astonishingly circumspect.

"I'm not entirely surprised. The more I think about it, we probably didn't screen that guy as well as we should have. Aretta needs to do a better job checking those people. But there's no point crying over spilled milk. Stay there as long as you must. Help Aretta properly screen the next person. And let's get the hacking activity going again as soon as we can. We've got twenty-five million to replace. And be careful down there."

Annoyingly, she had recently adopted the habit of just hanging up when she was done speaking. That left no opportunity to ask what prompted her warning and caused him to sleep fitfully that night.

The next morning, Jennie resumed her probe of the incident, tracing every formula on the Dark Web.

Meanwhile, Wendal huddled with Aretta as they talked about possible sources of skillful hackers, checked out various chat rooms, and researched social media patterns. They identified a half dozen potential candidates before the end of the day, and Aretta put in motion first interviews for each. She used resources from the extortion side of her business. They were experts at researching and finding personal weaknesses.

Their day stretched well into the evening. By the time Aretta dropped Wendal and Jennie at the lobby door of the Five Seasons, he felt restless and fidgety. He ate, but found the room service food unappealing and tasteless despite its meticulous preparation by an accomplished chef. Even the Australian wine seemed too dry to merit the label of "fine" printed on the room service card.

Surprisingly, video games failed to interest him either. He checked out the top-quality TV screen that served as an awesome monitor on the wall, but shut it off again despite its spectacular color and definition. The goings-on in Australia didn't compute right for him, but he couldn't figure out why.

He thought briefly about making a call or sending an email to a guy who might know, but decided he couldn't risk it. He had no way of knowing on whose telephone or computer Fidelia had downloaded the special software he'd invented. As soon as the app detected specific code words, it recorded the entire conversation. Fidelia knew how to program the app for the info she wanted. There was no way of knowing which conversations she was listening in on unless she told him.

Wendal slammed his fist into a cushion of the sofa—not in anger—rather more annoyed that his own brilliant invention had effectively stymied his room to maneuver.

He thought a shower might help and heard his phone ring while he was in the stall, but ignored it. Steaming hot water for almost half an hour helped, and he felt much calmer as he toweled himself dry. Relaxed enough to quaff a couple small bottles of fine scotch whiskey from the minibar, and watch a rerun of *The Big Bang Theory*.

He thought again of the ringing phone and checked for a message. It was Jennie.

"Good news, big guy. I did a little more digging on that mysterious algorithm that stole The Organization's cash. I think I've got something. Give me a call."

Wendal called her phone, but she didn't reply before it bounced to her voicemail. She must have fallen asleep. There was no point in leaving another message. He'd just catch up with her when she came up for breakfast.

The following morning, she didn't show up at his suite at the agreed-upon time. He ordered breakfast and rang her room phone when she still hadn't arrived. There was no answer, and he felt an unexplained sense of unease. That feeling switched to dread when a hotel security guard knocked on the door of his suite, a Sydney police officer standing directly behind him.

A maid had just discovered Jennie's lifeless body in her room. The guard remembered seeing Wendal walk into the lobby with the beautiful young woman the night before and shared that information with the police.

Now, the towering man in uniform stepped forward and wanted to know what Wendal could tell them about their relationship.

TWENTY-FOUR

Ft. Myers, Florida, Thursday February 27, 2020

Her office phone rang several times before Suzanne's Keurig finished brewing its first cup of coffee about six o'clock that morning. Dan Ramirez was poised to deliver his update from Chile and knew "first thing" meant she was probably at her desk. She juggled her bag, pressed the phone against her ear, and carried a mug of coffee to her desk without spilling it. There, she pressed the speaker button and let him know she was ready.

"James Fitzgerald is here with me in Valparaíso. A couple developments to report, ranging from important to curious. Where would you like to start?"

"Your choice. Fire away." Suzanne savored her coffee. She liked to inhale the hazelnut aroma when it was freshly brewed, and took a few seconds to indulge before she hunched forward to concentrate on every detail and nuance of the conversation.

"They've identified the guy who drugged and threw Mrs. Ortez off the apartment building balcony. As Carlos surmised, it was her son, Manuel."

An icy shiver rushed down her spine. Even though it had been their working assumption, it still rankled her they were dealing with someone so ruthless and devoid of emotion he could murder his own mother. Dan paused a moment, giving her a moment to absorb the significance. It was James who continued.

"Dan and his people are getting good cooperation from the Chilean police. They spent three days collecting videos and another two reviewing them until they found one where the low-life revealed his face." James paused. Suzanne could almost visualize his nod to Dan to carry on from there.

"Yeah. This one's experienced. He made only one tiny mistake. When he first got out of his car—before he pulled down his cap and wrapped a scarf around his face—a camera mounted high on an electric pole on the street captured him for a second. Just to be sure, the FBI people sent it to Quantico for enhancement. After they increased the definition, there's no doubt it's Manuel Ortez. He dragged her into the building and then left without her less than ten minutes later."

"Have they made any progress locating him?"

"Nothing concrete yet," Dan replied. "The police in Santiago know him, but not for anything like our fraud issue. He had convictions for burglary and extortion several years ago. Nothing in the past five years."

James jumped in again. "But we found his name, or variations of his name, on another two-dozen companies. Angela traced the payment details Supermarkets provided, and she's narrowed the number of banks involved down to five. Dan's people are working with the Chilean police and a judge here in Valparaíso. Later today, we're hoping to have court orders requiring the bank managers to release their records with all the contact details they received when the accounts were opened."

"What do you plan to do with that information?" Suzanne asked.

"The Chilean police tell us they'll get personal addresses and telephone numbers for all the names on the accounts," Dan explained. "They'll then follow-up on each of those to try to locate Ortez or the others named as directors of the companies. Hopefully, one of those bits of information will lead to our man."

"I'm afraid it all sounds quite abstract to me at this stage," Suzanne said. "Have we nothing specific about his home or current whereabouts?"

"Nothing we can rely on," James replied. "But one of Dan's people got some information we're checking out."

"Yeah, I wasn't going to share this with you because it's very early stages, but here's what we know now. Remember the young Spanish-speaking woman we added to my contingent at the last minute? Sophia Garcia? The one we had to meet in Miami on the way down? When we picked her up, she'd come directly from a party. Let's just say her outfit was a little revealing, and she had no time to go home and change before we left."

Dan Ramirez paused, apparently to choose his words carefully.

"Not unexpectedly, the morning after we arrived her attire drew a bit of attention from the local constabulary. I sent her out to buy more practical clothes, and the Chilean police sergeant assigned one of his guys to go with her. It seems the pair hit it off and didn't return with her new outfit for a couple hours. Since then, that fellow has been hitting on her continuously and tags along wherever she goes."

"Is he stalking her?" Suzanne asked, in a tone more severe than intended. She was short on sleep. Stefan had called late the night before, and they'd talked for more than an hour. She resolved to focus on the call and be more patient. The guys were probably just trying to give her the entire picture.

"Not really," Dan explained. "He's a little more like a puppy in heat. She finds his behavior sort of stereotypical Latino machismo. He's flirtatious. Keeps trying to impress her with his knowledge and connections. She encourages him, hoping he might eventually share something useful."

"Got it," Suzanne replied without enthusiasm, her patience waning. "So, how does all this relate to James's comment that you're following up on a possible lead?"

"Macho Man claims to know Ortez personally, as well as some of his friends," Dan said. "He claims a mutual friend saw Manuel Ortez at the airport two days ago, in a line boarding a flight to Uruguay. The guy gave his superior that same information, but his sergeant claims it's all bullshit. To be sure, I sent one of my people out to the airport with Ortez's picture and asked around. An airline employee confirmed she saw a man matching Ortez's description, but with another name. He was in line to board a flight to Montevideo. The airline employee was certain of it."

"So, the Chilean police sergeant might be protecting Ortez?" Suzanne asked.

"And that protection may come from even higher than the sergeant," James replied. "One of Dan's people and an FBI agent flew to Montevideo last night. They're following up on the name and passport details for the traveler to see if they can find him in Uruguay."

"But it's a long shot," Dan interjected quickly. "If the fellow isn't traveling on his Chilean passport, we may be on a wild goose chase. He might use different ID."

"Okay. I get it. You said you had a few things to share. I've only got about five minutes before my next meeting." She used her chipper "let's get this over with" tone so Dan Ramirez would sense her growing impatience without taking offense.

"Right. We're focused on the court orders and bank interviews here today. We'll also check out that lead for Uruguay. Now, the other curious bit is more gossip than anything, but I thought you might want to know. Our former colleague Wendal Randall has been arrested in Sydney, Australia."

Suzanne felt herself grimace. She'd always considered Wendal trouble but resisted an impulse to comment. Dan carried on into the vacuum.

"My contact at the FBI noticed an Interpol report that someone using the passport and identity they gave Wendal in the witness protection program was being held there on suspicion of murder. My guy at the FBI contacted the Aussies and confirmed the passport number and a fingerprint. It's definitely Wendal."

Suzanne finished the call saying all the right things, but her mind wandered to the new development. Wendal Randall, a murderer? The guy was a little weird, perhaps. But a killer?

TWENTY-FIVE

Fidelia had barely slept since her German friend, Klaudia Schäffer, called back with information about the mysterious IP address that was in some way related to both the CIA and The Organization's missing twenty-five million dollars. The story she'd told was troubling.

"What really had me stumped was where the message originated. It may have been directed to someone in the CIA, but all the evidence points to a highly secure IP address in Moscow." Klaudia's voice trembled slightly as she paused to either collect her thoughts or her courage. Fidelia couldn't be sure which, but she trusted her friend's intuition implicitly and sensed bad news to come.

"When we track the message with a GPS identifier, it seems to come from a building in the same general area as the Russian Federal Security Service."

"Are you kidding me?" Fidelia was incredulous. That was the outfit that had replaced the dreaded KGB. Its reputation was even more sullied than its predecessor's. There were undeniable links between the secret security agency and the Russian mafia.

"Yeah. Near the FSB. Nothing confirms the FSB is actually involved," Klaudia emphasized.

While her friend was trying to soothe her concerns, Fidelia's intuition rebelled. Unease wasn't a strong enough word to describe her discomfort with the news. Angst was a better one. Or dread. Maybe apprehension would be an even better word. Regardless of the precise definition of her nervousness, for the following nights, sleep became elusive as her worry intensified.

After Klaudia's call, she'd developed the seed of a scheme, and it was taking form. Complex and dramatic, to make her plan work she'd need brilliant technology, flawless execution, and a stomach of iron. She'd also take on enormous financial risk. Wendal Randall probably had the technology wherewithal. Her own business acumen was at its peak. But she didn't have the needed contact inside to do it quickly. Giancarlo Mareno hadn't divulged that information even to Luigi.

Before she could decide, her ringing phone intruded. It was Aretta in Australia with news of Wendal's arrest. Her voice an octave higher and pace a notch quicker than usual, she recounted that Sydney police discovered Jennie's body in her room at the hotel and didn't believe Wendal's pleas of innocence. What should she do?

"What happened?" Fidelia wanted to buy some time to think about this new predicament. It added unwanted complexity on multiple levels.

"One of my guys has a connection with security at the hotel. A maid found Jennie lying in her bed, undressed, when she let herself in to clean the room. They called the police. One of the detectives said it looked like a broken neck."

Fidelia cringed in sympathy. Her mind flashed to a video she'd watched years earlier. One that caught Wendal in the sordid act of erotic asphyxiation. Howard Knight had the evidence, and it vividly showed Wendal choking his victim as he reached orgasm. It was the leverage Knight had used to control Wendal at Multima, and the reason she always stayed on top when she had sex with him.

"Have you talked to a lawyer yet?" Fidelia asked.

"No. I just spoke with Wendal a few minutes ago. There's been no time. I can call the gal we usually use for our criminal matters here."

"Give her a try. I'm guessing the courts will claim Wendal's a flight risk and deny bail, but we're best to get the process underway." All sorts of alarm bells rang for Fidelia. She found her throat dry and her thoughts darting in a dozen different directions at once. She tried to focus. "Have you been to the hotel yet?"

"Not yet. I've sent a guy over there, though. He's checking to see if any computers were left behind. The police probably seized both, but the guy I sent is the one who knows the security guard. He'll get into both rooms if he can. I told him to gather up anything that might implicate The Organization."

"Do we have anyone there who can access the servers and wipe them clean?"

"No. Jennie and Wendal were handling all of that until we hired a new person."

"Okay," Fidelia said. "We have someone else here in Singapore. I'll get her working on it."

"Should I keep trying to find a replacement techie?" Aretta didn't wait for an answer to her question. "It's a shame losing that income when all our other sources are drying up because of the pandemic."

"I know. I saw the numbers you reported from the girls last week. It's effin' unbelievable. But don't do anything until we find out where Wendal's and Jennie's laptops are. If we recover them before the police, maybe we can go on. If the police have them, we'll have to lie low for a while."

Despite the early hour, Fidelia woke Wendal's other technology whiz, Suzy. They hadn't met since the woman arrived in Singapore, and she had no idea if the younger woman had the necessary skills, but she had no choice. Fidelia introduced herself and let Suzy wake fully before she spoke.

"There's been a complication in Sydney." Fidelia forced her tone to stay measured and calm. "Neither Wendal nor Jennie are available right now. I need you to clean up the files in Sydney—the ones we've been using to get into the banks down there. Do you know how to do that remotely?"

"It'll take a little time, but sure," Suzy replied. "What happened?"

"I'll tell you all about it. But first, I want you to get dressed, grab your laptop and meet up with the bodyguard I'm sending over right now. He'll be there in fifteen minutes. Wait for him on the first corner to the right of Stan Tan's house. He'll bring you here to do your work, and I'll tell you everything I know. It'll be safer that way." Fidelia's tone left no room for discussion.

She'd barely completed dispatching the bodyguard when her phone rang again. This time the screen announced Stan Tan. Fidelia swallowed hard before she said hello.

"I just got a call from Cambodia. Are you still interested in Howard Knight?"

"Howard Knight? Cambodia? Are you sure?" If he had the goods on Wendal, he just might have information about the other one too.

"Yeah. He's using an assumed name, of course. But it's him. We got a picture of the guy and ran it through some facial recognition software. My operative knows where he's holed up in a small hotel in Siem Reap. You want him?"

Fidelia paused to think it through. There was no way Howard Knight would help her voluntarily. He was past that. But he just might have the key to Wendal's concern about inside influence. Then she asked another question to buy some time.

"Are you able to smuggle him into Singapore alive?"

"With everything going on at the airport here these days, we'd need to bring him through Malaysia. There's a business aviation terminal at Senai in Johor, just across the border. We can bring him in undercover from there. Could have him here sometime tomorrow. Fifty thousand US should do it."

"Bring him in."

TWENTY-SIX

It finally happened. For countless hours, James and Angela had been working elbow-to-elbow at the dining-room table they'd converted into a communal desk.

The working arrangement was her idea. Get the hotel to rearrange the suite with the massive walnut table right below the oversized TV monitor on the wall. He never watched TV anyway. Most of the team was spread out across Chile, so there were seldom more than two of them and a couple bodyguards eating meals in the room. The bigger screen would make it easier to scrutinize the mounds of data.

They'd spent most of the past two days squeezed together, poring over public records.

It was nice. She used just a touch of perfume, and its scent stirred something in his spirit. He liked her giggle of delight when results from some obscure website produced the warming satisfaction of a positive lead for another one. And he loved her perpetual smile. Even when she encountered a disappointment, her frown lasted only a second or two before her eyes lit up again and a toothy smile spread. He found her energizing.

Well beyond the dinner hour, Angela murmured something. His eyes fixed on the screen, James didn't hear her at first.

"I said, I might have a hit," she repeated, this time more emphatically.

James shifted his attention to a section of the big screen where Angela pointed with her mouse. There it was: an address in Uruguay. Avenidas Cannes, 20. Punta del Este. The address appeared on a city tax billing listing Manuel Ortez as the owner.

While James reached for his telephone, Angela brought up the address on Google maps and took a satellite view of the property.

"It's not a mansion by any means," James explained to Dan Ramirez when he answered. "The home's nestled into a neat row of properties on a dead-end street. It looks well-maintained and unremarkable compared to other homes on the avenue. Do you think we might have something here?"

"We won't know until we check it out. I'll send the FBI and Chilean agents in Uruguay over there. It's a couple hours' drive from Montevideo, but hopefully, we'll find a trail."

They surely didn't have their man yet, but something magical happened regardless. When James set down his phone and looked at Angela, she sprang to her feet and raised her arm high in the air for a celebratory high five. Her eyes sparkled as he slapped her outstretched hand, and she leaned in for a hug. When he reached out to put his arm around her shoulders, she looked directly at him, raised her eyes, and parted her lips. Before he had time to think, their lips met, and she squeezed him tightly.

From there, it all became a blur. Within a minute or two, they'd shuffled to the sofa with mouths and arms seemingly locked as one. Moments later, he explored her body with his hands while their tongues probed desperately. Before he realized it, she unbuttoned his shirt and teasingly ran her hands across the hair on his chest. He undressed her completely in return and continued delicately stroking her breasts, then down to her thighs. Without warning, she pulled herself out of his grip, stood up, and tugged his arm in the direction of the bedroom.

It had been almost two years since his wife left him for another woman. The minutes after Angela guided him to the bed in his suite were the most intense he could remember. Their lovemaking had an edge of desperation, and he climaxed far too soon. Undaunted, Angela climbed on top and teased with her tongue and touch until he was ready again.

Their pace was more measured and deliberate the second time. His desperation morphed into tenderness, then a renewed passion. By the time Angela reached her climax, he was exhausted, satisfied, and in wonder. During more than twenty years with Diane, the chemistry with his ex-wife never once matched the fervor of his coupling with Angela. During his marriage, his sole dalliances—with a subordinate named Janet Weissel—may have matched the sexual intensity, but had never achieved the powerful connection he experienced with Angela.

She stayed the night and James slept soundly, satisfied and released from pent-up sexual tension. Angela awoke the next morning just as he opened his eyes. They looked at each other and broke into mischievous laughter. Then they held each other again in an embrace both seemed reluctant to break. A phone call shattered the bliss.

"We missed the scum," Dan Ramirez said when James answered.

"What happened?"

"All they found was an underage girl, mid-teens the agents guessed.

She called a lawyer before they even rang the doorbell. The agents had to conference with her and an attorney by phone, with her looking out through a window as they talked. The legal weasel wouldn't divulge any information other than her name and a declaration that the girl had the right to complete privacy as an Uruguayan citizen. Trying for a search warrant would be futile."

James and Angela both listened to the disappointing report. Her body slumped in dejection as the news settled in, and his initially buoyant spirit plummeted.

"So, we're back to square one?" James asked.

"It looks like it." Dan Ramirez's dejected tone left him searching for words.

TWENTY-SEVEN

Siem Reap, Cambodia, Saturday February 29, 2020

A faint click of an opening lock didn't alarm Howard. It was probably Chantou slipping quietly into the room as she had most nights for a week or more. As he turned toward the doorway and lifted his head from the pillow, they pounced.

Howard thrashed his arms and legs as two strangers leaped toward him, blocking anything else from view. One landed directly on him, using his full weight to restrain his movement. The intruder pressed a foul-smelling wad of fabric tightly over Howard's mouth and nose, muffling any attempt to cry out. Another pair of strong hands gripped a nerve near his neck. Within seconds, everything faded to darkness.

When Howard opened his eyes, everything was blurred, his mouth was dry, and he couldn't move. He slowly surveyed the damage. He was naked, wrapped in the sheets from his bed, and lying on a rough metal surface. The cargo area of a pickup truck, he realized, after his focus cleared. His arms were strapped tight to his sides in three different places. His ankles, knees, and thighs were also bound.

A mask covered his mouth and nose. It felt like one of those cheap, rough disposable paper masks that restricted his breathing only slightly. Beside him, his backpack bounced around in rhythm to the frequent bumps in the road, slipping and sliding as it jostled harmlessly out of reach. It looked full. Maybe his clothes were in there. Every muscle ached, and every bump in the road jolted him from the steel surface only to land again with a painful thud.

Cool gusts of wind caused Howard to shiver sporadically. It was still dark and clouds blocked most of the light from the moon. It felt as if the pickup truck moved along a gravel road; the tires tossed up loose stones and occasional debris, disturbing an otherwise quiet background. Like roads all across Cambodia, this one was poorly lit, and there seemed to be few intersections, no stops, and no lights.

The way they'd attacked and subdued Howard left little doubt his captors were not from any conventional police force. That meant someone from The Organization or local thugs. Perhaps friends of Chantou's cousin, Sammy? Neither possibility inspired much hope. In fact, for a guy seeking only to be left alone, it was terribly demoralizing.

The alarm tone on Howard's phone, somewhere in the backpack beside him, grew louder with each ring—reminding him the timing of his capture was frustratingly ironic. Only hours earlier, he had decided to move on from Aunt Martha's Guest House. He'd intended to leave that very morning as soon as it was light outside.

One more good intention thwarted by lousy timing.

———•———

It had been more than his growing unease with Sammy—and the cousin's complicated relationship with Chantou—that led to Howard's decision to move on. The atmosphere in Siem Reap had changed slightly. People looked at foreigners a second or two longer than usual as they passed in the street. Masks covered facial expressions and everyone now wore one wherever they went. It was difficult to judge moods or intentions.

Nods in greeting or cheerful hellos disappeared. Locals went out of their way to create space in crowded streets or shops. The only remaining tourists in town seemed to be hardy Eastern Europeans traveling in groups. Even they seemed less boisterous and animated as they steadfastly followed their tour guides around the town.

It had to be the COVID-19 virus causing all the change. Howard had found himself thinking more like the older fellow he'd chatted with at breakfast a few days earlier. As predicted, the guy checked out the morning after their conversation. His destination was Singapore, where he trusted the quality of health care.

Although Howard intended to move on from Siem Reap, he had settled on a different strategy. Anxious to avoid more flights and possible exposure to facial recognition software, he had concluded it was better just to avoid the virus.

The mountainous regions of Laos seemed more prudent. With care, he should be able to avoid contracting the disease. He'd wear a mask all the time. Touch only the items he must. Wash his hands continuously, and spend time with nature, sleeping in the outdoors like the homeless. And the country was only a three-hour scooter ride from Siem Reap.

———•———

That strategy would be moot if he didn't find a way out of his current predicament.

As that sobering thought sank in, the pickup slowed and shortly after veered off the road. The terrain became much rougher as Howard and his backpack bounced almost continuously on the hard metal surface. He arched his neck forward, trying to avoid the excruciating pain in the back of his head from repeated banging against the deck of the truck. The vehicle continued along a tree-lined laneway for some distance, then stopped abruptly in a clear area. Looking up, Howard no longer saw overhanging trees. They'd parked in an open area.

In the distance, a noise grew steadily louder. No one moved from the pickup, and he couldn't hear any voices from the cab, although the engine no longer ran. A few minutes later, no doubt remained. The sound growing louder was the hum of a small airplane, and it was getting closer.

Anxiously, Howard listened for the predictable thump of tires touching land, followed by a roar of the engine braking the speed of the aircraft on the ground. He heard the thump and a distant rumble but didn't hear the usual whine of tires at high speed on an asphalt tarmac. Instead, it sounded like the plane had touched down on grass or dirt.

It made sense. They were probably in some remote location, and a small incoming plane would have space for only two or three passengers. An opportunity for immediate escape seemed unlikely, and he silently cursed his bad luck once more.

The plane thumped more loudly along uneven ground in the field, its propeller gradually slowing as it drew nearer. Howard could see the top of it parked next to the pickup. With the plane's arrival, both doors of the vehicle opened, and people got out on either side. Doors slammed shut and two men peered over the side of the cargo area at Howard.

Both were Asian and inspected him as one pointed a bright flashlight into his face. He could only see their upper bodies, but both men had solid necks like weightlifters or football players. They made some comments Howard couldn't understand as the flashlight passed over his body from head to toe. The faint light revealed a few of the dark welts and bruises that spotted his now partially covered body. The aching wasn't likely to subside any time soon.

The plane engine idled but never stopped completely. A voice from the aircraft shouted out in Khmer and both men on the ground responded. There was an exchange for a minute or so before one of the men reached into the cargo area and snatched Howard's backpack, then

163

angrily tugged on the zipper to open it before he yanked out a shirt and shorts and threw them at his immobile victim.

The other man issued some form of command that sounded as if he wanted Howard to get dressed. How that would happen with the zip ties around him wasn't clear. After another exchange between the plane and the men on the ground, the two men climbed onto the pickup bed and removed the zip ties on his upper body. Howard struggled to pull on the golf shirt, barely able to raise his arms above his head.

Another shout from the aircraft and men on the ground reinstalled all three zip ties on Howard's upper body to assure he would still be immobile when they removed the lower ties. This gang must have heard the story of his brazen escape from The Organization's goons in Spain a couple months earlier. They were taking no chances this time.

After one of his captors roughly yanked Howard's shorts up his lower body, both men reached to reattach the zip ties but stopped when there was another shout from the plane. Some genius among them realized it was better to force Howard to walk up the stairs to the plane rather than carrying him up. The pair yanked him down from the pickup bed without losing his balance, then dragged him toward the plane, each gripping one immobile arm. He swore in anger but neither reacted.

They pushed him up the stairs as far as they could reach. From inside, the pilot reached down and tugged Howard upward as the two thugs on the bottom pushed up his lower extremities. Humiliated, he lashed out a leg, hitting one in the head. The bastard smashed the back of Howard's knees in retaliation.

Twice, they almost let him tumble backward, but the pilot found enough strength and space to anchor his legs. Eventually he dragged Howard inside the plane, with his scraped and bleeding stomach on the floor. Exhausted and realizing it was futile, he gave up his struggle with a muffled cry of exasperation.

The pilot commanded one of the men to climb the stairs. Between the two of them, they man-handled Howard into a seat beside the pilot, then reapplied the zip ties thrown up from the ground by the guy below. Once he was again immobilized by six zip ties around his arms and legs, the pilot buckled his seatbelt. In case of an emergency landing, Howard would be a moribund spectator to whatever might occur.

Without a word, the pilot closed the doors, revved up the idling engine, then spurted off to a darker shade of ground to prepare for takeoff. Howard had experienced a lot over his lifetime. Until that day, he'd never taken off in an airplane from a grass-covered runway and really had no desire to try. He lowered his eyes and studied the metal floor.

The engines wound up revolutions per minute to a furious roar before the pilot released the brake, and the plane lunged forward, picking up speed. The bouncing aircraft tossed Howard in all directions within the confines of the tightly buckled seat belt. Some potholes felt like deep ruts caused by rodents. At times, the tiny tires lost their grip in the soil, and the plane tilted sideways or bounced like a basketball and bottomed out whatever shock absorbers the airplane used to cushion bumps. One time, his head was thrown so violently in the pilot's direction, he was tempted to bite the man's just-out-of-reach right ear.

After a short while, the airplane slowly climbed from the ground, buffeted gently by the winds, until the pilot found a comfortable cruising altitude. From the interior, the plane resembled one used a few weeks earlier by the hired pilot that had carried Howard from Lourdes, in France, to Giancarlo Mareno's makeshift lair at the Innsbruck airport in Austria. It was that flight that had launched him on his current voyage of desperation.

Howard knew little about cockpits. He'd been a passenger a few times, watching pilots at work, but he knew enough to see they were flying unusually low. Intuition told him it was probably to avoid air traffic control. He'd read somewhere that planes flying below a certain altitude weren't required to file flight plans and were seldom monitored. He was also able to read a compass and saw they were traveling in a southwesterly direction.

Howard visualized a map of the region and mentally rhymed off potential destinations. Thailand? Malaysia? Singapore? Indonesia? Then he considered the geographic realities. Singapore and Indonesia were just too far for such a small aircraft. They'd need to cross the Gulf of Thailand, which spanned at least three hundred miles, and it was probably more than a hundred miles across Cambodia before they reached the Gulf. More likely, they'd stop somewhere in Thailand to refuel or perhaps transfer him to another plane. None of the possibilities eased his concern.

Beside him, the pilot ignored his captive and focused intently on control panels and switches, occasionally peering out the windows on either side. The sunrise became brilliant with little cloud cover, so the aviator wore wrap-around sunglasses that protected and hid his eyes. He made no effort to communicate, and his body language projected total indifference.

Howard closed his eyes often against the constant glare and eventually dozed from time to time. He had probably slept for only a couple hours before they snatched him from Aunt Martha's Guest House, and the ride in the back of the pickup had been far too harsh for sleep.

When engine speed reduced and the plane began its descent, Howard awoke startled. He had lost all sense of time as he snoozed and had no idea of the distance they'd traveled. Looking across the horizon, he thought a large body of water spread to infinity beyond a small parcel of land below. The pilot banked the plane to the right and an airport runway came into view. It was a significant airport, large enough to accommodate small jets for sure, maybe even large ones.

The pilot lined up an approach with a runway and continued a gradual descent until the reassuring touch of wheels hit the runway. Thankfully, this one was either cement or asphalt. Skillfully, the pilot brought the aircraft to a stop with plenty of runway remaining, made a left turn at the only access to the tarmac, and motored toward a terminal building. A bilingual sign announced Trat Airport.

With a reliable memory, Howard visualized a map of the region and recalled Trat was a small town at the Southern tip of Thailand on the east side of the Gulf of Thailand. They could be taking him almost anywhere if they planned to transfer him to a jet. As that thought formed, he realized the pilot intended to park not at the terminal but next to a plain white Learjet.

Once the plane had stopped, the pilot reached across Howard and opened the door, then stepped down to the ground. He was gone only a moment or two before he dashed back up the stairs and into the doorway. Behind him, two large Asian men wearing Khaki shorts and jackets also squeezed into the opened door.

"It takes me two seconds to reach inside my jacket and pull out my gun, another second to aim and shoot." The apparent leader's English was perfect, his tone matter of fact. He paused a second to let his message register.

"Each of my friends, here and on the ground, has weapons in their pockets and are equally proficient. We're going to release your zip ties. You're going to come down the steps and walk with us to the jet. One false move and we all reach for our guns. We get paid whether we deliver you alive or as a corpse. Got it?"

Howard nodded.

"Don't just nod. Say it. Tell me you understand," the leader said, louder this time.

"I understand. I'll follow you to the jet." Howard spat out his words defiantly.

"We've heard all about your escapades in Europe. Don't even think about trying that shit here."

The leader signaled for the man beside him to climb up into the cockpit. Together, the pair cut the zip ties and freed Howard.

Unsteadily, he made his way down the steps. As he touched the tarmac, four men fell into an informal formation, enclosing him from all sides. When the leader said go, they all stepped forward. After a moment's hesitation, the leader gave him a nudge from behind and Howard complied. At the stairs to the jet, one man mounted the steps and someone pushed Howard from behind to prod him forward. The others all followed.

The Learjet's bright interior was spectacular. Eight white leather seats formed two rows, four on each side, with an aisle in between. The leader pointed Howard toward the second seat on the left and told him to sit down and buckle up. With the click of his seatbelt, Howard felt a hand reach from behind, and again smother his mouth and nose with a foul-smelling cloth. Others were already reaching forward with zip ties when Howard lost consciousness.

TWENTY-EIGHT

Ft. Myers, Florida, Saturday February 29, 2020

Eileen buzzed Suzanne just before noon. Beverly Vonderhausen was holding on line one.

"I'm afraid I don't have much to report," Beverly said. "I spent the entire week with your supermarket industry lobbyist in Washington—a surprisingly well-connected woman, by the way. Every path we tried was a dead-end. Everyone claimed they didn't know anything about an investigation into Multima Corporation or money laundering issues related to Multima. You'll also be relieved to know virtually everyone expressed shock at any suggestion you or your company might be doing something illegal."

"We knew it was a long shot, but I really appreciate you spending so much time with the lobbyist." Suzanne injected as much enthusiasm into her thank you as she could muster, but didn't mask her disappointment. She continued after a pause to decide how much she should share.

"Dan Ramirez is coming up empty with his contacts at the FBI too. They called back the three agents Dan initially persuaded them to send to Chile. Higher-ups in the FBI called the exercise a high-cost, low-return investigation. Even Dan admitted the evidence they uncovered possibly linking Manuel Ortez to defrauding Multima was weak. James Fitzgerald and the forensic investigator argued otherwise, but they might be too desperate for a solution."

"Are you abandoning the Chilean search then?" Beverly asked.

Suzanne was exasperated with the entire affair in South America, but chose her words to sound more neutral.

"Last night, I pulled Dan Ramirez and most of his team back, but James persuaded me to give him and his forensic investigator another week. Dan left one of his team behind to protect them. I'm not convinced it's worth the risk, but James was more passionate than ever about seeing it through to the end down there. Against my better judgment, I acquiesced. But only until next Saturday."

"I still don't understand why the Chilean police aren't more aggressive." Beverly's tone conveyed more exasperation than her words. "Don't they have that guy's image on a video connecting him to a woman's fall to her death from an apartment balcony? I can understand they're not too concerned with Multima's problems, but don't they at least want to find him for questioning about the murder?"

"That's precisely James's argument. They matched his image using facial recognition software, and they know the woman was his mother. To most of us, it seems obvious there's been foul play. But the Chilean police aren't convinced." After a pause to take a breath, Suzanne changed her tone to become more skeptical, almost sarcastic.

"They think he may have had good reasons for taking his drugged or drunken mother to an Airbnb apartment late at night, and suggest her fall may have been accidental if she was under the influence of drugs or alcohol. It's bizarre, but they've pulled all their investigators off the case," she scoffed.

"I assume Dan and the FBI people have tried to influence the most senior levels at the Chilean Investigations Police?" Beverly asked.

"Oh yes. Dan even appealed to an FBI assistant director to make a call. He spoke to someone in the office of the Chilean Minister of Justice and reported back that he detected nothing out of the ordinary in either their process or reasoning. We're at our wits' end with this mess. Any chance you have a contact or two in Chile?" Suzanne knew she sounded desperate.

"Personally, no. But our firm has a partner who specializes in South American legal files. Let me reach out to him and see what we find. What you're hoping for is someone who can penetrate the Chilean police to see what they might be hiding?"

"Yes. Neither Wilma nor I feel we have enough to sway the European Central Bank on the license issues," Suzanne explained. "We can show them we made a grand effort, but that's really all we've got. We know the money was transferred. We know it was transferred because of fraudulent invoices. But we can't find the former Multima employee who processed the invoices, nor where the money went after its deposit into the Chilean accounts."

Unfortunately, Suzanne could ask little more of her attorney that morning because the ECB crisis was not the only one demanding her attention. The coronavirus was raging. Almost eighty-thousand cases had been reported in China. Italy's count had suddenly surpassed five hundred and most countries were reporting new cases. Although the US had only twenty-six COVID-19 patients that morning, panic buying had already started across the country.

Intuitively, American consumers seemed to sense a spread was inevitable and the current low numbers merely a harbinger of worse to come. Entire sections of Multima's supermarkets emptied within hours in some cities. Disinfectants, wipes, sprays, and cleaners were the first to go. Toilet tissue became a rare commodity in certain towns, with people stockpiling and physical fights occasionally breaking out in the checkout lines. Hoarders wouldn't share and those without became desperate.

Her daily videoconference with the management team at Supermarkets dealt with a bizarre assortment of urgent issues. They decided to negotiate a contract with a national private security firm to control unruly crowds forcing their way into stores. Management also agreed to allow some of those guards to carry weapons to protect employees from physical attacks.

Jeremy Front, director of store operations, insisted they move forward urgently with a project to install plexiglass barriers between cashiers and customers to protect their staff. Gordon Goodfellow, Supermarkets' president, supported the recommendation of his director of human resources to immediately increase the pay of store employees by two dollars an hour. Some staff had already declined shifts, fearing both the virus and irate customers.

They debated the wisdom of equipping each employee with face masks to follow a practice stores in Asia had already established. Debate became particularly acrimonious as some echoed the World Health Organization message that masks had limited value, while others maintained masks might reduce any spread of the virus from Multima employees to customers should they be infected but asymptomatic. Still others pointed out union objections on the grounds of individual employee rights.

Impatient, Suzanne cut short the discussion before it became even more heated. Uncomfortable using precious time to build a consensus during the crush of a pandemic, she instructed her team to have every store manager check the advice of local public health officials and follow that advice to the letter.

Next, Suzanne asked Michelle Sauvignon to describe the blitz buying campaign that had worked so successfully in Europe a few weeks earlier. The team embraced her ideas at once. Michelle also shared a few tips learned from China, Singapore, Australia, and New Zealand—all

A Web of Deceit

countries ahead of the US on the learning curve of how to cope with what was almost certain to become a serious pandemic.

Throughout the day, several directors checked in individually to learn what they could about Suzanne's odd run-in with the US Justice Department, all initially using vague pretenses of concern about the spreading virus to camouflage curiosity about her legal issues. All expressed support and confidence in her leadership, though tones of a couple belied continuing doubts. She worried their misgivings might intensify if she couldn't soon find a way to squelch the rumors and innuendo.

Eileen popped into Suzanne's office hourly with new stacks of reports to study, documents to sign, and yellow sticky note requests to return calls from media, industry associations, and competitors. Her executive assistant performed her job well and had already dispensed with all but the most critical of the messages.

She always waited while Suzanne thumbed through the stack, assigned an alternative respondent to most, and kept only those essential for the CEO to handle. On Eileen's last trip of the day, only one note fell into that category, one marked "urgent" in red and asking Suzanne to call Gordon Goodfellow at Supermarkets.

"Some bad news, I'm afraid," he prefaced. "Georgia State Police called a few minutes ago. Police in Canada found our missing former colleague from accounts payable. Kim Jones has died of a broken neck in a skiing accident in Banff."

"A skiing accident?" Suzanne's astonishment showed in her high-pitched tone.

"Yeah. That was my reaction too. Before I called, I took a walk down to the accounting department and broke the news to her colleagues. Not a single person ever heard Kim mention an interest in skiing. No one could even recall the last time she talked about getting exercise. That just wasn't her thing."

"Didn't the FBI tell Dan Ramirez she was booked on a flight to Miami but didn't show up?"

"That's right. And Miami would make sense. She used to vacation often in Latin America. She lived with a South American expat, according to her friends. Banff, in Alberta, certainly sounds out of character."

"Dan Ramirez is back in his office. Why don't you call him? Maybe he can get his friends in the Canadian Mounties to share a little more detail."

171

TWENTY-NINE

An airport hangar, Sunday March 1, 2020

The first sound Howard Knight heard that morning was a strong male voice singing out instructions over a public address system. Still groggy from whatever had soaked the foul-smelling cloth they'd pressed over his mouth, he raised his aching head from a cement floor and looked around the massive enclosure. A couple planes sitting at the opposite end of the huge building confirmed it was an airport hangar.

Howard lay off in one corner, still tightly bound by zip ties. Little movement was possible. The floor was cool and the building appeared deserted, with the parked aircraft occupying only a tiny portion of the cavernous space. The only smell Howard recognized was jet fuel, and it was a faint odor that lingered on the floor rather than a stench overpowering the senses.

The building was dark, although a hint of light teased through open windows used for ventilation well up the walls on the sides Howard could see. The only doorway was near the planes, tucked into a corner near a wide opening that let aircraft in or out. It probably wasn't used often. The thugs who'd captured him in Thailand apparently chose another warm location, likely another nearby country.

The public address system continued chanting for some minutes. Howard listened more intently, and the source of the sound became clear—a Muslim call to prayer. That clue didn't help narrow down the new location much. Thailand, Malaysia, and Singapore all had significant Muslim populations. A little further south, Indonesia, Bangladesh, or Pakistan were all within the range of the Learjet they'd used to whisk him out of the Trat Airport in Thailand.

He remembered nothing from the flight and had no sense of how much time had elapsed. The fog of whatever they used to subdue him left his thoughts scrambled and labored. In addition to the headache, he felt nauseated. And it seemed every muscle screamed for relief. He couldn't see much of his body, but it felt bruised or scraped in too many places to count.

His body also signaled that several hours had elapsed. He needed to relieve himself, but not urgently. With effort, Howard forced himself to raise his head completely from the concrete surface. Tilting his body slightly, a better view of another wall became possible.

After arching his neck to the left and as far forward as possible, then holding it there for a few seconds, he realized one of the parked planes was identical to the Learjet he saw the night they snatched him. If the guards were still around, they may have converted the comfortable seats in the aircraft into beds.

His suspicions were confirmed a few moments later as he still studied the plane. An Asian man appeared at the doorway of the jet and peeked outside, then took a long, slow look all the way around the building. He held a phone to his ear and listened rather than talked. As the fellow worked his way down the half-dozen steps to the ground, another man showed up behind him in the doorway.

Yawning and stretching as he poked his head around the doorway, the second man looked like he had just awakened. His demeanor seemed less aware and cautious as he tucked the bottom of his T-shirt into his pants and stumbled on his way down the stairway before he joined the first guy.

A dull gray van suddenly burst through the wide-open space at high speed and dashed toward the Learjet. It screeched to a halt only long enough for the two men to jump in before squealing tires announced its acceleration directly toward Howard.

A second vehicle entered the hangar, swung around the planes and followed the van, but more slowly. When the first van stopped, three men jumped out and guided some sort of cube van or small truck to a parking spot mere feet away from Howard's head. When they opened the doors at the back, a couple rolls of carpet tumbled from its gate and landed on the floor, rolling. Two men jumped in front of the runaway carpets and stopped them with their feet.

No one offered him food or water. In fact, there was no communication at all. Everyone seemed to know his role and performed it with speed and efficiency. Howard's faint appeal for attention was ignored. One guy stooped down, slapped duct tape across his mouth, and wound it tightly around his head in one practiced movement. Removal of that duct tape at some point was destined to be another painful experience.

There were no gasses or drugs this time. Instead, two guys grabbed a section of Howard and hoisted him to his feet. A third man wrapped him in a foam-like material that was heavy and dense. Encased tightly,

Howard watched them use more duct tape to secure the pieces and leave only space around his eyes and nose.

Finished, the men lifted him horizontally and slid him on his back into the truck. Two of the fellows climbed in afterward and dragged him to the front of the box where they left Howard lying on the floor, his head pointing toward one side of the box, his feet almost touching the other side. The truck bed was hard and its wooden surface rough, even penetrating the foam material.

Another odd apparatus was hoisted into the truck and dragged next to Howard. Then they eased the sizable device between Howard and the front of the truck box, creating a sort of bridge, enveloping Howard in carpet as though he too was inside a box. In the darkness, he could hear continuing activity for a few minutes more.

Grunting and tugging, the men threw the errant rolls of carpet back into the truck and conversed loudly in an Asian language Howard couldn't place. As they shifted rolls of carpet, the truck tilted and swayed, and each time, a carpet roll dropped to the floor or onto another pile. All this elaborate work around the special structure they'd inserted over Howard allowed him to breathe, but it also concealed they were carrying a passenger—a passenger who expected to see the light of day again but doubted it would be welcome.

THIRTY

Fidelia Morales got the call just after midnight. They'd found Howard Knight, smuggled him into Singapore, and currently had him stashed at the guest house on Stan Tan's property. Wendal was in jail in Sydney. One of his technologists had been murdered. The other young woman used a second bedroom in Fidelia's sprawling suite at the Five Seasons Hotel, so the vacant guest house was as good a place as any for her former lover.

"Is he okay?" Fidelia asked.

"Yes. A few scrapes and bruises from carting him about. Nothing serious. No medical attention needed." Stan Tan replied in his usual matter-of-fact manner. "Are you coming over?"

"In the morning. Let him sleep for a few hours. He'll be more useful. Did your guys give him food and water?"

"I doubt it. Hospitality is not their area of expertise," Stan replied, more dryly than usual. "I'll send one of my people to get him some western takeout and water. When should we expect you in the morning?"

"Mid-morning." It was better not to provide more details than necessary to the Singapore crime boss, even if he was an ally.

"Guards are already in position at the front and rear of the house. Do you want us to keep him secured overnight?"

"Yeah. Let him use a toilet. Feed him like you said. Let him wander about the house from time-to-time, then bundle him up in zip ties every few hours 'til I have a chat with him." Howard would eventually cooperate when he heard her idea, but it was always better to keep him off-balance.

Fidelia switched her attention to Suzy, the technologist. The cute young woman was a tolerable roommate. Petite, with short, black hair. Her perpetually wide green eyes always focused on a screen somewhere. Exercise didn't exist in her vocabulary, but she maintained a tiny waist and a well-proportioned figure. And she stayed in her room doing something with computers except for the rare occasions she surfaced to get some food or share information.

Information gave her reason to slip back into the living area as Fidelia prepared to head toward her bedroom suite.

"I found the twenty-five million that disappeared from our Australian bank feed on its way to Valparaíso." Her tone was detached.

"Where?"

"A place called Nicosia in Cyprus. It's a little island near Turkey—I checked."

It's actually a fairly large island. Fidelia had been there a dozen or more times, but there was no need to demean the girl, so she ignored the geography tip. "How did the money get there?"

"Our usual gate for the account in Valparaíso opened digitally with the correct password. But a millisecond later a foreign signal piggybacked on our entry and sent a digital stream that overrode our embedded instructions." Suzy looked quizzically at Fidelia to see if her dumbed-down explanation had registered. Fidelia nodded and the young woman continued.

"Although our stream was corrupted, Wendal embedded a detection device just in case someone ever attacked us that way. It was brilliant! On my screen, I could follow the trail of the transfer through twenty-three different bank accounts until it ended up in Cyprus. And the account where it's parked has hundreds of millions sitting there."

"No identifying details, I suppose," Fidelia murmured.

"None. A string of twenty digits blocks the account number field with no names, addresses, or other identifying markers."

"Is the bank's security good?" Fidelia wanted to know.

"Excellent. First-class technology, actually. I wiped my digital imprints, so I doubt they'll track us, but if we try to steal back our twenty-five mil, their system has a sophisticated digital tracking device. I'm guessing they'd know our IP address within a second or two."

Before dismissing her, Fidelia offered a warm smile, a word of thanks for a job well done, and a warm hug of appreciation. The girl trotted off to her room again, already focused on some digital dream. Fidelia made a mental note to contact Aretta in Australia in the morning. Was there any hope of springing Wendal from jail?

Without her ace technologist, Fidelia resorted to the second brightest technology mind in The Organization. It was just after noon in his time zone, and Juan Álvarez answered on the first ring, the sounds of a restaurant in the background.

"Sorry to interrupt your lunch, but I have a question. Who did our security coding on the accounts in Valparaíso?"

"I used our usual guy in the US, the one Wendal recommended. Why?" Juan's tone projected no unusual concern or curiosity.

"Apparently it wasn't as secure as he thought. Someone snatched twenty-five million from one of the accounts last week. You didn't notice that?" Fidelia's tone left no doubt about her displeasure.

"No! None of my people mentioned anything out of the ordinary." His voice conveyed an adequate amount of concern, maybe even fear. Fidelia imagined him leaping to a posture more alert and attentive.

"Find out what happened with your guy. If you have any doubts about his loyalty after you speak to him, make a change and make it quickly."

He didn't respond immediately, and Fidelia counted almost twenty seconds before his less-than-convincing reply.

"Your wish is my command, Fidelia. I'll talk to him tomorrow."

"Have you ever been to Singapore?" She used a more suggestive tone. Despite his penchant for teenage girls, he still responded well to an occasional romp with her. "Fix that problem with your guy in the US, and we'll find a way to get together for a few."

She ended the call.

THIRTY-ONE

Ft. Myers, Florida, Wednesday March 4, 2020

James Fitzgerald didn't concede defeat often, but he'd also learned years before that it was important to choose one's battles. Suzanne Simpson wasn't invincible and his sway with the board of directors was considerable, but it made no sense to argue again that they were close to a solution. It simply wasn't the case.

When she decreed they had only a few more days to solve the money laundering mystery, he understood her reasoning. Members of the board were already secretly chatting in private phone calls about her motives. To some, an inability to explain where the laundered funds ended up smacked of desperation to divert attention from the real issue. If they'd followed established checks and balances, the company wouldn't have lost fifty million dollars in the first place.

James didn't doubt Suzanne's integrity for a moment. He knew her well and had watched how effectively she took the reins when John George Mortimer named her president of the Supermarkets division. During the board's monthly financial review meetings, she always impressed him with not only her command of issues, but an understanding of each component's contributions to the well-being of the corporation. When she became chief executive officer of the entire Multima Corporation, her focus on compliance and financial stability increased a notch or two.

Suzanne had always preached a mantra that every leader's overriding responsibility was to "do the right thing." Equally important, she maintained they not only do the right thing but be sure their actions were perceived that way. He'd experienced firsthand her unwavering adherence to those principles.

When she'd learned James became involved in a brief affair with a subordinate, Suzanne summoned him to a dinner meeting in Fort Myers the evening before a meeting of the board. Coolly, and without emotion, she demanded he move forward his retirement date and resign at once as president of Multima Financial Services because of his indiscretion.

It took a while—and a nudge from a couple other board members—before she softened her stance and invited him to rejoin the board a couple years later in a non-operating role. He knew she was doing the right thing to push him out, and she did the right thing for the corporation when she welcomed him back duly punished and repentant.

His new involvement with Angela Bonner tread dangerously close to the line again.

He shouldn't have let it go so far. His original intention of kindling some interest from Angela during a trip to Paris was a flawed strategy. He hadn't foreseen their work together expanding from Paris to South America, with them cooped up together in the same hotel suite for two weeks. Suzanne may have detected some subtle shift in their manner during conference calls, or perhaps harbored some suspicion, or followed some female intuition. Regardless, her text summoning him to a Saturday morning meeting at headquarters the day he arrived made it clear he should come to the meeting alone.

Wilma Willingsworth also flew in from Chicago and was seated in the large conference room outside Suzanne's office with Dan Ramirez and chief legal counsel, Alberto Ferer. James greeted his old friends warmly. He doubted Ramirez had a secret he wouldn't share with him, and James had worked with Alberto to solve dozens of sticky legal issues over the years. Both were rock solid. Wilma held James's old job, and he courteously shook her hand before he sat down. Eileen popped in to see if they needed refreshments while they waited because their leader was on the phone with someone.

When she swept into the room a half-coffee later, Suzanne's manner was all business, her tone formal.

"We've run out of time with the European Central Bank. Monday's our deadline. Let's get underway then. James, bring us up-to-date with your latest from South America."

"We're still convinced Manuel Ortez is involved. His name, or variations of his name, appears on dozens of numbered company registrations. No bank manager would provide us with confirmation he owned any of the suspicious accounts or admitted to knowing him, but Angela Bonner is convinced the trail stops at him." James glanced at Suzanne when he mentioned the woman's name to see if she reacted. She didn't even blink, so he continued.

"After talking with authorities in the Cayman Islands, we were able to connect digital transactions between servers there and in Colombia.

Police evidence shows IP addresses in both locations ultimately transferred funds into the Valparaíso accounts where they usually sat for only a few seconds before transferring out again. Chilean police confirmed the funds went to more than twenty different locations in a dozen countries with no discernible pattern."

Dan Ramirez flashed a PowerPoint slide on a wall-mounted screen to show the flows with a series of connected dots and lines that created an image like colored spaghetti spilled on a floor. Then he picked up where James left off as though on a cue.

"Here's the bewildering aspect with all of the transactions. Once the money arrives in one of those destination accounts, it evaporates. We don't know how. The folks at the FBI think some ultra-sophisticated software must re-engineer its identity by cutting all the ID markers and morph it into a new identity that hijacks the funds. When they contacted the banks, none realized the money had passed through their systems. They showed no record of receiving the transfers and had no record of transfers out."

Wilma Willingsworth was the first to ask a question, and her furrowed brow spoke volumes. "If the European Central Bank's operating theory is that someone within Multima fraudulently stole from the company, then laundered it to avoid detection, doesn't this story almost give credence to their theory? To them, won't it look like only someone within the company would have the means to manage such a complex transaction from end-to-end?"

"Well, it certainly couldn't have been the accounting department section head who died in a skiing accident," Dan Ramirez answered. "According to the specialists in IT, her technical skills were limited to the scope of her job. She needed frequent coaching even to do that."

"Have we done a thorough screening of all our technologists?" Suzanne looked at her chief of security as she asked the question.

"Twice. My team interviewed every person on the team, more than one hundred people. OCD did separate interviews using their forensic technologists. We couldn't connect any dots at all."

The senior management team had scrutinized every aspect of the investigation and every piece of evidence they uncovered with a similar level of detail. They'd overlooked nothing. Dan and James patiently peeled back layer after layer of complexity for almost three hours. When it became clear there was no further avenue to explore, Suzanne looked at her watch before she brought their discussion toward a conclusion.

"Is it worth going to the ECB with what we have? Will they buy it?

Might they give us more time?" She looked each participant directly in the eye as she posed her questions.

Everyone voiced his or her opinion. They were unanimous. The cost of failure was just too great for any surrender. At the very least, they needed to beg for more time and convince the ECB it would be a mistake to prematurely withdraw Multima's European banking licenses.

"Okay, we're in agreement that we should appeal. James and Dan. Will you fellows carry the ball? I'm afraid the FBI's arrest of Wilma and I may taint any arguments we make. They know the FBI ordinarily doesn't arrest people on a whim."

James nodded and Dan voiced an "of course" before Suzanne offered them the company Bombardier Global 5000 jet for their trip, then stood to end the meeting.

As everyone shuffled from the room, Suzanne leaned in toward Dan Ramirez, and James heard her say quietly, "Before you leave, can you have one of your people check on Heather Strong? She expected to be here this morning but didn't respond to my text."

THIRTY-TWO

Singapore, Thursday March 5, 2020

Things happened quickly that morning. First, two Asian men entered the house and wordlessly released Howard from the zip ties. Then they left, locking the door behind them. As he gingerly limped about the bright living area, he assessed the environment and thought the new spot could be a pleasant enough place to be confined.

Moments later, the door opened again and a slight, polite Asian man entered. He made it clear to Howard that he was still in captivity, pointing toward armed guards standing outside both the front and rear doors. He introduced himself as Tan and told Howard he was being held in a guest house on his property for a friend.

"You'll be fine if you don't try to escape. There's no phone, and we can't give you access to the Internet for obvious reasons, but you have a TV, a stereo, and books to occupy your time. One of the guards will soon bring you some food and water."

"Where am I?"

"I can't give you any more information. My friend will tell you what you can know when that friend decides to tell you." The stranger's clever phrasing of the reply to avoid identifying the person's gender piqued Howard's curiosity.

"Are you with The Organization?"

"I can't give you any more information. Be patient and you should be fine." The statement made Howard's well-being sound less definite than the first assurances, but the man's eyes suggested a tentative smile behind the mask covering his mouth and nose.

With a slight bow and polite namaste gesture of farewell, the man backed out the door. A lock clicked solidly behind him. Just to be sure, Howard wandered over to the door and turned the handle. As he feared, there was no latch mechanism on the inside. A dozen steps to the rear door and he found another frozen handle without an inside lock.

Howard pulled back the window curtains to see a well-landscaped

182

yard in a tropical climate. Towering palm trees swayed in a gentle breeze. Dozens of orchids brightened meticulously groomed gardens with several varieties of plants and shrubs grown only near the Equator. He didn't see a clock anywhere, but the outside light suggested early morning. There was no hum of an air conditioner, but the room temperature was pleasing.

He tried to open a window, but found steel bars sealing it on the outside. The small house was surprisingly cozy. It reminded him of one where he took refuge for about a week with an empathetic and accommodating writer during his flight from The Organization in Portugal a few months earlier. A rueful smile formed on Howard's face as his buried memory of Katherine Page and her benevolent spirit resurfaced from some recess in his brain. He'd like to see her again someday. There had been a tiny spark of something between them that deserved another chance.

How life changed in mere months.

A knock on the front door interrupted his morning reverie. Immediately after, the lock released and the door popped open. A young Asian woman entered carrying a tray. Her eyes sparkled above a mask, but she said nothing before setting the tray on the only table in the living area. She fiddled with the plates for a moment before bowing slightly toward Howard and making her gesture of namaste. She left as quickly and quietly as she'd arrived.

For the next two days, the same young woman arrived with a knock on the door at breakfast, lunch, and dinner time. Every meal was western style. The food was delicious, and Howard struggled to finish because the portions were surprisingly large. Other than the uncertainty of captivity, he found the days relaxing and enjoyable. One of those fifty-cent beers from Cambodia might have been nice, but he wasn't about to complain.

On the third day of confinement, he heard an uncharacteristic knock on the door mid-morning. When he looked up to greet the young Asian woman, he was astounded to see Fidelia Morales.

Wearing a stylish beige pantsuit, low heels, and a colorful scarf covering her mouth and nose, she carried herself like a business executive. Her dark brunette hair had grown in the weeks since she'd left him in Martinique, and she looked fit, trim and relaxed. Behind her, two burly bodyguards stood menacingly with dour expressions.

She entered the living area without invitation and closed the door, leaving the guards outside. She looked directly at Howard for an instant but said nothing. She scanned the room and strode confidently around the living area to peek inside each of the three bedrooms and tiny kitchen.

Still holding the book he'd been reading, Howard watched her warily as Fidelia wandered about the house.

"More swank than I expected," Fidelia said finally as she released her scarf and smiled broadly, a charm offensive underway. Howard returned her smile with a genuine grin of good humor. He'd always been mildly amused when she used the term "swank." To him, it was a reminder of her humble Puerto Rican roots regardless of her current wealth.

"I guess you'll tell me what I'm doing here when you're ready." Howard's smile faded and his focus sharpened. She'd clearly abandoned her promise to leave him alone.

"You know me well. But let's chat a bit first, catch up with what you've been up to."

Fidelia plunked herself across from Howard on the sofa, her manner genuinely friendly but not inviting. She crossed her legs, folded her arms across her stomach, and waited.

"I was enjoying a quiet life of anonymity in Cambodia when your minions so rudely snatched me from my bed."

"That's what I understand. Chantou probably misses you." Fidelia smiled mischievously.

"How...?" Howard started, then realized she'd share nothing and changed his tack. "Yeah, but you probably also know I was about to move on from there anyway. It would have been nice if the mode of transportation and destination were *my* choices, though."

They sparred verbally for a few more minutes, politely and tentatively, each taking the measure of the other. Fidelia asked more questions and provided little new information. She chose her words more carefully than in earlier days, and contact with her large brown eyes was more direct, more penetrating.

She wanted to know how he found living in the Netherlands for a couple years and focused particularly on questions about the Dutch people, their habits, and lifestyles. For more than an hour, she posed question after question, as though she had conducted research for their meeting or gathered data about the country with some other intention.

When the young Asian woman arrived with lunch, she brought a large pizza and two plates. A quick glance at the pizza confirmed it was topped exactly as Howard had always liked, right down to the tiny anchovies scattered among the other toppings. Fidelia planned not only to stay for lunch but to send a message. As former lovers, they once took delight in surprising each other with special meals or gestures few others would know about.

But she gave no suggestion of softening her businesslike manner, no shifting of either tone or mood. Throughout lunch, Fidelia used her fingers instead of cutlery and chewed her mouthfuls entirely before posing another question. They were the same mannerisms she'd used for two decades whenever she was preoccupied or thoughtfully processing information.

They ate where they sat, each getting up to fetch another slice of pizza as one was consumed. She gave no indication of her reasons for kidnapping Howard in Cambodia, nor any inkling of why she broke her promise to let him go and live without harassment. Had Howard overlooked some signal when they'd talked after killing Giancarlo Mareno? Had she thrown out some subtle hint he'd missed?

When both had satisfied their hunger, Fidelia changed her questioning. How had Howard traveled from Martinique to Cambodia without detection by the authorities? He gave her a sanitized explanation, careful not to divulge any more details than essential.

Still, she homed in for more specifics than he wanted to share. Pressed, he gave her a brief description of his path to Barbados. For a little levity, he repeated the tall tale about getting caught in bed with a tour guide and beaten by her husband to provide cover for the injuries inflicted by Mareno's men. For the first time, she laughed.

"Howard, you scamp. You'll never change!" Fidelia's tone conveyed appreciation, and her laugh was warm, deep-throated, and genuine. It morphed slowly into a smile that lingered, the smile she had used to charm hundreds of men and women over an arduous career. Howard said nothing and smiled in return. There was little doubt she'd soon get to her purpose, and she didn't disappoint.

"Let's go back to your first question. Why did I bring you here?" Her tone remained friendly, but her expression hardened, losing the smile and intensifying her gaze.

"I know I promised to let you go free. Giancarlo's quarrel with you wasn't mine. You ended a lot of careers when you became a stool pigeon, but you actually helped mine. When I was able to get to Central Asia and contact Giancarlo, I influenced his choices of the guys who replaced the ones jailed by your testimony. You were wrong to break the code of silence, but I benefited from it. So, I'm not looking to punish you. That's what I told you in Martinique, and I still mean it."

Fidelia had reverted to the staccato delivery first formed as a young Latina trying to be heard in a harsh environment and then honed during law school. Howard asked the only logical question.

"So, what is it you want?"

"I need your help. Even though you've been away for a few years, nobody knows more about Multima than you. I remember the hundreds of hours you spent researching every tiny detail about the corporation. I know you desperately wanted to seize control of the company. And I recall how Mortimer outmaneuvered you. I also remember Janet Weissel was once a resource you planted inside. Did you control anyone else?"

Howard took several seconds to consider his options before he replied with a single word, "Perhaps."

"Is that person still with Multima and do you still have the power to control them?"

"Yes, to the first," Howard answered before he took almost a minute to consider his answer to the second part of her question. "I may have the power to control someone. But it all depends what you want to do. I told you before. I no longer have an appetite for The Organization's shenanigans."

"I want you to help me with Multima one last time. If you agree to help, whether we succeed or not, I'll call off both Interpol and The Organization."

Howard took a moment to process her simple statement. It might be more complex than her tone implied. "Interpol I can buy. No doubt you have the power and influence to have the Red Notice for my arrest disappear with one phone call. With The Organization, I'm not so sure."

"You can be sure. My consolidation of power is complete and absolute. Luigi is keeping the Americas in check, personally. Europe fell into line before you left Barbados. The house you're staying in belongs to the Asian strongman who keeps everyone in line on this side of the Pacific."

"Impressive. And if I should decide to pass on your offer?"

"Stan Tan will unlock the door. You can leave when you choose, and you'll take your chances again. No call to Interpol. I won't pursue you, but others may. Same as the last time."

Howard squirmed involuntarily with a reminder The Organization had the reach to find him anywhere, just as they had in Cambodia. He was tired. The constant running in fear had worn thin long before. Was it possible to dream of living a carefree life with a woman like Chantou or perhaps a Katherine Page? A life free from the rigors of constant pursuit? He swallowed hard before he asked only one more question.

"What's your plan for Multima Corporation?"

THIRTY-THREE

She woke from terrifying nightmares. Tears appeared from nowhere unexpectedly. She felt on edge and nervous continuously. Suzanne's last few days had been a blur of distress, horror, and grief. It began within an hour of her team meeting.

They had decided James Fitzgerald and Dan Ramirez should fly to Germany and plead with the European Central Bank for more time. Before their flight left, Dan called with the first shocking piece of information.

"Heather Strong is dead."

His voice faltered as he shared the news, clearly affected by a tragedy so close to home.

"I sent one of my people to her condo out by Lakes Park. There was no answer when he rang the doorbell, and he couldn't find a building manager. Just as he was about to leave, he noticed a crowd gathered outside the back of the building and a lot of police activity. My guy mentioned who he was looking for and they let him inside the yellow tape. Her body was a mess, but there's no doubt it was Heather."

Suzanne's hand shook holding the phone. Tears flowed down both cheeks and she gasped for words. The security chief gave her time to absorb the shock and get control of her emotions. Her head shaking in disbelief, she reached for a tissue and took a deep breath before she managed a simple question.

"What happened?"

"My guy says they can't be sure until there's an autopsy, but it looks as if she was beaten severely before she fell—or jumped—from the balcony of her penthouse suite."

Word of Heather's death spread through the office almost immediately after Suzanne personally announced it to the assembled finance team. She told them the office would close early to let employees deal with their grief, but it had little effect as small groups formed around the office crying, hugging, and trying to console one another.

Informally, the Lee County Sheriff's office agreed to pass bits of information to the fellow Dan Ramirez had sent out to check on Heather. He was a retiree of the office, and his former colleagues knew they could trust his discretion.

When the police tracked down a property manager and got into Heather's apartment, they discovered a mess. Upended furniture. Drawers opened and rummaged through, the contents discarded around the rooms. A wall safe in a bedroom closet hung open and empty, with a key inside the lock. Blood was splattered across the plush carpet of a bedroom and on the marble tiles of the living area. No blood was detected on the balcony, but a stained bed sheet lay crumpled in a corner beside the balcony door.

Dan Ramirez delayed his departure for Europe to liaise with his staff, Suzanne, and the now-alarmed board of directors.

Minutes before a scheduled videoconference to brief the anxious executives, Beverly Vonderhausen called Suzanne's cell phone. The attorney was agitated and barely masked it.

"Some bad news to start your weekend. I heard back from one of the contacts your lobbyist in Washington made available. She learned the Justice Department is about to issue a warrant for your arrest again. They now list bank accounts in Argentina but it's essentially the same charge as last time. And apparently again at the behest of someone close to the White House."

"That's unbelievable!" Suzanne didn't know whether to curse or cry. With a pandemic creating havoc for her businesses around the globe, and some nefarious element murdering her staff, the US government had time to prosecute her for a fraud that had cost her company fifty million dollars. The whole scenario was ludicrous. Thankfully, her lawyer waited patiently, giving her time to regain her composure.

"So you got this scuttlebutt off the record, right?" Suzanne confirmed.

"Yes. She wouldn't give me the person's name, but it's a well-informed, reliable source. I wish I could advise you what steps to take next, but there isn't much we can do until they issue a warrant, probably tomorrow."

"I should expect the same treatment? A perp walk? Media? Bond of ten million to get out?"

"Can't say. If they do it tomorrow, don't be surprised if it's a repeat performance. Since your offices are closed on Saturdays and Sundays, they might just visit your home and arrest you there. Bond will depend on the judge they assign, but you should expect at least the same amount.

After the embarrassment they suffered from dropping the charges a few weeks ago, I doubt they'll make it a media event this time. Would you like me to come to Fort Myers and be with you when they arrest you?"

"Thanks for the heads-up, and I appreciate your offer. Let me think about it and get back to you later."

Alberto Ferer was the board secretary, as well as chief legal counsel, so it was he who did a roll call of the directors and noted any absences. Suzanne's executive assistant had impressively rounded up almost the entire board for a hastily convened videoconference.

Looking deeply into the video feed squares on her monitor, Suzanne watched the reactions of each director as Alberto performed the mundane task, and she thought about her opening comments. She noted James Fitzgerald's calm, composed demeanor. His face was impassive, his hands crossed comfortably on a desk. He always looked unfazed by any crisis around him. She knew others on the board of directors were not so sanguine.

"Thanks for getting together on such short notice. We've had more troubling developments on the money laundering issue. I'll brief you on the latest news first, bring you up-to-date on our internal investigation, then answer any questions you have."

Suzanne carefully monitored the facial expressions in each of the small blocks as she painstakingly drew a picture of the latest unfolding corporate crisis.

With sensitivity, she told them of Heather Strong's death. It was much too early to guess whether there was some relationship to the money laundering allegations, or a robbery that went out of control, or some other unknown issue.

Two Multima employees had recently died in mysterious circumstances. Suzanne re-emphasized only hours had passed since the latest tragedy, underscoring her inability to fill in all the details for them. Of course, the reminder also signaled that she was still dealing with the shock of the incident. It might make it easier for her audience to overlook minor lapses or inconsistencies and be less judgmental about any perceived emotional weakness.

Beginning with an overview of the deaths, Suzanne explained for a second time—forthrightly and candidly—their discovery of some transfers of money to accounts in South America. She reviewed the amounts fraudulently stolen from the company. And she expressed regret some of the losses had started under her watch at Supermarkets. As a final mea culpa, she apologized that Multima's control systems had been ineffective, and assured the board they'd been tightened already.

From there, she moved on to her request for help from the FBI in both the US and Latin America. She mentioned the added security precautions Dan Ramirez had implemented at headquarters and around its supermarkets to protect employees and customers. She took care to point out that bodyguards had recently been assigned for people involved in the investigation, such as James Fitzgerald and Wilma Willingsworth.

When she asked James Fitzgerald to give an overview of his investigative work in Latin America, he performed splendidly. With his soft-spoken manner and calm demeanor, he provided just enough information to assure the directors they were dealing with a sophisticated fraud and to reassure them Multima management intended to use every tool possible to get to the truth.

After that, Suzanne informed the board of her decision to dispatch James and Dan Ramirez to plead for more time from the European Central Bank. Several brows furrowed on the screen in front of her with that news. Adding to their concern, she threw out the tip from her attorney that she might be arrested again in the coming hours. She spared them the details of subterfuge needed to get the info and took care to show no alarm. It seemed a suitable point to welcome questions.

"Why do you think both the ECB and the Justice Department continue to consider the matter a case of money laundering rather than a fraud against Multima?" It was the Chairman of Bank of the Americas who posed the question.

"That's precisely the point we're trying to understand. Multima Corporation is clearly a victim in this case, yet they continue to pursue some of us personally." Suzanne took care her tone reflected bewilderment, not persecution. "Heather Strong's death today may be related in some way. She too was arrested last month, and the FBI will almost certainly try to link her death to the fraud, but we have no evidence of that."

"If you're arrested and can't post bond—for whatever reason—who will manage Multima Corporation in your absence?" That question came from Chuck Jones, an independent director from Chicago. For several months he had been pressing Suzanne to develop a succession plan. With all the other cascading crises, it hadn't happened.

"If I'm unable to manage day-to-day, as secretary of the board, Alberto Ferer will become interim CEO. The board has the right to vote to either accept him in that role for a prolonged period or name an alternative." Suzanne felt a chill in her spine as she outlined the emergency plan in the company bylaws, hoping fervently there'd be no need for either step.

Questions continued for almost an hour. Suzanne dealt with them patiently and kept her composure throughout. Faces in the little squares on her monitor gradually reflected less worry and angst, though everyone realized the gravity of the situation. When she asked if there were any further questions or concerns, another director from the Midwest raised his hand.

"A comment before my question, Suzanne. A thought occurred to me while we've been discussing this tangled web the company's wrapped up in. You might want to check with your attorney, but it seems to me you don't need to sit around Fort Myers waiting for a visit from the Sheriff's Office. Now my question. Is everything going okay with our new office in Montreal?"

"I'm not sure. Perhaps I should get up there soon and report back to you for the next meeting." Suzanne waited until the video screen fell completely dark before she allowed a smile to creep across her face and her spirits to lift.

Beverly Vonderhausen at first chuckled when Suzanne questioned the oblique suggestion offered by the director from the Midwest. Then, she solemnly stated she couldn't legally offer her client that kind of advice. However, she could confirm that Suzanne had no legal obligation to stay in Fort Myers.

Within minutes, their plan was underway. Suzanne dashed home to pack a bag with enough clothes to tide her over for a week. Alberto Ferer jumped into his little sports car and sped off to do the same. Her director of corporate communications hastily ditched his partially finished cocktail at a downtown bar when he received Eileen's call.

They all met at Page Field at the agreed-upon hour. Multima's Bombardier Global 5000's engines were idling outside the terminal building of the private jet port, the stairway lowered to welcome passengers. The pilots saw no problem delivering Suzanne and her companions to their destination and returning to Florida well before Fitzgerald and Ramirez needed to depart for Europe later that evening.

As they soared into the dark Southwest Florida sky, Suzanne felt a weight lift from her shoulders. It was temporary, to be sure, but enough to rekindle hope a solution to the entire matter might soon be within reach.

THIRTY-FOUR

Fidelia's grand scheme was coming together. Even the stock markets cooperated. Her useful phone app reported a decline of 3.6% in the Dow Jones Industrial Average for the day. The spreading coronavirus was to blame. Closer to her temporary home, Howard Knight caved as expected. She let him stew over her proposal for a few hours, but had little doubt his keen analysis of the options available would lead to his eventual submission.

"But I'm going to condition that help," he insisted. "I'm tired of harassing Multima Corporation. Suzanne Simpson is a good person, and she doesn't deserve it. If you give me your word we'll do this without hurting her or the company, I'll do it. Otherwise, I'm walking out and taking my chances."

Fidelia gave him that one. She could always decide later who might be spared in battle.

Sexual promises or innuendo weren't necessary with her former lover either. They were both past that, it seemed, and she wasn't sure how she felt about that reality. He'd changed since they'd been together. Logic and critical thinking had become more important to him since she'd last spent any quality time with him—about three years earlier.

The guy was puzzling. His mind was brilliant, probably the smartest person in any room. His memory was infallible. And his depth of understanding of business and economics impressed even the world's most respected professors. He'd stashed away hundreds of millions of dollars in offshore bank accounts and should be able to hide away in some remote part of the world and live in extravagant luxury.

But he'd made the worst possible choices when it came to his personal life. The wife he'd abandoned was the daughter of a rival in The Organization. She had constantly hounded Howard for more freedom, more money, and more status symbols. Howard was ripe for picking way back when Giancarlo Mareno first gifted Fidelia to him for a night.

The guy was so desperate for a good, unconditional lay that he spent the next two decades clandestinely traipsing around the world for secret rendezvous with her. She actually fell in love with the dope over time. Even ran away with him when he had to flee The Organization after the fiasco with Multima Corporation.

However, it was all over for her the moment Howard agreed to double-cross The Organization and tell all to the FBI after rogue agents had captured and abducted the pair in Argentina. Fidelia knew right then that he would live his life as a desperate fugitive for as long as Giancarlo Mareno was alive.

Still, she gave him a reprieve in Martinique after they finished off Mareno. Again, the guy was too stupid to follow her advice. Instead of contacting the FBI from Martinique and getting settled in witness protection somewhere, he opted for some form of anonymity in one of the riskiest parts of a pandemic-plagued world.

If he'd followed her advice, there wouldn't be an Interpol Red Notice outstanding. The FBI could have killed that easily. He would have never needed to travel halfway around the world to hide. That kid in Cambodia who gave them the tip would have never made his acquaintance. And Fidelia would have honored her promise not to pursue him.

So, she felt no guilt about using him to design her next maneuver, and she had no doubt he'd stay until she was done with him. She'd already tested him twice. Stan Tan unlocked the doors to his guest house immediately after Howard accepted her offer, and he knew he could walk away. He stayed.

As Fidelia instructed, Tan also gave Howard a thousand Singaporean dollars to go out shopping for a new wardrobe. She had him watched, of course, but the guy showed no inclination toward escape, made no suspicious stops, didn't even visit a TVB Bank branch to take out more cash. He just came back to Tan's place loaded with bags of clothing and shoes.

Klaudia was another matter. Fidelia truly felt badly about breaking their agreement. Her German-Russian friend had kept her part of the bargain and loathed to change it.

"Just like you demanded, I stopped helping the *Bundesnachrichtendienst.*" Since they'd first parted two years earlier, Klaudia had secretly helped the German secret service wage war on human trafficking activities of criminal elements like The Organization. "That work was important to me."

"I know. I feel awful asking you to work with us again, but it's just this one time. It's probably only for a week or two. I'm desperate for your expertise." Fidelia leaned in closer to the little green dot above the video screen to emphasize her point.

"I'm already swamped at my new business, Fidelia. I'm hiring staff, working twenty hours a day and still not keeping up with demand. I really can't handle anything more." Klaudia slammed her fist on a desk for emphasis.

"I understand. And I'm glad the five million I paid you to cease and desist with the *Bundesnachrichtendienst* has made you so successful so quickly. But here's why I need you. You remember Wendal Randall?"

"The idiot that got my ass carted off to Guantanamo for a stay with the FBI? Don't tell me you're involved with him again!" Klaudia's tone was more hostile than expected.

"Actually, yes. It was he who developed the technology that let me take over from Mareno. I'm working with him on a few things," Fidelia said cheerfully and with enthusiasm. "And I desperately need you to collaborate with him one more time. It may be a matter of life or death."

Klaudia sighed and sat back from the webcam. Coolly, and with deliberate gestures, she first considered her response, then looked her friend directly in the eye.

"You gave me your word, Fidelia. I don't need your money and I don't need the drama of The Organization. I'm out and I like it that way. You had your chance to get out and enjoy a life of leisure as few others could. Instead, you not only got involved again, you had to go for the whole enchilada. I'm not interested. You'll need to find someone else to help you."

Lacking the leverage she had over Howard, it took a few days, two more tense conversations, and another million dollars. Her friend finally relented and agreed to meet them in Sydney, Australia.

Wendal Randall was the most problematic. Aretta Musa spent several days and called in favors. Australian authorities were preoccupied with the spreading pandemic. Many of the government and legal employees were working from home, taking leave, or simply not showing up for work. Everything moved more slowly than usual—including their system of justice.

Wendal did little to advance his cause. He refused to talk with the first lawyer Aretta arranged. The female barrister was too young and inexperienced for his liking. He dismissed her summarily during their first meeting, telling her to contact Fidelia immediately to get his incarceration "fixed."

After a few days, Aretta was able to persuade the top criminal lawyer in Sydney to take the case. It took a while because the arrogant jerk didn't bother to return calls from people he didn't already know. Aretta was finally able to penetrate that wall and remind him that he did indeed know her, and was a valued and frequent customer of one of her best call girls. One who kept video records of her exotic sexual liaisons.

Even after the implied threat, the scoundrel had the temerity to demand a non-refundable retainer of one-hundred thousand Australian dollars. Fidelia caved and told Aretta to deduct it from the next monthly remittance. The wily barrister proved his worth when he sprang Wendal from custody after only one day on the job. Of course, a digital ankle bracelet was required by the authorities. Plus, Aretta had to assume personal responsibility for his appearances in court. But the court deferred his case for thirty days.

There was a downside, however. Wendal was a crucial element in her technology equation. Without him, success was far less than assured. With him, she was confident the assembled team could work its magic. Especially with Klaudia's language and technology skills. With him unable to travel, they had no alternative but to bring everyone to Sydney. So that's what they would do.

Her tech genius now rested comfortably in the remote house where Oliver Williams had died, with heavily armed guards inside the house and around the property. Their job was to ensure no one got to Wendal, but also to be equally confident the subject of their concern didn't step outside that home.

When Fidelia explained her scheme, Stan Tan helped too. He saw an immediate win for his Asia businesses, but he wasn't prepared to leave Singapore. The spreading virus spooked him. Singapore was the only place he wanted to be. He offered to make two of his best technicians available for the project and to arrange and pay for a private charter to Sydney as his financial contribution. Fidelia accepted the jet travel and thought one technician would be adequate.

In New York, Luigi was disappointed she wouldn't allow him to be part of the fun.

"With that many people operating right under the nose of the Australian government, lots can go wrong," he protested. "We were planning to meet up at the end of the month anyway. Why don't I get a commercial flight over, bring a couple extra men, and meet you there? Everything's quiet here."

Fidelia resisted a chuckle at his intensity. Security shouldn't be an issue. The more important challenge would be channeling the competitive tendencies of Wendal and Klaudia. Her friend had described with passion the couple's many spats working to hack the phone companies in South America to successfully track down Howard and Fidelia for the FBI. But she didn't need Luigi for mediation. And he knew little about either hacking or the stock markets.

Thinking about the stock market reminded Fidelia of one more detail to follow-up on before they met the charter jet for their overnight flight. She hit the speed dial on her phone for Juan Álvarez. It was still morning in Uruguay.

"The servers in Valparaíso are all working fine now." His tone was confident but slightly more brusque than usual. The tone of a man who hoped there weren't many more questions to follow.

"And the situation in San Francisco?"

"It'll be handled tomorrow. When I had a little chat about the last problem, he didn't leave me comfortable it wouldn't happen again. So I'm making a change. I'm just waiting to hear back later today from a potential new one, a gal this time. Then I'll give the order."

"You're sure no traces will be left behind?" Fidelia needed another sixty seconds for the malware to load according to the instructions she remembered from Wendal. Keep him talking.

"Nothing. I hired out the job. You know how it is in America. We can just give a guy five hundred bucks and he'll take care of the job and forget we ever met. All the equipment will go to the new woman, and we'll wipe everything clean before delivery."

Still thirty seconds to go. "Any signs of the pandemic in Uruguay so far?"

"None, yet. But we're already seeing a drop in business with the girls. It seems a lot of guys are getting nervous about getting too close. Sex's dropping off right now. You must have seen the numbers."

"I did. I just wanted to make sure you remember I watch the numbers carefully."

Just over seventy seconds had elapsed. That was all she needed. She hit the "end" button.

THIRTY-FIVE

James Fitzgerald started their videoconference. "They gave us almost another month—until April 3." He hoped his smile conveyed at least some of the relief he felt more powerfully than his words. "They won't shut us down in Europe 'til then."

"Nice work, guys!" Suzanne's praise seemed heartfelt. She looked as if she wanted to give them both big hugs. Thirty days could be a game-changer.

"James did an outstanding job explaining things," Dan Ramirez piped in. "But we both credit you for delegating the task to us. You were right. The ECB people confided their concern that either you or Wilma might be too close to the transactions and have a vested interest. When you showed enough confidence to have a couple non-executives make the case, they resisted but with less intensity than we feared."

"So, you've bought us some more time. Where do we go from here?" Suzanne wondered.

Dan Ramirez answered first. "Let me explain what the Lee County Sheriff's office shared with us. Heather Strong was definitely murdered. An autopsy shows she was dead before they threw her body from the balcony. Several broken bones. Missing teeth. Battered face. All signs of a violent interrogation. This was no robbery gone wrong. Somebody was definitely on a mission, and serious about it."

"That's awful." Suzanne's expression reflected the horror she felt, but it took only a second for her jaw to reset and her blue eyes to intensify their gaze at the webcam. "Am I too quickly jumping to a conclusion that she might have been more involved in the fraud than we realized?"

"Maybe. We don't know," James resumed. "When we first heard the news, Dan and I had the same reaction. We assumed she must have been involved in some way. But there's a chance she became a target not because she was directly involved in the fraud, but because she was getting too close to discovering who was involved."

"The FBI is having trouble making a direct connection between Heather Strong and Kim Jones, the woman who had the skiing accident in Canada," Dan carried on. "They're not finding a record of any personal texts, emails, or phone calls between them since Heather moved from Atlanta to Fort Myers. Weekend personal meetings were possible, but no evidence has surfaced to suggest that was the case."

"But two sudden violent deaths of Multima employees within days of each other are suspicious." Suzanne's tone had hardened. She clasped her hands together and her shoulders tensed.

"We share your concern. It is suspicious. But police in Alberta maintain Kim Jones's facial injuries and broken neck are consistent with a high-speed fall. And they found nothing unusual about her wardrobe or ski equipment to suggest anything other than an accidental fall," Dan said.

"Did we find out anything more about that trading frenzy with Farefour shares last month?" Suzanne shifted the subject and James was prepared. He'd expected she'd want to extract some benefit from her agreement that Angela Bonner could join the pair for the trip to Europe.

"Yes. We touched down in Paris to let Angela off, and she was able to spend some time with a couple of her contacts there who specialize in forensic investigations." James took time to establish their credentials. "One of the firms also has some business with the European Central Bank from time to time."

"Hmm. Interesting." Suzanne was hooked.

"Angela gathered two significant new pieces of information," James continued. "There was also an unusually large amount of activity in Farefour options on the London Stock Exchange that same morning."

"London? Farefour's operation there is so small it barely merits a listing on the LSE." Suzanne's brow furrowed as she leaned toward the webcam.

"Yeah, I hadn't even seen it in the financial statements," James said. "Angela confirmed with Michelle Sauvignon that Farefour acquired Countryside Shops about a decade ago. Countryside shares were popular with retail investors who were also usually local customers. So, trading volumes are usually quite lethargic as you said. That's why the frenzy of activity was so unusual."

"Fair enough. So, what happened with the options trading?"

"At the same time as Farefour shares were tanking, sophisticated options algorithms were offering lower 'put' positions on Countryside shares which were also dropping dramatically," James explained. "When prices bottomed midmorning, whoever owned all the options exercised them. Millions of dollars changed hands in an instant. Then the price of Countryside shares rocketed higher."

"So, we're talking about a pattern with the Countryside shares that mirrors the experience with Farefour's shares," Suzanne said.

"Right. But something strange occurred. When Angela and her friends traced the transactions, they discovered a different IP address handled all the Countryside transactions. None of the transactions matched the IP address used to create the Farefour debacle. However, when they followed the transactions all the way back to a physical address, they ended up at the same empty office as the transactions for Farefour. Why might someone use two separate internet protocol addresses to both buy and sell the same stocks from the same room?"

"Could one person or group work for two separate interests?" Suzanne asked.

"Angela's thoughts precisely." James took a moment to admire how quickly Suzanne had figured it out. "Both activities look very much like a test. Someone wanted to see how the algorithms interacted. Both IP addresses made a big profit that day. Our guess is they were doing a practice run. The next time we might see a scenario where one would compete with the other."

"One would win, the other would lose. Either way, we lose. We end up with a powerful minority shareholder who may be impossible to please. And we also have an unhappy investor or group of investors who may be tempted to play more games to exact financial revenge. Is that right?"

"Exactly," James replied. "If they play that way with Countryside or Farefour, we have a pain in the butt. If they use the same strategy with Multima on the New York Exchange, you could lose the company."

"You said you had a couple things," Suzanne said dryly.

"Right. I mentioned Angela's contact also did some work with the ECB," James said. "One of their technologists analyzed the IP addresses used by the ECB to reach its conclusion that Multima is involved in money laundering. They found that about twenty-five percent of the payments were routed from banks in Valparaíso through the two IP addresses used for the stock manipulation in both Paris and London."

"Are you kidding me?" Suzanne's gaping mouth registered the shock James expected.

"I'm completely serious. Angela got her friend to promise he wouldn't disclose the information about the overlap to the ECB," James assured her. "If he does, your legal problems worsen exponentially. You'll have not only the Justice Department crying foul, but the Securities Exchange Commission will also almost certainly have to launch a stock manipulation investigation. Investors will bail out and Multima share values will plummet."

THIRTY-SIX

Sydney, Australia, Sunday March 8, 2020

After Howard agreed to work with her, Stan Tan delivered a new laptop to the guest house within minutes. Internet access was disconnected, but someone had loaded Multima annual reports for the past ten years onto the operating system, and Fidelia called to ask him to study them before they left for Sydney.

Later, traveling to the private jet by car, Fidelia had quizzed him about what he'd learned from the reports. Satisfied he'd done her bidding, she first suggested he sleep as much as possible on the plane.

The quiet corporate jet was comfortable, and the symphony music broadcast through a high-quality headset was therapeutic for the few minutes he could listen. But instead of letting him rest, Fidelia changed her mind and demanded more than three hours of planning, huddled over a small table between them. Their voices were as quiet as the continuous low whine from the engines allowed. Fellow passengers were excluded from their dialogue.

It was unlikely Fidelia had conceived the idea initially. She just didn't have the technology smarts for such a brazen attack on so many fronts. The architect must have been someone like Wendal Randall. As she walked Howard through the steps they'd planned—using layperson's language—he thought he spotted the technology genius's fingerprints. The concept was brilliant, but the scheme still had some fundamental flaws.

Fidelia didn't truly understood how options worked on the stock markets. While her explanation showed a good working knowledge of both the theory and practical execution of options, she'd overlooked a couple basic principles. It was already too late to be buying options on Multima shares. The price had already plummeted too far. It would be almost impossible to buy enough options at a price that made sense at this late stage. A few weeks ago it might have worked.

Undaunted, Fidelia demanded alternatives. As Howard worked through his mental checklist of alternative approaches to achieve the same goal, he came up blank. Twist after twist, idea after idea, no matter how he massaged them, each alternative concept had a fatal flaw.

Fidelia continued to press. Could they buy shares in one place and sell them in another? What if they used smaller chunks and did more transactions? If they penetrated a larger broker, could they buy the shares more quickly and turn them around at once?

Howard walked a delicate line. He couldn't let Fidelia fail. Despite her assurances of his release when they finished the project, he wasn't naïve. If they failed, she would finish him off just as he watched her blow out the brains of her former boss Mareno with cold, unemotional eyes and an unwavering demeanor.

Patiently, he processed her ideas, tried to mold them into more workable concepts, and precisely explained the problems she would encounter with each new twist. Still, the extraordinary technology and fundamental concept could work. It was brilliant in its simplicity, and there was little doubt someone could perfect the technical execution.

The fatal flaw, in Howard's mind, was the oversized scope of the objective. He couldn't get his head around the possibility of executing the scam through fifty different banks and brokerages and two separate stock exchanges simultaneously without triggering an alarm somewhere that would abort the whole thing.

Fidelia got it. Eventually, she came to realize Howard was exercising his mind and digging deep into his knowledge and experience. She didn't seem perturbed as he shot down one avenue after another. In fact, five hours out of Sydney she suggested he sleep on it. She smiled with the radiance and warmth only she could create as she touched his knee and assured him she had no doubt he'd eventually find a solution.

Damn it. The woman still has it.

When he woke up a couple hours before they arrived in Sydney, he glanced across the plane and noticed Fidelia still hard at work. With her laptop on her lap and her shoulders hunched forward in concentration, she was a picture of intensity as he gazed at her for a few minutes.

For as long as he'd known her, she'd been that way. Driven by an overpowering desire to succeed, she read voraciously. Books, magazines, newspapers—and, more recently, her telephone and laptop—all consumed much of her free time. In the two decades they'd been a secret item, he had never seen her watch a movie. She used television only for news, never entertainment. Most impressively, she retained almost everything she learned.

Gifted with a great memory himself, Howard still marveled at her ability to learn and absorb information in completely new areas of interest. He remembered a couple years when she was fascinated with the history of the Incas and read every book she could find—in English or Spanish. For a period, Russian history enthralled her, and she even learned a smattering of the language in the process. Then, he recalled a time she studied leadership, watching videos and reading nearly a hundred books on the subject.

But it was her obsession with business and investing where they shared the most common ground. He couldn't avoid a small smile when he thought about the times she brought up some unknown company name she'd spotted somewhere and wanted to dissect its balance sheet with him into the wee hours of the morning.

It was during those learning sessions he realized Fidelia was becoming a very rich woman. He knew how she earned her money in those days. Giancarlo Mareno rewarded her handsomely for recruiting and managing women across the globe. Back then, Howard was ambivalent about it all.

To him, prostitution was just another business. The women recruited by Fidelia for The Organization were simply assets used to produce revenue. There were good business reasons to treat the women well and keep them healthy to generate the biggest profits. But like all assets, they depreciated over time. So, it never seemed unreasonable to him that they'd get rid of low or non-producing assets one way or another.

Fidelia never once showed any regret or remorse about her work or the effect it had on exploited women.

Howard couldn't recall the exact trigger for his change in outlook, but his mindset about women, human trafficking, and prostitution had gradually evolved about a decade earlier. Maybe it was the Catholic education his mother insisted upon, or a guilty conscience about the misery prostitution caused. Whatever the reason, several years before he decided to escape the clutches of The Organization, he'd already crafted a scheme to pilfer hundreds of millions from its massive reserves to help women.

Giancarlo Mareno's death triggered the beginning of Howard's clandestine payout of that accumulated fortune to charities focused on the health and well-being of girls and young women everywhere. Fidelia had been mildly amused when Howard divulged the half-billion-dollar skim of The Organization's wealth. But she'd also promised to leave him alone, to no longer pursue him to reclaim the lost fortune.

Underhandedly, she broke that promise and put him into another no-win situation where he was once again forced to help the criminals.

His current unease seemed justified. This time, The Organization's target was bigger, more powerful, and more ruthless—and once again drew the leader of Multima Corporation into their crosshairs. He knew Suzanne Simpson well. He'd known her before John George Mortimer. In fact, Howard had led the company's founder to a business acquisition that eventually brought Suzanne into the Multima universe.

She was a brilliant woman, and he admired her leadership and people skills. She was a genuinely nice person. It came as no surprise that she succeeded Mortimer and became the chief executive officer. But Howard had never envisaged her in that role.

When he first convinced Mareno to invest in Multima—intending to eventually seize control of the massive corporation—Howard had planned to install a pliant executive. He wanted someone who would turn a blind eye to money laundering and help The Organization surreptitiously move hundreds of millions of ill-gotten gains out of the US to secret offshore tax havens.

It was a good takeover plan that Howard had studied and stewed over for years, watching always for an opportunity to get control and oust the founder. When a chance came along, Howard seized it. He came within a hair of outright control before the wily old scoundrel, Mortimer, outfoxed him with a clever conversion of company shares. That was the mistake that had caused Howard to flee The Organization before Mareno could exact his punishment for the loss of a billion dollars from the crime boss's fortune.

Ironically, Fidelia now wanted him to help execute a plan that leveraged Multima's current unfortunate dilemma with both the European Central Bank and the US Justice Department—an accusation of money laundering.

Fidelia glanced up from her laptop screen and interrupted Howard's reverie of memories. She motioned for him swivel his seat around to face her as she did the same.

"You'll be meeting up with an old acquaintance in Sydney." A smirk slowly took form. "Wendal Randall will handle the technology issues for our scheme. He's already there."

Unsurprised, Howard acknowledged her comment with only a nod.

"With Wendal, anything I should watch for?"

Her question took Howard by surprise. "I honestly don't know. He's a real enigma. The guy's a genius, but his character is more complex than I can pretend to understand. I never detected either power or greed as his motivators. But he's a strange bird."

Howard took a sip from his coffee to buy a little time to collect his thoughts.

"You'll remember, I controlled him with fear. He dreaded the possibility I'd release the damning video of him in bed violently choking Janet as he reached orgasm. Other than that, I think his most powerful motivator was his ability to convert an idea into a digital reality. His eyes always lit up when he saw a chance to create something new—something no one had done before. I don't know if those characteristics merit trust or suspicion."

That satisfied her and she swiveled around to face the front of the plane again, head already bowed as she studied some message on her screen.

At first, Howard felt a tingling in his spine when he heard Wendal's name and realized his intuition was sound. The guy might be a computer genius, but he was also trouble. He'd used the hapless technologist to infiltrate Multima originally, and it hadn't gone as expected. The guy the business media liked to refer to as the Steve Jobs of his generation ran his budding technology company into the ground.

Howard eventually convinced John George Mortimer to buy the distressed company. Multima's founder saw the benefit of owning Wendal's sophisticated technology to manage his supermarkets' inventories, but didn't have the liquidity to pay for an acquisition. That's when The Organization was able to get a piece of Multima in return for the cash to buy Wendal's struggling company.

It went well for a few years. Then the nasty video incident came along. Howard shuddered as he remembered when it suddenly surfaced. Wendal was caught on video almost choking a woman to death during sex. It was a useful tool for Howard to have, and it kept the wayward genius in line for several years.

But it didn't end there. The guy stupidly became embroiled in a ridiculous internal dispute. When Suzanne Simpson refused to share private payroll records from the Supermarkets division with Wendal, he hacked her system. Naturally, the FBI got involved and it was that momentous mistake that eventually got the technology prodigy clandestinely carted off to Guantanamo Bay when he tried to re-enter the US from a business trip—with a prostitute in tow.

Why the FBI took such drastic covert action for a relatively minor offense remained a mystery. Perhaps it had something to do with Mortimer. Multima's founder fired Wendal before charges were laid or any media became aware of the computer genius's disappearance.

Howard himself didn't waste much time thinking about it, but the whole circumstance still seemed a little weird.

As the chartered private jet slowed its engines and began its gradual descent into Australia, Howard took a deep breath and tried to clear the fog from his brain. Fidelia would expect him to fill in all the little details of her overarching grand scheme and Wendal would be of little help.

However, failure was not an option.

THIRTY-SEVEN

Wendal's hands still trembled a day after his release from a Sydney jail. The entire experience reminded him too acutely of his horrible experience with the FBI and the night they spirited him and the German women out of the US and across the Caribbean to the notorious CIA facility at Guantanamo in nearby Cuba.

This current fiasco didn't involve travel anywhere other than from his suite at the Five Seasons Hotel to the Sydney jail, and then almost two weeks later to this house in a secluded area. But it had been almost equally nerve-wracking. The police didn't believe his claims of innocence in all matters related to Jennie's unfortunate death. But, in truth, he hadn't seen her for hours before her murder and at no time after her death.

Their questioning had been long, insistent, and sometimes just plain rude. To Wendal, it seemed they refused to even consider the possibility someone else might be involved. They didn't actually say it, but they certainly gave the impression they were prepared to just throw away the key to his cell and leave him there.

Fidelia had been of little help. If she were a true leader of the most powerful criminal element on earth, surely she could have sprung him from jail long before she did. Then the woman who claimed to rule The Organization had the temerity to pop by the house for a visit—a house where a black Australian woman confined him as though nothing untoward had happened.

"Are you alright?" Fidelia asked the question as she walked across the room gazing everywhere but at him, then plunked herself on a sofa facing Wendal.

"Do you mean am I injured? Or am I unhappy? Or am I facing charges that could see me in prison for years to come? No. I'm not all right. I'm pissed."

"Their reports say her neck was broken." Fidelia said it very calmly. Then she let the comment just sit there, waiting for a response from him. Her black eyes flashed something less than anger but no hint of sympathy.

"They didn't tell me the cause of death. They didn't tell me anything. All those bastards did for two weeks was accuse me of murder and ask the same questions fifty thousand different ways."

"I once saw video of you having sex with a woman. Choking her. Gripping her throat tightly, suffocating her as you got your rocks off. You almost killed her. How is this one different?"

"How?" Wendal said, then stopped as quickly as he had started. He blanched as the realization set in. Of course. Fidelia had been Howard Knight's companion for some time. He must have shown her the damned video. Wendal chose his words as carefully as possible after he recovered from the initial shock of the accusation.

"First of all, I didn't have sex with Jennie that night. Yes, we had the occasional romp, but not that night. Second, I'm guessing you're talking about a video Howard Knight had in his possession, although he told me he destroyed all the copies. I made one mistake as a young man and never tried that kind of sex again—with anyone."

"Then who do you think did it?"

"I have no idea. Who killed Aretta's technologist? Maybe if The Organization had taken that incident more seriously—and dealt with the culprit—I wouldn't have spent two weeks in jail for nothing." At once, Wendal regretted his sarcastic, accusing tone but made no apology for his anger.

"Maybe." Fidelia wasn't prepared to concede the possibility. Nor did she soften her expression. "You're out of jail now. We've hired the best attorney in Sydney. And he's sure it's only a matter of time before you're completely exonerated. I want you to get a good night's sleep because tomorrow we'll begin a new project."

"I'm not interested in any new project." Again, his tone came out angrier than he intended.

Fidelia stood up and started toward the door without saying a word. Her steps were purposeful and her face unsmiling. A bodyguard also moved toward the door, and a woman opened it just before Fidelia arrived.

"No!" Wendal screamed out. "Don't leave. I'll do whatever you want!"

He dashed across the room after her, but the male bodyguard stepped in his path. With both hands, he gripped the top of Wendal's shirt and physically lifted him off the ground. Then he carried him over to the sofa and tossed his captive against the furniture like he was a toy doll. It was humiliating.

The bitch made him wait alone for eight hours. He couldn't eat, drink or sleep. All he could do was fret about his dire circumstances and curse his immature outburst.

Aretta visited just after dawn the next morning.

"She canceled the lawyer's retainer last night. You're on your own from here. Rather, you're on your own with my million-dollar guarantee you'll show for the next hearing. I'm not happy about that."

"Did she leave Australia?" Wendal wanted to know.

"Planning to leave this morning. She's pissed. She brought some financial genius with her from Singapore and hired a computer whiz from Europe to work with you. She already told them it's off. The woman from Germany hadn't even landed when Fidelia sent her a message. What the fuck were you thinking anyway?" Aretta stood up and shook her head in amazement as she asked the question.

"I wasn't thinking. I admit it. She messed with my mind. With all the other stuff going on, I screwed up and lashed out at her. I tried to apologize, but she wouldn't listen. I'll do whatever she wants. Can you get her to come back? I'll beg for forgiveness. I will."

Aretta continued to chastise him for a few minutes, but her manner softened, and her tone gradually became more accommodating. Apparently, she'd heard enough and told him to have some breakfast. She'd see what she could do about Fidelia. Wendal followed her instructions.

Hours later, Fidelia's bodyguard burst through the doorway. He slammed the door behind him as he charged toward Wendal, who cowered in fear. The Chinese thug grabbed him by the throat and snatched Wendal from a chair violently. With one hand, he clutched Wendal's right shoulder and with the other slapped his face—hard and twice on each side.

"When Madame asks you to do something the next time, or any time, your answer will be yes ma'am, immediately. If not, she has promised me I can pull you apart one limb at a time, and I'll do it with pleasure." The burly man bared his teeth as he stared at Wendal. His eyes looked so animated Wendal wondered for an instant if he was on cocaine or some other drug, but he kept his thoughts to himself.

A few moments later, with a dramatic smack on the door, Fidelia burst in with Aretta in tow. Wendal's hands began trembling again.

"I heard you had a change of heart." Her manner was more domineering than Wendal had ever seen. No smile. Black eyes cold as coal. Her jaw taut and shoulders rigid.

"Yes, Ma'am." Wendal glanced at the bodyguard, still only feet away.

"Whether you rot in a prison cell in Australia or not is entirely up to you. Frankly, I no longer give a shit one way or the other," Fidelia glared at him with a combination of hatred and disgust. She held her expression for more than a minute without another sound as Wendal felt sweat break out on his brow. His hands continued to tremble.

"You're going to create technology magic over the next few days. You're going to do it with some of the most brilliant minds available, people you already know. And you're going to make it work on the first and only chance you'll have. If you fail, your collaborators and I will drive to a jet we have leased and leave Australia. Aretta will forfeit the million-dollar bail and bury you somewhere in the Outback. Do we understand each other?"

Wendal nodded. Fidelia's bodyguard moved one step closer, his face devoid of emotion.

"Yes, ma'am," he added quickly.

Fidelia stepped forward into the living area and motioned for someone to follow. Howard Knight stepped into the room next, followed by Klaudia Schäffer, Suzy, and a Chinese guy.

Wendal felt faint and almost collapsed, but said nothing.

THIRTY-EIGHT

Sydney, Australia, Monday March 9, 2020

Fidelia Morales realized the incongruity of her motley crew working together. Howard. Klaudia. Wendal. They all knew each other. Circumstances had thrown them together before. Under extreme pressure, Wendal and Klaudia had once demonstrated an ability to collaborate masterfully despite an underlying dislike and mistrust of each other. Fidelia had learned to implicitly trust her Russian confidant from the time they ran the prostitution business in Europe together years earlier.

Now, sheltered in the secluded country house of her deposed former Australian country head, Fidelia needed a miracle. Luigi had pleaded to join her in the mission, but she denied him. Instead, she made Aretta Musa responsible for their security down under. That was paramount.

———•———

For the moment, Sydney police appeared no longer interested in the late Oliver Williams's home. Yellow police tape surrounding the place had disappeared days earlier. As Aretta had predicted, detectives quickly concluded Williams's murder was probably targeted—a code for organized crime settling a score. Typically, police departments around the world have little time for, or interest in, solving crimes perpetrated on criminals by other criminals. Sydney's cops were no exception.

Aretta planted almost thirty thugs in a large geographic area surrounding the enclave. The first line of resistance was several miles away at the nearest intersections leading into the upscale neighborhood. None of her assigned bodyguards there had vehicles. Instead, Aretta drove them to nearby heavily wooded tracts or parked them behind buildings or signage where they could spot any incoming police traffic well out of the public's view.

Another dozen took turns driving through nearby neighborhoods to watch for signs of anything unusual. Fifteen men and women hid in bushes and behind trees in the spaces close to the property itself. Another half dozen watched the doors and windows from inside the sprawling house. Aretta reminded everyone their job was to alert her and then apprehend anyone approaching the house.

As she issued orders in small groups, Aretta also took pains to emphasize the same instructions applied to anyone trying to leave the property as well.

—•—

Prices on Asian stock markets were plunging when Fidelia checked her app. Price volatility was key to her scheme, and it looked as if it had started. Now, she needed the team to gel quickly and get the results she expected. They'd have only a few days. A pep talk would get them going. She looked first at Wendal as she spoke.

"Wendal will take the lead. He developed the app we're going to use and knows its capabilities." She shifted her gaze to the latest arrival seated to her left.

"Klaudia Schäffer will bring technical knowledge and expertise she learned in the Russian secret service. She'll support Wendal and make recommendations to ensure his little worm is airtight and can penetrate even the most secure websites." Fidelia looked next at Howard Knight facing her across the table.

"The smartest guy I know in the business world will determine the exact timing. Howard will decide when we flip the switch. No matter how well Wendal's pet worm is performing, everyone follows Howard's command." She pointed at him and tipped her head in respect.

"Everyone else, you're all brilliant people. That's why Stan Tan or Wendal hired you and why you're here today. We need you to use your programming and coding skills like never before. We need you to work tirelessly for the next few days. Sleep when you must. Eat and drink when you need to. But we need you to devote your souls to the success of this project." Fidelia paused to let the importance of her words sink in.

"Before we left Singapore, I opened numbered bank accounts in Macau. Each with one million US dollars as an opening balance. If we succeed—as I expect we will—I'll give each of you a password for an individual account. You can change the password the day after we succeed and keep all the money in the account."

Fidelia listened to gasps of astonishment from the group around the table. It appeared they had trouble even imagining the magnitude of their good fortune. If they succeeded. Her smile broadened to show her confidence in their abilities.

She'd already arranged with Wendal that he'd begin with a technical briefing for the team and let them all prepare a new hack they would test the following morning. While he projected his schematic drawings and screenshots on a bare wall, Fidelia motioned for Howard to follow her to a den off to the side of the spacious living area.

The room was designed for the home's previous occupant. Oliver Williams had spent thousands on the construction of a room akin to a bunker. All four walls were thick and filled with sound-deadening materials. A jackhammer could probably work outside without disturbing the stillness of the room.

Williams apparently liked dark colors. Walls were all a somber shade of brown, the ceiling beige, drapes on the bullet-proof windows the color of rich, black soil. He must have held meetings there because a couple black leather chairs faced the desk. Fidelia took the only chair behind the desk and pointed Howard in the direction of another.

"Have you reached out to the FBI?"

"Yes. It took a while, but I sorted through the bureaucracy and finally found one guy from the witness protection program. He was pissed I was using an encrypted line he couldn't trace, but eventually he listened to my story. I told him my sad tale with only a few embellishments and let him know I wanted back into the program. He reluctantly agreed to review my file and talk with his superiors." Howard paused for a breath, but Fidelia chose to just smile at his weak attempt to lighten the mood and wait for the rest.

"We talked for an hour, but I couldn't get his agreement to track down Dan Ramirez for me. Said I should give him any crucial information about Multima that I wanted to share."

"Of course you declined his request." Fidelia raised her eyebrow slightly as Howard simply nodded once.

"You were right about one thing. Until the Interpol Red Notice is withdrawn, they feel legally obliged to hold me and return me to the Netherlands. They won't discuss re-entry into the witness protection program until that's out of the way." Howard's expression was blank, but Fidelia recognized his acquiescence was sealed.

"I'll get Klaudia to track down Ramirez's number. There's only a handful of telecom networks in the US, so she should be able to find him in a few hours. You're sure he'll cooperate?"

"I can't be sure, but I think it's better to try indirect communication first. Ramirez is the very definition of pragmatic. His years at the upper echelons of the FBI demanded it. He carries far more influence in the company than a typical chief of security. Some claim he was John George Mortimer's closest confidant. If he buys in, she'll agree. She's a listener and listens more to Ramirez than anyone else. I can't imagine that's changed in the past couple years."

"Okay. We'll track him down so you can talk to him. Now, why don't you listen to the rest of Wendal's spiel so you'll know what happens when you unleash the chaos." Fidelia smiled just enough to convey restrained satisfaction.

Much earlier that morning, she had already drawn Klaudia into her confidence. The woman grasped the nuances during their hushed and secret conversation in the same den. Before the others woke up, she had already installed an app that recorded every digital conversation originating in the house. Whether communication was by voice, email, text, or messaging service, they were all recorded in an app that uploaded to a site in the cloud. Klaudia could monitor and retrieve them using either keywords or a multitude of other search tools.

It was time for Fidelia to test the test. Late evening in South America, Juan Álvarez was probably finishing his dinner at some swank establishment in Uruguay.

"Luigi tells me your guy in San Francisco had a serious accident," she said nonchalantly.

"Yeah. His car didn't take a curve correctly and ended up on fire at the bottom of a cliff. I've recruited the new one. A girl from Costa Rica. She'll be fine." The head of Latin American operations sounded more than a little cocky and self-assured. That was somewhat typical of him, but Fidelia detected no remorse or sense of responsibility for the earlier problem that had occurred on his watch. And there was that other issue.

"Luigi also tells me a couple employees of Multima Corporation recently met unfortunate ends. What can you tell me about them?"

"Nothing," Álvarez said a little too quickly. "I don't know what you're talking about."

"Both sounded to Luigi like hits, and he knows we weren't involved. When that happens on our territory, he takes a personal interest. You sure none of your people got carried away?" She gave him a crack of wiggle room.

"I'm sure. Only my guy from Mexico was in the US to take care of the techie. No one else would dare go there without my permission." Juan's voice regained his confident tone.

She switched the subject to Latin American issues and chatted amiably with him for another few minutes, careful not to leave any reason for him to feel either discomfort or concern. Then she expressed her last thought as casually as possible.

"Stay in Chile for the next few days. The heist I told you about is coming together. I don't want to be tracking you down on some beach in Uruguay when I give the word to go."

As usual, Fidelia ended the call with no further comment.

THIRTY-NINE

Montreal, Quebec, Monday March 9, 2020

Accustomed to living life at pace quicker than most, Suzanne considered herself supremely adaptable. However, when she accepted the role of CEO at Multima, it never once occurred to her that a pending arrest might be her first thought one morning. Today, she had bolted awake at four-thirty with her body covered in perspiration, distressed about precisely that possibility.

She considered the hotel gym rather than running outdoors when she saw snowflakes from the window of her suite. But it had been years since she'd run outdoors in cold weather, and she decided to recreate some of her fondest experiences growing up in the province of Quebec.

Snow that morning had been sticky, with air temperatures just at the point of freezing. She bundled up carefully with a ski jacket and scarf about her neck to keep warm, thankful she'd remembered to pack earmuffs. Her newish running shoes had good tread on the soles.

Still, she had to pay attention to the slippery sidewalks and splashes of a salty snow and water mix thrown up by passing vehicles. The combination wasn't great for organizing her thoughts for the day the way she usually did on a forty-five-minute run. Regardless, she had much to process.

As if the legal issues weren't enough, Stefan refused to give up. She had tried letting him down gently before she left Paris, and more forcefully dampened his expectations when they spoke for an hour by phone the previous week. Now, he heard his university might soon close for the pandemic and wanted to meet up with her in Canada. As much as she genuinely liked the guy, his suggestion was among the first issues she moved to the bottom of her morning priorities.

The run proved exhilarating. She loved fresh air in her lungs. Her cheeks stung from the cold but turned a more youthful pink when she warmed up again. Muscles evolved from stiff to pliant as she ran. Random ideas and concerns popped to mind, but Suzanne didn't risk organizing them. The slightest hesitation or distraction could easily cause a fall or worse, so she respected the risks of a Canadian winter that day.

She had persevered, finished her morning run, showered and had a quick breakfast. It wasn't yet six-thirty. If she could apply a dash of lipstick and a little foundation to cover the worry lines, she'd have enough time for a second coffee. Their Canadian unit presidents planned to collect her and Alberto Ferer in the front lobby at seven.

A second mug of coffee would also give her a chance to organize the random thoughts that had sprung to mind as her adrenalin surged while jogging the streets of downtown Montreal that bitter winter morning. She swept the still-steaming mug from the dispenser and took a seat by the window, looking out over an abandoned Catholic church on Boulevard René-Lévesque below. *So many thoughts to filter.*

——•——

The FBI showed up at Multima Corporation headquarters the morning after Suzanne left for Canada. Of course, that was one day earlier than expected by the secret informer who'd tipped off her attorney. It was the same pair of agents, and they appeared more than a little uncomfortable when Eileen met them in the building's lobby. They asked for Suzanne and explained they needed to have a word with her again.

When Eileen advised them Ms. Simpson was away from the office, they pressed for details. One asked if they could reach her at home. Despite Suzanne's explicit instructions, the executive assistant decided she would first try to divulge as little as possible, so she simply replied that her boss was away on a business trip to Montreal.

The agents pressed some more and wanted to know how they could contact her. Eileen followed her boss's orders even though she dreaded it. She recited the name and number of the hotel where Suzanne was staying and gave them the number of Multima's Montreal office.

After a deep breath, she also divulged Ms. Simpson's coveted private cell number. She couldn't remember the last time someone pried that information from her, but that's what her boss wanted. As instructed, she also told them she expected Suzanne to return to Fort Myers on the weekend.

——•——

Suzanne had asked her executive assistant to check the media as much as possible to see if the FBI gave out any information. No leaks had been reported so far.

Since her arrival in Montreal, Suzanne had also talked with her attorney, Beverly Vonderhausen, every few hours each day. Her lawyer continued to make repeated calls to her contacts in Washington to see what she could learn. So far, she'd been unable to penetrate a fortress of silence. Even the trusted source who gave Beverly the tipoff the previous week was now ignoring her calls.

Dan Ramirez was back from Europe, and he'd already touched base with all his old cronies, searching for some insight into plans by either the FBI or the Justice Department. No one was talking. Dan had been the last person Suzanne spoke with Thursday evening, and he promised to get on the phone again Friday morning. Suzanne reminded him she'd need to decide about a return soon. The FBI would probably be looking for her again on the weekend.

As usual, Dan gave assurances he understood the urgency and she could count on him. Also, as usual, he had a bit of gossip to share. Someone had tried to reach him a couple times. He left a message saying only that he would try again later. The phone used by the caller was encrypted and left no number identifier, but the voice on the recording sounded strangely like Howard Knight's.

"Have you ever heard from him since he disappeared from that board meeting four or five years ago?" Dan Ramirez wondered.

Dan prefaced that question by categorizing it as gossip, so Suzanne hadn't felt bad about gradually switching the subject and never actually giving him an answer. He knew she liked to listen to gossip but rarely added to it, and answering him wouldn't give him clarity either way.

Jolted back to reality by her bodyguard Jasmine reminding her it was time to leave, Suzanne gulped the remaining coffee, grabbed her bag, and dashed out the door, then down the elevator to the hotel lobby.

Alberto and Multima's Canadian business unit presidents greeted her warmly. Bob McKenzie was responsible for the Canadian Supermarkets division, and Doug Burns oversaw Financial Services. After quick handshakes, she dragged a tiny bottle of hand sanitizer from her bag and offered it to everyone as they shared a hearty laugh. Adequately protected, she led her team to the stretch limousine waiting in the short circular driveway outside their hotel.

Everyone piled in through the rear doors except bodyguard Willy, who sat up front with the driver. Their trip to Aeroport International

Pierre Elliott Trudeau was a short one, about twenty minutes, and Suzanne used the travel time for social chatting. Although the group had been together for most of the previous two days, meetings had been structured, tense, and rushed. There'd been little time for Suzanne to catch up with the personal goings-on of her Canadian leaders, and she liked to devote a few minutes of each personal interaction to keep her relationships strong.

She'd oohed and aahed at photos of Bob's latest child, a baby boy added to his family of three older daughters. Doug wasn't to be outdone and scrolled through a dozen pictures of his family's latest addition, a tiny toy poodle. Alberto watched, bemused.

Multima's Bombardier Global 5000 sat at the entrance of the private jet terminal. Back from Europe, a new, refreshed crew had them boarded and on their way within minutes. The flight to Billy Bishop Airport on Toronto Island took only an hour, but Suzanne used the time for final preparations. Their most important meeting of the day—by far—was with the Toronto Stock Exchange. Pre-meeting discussions to prepare didn't go well.

"We need to deal with the European Central Bank threat right up front," Bob McKenzie said. "Canadian regulators have better and closer relationships with their European counterparts than Americans. If we try to gloss over the matter, they'll cut us off at the knees."

Alberto Ferer listened until McKenzie had made his point, but didn't conceal his haste to shut down the idea. The second his Canadian colleague finished, Alberto lunged.

"As chief legal counsel, I can't recommend that at all. Multima is a victim of fraud. That's our position. Letting the Canadian authorities know we're fighting a legal battle in Europe muddies the waters too much for Multima Corporation and for Suzanne personally. We shouldn't bring it up at all."

Taken aback by the harsh immediate reaction, McKenzie looked at his colleague Doug Burns, his animated dark green eyes begging for support. Both knew the delicate tightrope heads of subsidiary companies were forced to walk. While they might know far more about a subject matter and sensitivities in their local markets, they could never alienate powerful staff around a CEO. Consequences could be career altering.

"Your concern's a valid one, Alberto. But I think Bob's point might also be expressed another way," Doug said. "Whether we introduce the subject or not, we need to be prepared to deal with it. The relationship between Canada and the EU is much tighter than many people realize.

Right now, I have a personal friend living in Switzerland. He's there helping the ECB and other central banks develop new international banking rules. It's inconceivable the ECB threat won't be raised at some point in our meeting with the TSE."

Alberto held firm. "Well, then, we'll deal with it if they raise it. Tactically, I see no merit in us bringing it up. It'll simply give them a reason to delay a decision. That's what these regulators and stock exchanges always like to do."

Suzanne may have already leaned in one direction, but she realized the importance of debate and usually encouraged folks to offer differing viewpoints. She let the males satisfy their egos with arguments for and against early disclosure until faces started to redden and voices rise an octave or two. It was time to bring the debate to a close. Suzanne looked first at Alberto as she spoke.

"You all make very reasonable arguments, and I realize this money laundering issue creates complications for every aspect of our business and for my personal circumstances. I've been the head of a Canadian subsidiary company and know the challenges." She shifted her gaze to Bob McKenzie as she conveyed her decision.

"We'll put my personal circumstances aside. That's what a good leader does. We'll defer to the judgment of our local experts. They're the ones who will live longest with the impact of their recommendations."

For the rest of their short flight, they drafted an opening statement for Suzanne to deliver. She wouldn't read it aloud, of course, but she needed only to read the final draft twice to be sure the entire message was locked in her memory.

When they touched down at the island airport across from Toronto's impressive skyline, everyone aboard took a few moments to gaze across the harbor and admire the impressive center of Canadian commerce. From the jet's parking spot, Burns led the way to an underwater tunnel with a moving sidewalk. After a brisk twenty-minute walk, the group surfaced from an escalator exit onto Queen's Quay. With the cold weather, they descended into Toronto's underground PATH system for the half-hour walk to the Toronto Stock Exchange to seek approval for listing Multima Corporation.

Once approved, Multima would instantly become the third-largest publicly traded company in Canada. The TSE could then celebrate an image victory everyone agreed they desperately wanted.

Apparently, someone didn't realize that.

A security guard called the office of the exchange's CEO to

announce Suzanne's group's arrival. After a moment, he frowned and turned on his swivel chair to hide his conversation. He spoke quietly and took pains to partially cover the phone to muffle the sound of his voice. His shoulders became tenser as he listened, then his arms became more animated as he protested something more loudly. It took him a moment to collect his thoughts before he swiveled back in the chair and stood up to deliver his message.

"Mr. Argenter is not available. I'm sorry."

Alberto looked at Suzanne, who arched her brow but said nothing. The chief legal counsel stepped closer to the security guard's reception area and quietly insisted they had a confirmed appointment. It was to no avail. Despite his repeated insistence, the security guard was unmoved.

Eventually, Alberto convinced the man he should contact the TSE's chief legal officer, who agreed to come down and meet them. It took almost an hour before a large, red-faced and visibly shaken man approached them and introduced himself as Larry Peabody.

"I am so sorry about this. Please, step over here. I'd like to have a word with you privately." He led them to an arrangement of leather sofas in a corner away from foot traffic and looked around carefully once they were seated.

"I apologize again," he said. "Nothing like this has happened before."

"Let's just get to the point, Larry. What's going on?" Alberto spoke softly, but his manner showed exasperation. Suzanne smiled at Peabody with a resigned shrug of her shoulders to diffuse some of the building tension. This guy was just the messenger, after all.

"Like I said earlier, we've never had a situation like this. I spoke with Mr. Argenter. He realizes you had a meeting scheduled with him this morning, but he chose to cancel it based on a conversation he had earlier today. I asked him to meet with you to discuss it, but he refuses to budge."

"Is there some concern about the TSE listing we planned to finalize and announce this morning?" Suzanne asked before Alberto could say something to make the situation even more tense.

The man nodded, clearly trying to decide how much he was prepared to share. After a moment, he took a deep breath, looked first toward the ceiling, then directly at Suzanne. "Everything I say is off the record. I'll deny saying it, if necessary."

Alberto and Suzanne both nodded in agreement. Peabody clasped his hands together for courage and chose his words slowly and carefully.

"Argenter received a call from the Ontario Securities Commission the moment he arrived in his office. The US Securities Exchange

Commission was also on the line. It was the SEC that initiated the call."
Peabody paused and looked around the room before he carried on.

Suzanne noticed his concern and asked if he would be more
comfortable speaking only with her and Alberto. While he thought about
that offer, she added a reassuring thought.

"I'm okay with my team hearing anything you have to share with
us—no matter how sensitive it may be. You can be sure everyone will use
complete discretion. Our management team is completely transparent
with each other."

"I know what a great reputation you and your company have. You're
often used as an example of integrity, ethics and success for companies
here. That makes what I have to say so awkward. But here it is. The SEC
got a call from someone very close to the White House. The person who
called ordered the SEC to kill your TSE listing. According to Argenter,
the exact words were 'It's not going to happen. Period.' That's all I can
tell you."

Suzanne and her Multima entourage were speechless at the
admission. Argenter had been so humiliated by the attack on his
authority and the independence of the Canadian securities markets he
was too embarrassed to meet with them. It fell to Peabody to carry the
devastating message.

Suzanne recognized the man's predicament and tried to massage
his ego.

"I can only imagine how Mr. Argenter felt. I'm a dual citizen, you
know. I'm still Canadian even if I live in the US and earn my money
there. Did Mr. Argenter get any background into why someone close to
the White House would take this position?"

"Some. He wasn't prepared to share it with me though."

Peabody's discomfort was apparent. Flush face. Eyes darting about
nervously. Hands wringing continuously in his lap. But he kept his voice
calm and his tone soft.

"Mr. Argenter hasn't let the matter slide. He's on the phone right
now with the Department of Finance, and I know he already talked with
the Minister of Foreign Affairs."

After only a few more minutes of the fellow's excuse-making and
apologizing, Suzanne had enough. Snatching her bag from the floor, she
stood up, thanked the man for his time and strode resolutely toward the
doorway without looking back.

From the Toronto Stock Exchange, Suzanne led her associates
a couple blocks south. Alberto walked beside her, the others trailing

closely behind, but out of earshot given the busy Bay Street traffic flow. They commiserated on how badly their elaborate planning had turned out and expressed mutual shock at the callous disregard shown by the TSE management.

"It's good we aren't wasting the entire day," Suzanne said when they'd satisfied their mutual need to vent a bit. "Eileen organized the meeting of the board for three o'clock, right? Should we do it from the suite Eileen booked at the Royal York or fly back to Montreal and videoconference from there?"

"I'd pick your first option," Alberto replied. "There's always a chance those guys at the TSE will get their act together later. If they change their minds, we'll be close by."

Alberto needed a win, so Suzanne decided they'd stay. The team used the three hours between the TSE rejection and their board meeting to make calls. Alberto phoned his legal contacts in the US and Canada. The Canadian country heads networked with acquaintances at lower levels of the TSE to learn what more they could. Suzanne called the office of Canada's Prime Minister. When they met up again at her suite in the century-old hotel for their board meeting, no one had any concrete news to share.

When Suzanne saw all the expected directors were on the videoconference, she laid out the current dilemma in bold and candid terms.

"Our situation is about to become worse. The TSE wouldn't meet with us this morning." She walked her directors through the morning's events and summarized the follow-up calls the team had made in the ensuing hours.

"The Prime Minister's office promised to investigate pressure reportedly coming from the US and attributed to someone close to the White House. But it will take time. There are no leaks so far, but I would expect CBNN or some other outlet to report on the TSE rejection before the day is over." Suzanne paused just long enough to let the severity of the situation sink in.

"Also, I'll be served with another warrant for arrest as soon as I return to the US. We should expect that will also be very public. All this—on top of the suspicious death of our CFO—will almost certainly put pressure on our share prices. Those are the reasons for the item I added to our agenda, and I'd like to deal with it first."

A few of the board members looked down at their notes, a couple gazed off into space, and one peered directly into his camera before he spoke. It was Chuck Jones, the director from the Midwest and very close to James Fitzgerald.

"Why do you expect to be arrested, Suzanne?"

"FBI agents visited headquarters asking for me. They requested I contact them when I return to the US."

Chuck Jones made no reply. Instead, he raised his eyes as though looking for divine inspiration or the patience to deal with the news. It wasn't clear which.

Alberto Ferer shuffled some papers, head down, and squirming uncomfortably in the chair across from Suzanne. None of the other directors seemed compelled to say anything, so she continued.

"One of the defensive tools I recommend—just in case there should be a run on our stock price—is buying back shares." She glanced at the notes in front of her before she raised her head to continue. "We currently have more than two billion in cash and treasury bills set aside for emergencies. Wilma Willingsworth spoke with our consortium of banks yesterday and confirmed our unused five-billion-dollar credit facility is available. Is that correct?"

Suzanne nodded toward Wilma's image from Chicago on the screen and waited for a reply.

"Yes, Bank of the Americas convened a special virtual meeting with the participating banks yesterday. I explained the circumstances surrounding Heather Strong's death and let them know Suzanne had informally asked me to handle temporarily the CFO role again."

Wilma paused to see if there was any reaction from her fellow board members. There was none. Each displayed expressions that masked any emotion.

"I told them we were considering a resolution to buy back Multima shares if the value plummeted, and they all agreed that was a reasonable strategy. Of course, Multima shares are the collateral they hold if we use that line of credit. They win if we use it by drawing down on the loan. They protect their collateral and earn income. The rate of interest we pay on the loan is only LIBOR plus a quarter percent, but it's still income for them."

Wilma couldn't suppress a grin of satisfaction as she delivered a not-so-subtle reminder of her negotiating prowess. It was she who'd initially persuaded the banks to accept a rate only a quarter percent higher than the rate banks charge each other for loans. Suzanne granted her a moment of silent triumph before she carried on.

There was serious discussion among the meeting's participants for about fifteen minutes. Four directors had questions or comments.

Suzanne handled each of the responses and thoughtfully acknowledged the comments. None were particularly contentious, and none conveyed either a message or tone that suggested anything other than probable support before she read the motion formally and called for a vote.

She glanced at each of the faces on her screen. Chuck Jones still stared off into space, absorbed with something. Suzanne chose a safe route.

"Are there any concerns anyone would like to raise before we make a motion on the share buy-back and vote?" She deliberately waited a second or two longer than necessary. Others might see the image of a distracted director who was usually highly attentive and engaged. Chuck Jones spoke after a couple seconds.

"I'll certainly support the proposal when it comes up for a vote, and after the buy-back plan is announced I'll probably buy a few shares personally in the open market as well. But this insinuation that someone in or near the White House is involved is a genuine concern. Does anyone around the table have a guess at why Suzanne is being targeted this way?"

Ruth Begin from France raised a finger to announce her intention to answer. Ruth was a close friend of Michelle Sauvignon, and Suzanne had added her as a new director a few months earlier at Michelle's request— and to diversify the predominantly male board she'd inherited.

"We know misogyny pervades the current administration. Could this be just another attempt to weaken a proud company led by a female until we—the board—are forced to make a change in leadership?"

No one answered immediately. With the almost unlimited, erratic, and foolhardy decisions and actions taken by the current US administration, no possibility could be discounted without at least a moment of thought.

"I don't think it would be that blatant," Chuck Jones countered. "When I first heard about Suzanne's very public arrest a few weeks ago, that was my first inclination, too. But when they abruptly dropped the charges, that premise no longer made sense. I began to wonder if there wasn't some power in the background trying some corporate maneuver. We've all heard the rumors about the shady backgrounds of some of the people around the President. When the charges were dropped the day after Giancarlo Mareno's murder was announced, I wondered if there might be a connection between the two events."

"I wondered that too," Alberto Ferer said. "But we haven't had any demands, warnings, or other indication that The Organization has raised its ugly head again."

"That's interesting," Chuck conceded. "But it doesn't rule out that someone else might have inherited an interest in attacking Multima. Do we know who has filled the leadership vacuum Mareno left behind?"

Suzanne shivered at the thought. But the conversation was headed into purely speculative territory, and she had a real company to run.

"Chuck has raised some great questions for all of us to ponder offline, but I think we should come back to our initial discussion. Alberto, will you please read the formal motion to buy back shares to a maximum amount of five billion dollars at the discretion of the chief executive officer?"

Her chief legal counsel—who also served as secretary on the board—read the motion aloud, then asked for votes. The motion carried unanimously, and he noted the decision on his ever-present, yellow legal notepad.

Suzanne moved the discussion to three urgent expenditures Multima planned to make in response to the pandemic. All were technically within her authority to decide, but her style was inclusive. She preferred to deal with any dissension early and welcomed input and feedback. None of the directors objected to the immediate two-dollar-per-hour increase in hourly wages for all Supermarkets' staff working in the stores.

All agreed with her decision to hire security guards to control customer access to stores. Her decision to link purchasing departments globally for greatest leverage and pricing power drew actual applause from three directors.

With one last glance at each of the images in the little boxes on her screen, Suzanne asked if any directors wished to discuss other issues or concerns. Chuck Jones raised his hand.

"I don't want to sound like a broken record here, but I have one last thought for you to consider. The FBI seems complicit in whatever is going on with someone close to the President. We're a Canadian-headquartered company now, right? Even if the TSE hasn't granted us a listing on the exchange there?"

"That's right," Alberto confirmed.

"Then maybe we should ask the Royal Canadian Mounted Police to make some discreet inquiries."

Suzanne felt a tingle of discomfort. "Good idea. I'll ask Dan Ramirez to do that." She took care neither her expression nor tone gave her away. But she had confidentially asked the Attorney General of Canada to make exactly that request.

FORTY

"Yesterday the board approved a five-billion-dollar buy-back of Multima shares," Howard Knight announced confidently to Fidelia. "I confirmed it with two sources, both well-placed to know."

"How do you confirm it with your sources? Do you just tell them it's Howard Knight calling?" Her smile was mischievous.

"No," he snorted with a laugh. "I haven't been good old Howard for a couple years. Don't know if anyone would recognize the name. I've learned to use the Internet. I checked two sites that monitor company filings with the US Securities and Exchange Commission."

"That makes your idea even better." Fidelia smiled more warmly. Perhaps it had been a dumb question, but it showed she was dissecting every tiny element of the stock market attack he recommended—apparently her sole motivation for abducting him from Cambodia. "When do we make an approach?"

"I think we'll need to hang on for a couple days yet. Suzanne's a prudent one. Although she has the authority to buy shares, she'll know things will get worse from here. Yesterday's tick down in the markets was only a warning. The market's volatility index is soaring. My guess is the end of the week, maybe even early next week."

Howard had already determined the trigger for their major action would be an inevitable crash of global stock markets as investors around the world woke up to the economic carnage the growing pandemic was about to cause. He couldn't pick a day it would happen—yet. But he'd already convinced Fidelia a downturn was about to unfold that was more devastating than any the current generation of investors had ever seen. It would give them cover, and they'd capitalize on it.

Howard watched Fidelia process his opinion and timing. She displayed neither alarm nor discomfort, but he wanted to test it anyway. His future rode on the success of the coming operation whether he liked it or not.

"How do you feel about the technology side of the equation?"

"Wendal's worm is working fine. His team has hacked into more than fifty brokerages. They did a test last night. All the funds arrived in Valparaíso as expected. They're going to do another test tonight." Fidelia appeared confident, but not entirely. Her staccato delivery conveyed a trace of doubt.

"Did you ever find the origin of the problem with those funds that ended up in Cyprus? The ones you asked Klaudia to work on?"

"Not yet. Wendal assures everyone it was a one-off mistake caused by the techie Juan took out in San Francisco. Klaudia thinks that's probably the case. She's still sniffing around to see if there's more there, but keep that to yourself," she said, frowning.

"We're talking about a ton of money here. You know your losses will be enormous if anything goes wrong, right?"

"I realize the risk. It wouldn't completely wipe out The Organization's reserves, but it might come close. You know I don't like risk, but this one is too important. As Giancarlo used to say, sometimes you have to put it all on the line."

Both grew quiet at the mention of their former boss and the most powerful man in the underworld of crime for a generation. Howard took a deep breath and slouched back casually in the plush leather sofa. So much had changed in such a short time.

Fidelia stood up and paced in front of the sofa as she gathered her thoughts. Howard watched. He knew her mannerisms. Pacing like that betrayed her confident words. Something was bugging her. Some piece hadn't yet come together in her mind, but he remained silent.

After a moment or two, she drew a breath and looked as if she wanted to say something. Then Fidelia paused, stopped pacing, and peered out a window. She held that position for another couple minutes before she asked.

"Our success hinges on her. Why are you so sure she'll sell at the price we want, when we want?" They'd talked so much about "her" the past few hours that neither needed to name the object of their conversations now.

"She has a secret addiction. She'll do almost anything to keep that nasty habit hidden and protect her pristine image." Howard took care to keep his tone neutral.

"How long have you known?"

"Years. Her marriage ended in divorce because her husband could no longer tolerate the losses. She wagered online excessively at one of

Giancarlo's sites and accumulated huge debts. Millions. She didn't realize it. But The Organization effectively had her in its pocket from then on."

Fidelia appeared satisfied. Her body language remained neutral and her facial expression relaxed as she pondered his revelation. Her dark eyes remained partially hooded as she consciously hid any sign of the direction she was leaning. He'd seen her do that many times before. Like Mareno before her, she had learned to take whatever time she needed to make a decision and felt no need to fill gaps of silence.

Fidelia took a seat again and drifted off with her thoughts for a while longer. Then, she crossed her legs, crossed her hands in her lap and sat perfectly upright. Every movement suggested she'd made some kind of decision. Still, she took another moment.

"Okay. I'll wait until you decide the time is right to contact her. But first, I want to do another test with Wendal's worm tonight to be sure everything's ready. Don't say anything."

Fidelia rose again from the sofa, her new signal that it was time for Howard to leave the den. A thought crossed his mind as he followed her example. It might be more accurate to call that room a lair rather than a den.

FORTY-ONE

Wounds to Suzanne's ego healed more quickly than her male colleagues' bruises. Before midnight rolled around, she'd made multiple calls to Eileen back in Fort Myers. After the virtual meeting with the board of directors, in the wake of that aborted session with the Toronto Stock Exchange, she'd also spent hours strategizing with her Canadian business leaders and Alberto. They had focused on how to repair the damage from the TSE rejection and reached few conclusions.

She enjoyed a couple glasses of red wine when they ordered dinner to her suite, but the guys seemed to need more. There were four empty bottles on the table when she kicked them all out as an ornate grandfather clock struck twelve. Sleep came quickly despite the turmoil and she awoke refreshed when her phone alarm sounded for a five o'clock run with the bodyguards.

Jasmine thought it too dangerous to run in Toronto's miserable winter weather that morning. It was raining quite heavily, with the temperature only a few degrees above freezing. She sent Willy down to see if there was ice and he reported the streets were wet but not slick. Suzanne chose to give it a try. They set off south on Bay Street, bundled as warmly as possible in waterproof running rain gear they always carried with them.

Jogging at a modest speed and hopping over puddles of water, they reached the waterfront of Lake Ontario in about ten minutes. In summer, the rejuvenated stretch along the lake was a magnificent place to walk, run or ride. That day, not so much. Suzanne led them along the smooth terraced trail in a westerly direction toward the landmark Cinesphere of Ontario Place. Strong winds blew pelting rain into their faces with such force it stung. Even Willy spit out a curse from the discomfort of one particularly strong gust.

About ten minutes into their run, Suzanne gave up and motioned for everyone to turn back. Their rain gear proved no match for the conditions, and icy water had seeped through almost unchecked. They were drenched to their skin and shivering when they stopped at a red light on the corner of Bay Street beside an entrance to their hotel.

It took about an hour for Suzanne to warm up. A steaming shower helped, after which she wrapped herself in a plush white robe from a closet in the hotel suite and drained two black coffees as quickly as she dared.

With breakfast finished and emails all caught up, Suzanne took to the phone. She reached Dan Ramirez first. He was in his car en route to the Fort Myers headquarters.

"Any progress with your connections at the FBI?"

"Not much. My contacts in Fort Myers took no time at all to make sure I knew about the complications serving you with a warrant." Dan spoke with his usual flat and unemotional tone of voice.

"I can imagine. Sorry for any strains this puts in your relationships over there, but I was wondering specifically about new information related to our deceased employees." Suzanne immediately regretted the insensitive tone and switched gears. "I was a little more abrupt there than I intended, Dan. Hope you understand. This business with Heather Strong and Kim Jones has me more spooked than I realized."

"No problem. I understand completely. With Kim Jones, we're coming up empty. The RCMP in Alberta is just too willing to accept an accident as an explanation. I sent one of my people up there—a very persistent woman by the way. She tried every technique in the book to get them to expand the investigation. The local police just don't see either motive or means. They're already overworked, and this additional death of a foreigner just adds to their burden."

"How about Heather's case?"

"We know the apartment was ransacked, so the police think robbery could be a motive. They did pick up a fingerprint and checked it in the national database. They found a match. The print belonged to a convicted small-crime felon out of Miami. They're looking for him, but have no last known address or any other leads so far."

It became apparent Ramirez couldn't enlighten Suzanne on either issue, so she tried another tack.

"A few days ago, you mentioned you'd received a message from someone with a voice like Howard Knight's," Suzanne ventured. "Is there anything more I should know?"

"Not with that call. It was bizarre though. I had my people check a voiceprint we had on file, and the voice was definitely Howard's. But there's been no further communication since. An interesting bit on Wendal Randall though."

"Oh? Have they found him guilty of murder?"

"No. Still just charged with murder, but free on bail in Sydney. Someone posted a million-dollar bond to assure he appears in court. Wendal never had that kind of money, so the FBI asked the Australian authorities to poke around and let them know who came up with the funds. They're still waiting for a reply."

Their conversation returned to Suzanne's predicament. She told him she was prepared to stay in Canada as long as necessary. If the FBI wanted her badly enough, they might have to extradite her to force a return. They ended their call with Dan's promise of continued efforts to see the entire messy issue resolved.

James Fitzgerald was next. Suzanne reached him at his home in a Chicago suburb, sipping his first coffee of the morning and watching the CBNN business news channel.

"There's all sorts of speculation this morning," he responded to her inquiry about any good news. "They're calling yesterday Black Monday because of the severe contraction related to COVID-19. Some of the talking heads are speculating it will get worse every day this week. Others maintain it's just a hiccup."

"You were very quiet during the discussion yesterday about buying back Multima shares."

"You know I'm opposed to buybacks philosophically." As she expected, James chose his words carefully. His tone seemed resigned. "Usually, I think it's management's way of propping up share prices to get the largest bonuses possible. I wish they weren't allowed. That said, I think you made the right decision. Multima shares are about to plummet for a few reasons. When they do, if you buy back shares at a low price, the company will win. Ultimately, shareholder value will increase."

"Should I personally buy once the buy-back is public?" Suzanne chose a tone conveying curiosity rather than one seeking advice.

"If I were in your position, I would. You'd need to declare it, of course. Despite all the pessimism around this nasty pandemic, supermarkets will surely be one of the winners. In Europe, our financial services will take a huge hit if we can't turn the ECB around. But Multima has a strong foundation. Your personal investment horizon is really decades, not years."

They parried back and forth for a few moments longer on the investment question, then Suzanne shifted abruptly.

"If you wanted to take over Multima, where would you strike?"

"Well, you know I have no intention of trying to take over your company." James laughed, apparently to cushion the harshness of his words. "But you're vulnerable. That's a fact. If I were interested in taking over Multima, I'd make sure you were not only arrested but also incarcerated. The value of the company would become impossible to validate because you have no established successor."

Suzanne could almost feel James cringe as he made his startling claim. He'd already warned her about succession planning several times since she assumed the role of CEO.

"Let's keep Angela doing her thing. Maybe she'll identify the culprits," Suzanne offered in farewell atonement. "I think she does great work, and she's worth whatever we're paying her."

Moments later, Suzanne reached Wilma Willingsworth in Fort Myers. The president of Financial Services was in her former office, most recently occupied by Heather Strong before her sudden death.

"Have you found anything?" Suzanne wanted to know.

"You're not going to like what I have to say." Wilma paused and cleared her throat. "It's looking like Heather Strong might have been involved. OCD's managing partner called me today. They have uncovered some incidents when the question of fraudulent transactions came up and Heather may have looked the other way."

"What did they find?"

"Buried in a bottom desk drawer, someone found an auxiliary hard drive that was encrypted. The technical people are still trying to recover the files, but there's an indication a separate set of books might have linked into the Multima server. Some of the files they discovered are for transactions with Latin American companies. It's too early to say for sure. She may have just copied some transactions she wanted more info about."

Suzanne made a mental note to share this disconcerting discovery with Dan Ramirez as soon as she could. It merited verification. Then she pressed Wilma for her opinion on the resolution to buy back Multima shares.

"Did we make the right decision?" Suzanne used a tone that implied not only uncertainty but regret.

"Maybe." The woman considered one of America's most influential women in the world of finance sounded doubtful at best. "It's a question of timing. If you seize the right time, shareholder value will grow and you'll be a hero. Choose the wrong moment and you're out on your ass."

"Can I count on you to tell me when the moment is right?" Suzanne took pains to sound objective.

"Of course."

There may be a silver lining in this cursed pandemonium after all.

FORTY-TWO

Sydney, Australia, Wednesday March 11, 2020

Klaudia secretly performed another test run for the amazing new app on Tuesday evening, Sydney time. The next morning, Fidelia gathered her entire group around the large circular dining room table at the late Oliver Williams's secluded house to review where everyone was in the process. They drank tea or coffee, with muffins—and some American-style donuts one of the security people brought in.

The tech resource from Singapore reported a major bank in Vietnam and a brokerage in Japan had each discovered evidence of the first test and had already repaired the gaps in the systems the team had hacked the previous day. They'd need to find another entry point. Both were quite basic security systems, and the techie expected to find another way to hack their servers before the end of the day.

Fidelia wondered why only two of the fifty institutions tested discovered the problem.

"Security teams in banks and brokerages are overworked and underpaid. Most companies reconcile their account balances overnight and see results the next day. If there's only a small variance for one day, staff set the matter aside to see if there's a recurrence," Wendal explained.

"We did tests two days in a row. Does that mean some other banks might become more alert now and fix their vulnerabilities?" Fidelia asked.

"Maybe. But not likely. First, they'll look for a pattern. If nothing else shows up over the next few days, they'll usually assume an error was made somewhere and expect someone in their operations groups to make an adjustment at the end of the month. Those two who checked out the small variance—and tracked where it occurred so quickly—are exceptionally efficient." Wendal added a nod of admiration as he complimented their foes.

"When we do the real thing, what happens if we find another server has been fixed?" Fidelia creased her brow and gave an edge to her tone. This technology twist could become a problem.

"We'll have to do the same as our friend from Singapore is doing today. Find another way into the server." Wendal shrugged. "It should only delay us a few minutes. We can also divert the transactions to other banks if we encounter resistance that creates time pressure for completion."

Fidelia let the matter rest for the moment. She'd chat with Klaudia later and see if she had any better ideas.

Suzy—Wendal's technologist and occasional plaything—reported the transactions through Valparaíso went smoothly both times. No funds had disappeared the way they had a couple weeks earlier. Fidelia remembered too clearly the twenty-five million diverted to Cyprus and still not found. But Klaudia was working on that behind the scenes.

Howard provided an overview of global stock market activity and conditions. He drew everyone's attention to the rising VIX index—a measure of investor volatility on the American stock exchanges. Investors were becoming more worried, and the most astute professionals had already bought hedges against dramatic drops in their portfolio values.

Wendal detected her unease and had thought more about his earlier answer about bank security. After Howard's update, he held a finger in the air to add a comment. He suggested both teams focus on penetrating at least six more banks they could use for back-up in the event others thwarted their illicit entry. Fidelia nodded agreement before she motioned for Klaudia to follow her to the soundproof den.

"Two things you need to know," the German-Russian woman blurted the moment the door was closed. They were still standing in the center of the spacious room and remained there while she relayed her message.

"I found the twenty-five million you lost a couple weeks ago. It's in three different bank accounts in Malta, Macau, and Monaco."

"Great work! What happened?" Fidelia leaned forward to catch every word.

"In Valparaíso, I discovered an app with a worm very much like Wendal's. The app is buried deep in every account you use there. But this one seems even more sophisticated than Wendal's. Whoever planted it can switch it on and off at will. That's why some of the cash was diverted and some wasn't."

"Makes sense. Did you figure out who turned it on and off?"

"I don't have a name, but I do have an IP address. It's in Santiago, Chile, and the same IP address manipulated all the accounts in Valparaíso."

"So, someone turned on an algorithm operating in the background. It took money from our account in Valparaíso and deposited it to an account in Cyprus that belongs to an unidentified numbered company. How did the money get from there to Malta, Macau, and Monaco?" Fidelia wanted to know.

"Each of the transactions from Cyprus to the other locations was an individual command. And they all came from one IP address. In West Virginia. From an IP address located close to the American CIA headquarters."

Despite her earlier suspicions, Fidelia gasped as she heard the news. Their entire project was now in jeopardy. She hadn't planned for an eventuality that someone could steal the money her team was pilfering from others.

Worse, perhaps some mole in the CIA was involved and poised to financially ruin The Organization should Fidelia continue with her grand scheme. Klaudia wisely gave her a moment or two for the news to sink in. She sighed before she carried on.

"You said you had two items." Still standing, Fidelia braced for more bad news.

"I got an alert on the app you planted digitally in Juan Álvarez's phone. The trigger was 'Fort Myers.' The app recorded an entire conversation, but it lasted less than fifteen seconds. No names were used. In Spanish, a voice said the work in Fort Myers was done. Álvarez' replied, "Okay, good job.'"

Fidelia felt the blood drain from her brain, and she became faint, but didn't allow herself to panic. Instead, she took three or four steps and sank slowly into a plush leather chair behind the desk. She needed some time.

"Please get me a bottle of water from the kitchen," Fidelia instructed.

Was her scheme literally falling apart? It was bad enough for Juan Álvarez to be involved with something in Florida, but the mysterious worm Klaudia had discovered might also be his handiwork. She had trusted him completely and moved him up the ladder to oversee her Latin American empire. How had she missed the signals? How had her judgment failed? Who else was working with him?

And then it dawned on her. Klaudia's secret tests had not been diverted to other accounts. Why would they leave small test amounts behind if the accounts were controlled by an app? Were the amounts too small to trigger action? Or, did it mean someone inside the late Oliver Williams's former house had tipped Juan about the tests?

Shock turned to anger and Fidelia smashed her hand down against the desk, causing a louder than intended bang. Her face regained its color. She willed herself to keep calm. It was almost midnight in South America, but she hit the speed dial button with conviction.

"Sorry to bother you at this hour." Her transformed voice and demeanor belied her anger. With effort, she made her voice almost seductive, suggesting an entirely different purpose for her call. "Where are you?"

"Valparaíso. To what do I owe the honor of your call tonight?" Fidelia could almost visualize Juan Álvarez's charming smile, rumpled hair, and mischievous dark eyes as his voice flirted in return.

"Somebody made a mistake and transferred some funds into the Valparaíso account today. Are you able to see it there?" she asked.

"I don't think so. We've set that up to give me an alert so I know to move the money." His fingers pattered on the keyboard in the background. "What's this? Yeah, there's money there and the alert is shut off. Let me talk to the new girl in San Francisco about it."

Fidelia doubted the story. Juan would never have trusted a new resource with access to the account settings during her first days. *A slip-up?*

"I told you earlier. We've got a project materializing. It's big. Again, I want to be sure you'll stay in Valparaíso for a few days in case I need to reach you urgently. Are you at the Hotel Casa Higueras?"

"Yeah. Now that those clowns from Multima freed up my usual suite, I'm back home."

"Sit tight. I'll be in touch." She ended the call, anxious to compare notes with Klaudia.

Clowns from Multima? Was that a careless post-dinner slip after a couple glasses of wine? She was too quick to hang up. She should have drilled down to what he knew about a Multima team and what they were doing in Chile. Instead of calling him back, Fidelia made another mental note for her talk with Luigi.

Klaudia returned with a chilled bottle of water, condensation already forming on the plastic, as Fidelia set down her phone. She told Klaudia to call in Aretta and then take a seat. They had work to do. Her rapid-fire commands left no room for discussion.

"Aretta, get a car and two bodyguards around to the front right away." Fidelia paused while the Australian woman picked up a phone to follow orders. She looked over at Klaudia and continued her instructions.

"I need you to leave right away for Chile. There's stuff going on there that might jeopardize our scheme." Fidelia looked deeply into the woman's eyes, searching for any hint of fear or hesitation. She found none but added assurances anyway. "You won't be in any danger. Luigi and his team will meet you and get you direct access to our servers there."

Klaudia nodded her understanding. Still, there should be a back-up, just in case.

"Take Suzy with you. You'll have a lot of entries to handle and she seems very capable. I'd prefer to have her here, but there's no choice. We'll have to talk by phone as you travel and after you get in."

Fidelia switched her attention to Aretta and stood up as she talked to signal urgency.

"Leave right now. Rent a jet to get Klaudia and Suzy off to Valparaíso today. Make the calls after you're well clear of here, but travel directly to the airport and put these ladies on a plane. Deduct the expense from this month's remittance. Now get out of here quickly. Both of you."

She took a sip of water, picked up her encrypted phone, and hit the speed dial for Luigi. As she waited for the rings, she glanced at her watch. One in the morning in New York. Too bad. Luigi needed to find a jet and head to South America at once. Before he answered, there was a loud knock at the door of the den, and one of the security guys popped his head inside the door.

"The outer perimeter just called. Two police cars en route at high speed. Both unmarked. We have three minutes before they're here."

"Stay awake, Luigi. I'll call you back as soon as I can."

FORTY-THREE

Montreal, Quebec, Wednesday March 11, 2020

The Toronto Stock Exchange wouldn't budge, so they had no reason to stay in Toronto after the board of directors' call. Suzanne's team traipsed back across the moving walkway in the tunnel under Lake Ontario to Billy Bishop Airport. Late Tuesday evening they arrived back in Montreal.

Dejected, Suzanne suggested they each arrange a late-night meal on their own and reconvene in her suite in the morning for breakfast. Within minutes of arrival, she opted for bed. She slept well despite the challenges and awoke rested for her early morning run.

It was colder in Montreal. There was snow on the ground, and the wind continued to howl, but Suzanne and her bodyguards managed five miles in the streets surrounding Le Centre Sheraton and out past Le Stade Olympique. A gigantic shell, the stadium was open in the center and featured a massive, inclining mast that hung over one end of the seating area. Love it or hate it, the landmark had dominated Montreal's downtown east-end since the 1976 Games.

Suzanne liked it. She always marveled at how the island-city had blended new, innovative building designs with centuries-old enclaves in Vieux Montréal. She always felt a vibrancy and energy in the city and ended her run refreshed, her spirit rejuvenated.

As she stepped out of the elevator to her floor at the hotel, a butler greeted her with a welcoming smile, handed her an envelope, and offered to bring a mug of coffee to her suite.

Before she changed her running outerwear, Suzanne tore open the envelope. It was a message from James Fitzgerald. Could she please call him urgently? Suzanne hit the speed dial button, and James answered on the first ring.

"We've made some progress. Do you have a few minutes now to discuss what Angela found?" James's usual soft-spoken tone was elevated and he almost spit out the words.

"I'll probably be briefly interrupted with the arrival of my first coffee of the morning. Other than that, fire away."

"Angela spent yesterday online and in conversations with a couple resources she cultivated in South America. I'll let her explain it."

"We may be closer to tracking down our mysterious Manuel Ortez. We were headed down the wrong path before. We based all our assumptions on a premise that Ortez was Chilean because of his mother in Valparaíso. We got a clear picture of his face in the security video and tried to track him down in both Uruguay and Chile using that name. That's why we came up blank everywhere."

Suzanne played a mock piano concerto with the fingers of her left hand on the large dining room table, and her toes tapped nervously on the floor. She wished the woman would get to the point, but said nothing. A moment later, Angela continued her narrative.

"It seems Señor Ortez also has another identity—one he uses much more often and more broadly. We think Manuel Ortez is also an Argentinian citizen named Juan Álvarez. One of my contacts in Colombia came up with a match of his photo from a check-in to a hotel in Medellín."

"Have you been able to confirm that?"

"Not yet," James replied. "It sure looks like the same person, but we sent the file over to Dan Ramirez. He's going to get the FBI to run it through their facial recognition software. One curious thing: her guy may have slipped up using his passport in Medellín. Dan Ramirez found it curious he used a passport instead of an Argentinian Identity Card. That's apparently what most South Americans use for travel within Latin America."

"Coffee's here, just be a minute." Grateful for the interruption, Suzanne processed the information while she answered the doorbell. Despite James's and Angela's obvious enthusiasm, were they now headed off on another fruitless mission?

"Sorry, about that. You mentioned a hotel in Colombia. Have these passport records shown up anywhere else?" Suzanne wanted to know as they resumed.

"That's what's so encouraging." It was Angela again and her tone was more emphatic. "Yeah. I shared the file with a resource we've been working with in Buenos Aires. I can't tell you how, but she was able to hack a server at the National Registry for People. I know it sounds weird, but that's its name. But I digress. The important bit of information here is that she couldn't find a record of any passport for any Juan Álvarez. It's a fake."

"And why is that information encouraging?" Suzanne was losing her patience and reflected it in a tone that was not only skeptical but also a touch sarcastic. She softened her comment at once. "It seems to me a fake passport is problematic. No?"

"Under usual circumstances, that would be the case." Angela continued, unfazed. "But this must be a very good forgery because Juan Álvarez has used it in several countries. We got lucky. Not only was he careless, but someone in that hotel in Medellín was unusually thorough. Instead of copying only the first page—with the basic identification details—the hotel clerk scanned all the inside pages too. Twelve of them. That's where the entry and exit stamps of other countries appear."

Angela paused for breath and James Fitzgerald took over.

"You'll be surprised where he's been during the past five years. Malta, Cyprus, Macau, Monaco, Russia, and he lived for a year in Uzbekistan. None of those places are popular South American tourist spots. Dan Ramirez thought the travel destinations might be the most important clue about the guy."

"I see. That connects obliquely to your theory that Manuel Ortez is the son of a Russian father. The other places are all popular places to hide money. But how does Uzbekistan fit into the equation?" Suzanne tried to sound more interested and engaged, with more empathy for the pair's enthusiasm.

"We haven't figured that part out yet," Angela replied. "But we will."

"So, all we can do is wait for the FBI to confirm the identity? What then?"

"Dan Ramirez has already talked to the Argentinian national police. He has a connection there from his days with the FBI. His contact agreed to try to locate Juan Álvarez and invite him in for a chat."

"Okay. Good work." Suzanne managed slightly more enthusiasm as she brought the call to an end. "Keep me posted on developments."

"Angela has one more bit of information you might want to be aware we're working on," James interjected before she could leave the line.

"Yeah. We're still trying to figure out precisely what it means, but it seems important. Late last night, I got a text from one of the bank managers we met in Valparaíso. Two of the mysterious bank accounts that received Multima funds fraudulently showed activity again over the past couple days. Each account received relatively small sums, one Monday and the other yesterday. Neither transfer related to Multima. But here's the strange thing this woman noticed: The amounts were not immediately transferred out again like all the other times. The funds are still sitting in those accounts."

"We're sure the funds didn't originate with us?" Suzanne wanted to confirm. It was James who answered.

"Yes. We're sure. Whether the bank manager was supposed to see the source or not, she saw the amounts were converted from Singaporean dollars coming from an online brokerage in Singapore."

"Is there any significance to either fact?"

"We're not sure," James continued. "The bank manager drew both to our attention. She thinks there might good reason to dig deeper. The bank account is in US dollars, and she checked. This was the first time any currency other than dollars was deposited and the first time there was a marker naming the original source of the funds. All the other transfers were cleansed of any ID except that of the transmitting bank."

Suzanne remained silent. Why would a brokerage from Singapore transfer funds to a bank account in Chile? Twice?

Angela filled the silence. "Our current supposition is that someone is about to initiate a new type of fraud from another part of the world. These transfers were probably tests. But we can't be sure."

"How does this information help our situation?"

"Now that the bank manager is aware of unusual activity in the accounts, she can bubble it up to Chilean authorities," Angela said. "She already did that yesterday. There's now around-the-clock digital monitoring on the accounts. Every transfer out will carry a digital marker that traces where the funds ultimately end up in real-time."

"We may be able to see exactly in whose account the funds end up," Suzanne whispered almost reverently. "Impressive. Both of you. Your diligence has been nothing short of remarkable and I don't have the words to tell you how much I appreciate it."

Her voice broke involuntarily for just a second.

"Thanks, Suzanne. We're not there yet. But I think we will be soon," James replied in his trademark soft tone.

Were they finally edging toward resolution?

By the time she finished dressing for the office, she had already caught new banners and audio reports from CBNN on the TV monitor in the background. Global stock markets had started the day underperforming due to the spreading pandemic. New York was expected to open lower and another day of market turbulence was likely. VIX, the volatility index, was now at the highest level in nine years—a certain predictor of future turmoil. Suzanne called Wilma in Florida.

"I see the VIX is up again. Are we getting close to pulling the trigger to begin buying back shares?"

"It looks like it. Surprisingly, our shares are holding up well so far. I think people realize we're going to post great results with all the panic buying in our supermarkets. They may be nervous about some businesses, but we look safe at the moment. The only reason for a drastic, immediate downturn would be some unforeseen news that blindsides us."

Within an hour, CBNN broadcast the bad news. Suzanne saw the bright red banner crossing the TV screen in her Montreal office.

FBI AGAIN ISSUES WARRANT FOR MISSING MULTIMA CORPORATION CEO REPORTEDLY HIDING OUT IN CANADA.

She blanched, her stomach churned, and her heart sank. It was the worst possible time for bad publicity. Beverly Vonderhausen came on the phone only moments later.

"I have no idea what's going on!" Her wavering voice suggested she was close to tears from anger and frustration. "Your assistant already told them exactly where you are, and when she expects you to return to the US. I can't believe they're doing this to you again."

"Dan Ramirez heard from his contacts at the FBI that they were under more pressure to arrest me, but he never suggested they planned to go public," Suzanne complained.

"It's bizarre. Has anyone from any of the Canadian law enforcement agencies contacted you there?"

"No one. I was in Toronto for a couple days, but there were no calls to the office here, nor any messages left at the hotel. Who do you think is behind this?" Suzanne almost pleaded.

"I'll make a few calls. See what I can find. I'm so sorry this has happened, Suzanne, but I still think you're better off staying there if you can. Something truly underhanded is going on with your case in our system of justice."

Dan Ramirez phoned later that morning with expressions of regret. He was shocked and humbled. "These are guys I worked with for over thirty years at the FBI. We know each other. I've never been betrayed like this before, and I'm at a loss for words. What they're doing is wrong—and they know it."

"Believe me, I understand your angst, but we'll all have to tread carefully over the next few days. Beverly thinks I should stay here until they force me back. What do you think?"

"I understand why she recommends it, but you'll need to make the call. I'm guessing if you come back, they're going to keep you inside for at least a few days. Risk of flight and all that stuff. Canada has an extradition treaty with us though. The authorities there may have to send you back if the US courts require it."

"You're up-to-date on the developments with James and Angela?"

"Yeah. They called me right after they spoke with you."

"It seems the best possible way out is to stay close to the Chilean authorities watching those accounts in Valparaíso. Would you agree?" Suzanne needed reassurance.

"One hundred percent. I'm on it personally. Don't worry, we'll sort this out."

"Do you have any resources on the ground in Valparaíso? Or are we relying on your Chilean contacts entirely?" Suzanne's inquisitive tone was designed to plant a seed of doubt.

"Right now, all our people are back here." Dan paused a second to consider her questions. "You think I should send people back down?"

"You always know what's best in these situations, and I'll follow your lead. Call it intuition—or just a weird feeling—but I sense something might be developing there again. It might be a coincidence, but I wonder if Angela's information about new activity on those mysterious bank accounts might be a harbinger of some new undertaking."

"Yes. I see your concern. If I rely entirely on the Chilean authorities, they might bypass us for any number of reasons. Maybe we should get a couple Spanish-speaking people down there tonight."

"Since your contacts at the FBI are feeling a little uncomfortable about the way the Justice Department is treating me, might they feel rogue enough to send their people down with yours?" Suzanne smiled as she used the rogue cop reference. She often teased Dan about his mysterious connections from a former life.

"Can I use a Multima jet? They won't want to bubble up a travel request for approval."

"Done. Set it up with Eileen."

Suzanne shut off her phone and instructed the receptionist for the new Canadian headquarters to hold all calls. Next, she hit the speed dial and spoke with Alberto Ferer for over two hours. They examined every one of the many moving parts from a legal perspective.

Then they dragged in Edward Hadley, who had been monitoring media reports all day. He painted a picture of reputation damage and potential customer loss of confidence using brilliant descriptions and colorful language. His normally demure manner became assertive, and his final recommendation was delivered almost as a demand rather than counsel.

"I don't see any way to get this image catastrophe under control without a great media interview—the best interview of your life."

Suzanne opened the videoconferencing app on her laptop, switched to the TV monitor on the wall, and tracked down James Fitzgerald, seeking his advice.

"You already know where I stand, Suzanne. I recommended it the last time, when the legal folks objected. I recommend it again. No one can quell the storm but you, and I've no doubt you can do it."

The final party to join the damage control meeting was Beverly. Suzanne outlined the consensus. She needed to schedule an interview with CBNN as soon as possible.

"I get it. I won't try to persuade you not to do it. Let's spend a couple hours now. You, Alberto, and me. We'll give you the best legal preparation for the interview we can. The delivery will all be up to you."

Edward Hadley dashed out of the room, determined to have Suzanne sitting for an interview during the crucial eight o'clock morning hour with Liara Furtamo. She was the toughest interviewer in the business world. But only a brilliant interview with her could change the negative tide of investors' opinions forming around the bad news.

FORTY-FOUR

Sydney, Australia, Wednesday March 11, 2020

Howard was the first to jump when Fidelia shouted out the word "police" that afternoon. The outer perimeter security called to warn police were en route—and would arrive at Oliver Williams's former house in about three minutes. Following his example, the entire group leaped into action. A day earlier, Fidelia had not only outlined everyone's role in such an event, she'd forced everyone to run through practice drills. Twice.

Before the call, Aretta, Klaudia, and Suzy had already grabbed their laptops and dashed out the front door. Their car pulled away immediately after.

Howard scooped both his laptop and Wendal's under his arm, and dashed for the back door. In his peripheral vision, Fidelia jammed her iPad into her bag and ran. She was already ahead of him by a dozen steps. A bodyguard had the Asian guy's computer under one arm and was breathing heavily only a step or two behind Howard.

He didn't look back but expected the Asian guy from Singapore, the two local bodyguards, and Wendal were rushing about inside as instructed, opening bottles of wine and beer, pouring snacks into bowls, turning on a television, and making themselves look like a few friends casually relaxing around a living room on a Wednesday evening.

Fidelia jumped into the rear seat of a small SUV parked just outside the kitchen door, with one bodyguard joining her from the other side. Howard took his assigned spot in the front seat next to the driver and hadn't closed the door completely when they lurched across a small green space and raced toward a narrow track in a densely wooded area behind the mansion. Howard wasn't sure the vehicle could actually squeeze between the large trees on either side of a gap they hurtled toward. For safekeeping, he nervously secured his seatbelt and tucked the computers on the floor.

The bodyguard driver was masterful and guided the vehicle through the narrow tree-lined opening with inches to spare. With some effort, he also kept the small vehicle upright as it fishtailed along a dirt path with dips and bumps, throwing up behind it sand, stones, and an assortment of unlucky weeds and tree branches.

In the first two hundred yards, Howard's head banged against the inside roof of the SUV twice, and Fidelia clutched his shoulders from the back seat to cushion her forward thrust during an erratic stop at a protruding rock. At a temporary low speed, the four-wheel-drive SUV crawled up and over the obstacle with ease.

Their ride through the woods lasted about ten minutes before they emerged from the wooded area to join a paved two-lane highway with limited traffic. The bodyguard riding in the back seat used a burner phone to let his colleagues know their progress by time and landmarks. Only a few miles down the road, the SUV jerked off the highway with a thud as it plunged downward through a drainage ditch, then darted toward a helicopter parked about a hundred yards off the highway.

Rotors were already whirling. One pilot reached down with an outstretched arm to help Fidelia, then Howard, up and into their seats. Before their seatbelts were buckled, the helicopter left the ground, swaying from side to side as wind currents jostled them gently through a vertical ascent.

Inside, it was too loud for any conversation, but Fidelia mouthed that their ride would take about an hour as she held a single finger up. They headed in a southerly direction. Howard saw the Pacific Ocean out his window to the left for much of the flight, and it was only after they passed over a coastal town about forty-five minutes away from Sydney that the pilots veered gently to the right and headed inland.

Fidelia's forecast proved correct as Howard felt the tug of descent almost precisely when she predicted. Minutes later their pilot maneuvered the aircraft down into a field covered with brown grass, next to a much larger SUV with a driver and yet another bodyguard watching their landing.

Howard and Fidelia sat in the new vehicle's rear seat with their collection of computing devices and their security detail in front. That ride was considerably more comfortable and less adventurous than the trek through the woods.

As soon as they were in motion, Fidelia hit a speed dial number on her phone and said hello to Aretta, before she switched the phone to speaker mode. The Australian and her companions had successfully evaded the incoming police detail. Bodyguards had warned them to duck low in their seats as police cars sped past, showing no suspicion.

Their private jet was preparing for takeoff to Chile as they spoke.

Fidelia hit the speed dial for the burner she left with Wendal. From the speakerphone, Howard heard only "I'll have to call you back" before a silent click of disconnect.

"The police must still be there. We're only about a half-hour drive from our final destination. It's a house The Organization uses as a getaway location for johns on a budget. One of Aretta's innovations— affordable weekend packages with women and secluded accommodation all included in one bargain price." Fidelia snickered mockingly at her categorization of its purpose.

"We'll have Internet and good telephone connections there?"

"First class. We'll stay there for the duration. We can't risk the Aussie police acting on an Interpol Red Notice for your arrest at this stage, can we?"

"The others will join us?" Howard wanted to know.

"I hope so. I'll have to check with Wendal later to be sure there were no complications. If all's clear, the fellows outside Williams's house will bring Wendal and the guy from Singapore down. Hopefully, we'll have everyone here in the morning."

Once they were settled into the temporary new accommodations, Fidelia contacted Luigi again and Howard overheard her instructions. Luigi was to borrow the usual private jet and head for Valparaíso, with a stop in San Francisco to pick up a gal Klaudia Schäffer had used to help track down a mysterious IP address in Chile. It would delay his arrival by a couple hours, but Klaudia considered the woman crucial to their mission.

In Valparaíso, Luigi was to meet Klaudia and Suzy at the airport and get them all to a safe hotel with high-speed internet access. There, she wanted Luigi to take control of the Latin American servers with the help of Klaudia, Suzy, and the gal from Silicon Valley. He was to use whatever means necessary to carry out the task. Howard listened in from time to time as their detailed planning stretched more than an hour.

Remarkably, Fidelia curled up on a sofa, laid her head against a puffy cushion, and fell asleep within moments of saying goodbye to Luigi.

"Did you sleep?" She moaned in greeting as she woke up a few hours later and stretched from her curled position on the sofa.

"Not well. A little too much excitement for an old fellow like me." He grinned as he said it, and Fidelia responded with her teeth flashing brightly. Her smile was warmer than he had seen since their first meet-up in Singapore. This morning she appeared rested and ready for whatever the day might bring.

"I need to call Juan Álvarez again." She looked at her watch and frowned at the time. "Will you be a sweetheart and make me whatever you're drinking while I call?"

Moments later, Howard looked over from the kitchen to see Fidelia seated at a table with her phone on speaker. Her posture was upright; she was in deep concentration. Her voice sounded cheerful and relaxed as she spoke with Juan. She used the first minute or two for typical small talk and casual interaction, then switched to business with a natural and unhurried pace.

"You'll need to avoid any activity on the accounts tomorrow. We're going to buy some Multima shares. The algorithms will start in France—just like last time. But we'll buy much more. We're not sure, but as we hit purchase limits, we may need to flow some funds from Macau to the brokerage in Paris through Valparaíso. We can't afford any mix-ups, so it's best for your people just to take a day off and let us manage the accounts from Singapore. Sit tight there at Hotel Casa Higueras."

Howard noticed Fidelia's intentional deception about their location and raised his eyebrows in curiosity.

"Sure." Juan's voice enthused after he listened to her instructions. "I'll be here and keep all channels clear. If you get control, we'll have all the business we can handle, right?"

Juan laughed after his comment, and Fidelia humored him with more small talk for only a moment. As usual, she cut off the call when she finished.

"You're running just the Paris algorithms today, right?" Howard asked nonchalantly.

"Let's see. Unless we get Wendal here and set up, we might not be able to test anything. But assuming they arrive this morning, he should have enough time to launch the program before the Paris stock exchange opens."

Fidelia's tone and manner seemed peculiarly unconcerned. He tested her resolve again.

"I wouldn't be at all surprised to see the markets plummet today. I sense a real panic forming. Are you ready to put it all on the line?"

"I'm ready to begin drawing vermin out of the woodwork. We'll soon see how much we'll need to put out."

Howard found her answer to be an odd one. His puzzled expression implied a more precise question might be which vermin was about to become her next victim? There was little doubt he'd find out soon.

FORTY-FIVE

Suzanne had been sleeping soundly, and it took a few seconds to realize she was listening to the voice of Howard Knight when she answered her private cell phone about one o'clock in the morning.

"Don't be alarmed by either the volume of trades or pressure on price you'll see today in Paris and later in New York. I know it's a big ask at this point, but you need to trust me."

"Why?"

"This has nothing to do with Mareno. He's dead. Temporarily, I'm working for a person who has a different score to settle. As a condition for helping this person, I got their commitment to not materially harm Multima. What we're doing might even help you in the longer term."

"Again, why?"

"I'm finished with The Organization. What they did to you before was wrong. I get that. And I see this as an opportunity to at least make some small amends while my current master accomplishes their goals."

"Who is your current master?" Suzanne had noted Howard's uncharacteristic use of neutral pronouns.

"I can't tell you that. Here's what I will tell you. There will be pressure on the price of Multima shares all day today. Don't worry. The combined entities won't buy enough to challenge your control. Tomorrow, you might even see a slight recovery. Next week will get worse. We'll run the price down to about $33."

"Why?"

"That's your signal to begin buying Multima shares for your personal account. We know you have a million dollars set aside for that purpose. Do it. But pay a dollar or two premium to boost the price. Cooperate, and your problems with the US government and ECB go away. Fail to act precisely as I've described and a little-known financial analyst from a little-known firm in Pennsylvania will become a momentary national celebrity again as he trashes Multima until your shares plummet into the teens."

Suzanne became speechless as her entire body froze, almost paralyzed with fear.

"Why are you doing this, Howard?" she gasped.

"We also know you got board authorization for up to $5 billion. It's there on the SEC website. So, be sure your CFO spends those big dollars to buy back your shares at generous values, or you'll still get to watch that financial analyst do his dirty work on CBNN."

Suzanne regained her composure but said nothing as she processed his threats. Then he added his clincher.

"The market's going to like the buyback. Prices will recover quickly. You'll solidify your hold on the company. Understand, we'll be dumping all our shares as the price moves up. My master promises no further harassment after that. Your nightmare finishes."

"As you said at the beginning, it's a big ask. Why should I trust you now?"

"My master accomplishes their goal whether you cooperate or not. If you don't follow my instructions, it just takes a little longer, and they have lots of patience. They might even become enamored with the company and want to become a partner again." Howard kept his tone even, but subtly emphasized the word partner to be sure he had her attention. Then he waited.

"And if I cooperate, your master settles his or her score with more impact?" Howard didn't react to her bait and continued waiting for a reply.

"I'll think about it," Suzanne conceded.

"Have fun with your interview later this morning. I know you'll do great and we'll be watching," he said and hung up.

She couldn't sleep after Howard's call as she weighed his threats and the alternatives.

About four, she called Jasmine and canceled the morning run. It wasn't so much the angst she felt about her dilemma. Rather, it was the anticipated tsunami of activity until seven o'clock that morning. A live interview with CBNN was set for 8:03 a.m.

She had emails, breakfast and morning rituals out of the way by six, when her bodyguard Jasmine announced the hairstylist had arrived and was waiting outside the door of their suite at Le Centre Sheraton. They had been lucky to find her, and the woman did both hair and make-up. Fortunately, she also owned a popular shop on nearby Sherbrooke street and had agreed to squeeze in an appointment to prepare Suzanne for her TV interview. She'd worked with plenty of celebrities and knew instinctively the steps she should take to portray her subject most favorably under the harsh glare of studio lights.

While the stylist performed her magic, Suzanne studied her prep notes for the umpteenth time. Edward Hadley had prepared pages of hypothetical questions Liara Furtamo might raise during the interview. For the entire prior evening, he had peppered her with questions. A master communicator, he adopted Furtamo's trademark style, asking tough questions in the nicest possible way and often setting a potentially devastating trap.

Alberto and Beverly Vonderhausen sat in for the full session and interrupted whenever they heard an answer that might become legally troublesome. Edward suggested more positive spins she might consider, projecting most favorably with CBNN's influential business and investor viewers around the globe. They videotaped her responses to highlight body language pitfalls and accent her best features. Together, they trimmed and shaped her responses to emphasize clarity and avoid mistakes. It continued until about midnight when everyone considered her adequately prepared.

This morning's review of questions and answers served only as a refresher so she could access—without hesitation—the optimum responses, tone, and mannerisms. Suzanne felt prepared and confident but knew that could easily evaporate. The little red light on the TV camera would instantly remind her several million people were dissecting every word she used and might make decisions that could shift hundreds of millions of dollars one way or another.

Jasmine announced the arrival of the car to drive them to the studios just as the stylist-makeup artist put the final touch of mascara on her naturally long eyelashes. Suzanne was delighted with the result and passed four hundred Canadian dollars to the woman in appreciation for the early start and superb workmanship.

Before leaving the suite, Suzanne took time for one last look in the full-length mirror. Edward recommended she wear a navy-blue suit. She smiled into the mirror as she recalled how he rhymed off his list of reasons during their preparation session.

"Navy blue elicits a positive response from most TV viewers. It implies authority, confidence, trust, honesty, reliability, and credibility," he'd insisted, pumping his fist in the air.

She brought one with her whenever she traveled. Navy blue was versatile. As she loosely knotted a contrasting pale blue scarf around her neck to add a more feminine touch, she nodded to herself. She looked good. Navy blue highlighted her new blonde hair color, and the skirt's length showed just enough thigh to satisfy the CBNN viewing audience. Furtamo's skirt would surely slide even higher.

The drive from Le Centre Sheraton to the studios for local French-language network NTV usually required between twenty and thirty minutes at that time of the morning. Edward Hadley asked them to allow longer. CBNN contracted with the local TV studio and always liked to have at least a thirty-minute cushion before the actual interview. Suzanne used the short travel time to catch up on emails and text instructions to Eileen back in Fort Myers.

One message in her inbox caught her eye, from two hours earlier, marked "urgent" and with a subject line all in uppercase.

RUN ON FAREFOUR AGAIN. CALL ME PLEASE.

She called James.

"We've got problems over in Paris with our Farefour subsidiary. It looks like algorithms are running down the price of our shares again, but it's hard to tell for sure." His tone was calm but somber. "All the Asian and European markets are getting scalped today."

"What's the damage so far?" Suzanne asked.

"It's a little after three in the afternoon over there, so they have about two-and-a-half hours of trading left. Volume for the day is already about twice as much as usual and the share price is down more than twenty percent."

"You said the market's down. How does our twenty percent compare with the overall market?"

"We're down about double the EuroNext index. It's off about ten percent but will probably go lower. No reason for panic, but I wanted you to be aware before you did the interview. It might come up."

When Suzanne and her entourage arrived at the NTV studios, two technicians greeted them with typical Quebecois charm and good cheer. They were surprised, then delighted, to learn she spoke French and chatted amiably as they guided her into the studio and positioned her before a couple cameras.

Suzanne was accustomed to the preparation needed and carried on chatting as they clipped a tiny microphone to her jacket and tested for sound. Multiple variations of lighting followed until the director in the soundproof room off to the side gave her a thumbs up. About five minutes before the live interview was set to begin, Liara Furtamo's face appeared on the monitor. She was in CBNN's New York studio with technicians bustling about her in preparation.

When Liara saw Suzanne's image appear on her monitor, she waved a friendly hello with her smile dialed up to maximum charm. A neutral observer might think they were best of friends reuniting for a night on the town.

A voice connection was established only a moment before the interview started. Edward Hadley once told Suzanne they did that with satellite feeds to save cost. Transmission of sound and image was considerably more expensive than images alone. Even the big TV networks needed to find ways to trim costs these days.

With her big brown eyes looking directly into a camera and a megawatt smile fully engaged, Liara Furtamo wasted no time.

"Tell me, Suzanne Simpson. Why are you hiding out in Canada?"

Damn, Hadley is good. First question—just like he predicted!

"I'm not hiding out. The FBI has known I'm on a business trip to Canada since they visited my office in Fort Myers last week and spoke with my executive assistant. She told them I'm in Montreal on a recruiting mission for our new headquarters and gave them the office phone number here and the number for the hotel where I'm staying. They asked her to relay a request that I meet with them when I return. I have no record of an attempt to contact me."

"Then, why is the Department of Justice treating you like a fugitive?"

"You'll need to ask them that question. As you may know, the FBI quite publicly arrested three of us a few weeks ago, then dropped all charges two days later. We also find that very curious. After all, Multima has been the victim of a fraud. Our internal security people have traced the fraudulent transactions to an individual in South America. Why is the FBI not pressing the authorities in Chile to apprehend and arrest that person?"

Suzanne took care to look directly into the camera and show measured defiance.

"That might be a good question for the police, but we don't have them here. So, when do you plan to return to the United States to defend your position?"

"I'll return when my work here is finished. Quite frankly, a public arrest followed immediately by dropped charges, then rumors and innuendo leaked anonymously to the media about an arrest, don't give me a lot of faith our system of justice is behaving the way it was intended. Remember, Montreal is now the global headquarters for

Multima. Whether I'm here or in Fort Myers, I can perform my job for shareholders equally well."

Suzanne softened her tone and smiled confidently as she waited for the next question. The camera had zoomed in tightly on her face as she answered. Now, the monitor showed a split screen as Liara mentally wound up for her next attack.

"Prices for shares in your subsidiary, Farefour in Europe, are down almost twenty percent this morning. Some analysts suggest that's due to your legal problems. Are you serving your shareholders well by quarreling with the Justice Department?

"I'm not sure quarreling is a term I'd use. Neither the FBI nor the Justice Department has made any effort to contact me. If they were to call, I'd strongly request they follow-up on the leads our security people have given them. Criminals are stealing money from our shareholders, and we're working hard to track them down and bring them to justice. Let me also reassure Multima shareholders that we will do all we can to support the value of their holdings. I can tell you we advised the SEC a few days ago that our board of directors has authorized spending up to five billion dollars to buy back outstanding shares in Multima Corporation. We'll do that at the right time and pay market prices for the shares we buy."

"As its CEO, would you buy more shares in your company right now?"

Suzanne looked directly into the camera again. She needed to say this without blinking.

"I would certainly do that. I have every confidence in the future of Multima Corporation."

"Changing direction, how is your company performing in the marketplace right now?"

"Our last quarterly guidance was in early January before the pandemic hit. In Financial Services we don't expect to see much variation to finance volumes and profits we projected back then unless it becomes necessary to significantly shut down the economy as they've done in China."

Suzanne paused a second, her eyebrows arched slightly, to give time for the seriousness of that comment to register.

"On the Supermarkets side of the business, you've undoubtedly heard about panic buying in some areas. Our sales volumes for the current quarter will be up dramatically. The gross margin dollars we generate will be up too. But we're also incurring unprecedented increases in expenses. Labor costs, refitting stores with plexiglass, and other protective measures will probably offset many of those gains. We're expecting net profits to be only slightly higher, if at all."

"Won't shareholders be upset that you haven't effectively controlled costs and kept expenses under control? Especially when they consider the extra fifty million you've lost due to inadequate controls on your payments to foreign bank accounts."

There it was! Someone had fed Liara information Suzanne hadn't disclosed to anyone outside the company except the FBI. How she handled the question would be crucial. She chose to deal with the first part while she formulated a response for the second and pursed her lips slightly for emphasis.

"The two most valuable assets Multima has are its customers and employees. We make no apology for spending money to protect those assets. No expenses were made frivolously, and management approved and tightly monitored all necessary expenses."

Again, Suzanne paused to let her message and conviction set in.

"The precise amount involved in the purchasing fraud we encountered has not yet been determined. The total amount stolen from us is still under investigation, but I want to assure our shareholders that we have insurance against theft and fraud, and we expect to recover any amounts attributed to fraudulent payments to fake foreign suppliers."

Liara nodded with only a flicker of a smile to concede Suzanne had reframed her loaded question skillfully. Then she tried again.

"My producer got a message this morning from someone in the White House. That person implied you might know something about the suspicious deaths of two Multima employees during the past two weeks."

She let the statement hang there and waited. Suzanne fought to prevent her complexion from either blanching white in fear or flushing red with anger. They hadn't anticipated this question. She took three or four seconds to control her emotions and chose her words gingerly.

"Personally, I find it odd someone in the White House would comment on any Justice Department investigation. I thought everyone there took pains to keep the two very separate. Sadly, I have learned of two recent deaths, although I take exception to the term suspicious. One employee died in an unfortunate ski accident while on holiday in Canada. She was not an experienced skier and took a fall that proved fatal. Police in Canada say they see no reason to believe her death was anything but accidental."

Suzanne shook her head slowly as she spoke, then looked into the camera with more resolve.

"Our CFO also met a tragic end. I understand she fell from the balcony of her apartment a few nights ago. I also understand the police are investigating the circumstances. Our heartfelt thoughts are with the families, colleagues and friends of both women."

"Kind of suspicious though, when they both worked in the finance area of your company." Liara didn't wait for a response. Instead, she switched gears again. "Have you had any employees fall ill with the coronavirus?"

"Thankfully, not yet. However, should any employee test positive for COVID-19, we'll do everything possible to protect our customers and employees. We'll close affected locations and keep them closed until thorough, deep cleaning is complete. We're also asking our employees to wear masks now, even though health authorities say they're not required."

Before Suzanne could add anything further, Liara Furtamo flashed the alluring smile that her audience loved, thanked her, and signed off back to the main CBNN studio.

Edward Hadley and Albert Ferer both signaled enthusiastic thumbs-up approvals as the camera stopped recording and technicians swarmed toward Suzanne to clear the way for the next interviewees waiting their turn. A wave of relief washed down her body as she realized she had escaped the interview unscathed.

Back in the waiting SUV, Suzanne glanced at her watch: 8:32. The stock markets wouldn't open for official trading for another hour. Still, she scrolled to her phone's finance app to see how the futures trading responded to her interview. It was usually a good indicator of what would happen when the exchanges rang the bell to launch the day's trading.

In New York, it looked like Multima Corporation's shares would begin trading about seven percent lower than the day before. Then, to Paris. The full-day's results could well become worse—with Farefour Stores shares in Paris now trading over twenty percent lower than the day before.

FORTY-SIX

Sydney, Australia, Thursday March 12, 2020

Fidelia and Howard watched Suzanne Simpson's interview with CBNN in their new surroundings. After a few share prices from the Futures Market scrolled across the screen, Fidelia flicked the channel to a new network, then turned toward Howard.

"How did she do?"

"She did well. I liked the way she showed resolve and determination with the interviewer. Furtamo can be a tough one. Investors should be able to sense Suzanne's mettle and willingness to do battle if necessary. But we know it won't help her much in the short term, don't we?"

Fidelia didn't take her eyes off Howard as she digested his assessment. The tinge of sarcasm at the end was typical, and she took no offense. She changed the subject instead.

"I'll let Wendal sleep for another few hours, maybe until midnight. I don't want him making any mistakes when he starts to work."

Wendal and the Asian guy from Singapore had arrived only a couple hours earlier. He'd already set in motion the algorithms in Paris, but needed to sleep. The police investigation at Oliver Williams's former home took several hours to complete and created a lot of stress for the remaining occupants, although the *coppa* discovered nothing in the end.

After their arrival at the new location, and once the buying of Farefour shares was underway, they had celebrated the launch of their new venture with a modest takeout meal the bodyguards had picked up a few miles before the turnoff to their current secluded location. Then Fidelia had assigned bedrooms.

Unfortunately, Wendal still wore his ankle bracelet, so they had to assume police in Sydney knew where to find them. Fidelia and Aretta had already developed another escape plan in case the early-warning lookouts along the narrow highway detected any police presence.

"Have you heard from Luigi?" Howard stared off into space as he asked the question.

"Yeah. Luigi and his team got to Valparaíso a couple hours ago. They're scouting the Hotel Casa Higueras and figuring out how to get into his suite. It'll probably be another few hours before they begin." Fidelia still harbored an occasional doubt about Howard's commitment to her scheme, but had no regrets about him overhearing her instructions to Luigi the night before.

"How about Klaudia and Suzy?"

"They're still about an hour out of Chile. Their pilot had to go around some South Pacific storms, but Klaudia said they got some sleep and are ready to go on arrival." Howard listened but still stared off into space. Very uncharacteristic. "Do you want to get some sleep? You too were up most of the night. I can wake you when we begin buying."

Howard nodded and she pointed him toward a bedroom on the second floor, not the master. He shuffled off and made his way up the stairs. It was probably better he wasn't there for the next steps in the saga. If she found it necessary to modify their plan once the game started, she might also need to change the rules quickly. She had no intention of negotiating with him.

Fidelia shifted her attention to the television again where news of the spreading coronavirus dominated coverage on all the news channels. The World Health Organization had finally officially declared it a pandemic. Broadcasters adapted graphics similar to sports scoreboards to report developments. Over four thousand new cases yesterday, bringing the global total of people infected with the virus to more than 125,000. Almost three hundred new deaths yesterday, bringing the total deaths attributed to the disease to more than 4,500.

Another station carried red banners across the bottom of its screen, announcing that the US had now stopped all travel from Europe except the UK. Talking heads speculated that American authorities must think no one from Europe would consider traveling first to London and from there to the US. In loud voices that had become the norm for cable news networks, speaker after speaker sought to display his or her superior knowledge about the science of epidemiology, rarely listening for long to actual medical specialists.

In disgust Fidelia switched off the TV. She didn't have the gear for a run, but exercise was important. In her streetwear, she motioned for two bodyguards to walk alongside as she announced her departure. A scramble followed. Then the lead assigned by Luigi barked out Fidelia's orders.

"Grab an SUV and follow her. We need to be able to evacuate at a moment's notice."

One man left to carry out the command.

"Bring up another vehicle ready to take those inside."

Another man hurried from the room.

"Reposition the chopper monitoring the roads a bit further out."

The guy continued his orders as Fidelia moved out of earshot and picked up her pace for a two or three-mile walk. Speed was important. She wanted to get her heart rate elevated and adrenalin flowing. It was much more than a desire to keep her figure trim.

As a student at Colombia Law School, Fidelia came to realize her mind worked best when she exercised hard. Whether she was running or walking, her ideas flowed freely. Creativity seemed unlimited. Challenging problems found practical solutions.

Although her scheme was underway, she had yet to trigger the entire cycle. As she hiked along a country road at her quickest pace, she reviewed every piece in the puzzle. She visualized where each one fit. She thought about all the players—from Wendal sleeping in a bedroom nearby to Klaudia soon performing her magic in Chile.

Once more, Fidelia weighed the risks. Thought about every action that might go wrong. Considered alternative solutions to each identified risk. And then racked her brain for possibilities she hadn't considered. As she slowed her pace for the final few hundred yards on her return toward the secluded house, she switched her attention to Howard. He'd always been an enigma.

Even back when she thought she might be in love with the guy, she always harbored one niggling concern. How could someone with his intelligence make so many errors in judgment? It seemed that too often, despite his insight and analysis, he missed some tiny detail that turned magic into misfortune. His mistakes weren't always disasters, but they could be messy enough to fall short of a goal.

She could find only one element of her scheme that might inadvertently cause a hiccup. While Howard was considering her offer of freedom in exchange for advice, she let him extract only one concession. She'd resisted at first but eventually saw the merits in both his request and arguments. He'd insisted they pull off the heist without wreaking havoc on either Multima Corporation or Suzanne Simpson.

It was a noble sentiment. He felt guilty about the chaos he'd caused with Giancarlo Mareno and their repeated attempts to infiltrate—then control—the massive corporation. However, Fidelia didn't share Howard's softheartedness. Business was business, and sometimes there were unavoidable casualties.

She finally relented when she realized she ought to let him win something. After all, controlling an operating company wasn't part of her long-range plans. Hacking the systems of financial institutions was a far safer way to grow The Organization with far less work and risk. So she let him have that one. And that soppy concession was the only potential weak link in their elaborate scheme.

They'd do a test today, she decided. For the next few hours, she'd revisit her concession and see if she could prompt Wendal to tweak his app and let Multima orders for shares take priority over others. If they couldn't fix it, she'd have to break her commitment to Howard and let the market decide where the prices would go. At that point, his happiness would be of little consequence.

She'd give it just a few more days to decide.

FORTY-SEVEN

Valparaíso, Chile, Friday March 13, 2020

Luigi Fortissimo allowed himself a hint of a smile of admiration for the way Juan Álvarez crafted his protective cocoon. It took almost a full first day to identify all the muscle surrounding the head of The Organization's Latin American operations. Fidelia's chief of security recognized the basic protective structure because the guy learned it from people Luigi trained.

When Álvarez learned the fundamentals, he was too low in the pecking order for Luigi to train him directly. Instead, it was experts two or three levels below. Of course, over time the bright young fellow learned more twists and turns to protect his ass from associates and fellow partners in crime.

Luigi had met the guy a few years earlier. It was when Fidelia lobbied Giancarlo Mareno—his boss at the time—to promote Álvarez to run the prostitution business in Latin America. He did a security check on the South American that included a "personal interview." In The Organization, security checks weren't handled by online investigation or traditional interviews. Guys got their hands dirty.

In Álvarez's case, he killed the woman he had been sleeping with for two years. It was an honor killing. Luigi showed him a video of his sweetheart playing in bed with two of the guy's closest associates. The pictures were lewd and graphic. The girlfriend really seemed to enjoy her work. Of course, drugs helped feed that sexual appetite, but Álvarez never knew about that. All he saw was the damning video.

When Luigi asked what the guy was going to about it, there wasn't a moment's hesitation. He stormed out of the secluded warehouse where they'd met late that night and was gone for about thirty minutes. When he returned, he dragged his girlfriend from a car and violently threw her on the cement floor. Bruised and bleeding, bawling, and more terrified than any woman Luigi could ever recall seeing, Álvarez hoisted her from the floor and dragged her to Luigi's feet.

Politely, the guy asked Luigi to show her the video. The woman refused to watch. Álvarez grabbed her hair and forced her to look at the iPad screen Luigi held up for her to view. She screamed, cried, begged, pleaded for forgiveness, and promised never to do it again. Cruelly, her lover forced her to watch the entire twenty-minute video. Then he drew his weapon, pressed it against the side of her head, and pulled the trigger.

Álvarez let her body fall to the floor and wiped blood, brains, and gore from his face, arms and hands and turned to Luigi seeking approval. Luigi nodded.

"She wasn't alone in the video."

Young Álvarez looked startled at first, then understood the instruction. Said he'd be right back. Luigi had waited in the remote warehouse for less than an hour before another vehicle—an older model—returned and screeched to a halt at Luigi's feet. The young buck passed the test. He flung open the trunk of the car triumphantly and pointed to the two bloodied bodies of his former comrades in arms. Luigi simply nodded again.

Because of that interview, Luigi couldn't show his face around the hotel. Instead, he stayed in the rented vehicle and drank coffee while his cohorts circled the building multiple times. They all wore earpieces and their phone cameras were all the latest models. From time-to-time, one or another returned to the black SUV in the last crowded row of the parking lot and showed photos from a camera or sent video clips from a secure phone to Luigi's. They always spat out a few comments about their discoveries. Meanwhile Luigi made color-coded marks and circles on a floor plan of the hotel or on the charts and diagrams surrounding him on the rear seat.

The parade to and from the SUV continued throughout the afternoon and evening until they all broke for dinner at nine. It was about an hour's drive to a rented house in a village south of Valparaíso. Luigi forgot the name of the place, but it was perched high on a cliff overlooking the Pacific. When he and his team arrived, another group of six had prepared dinner, and they ate in shifts at the long table for eight.

They had pasta because the gang surrounding Luigi were all from New York. Most grew up in the same Italian neighborhood. They had all worked together for years. They knew each other's habits and movements as well as any crack navy seal team. And they all understood the importance of their mission and waited anxiously for Luigi to deliver the battle plan.

On a light-colored wall, Luigi displayed graphs, charts, and photos in a PowerPoint presentation. One his techies hastily threw it together in the rear of the SUV on the drive down. Every man had a role. Each had a defined target. Luigi talked and they listened. Each participant repeated his mission back to be sure nothing was missed. About eleven o'clock, Luigi ordered his men to get a couple hours of rest. He needed them alert and ready to perform at two in the morning.

Luigi himself didn't sleep. Instead, until one in the morning, he reviewed the entire plan with Fidelia—in almost the same detail as with the men themselves. She listened intently, asking questions every few minutes, double-checking his calculations, challenging his assumptions. He was prepared, and she sounded satisfied when he finished.

"Good work. You look ready. When do you attack?"

"We'll leave here at two. Arrive at the hotel by three—when bodyguards are always at their most vulnerable. Five minutes later we should be inside the suite. Ten minutes after that, we'll have Álvarez in the SUV, all the bodies in a truck, and the whole bunch leaving the parking lot. A little after four, we'll begin working on him. We should be able to have the information we need and your women working inside the server farm here by midmorning. Will you start buying today?"

"No, I've decided to wait a day or two. I want to be sure Klaudia gets what we need and it works as expected. There are a couple other loose ends too. Get your stuff done. We'll decide when we strike on the weekend."

Annoyingly, that's all Fidelia had to say. *We drag our asses all the way down here only to be treated like mushrooms—kept in the dark and fed shit.*

He slunk down in the dining room chair he'd used for the call and stretched out his legs. Álvarez was going to be a tough one, and Luigi relished a few minutes of quiet. Within hours, his adrenalin would be pumping. It was always that way during the attack. As they drove back, there'd be an emotional letdown and calm. Finally, he'd need to prepare for the guy's defiance, followed by screams for mercy and groans of excruciating pain.

Luigi never enjoyed the torture, but he always got the desired results.

He leaned his head back on the chair, closed his eyes for a moment's rest, and tried to relax. Thoughts of a coming weekend with Fidelia surged and ebbed across his mind in waves. His body tensed. Recalled images weren't quite as vivid and pleasurable as they once were. As great as she could be in bed, was she really worth the continual chase? Might it be better to be just the security guy?

He dozed for a few minutes before his phone alarm jarred him into action. Within moments, he alerted those closest to him that it was time to go and sent them to wake the others. The coffee-pot timers had done their jobs and two carafes brimmed with hot java to wake the gang up. Half asleep men lined up to fill the Styrofoam cups before they made their way to their assigned vehicles.

Travel to Hotel Casa Higueras at two in the morning was easy. Roads were deserted and Luigi noted they pulled into the hotel parking lot five minutes ahead of schedule. He gave the signal to start as soon as he saw the teams were all outside their vehicles.

Casually, the men spread out and walked unhurriedly in their separate directions. There were four side entrances to the complex, all monitored by video surveillance. Each camera was blocked with a hand-held device as a team approached. Plastic electronic cards—activated the previous day by a front-desk clerk for adequate compensation—all worked. Walkie-talkie messages confirmed four entries and neutralization of eight bodyguards.

Five minutes later, the lone security guard patrolling the hotel was disabled on the fourth floor as planned and his body dragged to a cleaning closet. Two minutes later, one-word codes confirmed each of the four teams waited in stairwells on opposite sides of the penthouse floor of the hotel near Juan Álvarez's suite, which had two bodyguards outside the door.

Sixty seconds later, a voice squawked into Luigi's ear. Two bodyguards had been overtaken and were no longer active. Their bodies were also stored in a vacant cleaner's closet. Almost three minutes after that, a voice confirmed two bodyguards inside the suite were neutralized and their subject was still sleeping. All under control.

Luigi signaled the drivers to start their engines and prepare to open doors. Forty seconds later, one man confirmed they'd moved the two unconscious bodyguards from a closet into the suite and the lock mechanism was disabled. As the first familiar heads popped out from entrances to the hotel, the drivers scurried around the SUVs opening all four doors and the rear storage compartments.

One huge team member carried a still body over his shoulder like a large burlap sack of potatoes. The others formed a protective circle around him as they walked quickly toward the parked vehicles in a remote corner of the dimly lit parking lot. Luigi dispassionately surveyed the action from the cover of a low-hanging tree as his guys executed maneuvers with military precision. He jumped into the front seat of his assigned vehicle last as all three SUVs accelerated from the parking lot.

Mission accomplished, he texted to Fidelia while they were still inside the city limits and had reliable cell service. *Headed back. Will begin in an hour.*

—·—

About a hundred yards behind the Hotel Casa Higueras parking lot stood a five-story apartment building. A day earlier, Carlos, the former Chilean police officer, had approached the tenant of a suite on a corner of the top floor of the building and offered the young woman ten thousand US dollars for a two-week rental. She was an artist who worked from home and paid about five hundred dollars a month for the place. It took only a few seconds for her to decide it was time to make a long-delayed visit to her parents in the countryside.

Dan Ramirez had been able to wrangle two FBI agents and added two members of Multima's crack security team. Carlos met them at the airport and helped them set up all their technology in the sublet apartment. Video cameras with powerful zoom lenses pointed out the windows. Recording devices monitored select conversations up to a half-mile away. Powerful laptop computers cluttered tables among old-fashioned devices like binoculars.

Carlos, and three members of the team, watched and listened to Luigi and his gang for the entire time they undertook their original reconnaissance to snatch Álvarez. The team upstairs had no idea who they were watching at first, but the guys were suspicious enough that they turned on all the equipment. When they overheard the name Álvarez in one conversation, their interest intensified.

They heard the guys report back to Luigi about Juan Álvarez's security detail—who they were and where they were positioned in the hotel. They even hacked photos of the bodyguards the men had transferred from their phones to Luigi. When the gang all left the hotel for their secluded retreat that first day, the team in the apartment knew as much about the target's security arrangements as Luigi himself.

What they didn't know was when some form of attack might occur. That's why everyone had slapped elated high-fives when the fourth member of the crack team returned after a shift in the bar of the Hotel Casa Higueras.

It had been Carlos's idea to get the gorgeous and engaging young woman from Miami inside the hotel as a plant. Midmorning, while events were just starting to unfold in the parking lot below them, Sophia Garcia left the apartment dressed appropriately to work in a bar. With her sparkling personality, she persuaded the manager of the hotel bar that she was a traveling student who had run out of money and needed a job for a few days until a wire transfer from her parents arrived.

Sales had been slow in the establishment with all the concern about the coronavirus. The manager was working the bar and serving tables alone that day. Sophia convinced him she had experience as a server and would work only for tips. Her appropriately low-cut top and short skirt also probably influenced the manager's decision. The fellow expected customers would reward her handsomely and boost his drink sales. No doubt her inviting manner also suggested she might reward him if he played his cards right.

She only needed work for a day or two, so he hired her on the spot and gave her five minutes of training before sending her off to the first table.

Of course, Sophia didn't tell her new temporary boss she was wearing a two-way communication device with a highly sensitive microphone concealed; nor that her long, curly black hair hid crystal-clear earpieces. The team in the apartment building could hear whispered questions and deliver answers or instructions with equal clarity.

Sophia had worked as a server through four years of college. She engaged customers easily and effectively, and served drinks with polish and charm. Within minutes, her new boss was busier than he'd been for days with customers seated and drinking at several tables scattered around the room.

Just after lunch, a lone male entered the bar, took a table in the farthest corner, and ordered a double vodka with tonic, tonic on the side. He was unusually tall, broad shouldered and looked like a football player out of uniform. Sophia was a fan of the Miami Dolphins, so she dubbed him Flipper and relayed that nickname and basic description to the guys in the apartment.

Sophia promptly delivered his order and engaged him in cheerful conversation, even flirting a bit. The fellow responded with broader grins, matching her wit and humor. She noticed his accent was closer to that of someone from Los Angeles than Chile, so she asked where he was from. His good humor changed abruptly. He told her it didn't matter, dismissing her with a casual flick of his hand.

While Sophia took orders from customers at another table, the team got back to her left ear. Flipper was part of the team they were watching.

He returned every few minutes to the one named Luigi, bringing photos and diagrams. He was the one she should try to tag.

As though on cue, Carlos also entered the bar, posing as a customer and wearing a hidden microphone. He took a table next to an open window where he had Flipper directly in his line of sight and a view of the garden outside.

After delivering an order of drinks to another table, Sophia still had a glass on her tray and stopped again at Flipper, who was transmitting files from his phone. She saw photos on the screen, but he was scrolling and transmitting too quickly for her to catch their contents. She set the glass on the table in front of him.

"This one's on the house." She leaned in enough to reveal cleavage almost to her nipples. Carlos watched the guy's eyes follow her motion.

"How come?" The guy reached for the full glass without hesitation. When Sophia stood straight again, his eyes lifted but only to the contours of her breasts.

"You look like my kind of guy." She giggled, smiled shyly, and leaned in toward him again. He reached out to touch her, and she stood straight and backed up a step.

"Now, now," she scolded him, mockingly. Playfully adopting the facial expressions of a schoolteacher, she wagged her forefinger. "Not when I'm working."

The fellow downed the glass of vodka again and hoisted himself out of the chair. He towered more than two feet above her. He tossed two twenties on the table and headed toward the door. Sophia gathered up his full bottle of tonic and scooted after him. Outside the bar, she called out. "Señor, you forgot something!"

Her smile was radiant and inviting as Flipper took a step back toward her, an outline of a smile forming. Sophia took a few steps toward him and reached out with the open bottle of tonic. She fluttered her eyelashes, tilted her chin downward, coyly crossed one leg in front of the other.

"Are you going to be around for a few days?"

"Maybe. You want to get together or something?"

"Yeah," she said. "I'd like that. Here's my number."

She scribbled it with a pen and a scrap of paper from her apron pocket and sidled up closer to him. With her left hand she held out the piece of paper for him and he leaned forward to take it from her. As she stretched upward on her toes to give him a kiss on his lowered cheek, she reached around and touched the middle of his back and suggestively drew her finger down the lower part of his spine. As Sophia's right hand touched the inside of his belt, she affixed a micro tracking device no larger than a dime.

"Don't forget to call." Her voice was husky and seductive. Flipper appeared quite entranced for a moment before he turned away.

Because of Sophia's masterful performance, when Luigi's contingent pulled away from the hotel parking lot with their victim before dawn, a large black SUV followed. Just as it had hours before. There was only one difference. On the first trip, there were only two in the tracking vehicle, and one of them remained behind, hidden in a densely wooded area near the house close to the ocean.

This time, there were four occupants in the trailing vehicle, and they monitored Luigi's team from a safe distance of more than half a mile to avoid detection. As the convoy raced southward in the darkness, the tracking device's signal in Flipper's belt guided Carlos and the team. Sophia compared their progress with a separate highly sensitive GPS monitor showing as much detail as the street view on Google Maps.

When Luigi's gang pulled up to the secluded home, the folks trailing them veered off to the side of the road and focused on every aspect of their quarry's arrival. The spy left behind in the woods the previous day counted and reported that twelve people plus one unconscious person got out of the vehicles. He reported each arrival headed in a different direction except the two who lugged the body inside.

When he finished his report Dan Ramirez's secret security team was confident they understood the details of the security perimeter. They knew the precise number of adversaries they faced. Carlos made an urgent call for instructions with an encrypted device.

FORTY-EIGHT

It was already mid-afternoon in eastern Australia when Fidelia got Luigi's confirmation of a successful snatch of Juan Álvarez. She cursed the loss of so many valuable security resources. The guys who ran countries or regions always surrounded themselves with the *crème de la crème*—their most elite and experienced. It would make the job of rebuilding the Latin American operations slower for the person she had in mind to replace the bastard. But she didn't dwell on it as she held her phone to her ear, pacing in circles under the only tree available for shade.

"Begin as soon as he's conscious," she ordered Luigi. Their phones were encrypted so no codes or delicate choice of words was needed. "I only need two pieces of information. Who is he working for? And what are the passwords? Keep him alive until we have both bits and Klaudia confirms the passwords get her in."

"Where is Klaudia? We never did meet up."

"I told them to stay on the jet overnight. The pilot assured me they'd be comfortable. He had auxiliary power to run the cooling system. They'll stay in Valparaíso while you do your work with Álvarez. Neither woman should know how you extract the info we need."

"How will I verify the passwords?"

"I'll text you her number when we're done. When it's light there, the pilots will get the women installed at a separate hotel with Internet access. It's all organized. No need for you to get involved. Just call her in a few hours to find out where she is and make sure she's ready. When you know where they are, get the woman you brought from San Francisco to join them. I want all three in the same room when we start."

"Will we buy today?" Luigi asked.

"Only a few shares—to test—if you can get Álvarez talking soon enough. You probably haven't heard, but global stock markets plunged yesterday. Everything. There was widespread selling of stocks at desperation prices. The media is already calling it Black Thursday. We lost a couple million from when we bought our shares. Howard Knight suggests we sit out today and see if there's any recovery before we strike."

Fidelia increased the volume on the TV. Howard had come into the room again and both wanted to listen to the forecasts of the talking heads.

"Some are quite good," Howard offered. "The analysts out of Asia and Europe generally know their stuff and don't seem as jaded by politics as their American counterparts. Politicization of business—like everything else in the US right now—is really weakening American investing expertise."

"What will Suzanne do today?"

"With Multima? Nothing, I expect. I told her we'd begin buying when the price bottomed in the low thirties. Prices in the futures markets suggest Multima will trade about thirty-five when the exchanges open. She's smart. She'll wait to see what happens during today's trading."

"If Álvarez doesn't break right away, we'll need to delay even further. It's too risky otherwise."

"Agreed. I don't know the guy at all, but it may take a while. I remember when Mareno tortured to get information. Sometimes it took days. The human body has a remarkable ability to survive even with severed extremities." Howard visibly quivered as he recalled some brutal scene and looked downward in disgust. "The biggest risk is him dying."

"Right. Luigi brought a doctor with him. Someone we use in New York. Hopefully, he'll keep the bastard alive long enough to get the passwords. It would be a shame to abort the whole thing at this stage."

Wendal Randall appeared on the stairway, still groggy from sleep, and made his way down to join them in the living room.

"What's happening?" His voice lacked his usual cocky tone, and the pronounced worry lines on his face suggested his question was more than a greeting.

Howard turned toward the TV. Fidelia paused before giving him a reply. She still needed Wendal's technology expertise...just in case.

"The stock markets tanked around the world yesterday. Newscasters speculate there's more to come." Fidelia saw an opening. "We'll probably delay today and wait until next week, but I'm considering calling off the whole thing."

From the corner of her eye, Fidelia saw Howard squirm uncomfortably in his seat, but her gaze was directed toward Wendal. He stopped in his tracks. A flicker in his eyes was almost imperceptible. The rest of his face displayed no emotion.

"Wow. That's a surprise to wake up to. Some complications?"

"No, I'm just a little spooked by this whole pandemic thing. That's why the markets tanked." Fidelia continued to watch Wendal intently, looking for any sign. "It's probably the stress. I'm going for a run. Maybe when I get back I'll feel more confident."

No need to let him know he's a cause of the stress.

FORTY-NINE

Montreal, Quebec, Friday March 13, 2020

Right after Suzanne returned to Le Centre Sheraton Montreal following her morning run, she picked up her phone and checked the stock market activity in Paris and New York. EuroNext was open and trading slightly upward. Farefour shares followed the market with a slight increase from the disastrous results of Black Thursday, as the TV talking heads were now calling the previous day.

In New York, only stock futures were trading that early in the morning, but the same trend applied. It looked like Multima Corporation and the broader market might recover somewhat on Friday. Her inclination was to sit tight over the weekend, but Suzanne learned early in her career that consultation breeds loyalty, so her first call was to Wilma Willingsworth, her acting CFO and long-trusted colleague.

"What are your thoughts on the timing for our share buyback at the moment?" Suzanne phrased her question to get Wilma's candid assessment, yet also leave wiggle room.

"At the moment is a good way of looking at it." Wilma laughed as she said it, but her laugh was tenuous, almost forced. "During my thirty years in the finance world, I've never seen anything like it. Rock-solid companies yesterday are treated like pariahs today and technology stocks that have never made a dollar of profit are trading at previously unimaginable prices."

"So we're with the pariahs?"

"No. Not quite. But we have so many moving parts right now, it's hard for investors to assess our true company value. I had a half-dozen calls over the past two days from major investors. This stuff with the Department of Justice has them spooked. They're not so much worried about the fifty million we lost in the fraud as concerned about what else might crawl out of the woodwork. Some of them pine for the good old days when John George Mortimer ran the company."

"You reminded them we're going to buy back shares to increase the company's value." Suzanne made her query a statement rather a question, assuming her colleague covered that basic issue and showing her respect.

"Yes. A couple hadn't heard the news or checked the SEC site, but the others were all aware. They're positive about that, and they're not threatening to jump ship yet, but we really need to get to the bottom of these money-laundering accusations."

"I understand. Dan Ramirez has turned up the heat with his old cronies at the FBI. He has a team back in South America now. I'm hoping to hear something from them soon. But what are your thoughts on when we should start buying back shares?" Suzanne refocused her colleague's attention.

"Everyone I spoke with yesterday agreed. The ones with more money than brains will push stock prices up a little today, sensing some bargain-basement buying prices. This pandemic has created so many uncertainties the people I spoke with thought prices would fall even more next week. I'd wait until at least then. We'll probably want to give the brokers a range even if we buy at market prices. For example, not to exceed thirty-eight dollars a share without approval or something like that."

"Okay. Thirty-eight sounds reasonable as a maximum. I'll follow your advice about when we should begin," Suzanne reassured her colleague, then prepared to sign off. "You're right about uncertainties. Believe it or not, the concierge here at Le Centre Sheraton told me there's a rumor they may temporarily close the hotel entirely. The provincial government has warned his management to prepare for an almost complete shutdown of all non-essential businesses and services."

Alberto Ferer called next. With no further meetings in Canada on his agenda, he had returned to Fort Myers and was in his office there. His tone was somber, and Suzanne stood and walked over to a window, sensing a need for brighter light.

"I went to Heather Strong's funeral yesterday afternoon. Her family is devastated. They told me how much they appreciated your call offering condolences. They're in shock and bewildered by the whole thing. And Dan Ramirez still hasn't been able to pry any information out of the county sheriff's office. They don't have a single lead they can pursue. Same with the RCMP up in Canada with Kim Jones's accident."

"Both are tragic, but it surely seems Kim Jones was involved, doesn't it?" Suzanne countered. "Her initials are on every payment we made to the fraudulent companies. Heather Strong is more bewildering. We don't know that she had any direct knowledge of the transactions, do we?"

"You're right on both counts. That's why the sheriff's office is working on a theory that Heather's death might just have been a divergence, that whoever threw her off the balcony was trying to draw attention closer to you. Dan Ramirez is over there right now. His contact asked to meet urgently, so they might have something."

The pair theorized and commiserated for another moment or two before dealing with Alberto's concerns about other pressing legal issues.

The pandemic might cause lawsuits if employees didn't follow the rules and customers fell ill after visiting Multima Stores. Financial Services had already sought advice about how to handle mortgage and credit card defaults, as well as missed payments, in the event the economy shut down as many governments suggested might happen soon.

They still had the issue brewing in Europe where the European Central Bank was withholding banking licenses for Poland and threatening actions in Western Europe. And there was, of course, the sticky issue at the Toronto Stock Exchange where they had been so rudely snubbed a few days earlier.

"Doug Burns has continued an off-the-record dialogue with Argenter at the TSE. They're chums from their college days. Burns claims Argenter was apoplectic about the snub when they chatted yesterday. Says the guy felt blindsided by the arrogance of the SEC order and he needed to buy time."

"That's what I suspected."

"The powers that be in Canada are furious. They're treating the nasty incident as an incursion on their sovereignty. They also heard someone quietly called in the US ambassador for a frank chat. Nothing definitive, of course, but she agreed to investigate."

"Good work, Alberto. Keep me posted on all fronts."

By noon, global stock markets had demonstrated the resiliency Wilma predicted. Trading in shares of Farefour closed in Paris slightly higher than the previous day. In New York, prices were holding steady about five percent higher. The trend validated Suzanne's decision to wait. She noticed a text message from Dan Ramirez, asking her to call him on a secure line. That was code for not just encrypted. He wanted no other ears in the room. Suzanne asked Jasmine if she would be a doll and get the concierge to make a latte.

"A lot is happening." Dan left out the small talk as Suzanne listened. "I heard from our people in Chile in the middle of the night. I held off calling you until I talked with my guy at the FBI.

Whether his pause was to regain composure or give Suzanne time to brace for the news wasn't clear. She drew a deep breath but said nothing. He continued.

"Just as the team expected, the suspects kidnapped the guy in the Hotel Casa Higueras about three this morning. Our tracking device worked fine, and the team followed the gang to the same house on the coast, south of Valparaíso."

"Have they got the authorities involved and apprehended them?"

"No. That was their intention, but I overruled them. I got my FBI contact to order his people to sit tight until we knew exactly why the gang grabbed the guy from the hotel. We got a listening device in there while everyone was in the city executing the kidnapping."

"And?"

"Most of what we're hearing you don't want to know. Suffice it for me to say, The Organization is involved. The leader is the guy who used to be Giancarlo Mareno's security chief. His name is Luigi Fortissimo. The FBI verified his identity with both facial and voice recognition software. Nobody's sure what his role is now that Mareno's dead, but he's clearly in charge of this mission."

"And what don't I want to know?"

"The Organization is treating the guy they snatched like a turncoat. It's messy. They're not nice people when they exact retribution."

Suzanne took a moment to process that. She stood again and moved toward the window and looked out at the vacant church as she listened. She didn't condone torture. That people in her employ were sitting idly by while someone was being tortured disturbed her on several levels.

"Shouldn't we let the authorities deal with this, Dan?" Her tone reflected a note of concern and despair.

"I won't say I told you that you didn't want to know. But, candidly, I don't trust the Chilean police. I think the only way we'll find out where Multima's money ended up—with a full explanation that absolves the company of wrongdoing—is to let the drama play out. We're recording everything. When the guy breaks, I think we'll have the smoking gun we need."

Suzanne took some time to think it through. Dan Ramirez knew her well enough to give her time to wrestle with her internal conflict. How could she justify standing by while any human being suffered pain that was probably beyond imagination? She turned away from the window with a view of the church and didn't speak for more than a minute as her mind raced. When she replied, her voice initially broke and when the words finally came out, they were forced and slow.

"The choices we make will ultimately destroy us. I can see that now. But the welfare of our twenty thousand employees and their families compels me to put the safety of the company first. I fear you're right, Dan. The only way we'll satisfy the authorities is to solve the mystery for them. And it looks as if the only way we'll know where our money has gone is to do what you suggest. I may not sleep nights for a while, but carry on. Let me know what you learn."

A CEO of a major corporation lives life at a pace far quicker and more demanding than most people can imagine. At the same time, they carry weighty burdens that affect the lives of both customers and employees. COVID-19 had become a constant reminder of that reality and immediately jolted Suzanne back to dealing with another crisis that was rocking her supermarkets around the globe.

Gordon Goodfellow, president of Multima Supermarkets in America, was on the phone mere minutes after Suzanne's emotional conversation with her security chief.

"The only good news I can share with you is that sales are reaching all-time highs every day, in every store, every hour that we're open," Gordon said. His voice was an octave higher and his delivery far quicker than usual, a sure sign he'd been surviving on coffee for the past few days. "I've given half the buying team the weekend off to recover. Some haven't slept in two days."

"Good idea. How about store staff?"

"We're better there. We keep a large reserve of part-time employees who usually only work twenty hours or so per week, so we're adding hours for those who want to work. We still have lineups in almost every store, but the checkouts are now fully staffed everywhere. Few are working over forty hours, which keeps the union happy."

"How about shelves in the stores?"

"Some are bare for much of the day. We moved a lot of floor staff to night shifts so we can clean and stock the shelves. Some are loading two tractor-trailer loads of goods onto the shelves every night. Still, certain inventory sells out before ten o'clock in the morning."

"How are the security folks managing?"

"We've needed police reinforcements in a few areas. It's bizarre how a few people are behaving. This pandemic seems to have brought out the worst in some. We've had a handful of injuries to employees, but they've been mainly pushing and shoving incidents. Not good, but manageable."

"If you haven't already done so, ask your store managers to deliver some flowers or a fruit basket or something to the injured folks. And you might want the HR people to call the insurance company and ask them to handle claims from those employees with both sensitivity and speed."

"Right. Deliveries of the gifts have already started. You were a good teacher, Suzanne. I'll get HR to make that call to the insurance people before the end of the day."

For more than an hour, Suzanne posed questions and Goodfellow brought her up to date on the crush of business Multima Supermarkets was experiencing nationally. She listened intently and offered tips or suggestions where appropriate. When they finished, she'd made note of a dozen action items her division president would have added to his to-do list for the day. Sleep for him that night might also be delayed.

After Suzanne checked the closing prices for Multima shares and the stock market generally on her phone, she scrolled down a summary of news stories on her various feeds. The news about the pandemic became more dire by the hour.

Canada's government had just warned its citizens to avoid all unnecessary travel and advised those abroad to return while flights were still available. CNN reported that schools were closed in sixteen states. Cruise ships had been ordered to discontinue all voyages from the US. The US government announced a "Families First Coronavirus Crisis Response Act."

The next headline to catch her eye was an odd one. The Transportation Security Administration announced it would allow hand sanitizers but would require special screening. A reminder of how emergency measures set in place after another crisis still lingered two decades later.

What lay in store in the aftermath of this one?

FIFTY

Precisely as Fidelia had instructed, Luigi called before they began to work on Juan Álvarez.

"This won't be easy. Ya sure you want to listen?" Luigi's tone sounded both deferential and admonishing at the same time. Clearly, he didn't want her there, even by phone.

"Yes." She kept her response simple, her tone emphatic. Everything was on the line. No matter how gruesome it might become, she was determined to hear the password for herself and let Luigi exact whatever pain it took to break the scum who'd sold her out.

It took a while. First, they applied electrical shocks to his testicles. Before it started, he had screamed profanities at Luigi that left no doubt about what was coming. During the torture, he wailed and pleaded for relief. She shuddered at his blood-curdling pleas of agony and moved outdoors to listen so Howard or the others wouldn't hear what was happening.

Luigi tried to reason with him when Juan regained his composure sometime later. Fidelia imagined him lying on the floor in pain and humiliation as her security chief calmly explained why it would be better for him to cooperate. The lowlife remained defiant and Fidelia gritted her teeth and braced for more.

Over the following hours, she listened while Luigi threatened him with what was coming next. Each time, she readied herself for an inevitable scream of excruciating pain. It helped if she held the phone as far away from her ear as possible, but only marginally. More than once, she was tempted to call Luigi off before resolutely accepting the reality that it had to happen.

Her own body ached and trembled as all his fingernails were crudely extracted. Four fingers were chopped off, one at a time. She cringed at each separation and almost cried out herself a couple times. Both of Juan's knees were broken, and Luigi threatened to completely sever his penis and shove it down the despicable traitor's throat if he didn't cooperate.

After the doctor did some more repairs and administered drugs, Luigi and his gang resumed their interrogation. Álvarez began talking. Luigi wanted to settle his own scores first and extracted the story behind the mysterious deaths of the two Multima employees and a name for the guy behind the IP address near the CIA in West Virginia. Fidelia grimaced in disgust as the guy confirmed he was following higher orders than hers. And she ground her teeth in anger when he divulged it was Wendal who provided the new algorithm.

"Álvarez is not Argentinian at all. He was born in Chile to a Chilean mother and Russian father," Luigi told her during a second break while the doctor treated their victim between rounds. "The son-of-a-bitch's been groomed by the Russian mob since birth."

It took another two hours, but eventually the victim revealed everything his torturers demanded, including the password Fidelia so desperately needed. It was a complex one. The guy must have struggled to even remember it as they chopped up his body. When he spat out the letters and digits, Fidelia punched them into her phone.

Álvarez collapsed again, and she shot a text with the password to Klaudia.

It worked. They got in.

A while later, they finally learned where to find the algorithm they needed. That was the most difficult info of all to extract because the guy's brain stopped functioning in English. It was indeed fortunate that Fidelia had listened in on the torture. When the low-life switched to Spanish, she was the only person to understand the guy's mutterings and translate them into English.

There had been misunderstandings in the process. Whether the guy forgot, continued to resist and intentionally deceive, or something got lost in the translation, Fidelia couldn't tell. But Álvarez was on his last breaths before Klaudia screamed out triumphantly by text that they were inside the system and fully in control of the algorithm.

Almost immediately after that, pandemonium erupted. She heard yelling and screaming in the background. Then Luigi's phone fell to the ground with a thud as Fidelia continued to listen. A cascade of gunshots blasted through the speaker of the phone. In shock, she listened as men screamed out in agony amid the sounds of breaking glass, shattering wood, and bullets deflecting off metal. The chaos continued for a minute or more. Then, an eerie silence. A few seconds later, the call disconnected.

Once she realized what had happened, Fidelia darted toward the house and hit speed dial as she ran.

"Get everybody up; we're leaving," she ordered. "Get the chopper here immediately, seven passengers."

She made another call as she rushed toward the house. As that call ended, a helicopter's loud drone approached, rotors violently chopping the air and its engine groaning, while dust from the ground swirled into the gathering group's eyes. Moments later, the rotors slowed but never came to a complete stop.

A pilot threw open the door and lowered an aluminum staircase as the assembled gang clambered aboard and took seats, starting from the back. Fidelia sat in the last seat available, behind the co-pilot. The chopper lifted before her seat belt was buckled, and it bounced about in gusty winds. Beside her, Howard sat silent, blissfully unaware of her inner turmoil. He watched her every movement but said nothing.

It was already dark when the helicopter touched down at the private airport. She chose the location because Aretta expected it to be deserted at that time of the day. No planes moved about. A dozen or more corporate jets lined the tarmac outside the small terminal that looked no bigger than a small house. She scanned the area for vehicles or activity and spotted only a few SUVs parked near the building.

Fidelia motioned for Howard to lead the way when the pilot opened a door, and she followed him down the steps only inches behind. At the bottom, she turned and signaled for everyone to follow her along a narrow sidewalk leading to a doorway into the building.

Aretta waited inside. Beyond her, going out another door, her security detail pushed and shoved ahead of them an older couple who might have been employees. Aretta led off the conversation as soon as the door closed behind the departing couple.

"They tested the router and Internet before we got here. Bandwidth is excellent, the signal is strong and the Internet is fiber optics. Should be enough for what you need."

"Okay. Wendal, you take the seat closest to the router. Howard, use that chair on the other side of the table, the one facing the TV monitor. Let's test a couple trades in London and Paris before they close. We've got about an hour," Fidelia instructed.

While Wendal fiddled with his laptop and the password set up for Wi-Fi, Fidelia noticed the TV screen was set to the local ABC affiliate. She glimpsed at the stock market data scrolling along the bottom of the screen. Asian markets had all closed significantly lower from Friday. More losses were in store for the rest of the world if that was any indicator.

Once he had everything connected, Wendal appeared furtive. His gaze darted about the room while he tried to grasp what was happening. Buying and selling a few million shares from a strange room in a remote building with people looking over his shoulder was not the plan they'd all discussed. A bead of sweat appeared on his forehead, and he quickly wiped it away, then studied a speck of dust on his keyboard. Fidelia flashed him a smile of reassurance when he looked up again.

Then, she glanced over at Stan Tan's whiz kid from Singapore as he pounded his laptop keyboards mercilessly for several minutes, shoulders slumped, head bowed, concentrating on numbers flickering across a tiny screen. He murmured something in Mandarin, then stopped and waited for something to appear on the screen.

He appeared perplexed, and keyed another sequence of numbers into his computer with a flurry, hands dashing across the keyboard like a concert pianist. When he stopped to watch the screen again, he smiled.

"It's there, Wendal. The worm you planted is working its way up the hierarchy. Bang! It found the account. We're ready to go!" He shouted it out with the same enthusiasm he might announce a video game conquest.

Wendal nodded. His face relaxed, but lines of worry still lingered around his eyes, and his jaws remained locked with tension. When he looked up and saw Fidelia watching him, he smiled. Not his usual cocky self. Relieved instead.

"Okay, buy ten thousand shares at market price from the Macau account," Fidelia instructed Wendal.

"Farefour or Multima?"

"Farefour from the EuroNext exchange in Paris."

Thirty seconds later, Wendal announced the purchase was complete. They bought the shares at thirty-three fifty-two. The brokerage account in Macau would pay for them Wednesday. He sat with his fingers poised for more instructions. She gave none, but raised a finger in the air to let him know she needed a minute. She motioned for Howard to follow her outside.

"I want to go now. Call her. Be sure she understands the precise timing you want her to do it and the specific price she's to use." Fidelia studied his eyes for any reaction. He nodded as he reached for his phone and made the call while she listened. It took less than a minute.

When they returned to the office there was some consternation.

"My email's been disabled," the Singaporean complained.

Wendal glanced down, hit a few keys, and muttered, "Mine too. What's going on?"

"Okay, Wendal. We're ready to go," Fidelia commanded, ignoring the question. "Queue up another hundred thousand shares of Farefour from Macau, then a hundred thousand Multima shares on the New York exchange from each of Malta, Cypress, Barbados, Macau, and Luxembourg. All at market price, all ready to buy the moment New York opens."

He followed her instructions and finished the tasks in just a few moments.

"Wendal, come with me," Aretta instructed as soon as he finished keying Fidelia's orders. She led him out a back door.

Fidelia pointed to the Singaporean, ignoring both Wendal and Howard. "You there, monitor the transactions and let me know when the worms attach."

By the end of their brief exchange, a private jet came to a stop in front of the building, its engines winding down. Even with the outside noise, Fidelia heard the three quick pops from the rear of the building before the engines idled down in front.

Wendal wasn't coming back. She scooped up the computer he'd been using and darted for the front door.

"We'll finish the rest of the transactions from the jet," Fidelia said, motioning for everyone else in the room to pack up and follow her. The Singaporean blanched in fear and did what he was told. Howard followed him. From the corner of her eye, she saw them forming a single file to climb the steps onto the jet. Fidelia's bodyguards followed Howard. Aretta calmly walked toward one of the parked SUVs.

Inside the aircraft, Fidelia pointed the Singaporean techie to a seat up front at a small round table on the left side. She motioned for Howard to take a seat at another round table in the far rear corner. The bodyguards didn't need further instructions. They sat down at seats on each side of the aircraft toward the middle of the plane.

Fidelia joined the Singaporean up front and huddled with him, connecting devices and poring over screens until the plane was comfortably at cruising altitude. She got up from her seat, used the Keurig to make a cup of coffee, and held up an empty cup to see if Howard wanted her to make one for him as well. He did.

Balancing two mugs, she worked her way back to the table where Howard sat studying the news feed on his phone. She made herself comfortable, took a sip of coffee, then brought Howard up to date.

"Everything's going smoothly so far. Are you still sure she'll do it?" She locked onto his eyes for any hint of doubt or betrayal. She saw none but still leaned toward him to catch every nuance in his words and tone.

"She'll do it. She made all the right protests of distress and agony that we're ruining her life. She's probably already contacted the broker. Should I now worry my fate might become the same as Wendal's?"

Fidelia smiled. Howard didn't understand her at all. That was okay. She softened her tone, forcing Howard to also lean in toward her to hear over the hum of the engines.

"No. You're safe. I couldn't have done it without those calls. And your brilliant idea about the final timing has probably saved Multima any lasting pain—just like you hoped. " Her smile disappeared and her flashing black eyes reflected her true emotions.

"Wendal betrayed me. He was double-dealing for the Russians. Working with Álvarez. We caught them just in time. I suspected, but Juan Álvarez confirmed it."

She paused for a few seconds to choose her next words carefully. This time her tone was less measured.

"Giancarlo Mareno always used to say that greed was our most subversive human character trait. We all have it. If we don't control it, eventually it consumes us. They all got exactly what they deserved. Álvarez was the worst. One of the reasons it took Luigi so long to make him talk was his languages." Howard leaned in again as her voice became softer, more reflective.

"As he neared the end, he lost his ability to understand and speak English. They had to pry the information from him. Sometimes he answered in Spanish, other times in Russian. They groomed him for his treachery from birth, and I missed all the signals."

"What happened?"

"I won't tell you how we learned the information, but the two of them inserted a computer code even more sophisticated than the one Wendal developed for me. He must have planned his treachery for months. Klaudia discovered it when she got access to the Valparaíso server. She recognized Russian code from her days with the KGB and traced it back through the algorithm. Those scum planned to steal all our money when we sold the Multima shares. Every dollar would have ended up in one of six bank accounts controlled by fronts for the Russian mafia."

Fidelia watched his reaction. His eyes were engaged and his expression somber, but he showed none of the visceral emotion she felt toward the two offenders. He was truly a spectator in it all.

"So, you'll sell the shares as we planned?" he asked.

"When your woman comes through, it will all be over in fifteen minutes. The algorithms are being programmed to trigger massive buying and selling just before the markets close. Ours will soon be ready. Bank accounts controlled by the Russians will pay for them when the accounts settle tomorrow. Klaudia found a way to reverse the direction of the worm they planted, and it'll happen just as the markets close. We know there's enough money in those accounts, and it will be hours before they realize what's happened. The Russians will take a one-day hit and never find their half-billion dollars again."

She grinned in satisfaction as Howard tipped his head in congratulations but said nothing.

Fidelia got up from her seat and returned to the table with Stan Tan's guy from Singapore. Within seconds, they were deep in conversation with hands flying across keyboards. It continued for hours, with only short breaks to get something to drink or use the facilities. The techie displayed no emotion. He kept his head down and only occasionally drew Fidelia's attention to something on his laptop screen as she watched, fascinated by the magnitude of her audacious scheme.

About thirty minutes before their scheduled landing in Singapore, she went back to sit near Howard again.

"The stock markets will close soon in New York. We've bought just less than ten percent," she said.

"You won't declare your position, I suppose."

She shook her head slowly.

"And the Russians might have their suspicions, but they won't be able to trace the purchases because the algorithm will self-destruct, erasing all traces of evidence," Howard speculated.

"Right. And Multima won't know because we used aliases for all the purchases. It might become useful later. You never know." Fidelia's smile was more mischievous than expected.

"So, my services are no longer required?" Howard's eyebrows rose in expectation.

"I can always benefit from your "services," as you call them. You're a genius and made my original idea work. But I know it won't last. I initially thought bringing you back for this job might rekindle some of what we felt before. But it didn't. You've truly changed. Your heart isn't in it at all, and that's okay."

"This time, you'll fix Interpol and leave me alone?" Howard looked hard into her eyes as he waited for her reply. His lips were pursed, with no hint of levity or a playful wink.

"Yeah. I already fixed the Interpol Red Notice for your arrest. Our guy there withdrew it yesterday. I'll get a name from Stan Tan for someone you can see for a passport. They can make you one for almost any country there in Singapore. And I'll give you a few thousand in cash when we land. Enough to tide you over until you're comfortable drawing down from your millions in the Caymans."

"Thanks. Everything's safe with me. You know that."

Fidelia shrugged. Her body tingled with an excitement she'd never experienced. For the first time, she felt the lure of power. She'd never experienced a high from drugs but imagined the euphoria must be about the same as the elation she felt right at that moment.

FIFTY-ONE

Montreal, Quebec, Tuesday March 17, 2020

Suzanne Simpson had spent all the previous day immersed in her work but still felt on pins and needles waiting for the price of Multima Corporation shares to drop as Howard Knight had ominously forecast in his bizarre phone call the previous week. But a quiet day for a CEO includes more reading, discussions, and decisions than most people deal with in a week. She compartmentalized it all quite well.

Among the barrage of information compressed into her time-managed day, Suzanne frequently visited the stock market prices on her phone to see how Multima was faring amid the turmoil.

Although share prices had dropped from the levels of Black Thursday, Multima shares remained in the thirty-four-dollar range. That was an almost fifty percent drop from only a few weeks earlier, but still above the thirty-three-dollar price forecasted by Howard in his clandestine call. One dollar per share might not sound like much, but it represented over a half-billion dollars of value to the company.

Suzanne woke up early that morning and spent an hour thinking about the entire situation before she left for her morning run. She focused on the question of when to buy more shares in Multima—for herself personally and as part of the stock repurchase authorized by the board. By the end of her run, she decided something must have gone wrong with Howard's odd plan to have someone he worked with drive the prices down and then push them back up quickly.

Logically, Monday would have been the day to drive prices lower. Investors everywhere were skittish after a weekend to think about the pandemic and panic in the stock markets. It would have been easy to engineer a significant drop in prices the first day markets reopened. That it didn't happen persuaded her to ignore Howard's advice.

So, her Tuesday morning began with a call to Wilma Willingsworth at Multima's headquarters well before the New York Stock Exchange was scheduled to start trading.

"When should we start buying back some shares? Is now a good time?"

"The five-billion-dollar question," Wilma said. "It might be. These next two or three weeks are probably our best opportunity. When we announce the results for the first quarter, we're going to blow away all the analysts' forecasts. We might drop a bit farther, but I have no doubt the prices will jump significantly when we announce our profits for the quarter. They'll be our best three months since John George Mortimer founded the company."

"Okay. I'll leave it to you to set the wheels in motion. I've instructed my broker to buy thirty thousand shares between thirty-four and thirty-five dollars at the open today. I'll announce that this morning. That might cause a bit of a bounce in the prices, at least temporarily. James thinks it important for me to keep our shareholders at bay during this market panic."

"Right. Good decision. What price range do you want me to use?"

It struck Suzanne as a rather odd question. They'd already agreed to buy the shares at current market prices, and Wilma's memory was like a trap. She remembered everything. So she waited for Wilma to explain.

"Whatever we start at will probably be the low end of the range, but I think we should give the brokers some latitude to follow the market up to an agreed maximum, maybe thirty-eight dollars, for example?"

Hadn't they already agreed to thirty-eight dollars? Suzanne thought about it a moment. With all the pressures these past days, Wilma must have forgotten. She gave her okay again for a maximum purchase price of thirty-eight dollars per share.

Before ten o'clock, Beverly Vonderhausen called.

"You won't believe this, Suzanne." Her voice had a surprisingly cheerful lilt as she paused for dramatic effect. "The Department of Justice has withdrawn the warrant for your arrest again!"

"Did you receive an official notice, or is it a tip from one of your friends in Washington?"

"The real deal. I received an email just a few minutes ago with a copy of the official notice attached. With this administration, nothing is ever definite, but this is as close as it gets to a reprieve."

"It's safe for me to go home?"

"One hundred percent."

Suzanne finished a later call with Eileen to coordinate the company jet arrival time and answered a half-dozen questions her executive assistant needed help with. When she finished, James Fitzgerald waited on the line.

"Some big news for you. It looks like I'll be moving a little closer to Florida," he said after Suzanne had brought him up to date on her Multima share decisions and the latest twists in her legal saga. She waited for more.

"Angela was just offered a job with the FBI she simply can't turn down. They loved the way she helped them solve the mystery of those fraudulent bank accounts and created a position for her at Quantico. She starts on the first of April, and we've decided to live together somewhere nearby."

"That's wonderful news. You make a great couple. And congratulations to Angela. I was impressed with her investigative acumen. I'll add a bonus to her invoice, too. She deserves it," Suzanne said.

"I'll continue to serve as a director of Multima until the end of the year, but I want to step away then. I'm getting too old for all this drama, and you really don't need my help anymore." He laughed in his usual self-deprecating way, but left little room for negotiation.

"I'll always need your help, James, but I'll also respect your wishes. Announce it whenever you're ready."

Trading in Multima shares remained brisk through the day, and phone calls with Atlanta and Paris reaffirmed business in the company's supermarkets continued at full throttle. If anything, the panic buying of grocery supplies—especially toilet tissue—had intensified. The outstanding profit results Wilma had predicted grew dramatically by the hour.

She checked the news as her day wound down. The pandemic worsened and travel restrictions came into effect between the US and Europe, China, and much of the world. It all made Suzanne grateful her jet would pick her up in Montreal by five o'clock. That evening she'd be back home in Fort Myers. In the meantime, calls continued. Just before she prepared to leave her hotel, Eileen patched through a call from George Argenter, CEO of the Toronto Stock Exchange.

"I've called to apologize for the way we treated you when you visited. I make no excuses, but at that time we felt we had no choice. I hope you'll understand. The Toronto Stock Exchange will be delighted to list Multima Corporation's shares. We received some new information today, and all approvals are in place. We can make it effective April 1 if you decide to go forward."

Suzanne didn't answer at once. She saw no reason to reward the bureaucrat for cowing to pressure from US authorities. But she didn't want to do permanent damage.

"I'm Canadian. I understand the challenges of sleeping with a giant elephant, so I take no offense. And I appreciate your offer, but I'll need to discuss that with the board, of course."

Her manner was polite but cool, and their conversation was short. However, she had no doubt the board would follow her recommendation they go ahead with the TSE listing. But maybe it would be best to hold off until things settled down with the pandemic.

Checked out of her hotel and traveling toward Montreal's airport to meet the company jet, she answered her phone when it rang again. It was Dan Ramirez.

"My contact at the FBI just called. I have some terrible news." His voice broke, and he paused, either to regain his composure or give her time to prepare. She waited with some trepidation.

"Wilma's dead. She shot herself."

"What are you talking about? I just spoke with her this morning. I don't understand." Suzanne's voice became so high pitched it sounded almost shrill. Her mind seemed momentarily to go blank.

"Before the guy in Chile was tortured, he offered up some information our people missed in real-time."

"What does that mean?" Suzanne tried to keep her tone even but expected it conveyed far more than her intense shock.

"They only learned the complete story when the entire team listened to the full recording after they got back here. They discovered a section recorded right after the thugs arrived at the secluded house—before our team was set up to monitor the conversations live."

"And?" The way she spat it out made her sound angry, but she left it that way.

"Wilma masterminded the entire fraud at Supermarkets. Between the recordings and some legwork by the FBI, they learned she had gambling debts. For some time, she was under The Organization's control. They forced her to set up the elaborate fraud within Multima to pay her debts and preserve her business reputation."

"Oh. My. God. I trusted her with everything." Suzanne couldn't believe what she was hearing. She managed to sputter a reply. "This all began four years ago? With the first phony invoices?"

"Yes. I've seen the evidence. The FBI connected all the dots and visited her home a few minutes ago. The moment they rang the doorbell, they heard a gunshot. She left behind a detailed note apologizing to her family and everyone at Multima, especially you."

Anger welled up and Suzanne fought hard to control it. Sadness for the loss of a friend and colleague shifted dramatically as she realized the depth of Wilma's betrayal.

"How did we miss the signals?"

"She was a brilliant woman who developed an addiction she couldn't find a way to overcome. She hid it well from all of us," Dan commiserated, his voice low. He too had failed to detect signs of her character flaw and clearly also felt some shortcoming.

"But Mareno is also dead. Why did all this happen now?"

"When Mareno dropped out of the picture, the guy in South America saw an opportunity to please someone close to the White House. He never divulged a name, but it was someone who has strong connections to the Russian mafia as well. Your recent problems with the Justice Department were all driven by this guy Ortez or Álvarez, for the Russians. Wilma was complicit every step of the way."

"How can you be so sure?"

"I've seen the letter she left behind. It's dated this morning. It said they forced her to give an order to buy back one hundred and thirty million Multima shares at the highest price possible, or they would publicly reveal her sordid history. She ordered the brokers to buy at thirty-seven dollars and ninety-five cents, starting at three forty-five this afternoon. I checked. That was the closing price in New York."

Suzanne quickly changed the screen on her phone. Dan's information was right. She spotted an email alert from Multima's broker confirming the purchase—all one hundred and thirty million shares in the last fifteen minutes of trading.

Silently, Suzanne did the math.

As her last act, trusty Wilma had given the Russian mafia, or The Organization, or whoever Howard Knight was working for, a seven-hundred-million-dollar payday. That was the difference between the price Suzanne herself paid for the shares she bought personally that morning and the price instruction Wilma gave to the broker to act on fifteen minutes before the market closed.

"Was Heather Strong involved too?" she asked.

"Heather Strong wasn't involved. Another thing Wilma apologized for. She didn't do it personally, but her masters killed Heather to divert attention from Wilma."

"And Kim Jones?"

"We learned nothing about her from the recordings or Wilma's note, but I think we can assume she was involved. Nobody wants to spend much more time investigating."

"Will this ever end, Dan?" This time, she buried her exasperation and sounded grounded.

"I know you're asking a rhetorical question, but I really don't know. Just before I called you, I watched an interview on CNN with a congressman from Florida. He demanded a full congressional investigation into the rumored White House influence on the administration of justice concerning Multima and you."

Suzanne sighed and slumped back in her seat. That meant many months of controversy and stress to come amid a pandemic and the already weighty responsibilities of her job. She took a deep breath and held it for a moment. Dan filled the silence again.

"And a little gossip to end our call? My guy at the FBI tells me Interpol rescinded the Red Notice outstanding for Howard Knight's arrest. No explanation. Just rescinded. On a sadder note, Wendal Randall's body was found at a small private airport north of Sydney, in Australia. It was a targeted murder."

As the corporate jet taxied for takeoff to Fort Myers, Suzanne finished checking her messages. An email confirmed her broker bought thirty thousand shares that morning and deducted more than a million dollars from her personal account. She had paid a price slightly higher than Howard Knight had demanded and surely triggered the rise that let Wilma pay an even higher price for the shares Multima bought. But there was no reason for anyone to know about that secret conversation.

Added to the shares inherited from John George Mortimer, Suzanne now controlled almost a quarter of all the company shares. Today those shares were still worth over four billion dollars. There was little doubt the price of those shares would eventually go up again. They'd almost surely return to at least the value before the crises brought on by The Organization, COVID-19, and whatever was going on between someone close to the White House and the Russians.

When things returned to normal—even if it took a few years—Suzanne would be one of the richest women in the world. Almost certainly, her personal worth would eventually exceed eight billion dollars.

After the plane hit cruising altitude, Suzanne tried to catch up on some reports she should read. But a few minutes in she began to cry. At first, the tears were little more than moist eyes. Before she realized it, they were gushing.

Suzanne glanced around the cabin of the opulent corporate jet. She'd told her bodyguards about Wilma, and Jasmine shed a few tears too. Her partner, Willy, stared off into space rather than meet her eye.

Cheerful, selfless, caring and kind, Wilma had been more than a colleague. She had been a dear friend, liked by everyone who knew her. It was impossible to imagine the demons she wrestled with that led to an addiction to gambling and eventually caused a massive betrayal to settle her debts.

As she cried and tried to figure it all out, Suzanne came to realize she actually knew the answer to the rhetorical "Will it ever end?" question she had asked Dan Ramirez.

In John George Mortimer's last months, she'd spent many hours listening to his words of wisdom and advice. Once, he emphasized what he had learned about people over his long career. "Our people are both our greatest assets and our biggest vulnerability."

Of course, for much of his business career, he didn't need to worry about hackers.

But the wisdom he expressed was profound. Howard Knight had once been a trusted, influential director on Multima's board. Wendal Randall had once been an admired leader of Multima's technology business. Wilma Willingsworth had been both a respected chief financial officer and president of Multima Financial Services. All three illustrated the dichotomy of individual brilliance and human imperfection. Together, they created a web of deceit.

But harboring anger or ill-will toward any of the three served no purpose.

Naturally, Suzanne and management at the accounting firm OCD would design new controls and oversight to be sure that kind of fraud never occurred again. But someone, sometime, would conjure up and try a new one. She'd try to select and promote people more carefully, perhaps with more psychological testing, but behaviors would change and some would inevitably succumb to temptation or greed.

It would never end. That was the correct answer. There was a reason the average tenure for an American CEO was five years and only one chief executive officer out of five lasted as long as ten years. The trend was toward even shorter tenure with burnout or ethical lapses accelerating the pace.

Was it all worth it?

By the time Multima's corporate jet passed above Washington, Suzanne had answered that question too. She had put the anger behind her, and even if she couldn't yet forgive any of them for their betrayal and harassment, she would carry on and prevail.

Thousands of people working for Multima—and the companies who sold products and services to her company—depended on her to keep it all on track. Their jobs, well-being, and happiness were all at stake. She wouldn't continue forever. But for as long as she could, those folks would provide all the motivation she needed to deal with the next challenges that forced her to live on a precarious edge.

But one rule was about to change. Regardless of the risks, it no longer made sense to block Stefan from her life. Corporate demands or not, she would get to know him better—much better.

ACKNOWLEDGEMENTS

My name appears on the cover, but my novels are always the result of extensive collaboration. Once I complete a manuscript, the polishing process starts with an outstanding team of editors who provide valuable input and suggestions. With the completion of each novel, I marvel at how much better the input from each editor made the final story.

Kim McDougall, Paula Hurwitz, and Val Tobin all helped me to polish the story with critical editing and proofreading that improved my story meaningfully. I owe an extra thanks to Val for suggesting the title. As always, any shortcomings in the book are entirely mine.

Next, I asked a few select people to read early drafts and give me critical feedback on content and style. Cathy & Dalton McGugan, Cheryl Harrison, and Heather & Dan Lightfoot all read early versions. Their incisive feedback and comments about the plot were of immense value.

Castelane performed superbly—as usual! Heartfelt thanks to Kim McDougall for her counsel, dramatic cover design, and pleasing book layout. Most important, I truly appreciate her expertise pulling it all together with unmatched professionalism and constant good cheer.

To the gang who are part of the Writers' Community of York Region, thanks for all the workshops, write-ins, encouragement, support and friendship among wordsmiths of all genres!

For family, friends, and readers around the globe, thank you all for a lifetime of support and encouragement. You're the people who inspire my unwavering confidence that anything is possible.

ABOUT THE AUTHOR

Gary D. McGugan loves to tell stories and is the author of *Three Weeks Less a Day, The Multima Scheme, Unrelenting Peril,* and *Pernicious Pursuit.*

After a forty-year career at senior levels of global corporations, Gary started writing with a goal of using artful suspense to entertain and inform. His launch of a new writing career—at an age most people retire—reveals an ongoing zest for new challenges and a life-long pursuit of knowledge. Home is near Toronto, but Gary thinks of himself as a true citizen of the world. His love of travel and extensive experiences around the globe are evident in every chapter.

FOLLOW GARY D. MCGUGAN

Subscribe to Gary's VIP Readers List:
https://www.subscribepage.com/garydmcgugan

Facebook
www.facebook.com/gary.d.mcgugan.books

Twitter
@GaryDMcGugan

Gary D. McGugan Website
www.garydmcguganbooks.com

Instagram
Authorgarydmcgugan

LinkedIn
https://www.linkedin.com/in/gary-d-mcgugan